DECEPTIONS

Book3 of the Ascendant trilogy

By Craig Alanson

Table of Contents

CHAPTER ONE

Master wizard Shomas Feany was up to his waist crossing an icy stream, holding his breath against the numbing shock and stumbling on smooth stones he could not see, when Lord Paedris don Salva de la Murta called him through the spirit world. As Shomas fought a wave of dizziness and pitched forward to splash face down in the stream, he considered that old rascal Paedris never contacted him that way unless the timing was bad.

"Lord Feany!" Captain Raddick screamed an alarm in sheer panic, rushing heedlessly back into the stream toward the unconscious wizard, though the two soldiers who accompanied Shomas had already acted to pull the man's face above the water. "Is he alive?" Raddick asked fearfully just before Shomas spit out a mouthful of frigid water. His question answered, Raddick helped the two soldiers carry the wizard onto dry land. "Get him out of these wet outer clothes," Raddick ordered. "And get a fire going, he must not fall into shock."

"Captain," a soldier named Thomas hesitated, for the Royal Army troop was making their way carefully through the lowlands north of the Taradoran border, and for the past three days had been struggling to stay ahead of a fast-moving orc invasion. "Dare we risk a fire here?"

"Better to risk being seen, than to risk our wizard falling ill or dying because we were afraid to act. I will trust you, Thomas, to make a fire that burns hot and clean."

Thomas nodded though he had doubts about making a fire without smoke, that required very dry fuel and as it had rained the past two nights, all the fallen wood in the forest was at least damp. "We will do our best, Captain. Liv! Help me-"

"No," Shomas wheezed. "No fire, not on my account. It is too risky, and I would rather be chilled than chopped in half by a filthy orc battleaxe. Help me up, Captain," Shomas grasped the man's shoulder, "walking around will warm me quicker than any fire could."

Raddick called over other soldiers to prop the wizard up while he walked in circles, breathing deeply and rubbing his hands together. With dry pants, a thick shirt and a woolen blanket wrapped around him, Shomas was soon ready to resume walking.

"Are you sure, master wizard?" Raddick questioned. He knew the wizard was sensitive about not being as fit as the soldiers, though the man was able to walk farther and faster every day since they had been forced to leave their horses behind. "The terrain ahead is steep," he gestured to the foothills they had begun to climb, "and becomes rocky above the treeline. If you were to faint again-"

"Blast it, Captain, I am not a woman whose corset is too tight," Shomas' face was red and not only from exertion. "I did not *faint*, I received a damnably unexpected message from Paedris in the middle of the stream! The message startled me, any communication through the spirit world can overwhelm the senses if you are not prepared for it, and, I became dizzy for a moment. Dizziness, not fainting," he insisted while wagging a finger for emphasis.

"Yes, Lord Feany," Raddick concentrated on keeping his lips straight lest his inner mirth betray him. "A message, through the spirits?" In his experience, while in the wilderness away from the royal telegraph system, wizards sent messages via various types of birds.

"A message, it is," Shomas searched for the best way to explain the deep, subtle magic to an ordinary person. "Paedris projected his consciousness, into mine, by traveling through the spirit world. We do not use that method often, or lightly. Only for messages of great importance, in times of great need."

"Oh," Raddick nodded to indicate an understanding he did not actually possess. "May I ask, does the message concern me, or is this wizard business?"

"It concerns us all, and *concern* is the key word, Captain. There is good news, I should tell you that first. Gather 'round, everyone," he raised his voice. "I don't want to repeat myself, I need every breath to climb this confounded mountain." When the full army troop was close enough for him to be heard without shouting, he related what Paedris had told him: the Royal Army had won a great victory at the Gates of the Mountains, wiping out almost the entire invasion force. Elements of the Royal Army were chasing enemy stragglers back across the River Fasse, or hunting down and killing the enemy within Tarador's borders.

Hearing the news cheered those soldiers with Shomas and he was glad of it. The army troop was there to assist and protect Shomas on his errand to find Koren Bladewell, their lives were at risk because of *him*. At times, Shomas felt guilt that he lacked the ability to throw fireballs like other wizards, though he knew his ability as a healer was unmatched. If he could wield magical fire, he could have taken care of himself in the wilderness rather than relying on soldiers. When Captain Raddick had informed him a massive host of orcs had invaded the dwarf homeland and was sweeping unchecked through the lowlands north of Tarador's border, Shomas had feared their vital mission would become impossible. Raddick asked what Shomas wished to do and the wizard had replied what he *wished* to do and what he *needed* to do were two different things. Onward was the only choice; the orcs being bold enough to risk a full invasion was proof that Tarador needed Koren returned to Linden as soon as possible.

New of the smashing victory at the Gates of the Mountains was cause for celebration by the soldiers, although as they were hiking up foothills toward the forbidding mountains in front of them, the celebration was confined to people taking extra sips of water from their flasks, giving the wizard congratulatory claps on the back, and offering small sweets they had secreted away in their packs. The back pats made Shomas wince, so enthusiastically were they given, and he refused most offered sweets as he knew such luxuries were coveted. He refused most sweets, not all, as not even a well-disciplined master wizard could resist honey-soaked dates and bits of chocolate. Chocolate! Walking farther into the wilderness with every step, Shomas justified eating chocolates as his last opportunity for a taste of civilization.

When the brief celebration was over, Raddick ordered the troop to again disperse, sending scouts out on all four sides, seeking as easier route forward and wary of ambush by roving bands of orcs. A discrete hand signal by Raddick told his men their captain wished to speak privately with the wizard. "Lord Feany," Raddick began quietly, "you said 'there is good news'. That implies there is also bad news. Please, tell me." Raddick could not imagine what bad news Lord Salva had sent to Shomas. The enemy had crossed the Fasse twice, with General Magrane counterattacking to throw the first force back across the river, and Paedris himself pulling down the great stones of the mountain Gates to crush the even second, even larger invasion force. Tarador was victorious, the enemy in disarray, and winter was coming. The peaks of the mountains to the north of Raddick were already capped with snow, surely all the Royal Army needed was to hold the enemy on the other side of the Fasse, and use winter to rebuild strength? By Spring, thousands of soldiers promised by the Indus Empire would arrive and Tarador could stand tall and strong against the army of Acedor.

"You might wish I had not told you, but you do need to know, Captain," Shomas warned the man. "Paedris fears the victory at the Gates only means the enemy will strike soon, rather than waiting for next Spring." He explained the court wizard's reasoning. "You see then, that it is all the more urgent we find Koren Bladewell. Paedris fears that without Koren, we are lost, and we have no time."

Raddick's face was white despite the exertion of climbing up the trail. "It would be best for us to keep this between ourselves," he glanced around to assure none of his men were within earshot. "Such an omen of doom would be a blow to morale."

"It certainly is not making me feel confident in our future, Captain," Shomas agreed gloomily.

Raddick walked without speaking for several minutes, scanning the horizon to the north. To the east and south, an orc host rampaged through the land. To the west, not all that far, lay the border of Acedor. And to the north lay the rugged, inhospitable mountains the dwarves called home. They would find Koren there, or not find him at all. Raddick feared to ask his next question, yet felt compelled to know the truth. "*Is* there hope for us?"

Shomas did not answer immediately. "Yes. Paedris has seen the vast hosts of men and orcs poised to cross the river, and he despairs for the enemy's numbers are unstoppable." Shomas took a drink of water and wiped the sweat from his brow. Only a short time ago he was shivering with cold, now he was soaked with sweat. He wished nature could make up its mind. "We have wizards on our side, but we cannot match strength with strength through magic."

Raddick had to smile at the irony. "You said we *do* have hope, master wizard? Yet you speak of an army that can crush Tarador, and their overwhelming strength in magical power?"

"Oh, um, yes," Shomas bit his lip. "Sorry about that. We do have hope, but such hope comes not from General Magrane, nor our Regent, or even Lord Salva and all the wizard fire our side can summon. The hope I speak of comes from Cecil, er, Lord Mwazo."

"The loremaster?" Raddick recalled with skepticism.

"Lord Mwazo is a powerful wizard, Captain," Shomas' tone reflected his continued irritation with people who thought the strength of wizards was measured only in terms of fireballs. "In many ways, Mwazo is the greatest of us all. That is in Lord Salva's estimation," he added, lest Raddick think Shomas was too defensive about wizards who could not mow down ranks of the enemy with magical fire.

"Forgive me, Lord Feany," Raddick bowed slightly, lower than he intended as he stumbled over a tree root.

"As you mentioned, Mwazo is our expert on lore, and in that capacity, he does not believe it is mere coincidence that Koren Bladewell is coming into his abilities at this time, this exact moment when the power of our demon enemy threatens to crush us all."

Raddick winced at the wizard's casual comment about Koren's abilities. When they set out from Linden, only Raddick and Lord Feany knew about Koren's secret, but along the way, it had become impossible to stop Shomas from mentioning the secret openly, and now all the soldiers with them knew their mission was to recover a missing wizard. "The spirits have brought him to us?" He guessed hopefully.

"I would not say that," Shomas cautioned. "The spirits do not *help* as you think of the term; our concerns mean nothing to them and all of history passes in the blink of an eye to the spirit world."

"Is the boy's power truly so great?"

Shomas shuddered despite being overheated from struggling up the hill. He recalled staring into the abyss when he, Paedris, Wing and Cecil had tested the nature of Koren's magical ability. "You cannot imagine the boy's power, Captain. *I* could not imagine it before I saw it, I had no idea it was possible for one person to command such power. I didn't realize such power existed! Lord Salva told us he felt the same, he was astonished and frightened, by the power that boy can command. Captain, when Koren Bladewell grows into his full strength and is able to control it, if he can control such immense forces, he could crush the demon as you could step on a bug, and seal the rent between this world and the underworld that feeds the demon. Yet, if the demon were to capture the boy, our enemy could seize Koren's power and unleash a demon army upon the world."

"Would it not be most prudent," Raddick lowered his voice even further, "for us to kill the boy and be done with it? You say as long as he lives, the enemy may find a way to use his power."

"Kill Koren? An innocent boy who has done nothing wrong? Have we not harmed him enough?"

"You think my words cold, yet I think of myself as coldly realistic, Lord Feany. My duty is to protect a nation, and, if you are to be believed," Raddick added as a hint he found the entire situation difficult to believe, "protect the entire world. The life of one boy is little compared to that of a *world.*"

"Captain, that is why I would never have made a good soldier; I cannot separate my sense of right from my sense of duty. I will lay your fears to rest. If Koren were to die, that would remove an immediate threat to Tarador, but only delay the inevitable end. The enemy has the strength to crush your army-"

"The princess, our Regent, has attracted promises of additional troops from our allies, not only soldiers but also ships, supplies and other aid. With Ariana as our leader, our allies have new hope. And they see the fall of Tarador would be the beginning of the end for all nations."

"Your princess is impressive, she is a clever girl. Unfortunately, we wizards have seen the enemy's full strength and we know that Acedor will overrun Tarador, despite the assistance of your allies. Koren's death would be trading a quick death by fire for a slower death that is just as certain. It is true that Koren is a potential threat, but the boy is a weapon, and a weapon can be used against you, or in your defense. Our only hope for survival, for true victory, lies with that boy."

"But, if it comes to him being captured by the enemy," Raddick pressed the point.

"Yes!" Shomas shot an unfriendly look at the Royal Army captain. "Yes, if it comes to that, you must carry out your orders, or we will all perish in fire. That is a last resort, only if the situation is truly desperate and you see no way to recover him from the enemy. Do you understand me, Captain? By killing that boy, you seal our fate just as surely as if you handed Koren to the demon on a platter."

"I see," Raddick shuddered also. "Well, then, we best find the boy soon. Are you feeling up to climbing yonder mountain?" Raddick pointed to a peak of gray stone that was tinted faintly orange in the late afternoon sun.

"Do I have a choice?"

"You could ask the spirits to guide us along a gentler route," Raddick teased.

Shomas groaned at the thought of climbing another, even higher and steeper mountain, "The spirits can," and he said a *very* bad thing that set Raddick to laughing.

Lord Mwazo unrolled the map onto the folding table in the wizards' tent, using dirty tea mugs and a sword to hold it flat. The situation was less than ideal; the portable table was not steady on the uneven ground, one of its legs was broken and had been inexpertly repaired, and Cecil was irritated that one of the mugs almost slid off the table, so he had to-

The table was not the problem, he admitted to himself. He was still tired, so deeply weary he slept most days away in the bouncing, lurching wagon as it traveled slowly down the rough roads toward Tarador's capital city. He was still bone-weary from the effort of clouding the minds of enemy commanders, making them think the Kaltzen Pass was lightly defended and so luring their army to destruction at the Gates of the Mountain. And then lending his remaining strength to Paedris, so that powerful wizard could pull down the twin rock formations of the Gates, trapping the enemy and burying many of them under tons of rock.

Nearly a week had gone by since Grand General Magrane's forces finished mopping up the last resisting pockets of the enemy army near the pass. Magrane now had his troops, and those of Duchess Rochambeau, driving the enemy westward across Demarche province, forcing the army of Acedor to choose between the steel blades and arrows of the Royal Army and the cold rushing water of the River Fasse. Many of the enemy had already chosen to risk the river and drowned, swept away downstream after jumping off the high bluffs. Three times, the enemy army on the west side of the river attempted to cross in two different places, and all three times they had been thrown back by Magrane's hard-pressed but victorious army. Lord Mwazo knew Magrane would eventually lose the fight and the enemy would gain another foothold on Tarador's side of the Fasse; the size of the enemy force was overwhelming and the utmost effort by Magrane's brave soldiers could not hold forever.

"Paedris," Cecil called in a soft voice, "we should go now. Do not say I am yet too weak to travel," he held up a finger to forestall the other wizard's protests. "I grow stronger every day, but the enemy's confusion lessens faster than I gain strength. If we are to cross the river and go west, we should do it now, while the enemy is still in disarray."

"Now *is* an excellent time, Cecil. An excellent time for you to drink that herbal tea I see you hid under your chair."

Mwazo made a sour face. "It tastes terrible, Paedris."

"That foul tea is *your* recipe, if you recall," Paedris retorted with a wink. "And you made me drink gallons of it when I last was sorely injured. It is good for you."

"I know," Mwazo grunted, reaching under the chair for the now-cold mug of awful tea. It even smelled bad.

"Go on, drink it. Don't sip it, that only prolongs the unpleasantness."

"Fine," Mwazo did not wish to argue, even more than he wished not to drink the tea. Tilting his head back, he swallowed the bitter and oily liquid in one gulp, then reached for the stoneware mug held out by Paedris. Gratefully, he took a mouthful of sweet lemonade, swirling around in his mouth to wash away the foul taste of tea. "Thank you. Now, could you show me where you plan to cross the river?" All the options looked bad to Mwazo. Places that were easy to cross were, naturally, well garrisoned by the enemy. Places where the enemy's watch was thin had fast-running rapids in the river, or high bluffs on the west side, or both. Beyond the river, much of the countryside was inhospitable, having been turned into a no-man's land by Acedor over the centuries. Tree cover was thin, water in the streams was contaminated and undrinkable, the ground grew thick with poisonous, itching plants and brambles with sharp thorns. It would be slow going at best, even for wizards. As they could not swim horses across the Fasse, they would be walking until they could steal suitable horses, and hope those beasts of the enemy were healthy enough for a long journey toward the enemy's lair. Just thinking about trudging across the grim landscape of Acedor made Cecil weary; it would be a long and arduous journey without joy, without comfort. And ultimately, without hope for himself and Paedris.

"Crossing the river would be difficult and dangerous, even for us," Paedris admitted.

"It would be less so if we were not so far away now," Mwazo complained. "I understand you and Magrane were anxious to get me away from the fighting while I was too weak to defend myself, but we have travelled too far from the border."

"No, we have not traveled far enough," Paedris said without offering explanation. "You should put away that map before you spill lemonade on it," he noted as Mwazo's hand shook and droplets ran down the stoneware mug onto the parchment map.

"I don't need a map?"

"No, you do not."

"Paedris, while I appreciate your confidence in my memory, I am not all that familiar with the enemy's land beyond several leagues west of the Fasse. It would be good to know-"

"You do not need that map, because we are not crossing the river."

"Not cross-" Mwazo saw the twinkle in the other wizard's eyes. "I assume you do not plan to dig a tunnel under the Fasse, and despite what people think, we wizards cannot fly, so what do you have planned?"

"Tonight, perhaps this afternoon, we will reach the upper tributary of the Pernelle river. My plan," he smiled, "is to board a boat there and float down to the sea, instead of riding in an infernal, bouncing coach on these rough roads. My back can't take another day of the luxury coach provided by the Royal Army." Paedris knew the coach Magrane had given to the wizards was the best available; those coaches with the softest springs were being used to transport wounded soldiers and Paedris did not begrudge those unfortunates that minor comfort.

"The sea?" Mwazo asked, startled. "A journey by ship would be preferable to walking or riding a horse, but how will you find a ship with a crew desperate enough to attempt such an insane voyage?" The sea even close to the coast of Tarador was infested with pirates from, or paid by, Acedor. Even Tarador's navy was mostly confined to patrolling within sight of shore, with the navy's efforts focused only on preventing an invasion by sea. The few ships of the Royal Navy had not the strength to fight piracy, and no naval commander would be rash enough to take one of his ships deep into the territorial waters of Acedor.

"We will find a ship and crew surely enough; do not worry about that, Cecil." He dug into a battered leather pouch on the dirt floor of the tent and pulled out a rolled-up scroll, untying the wrapping. "As to where will go ashore and our journey inland from there, we will need this map."

The princess let out a short, exasperated breath, louder than needed but she wanted to let the other occupant of the carriage know the future queen of Tarador was displeased. The carriage ride from the Royal Army camp on the east foothills of the Turmalane Mountains to the capital city of Linden seemed interminable. Ariana wanted simply to be back at the royal palace, but the journey over rough roads was *endless*. While she originally had insisted her carriage travel with the army contingent carrying wounded soldiers to the royal hospital, she had been persuaded after two days that her presence slowed the progress of the entire column and she was an unwanted distraction. Since then, Ariana's carriage and her guards had fairly flown along at a speed that threatened to shake the young princess's teeth loose. It had been a long and exhausting journey, not helped by her own deep sense of loneliness. At first, several of her advisers had traveled in the carriage with her, until those learned persons realized the new Regent was bored of talk about pressing matters of state. That day, as the speeding carriage came within tantalizing sight of Linden on its hilltop in the distance, Ariana had invited a young wizard-in-training to ride with her. By midmorning, Ariana had grown frustrated by the wizard's sullen and distracted attitude. "Lady Dupres," the princess began, "Olivia, I wish you would call me Ariana when we are in private. We are almost the same age, and I have almost no one I can really *talk* with. Everyone is so stiff around me."

Illustrating the Regent's point, Olivia stiffened in her seat. "Your Highness, if you were truly a mere 'Ariana', I would not be here."

"Oh," Ariana's cheeks reddened, chastened. "That is true, I suppose. You truly do not wish to be here?"

"Highness," it was Olivia's turn for embarrassment, "I do thank you for your hospitality," she said formally, wondering whether she should have said 'gracious hospitality'. "This carriage at least has some sort of springs to cushion us from the worst hazards of the road, while the driver of the wagon I rode in seemed to take delight in aiming for *every* pothole between here and the Turmalanes. But, no, I would not be here if the decision were left to me. All the other wizards are doing things that are *so* much more important!" She clenched her fists to show how being left behind was eating at her.

"Protecting the crown princess and Regent is not important enough for you?" Ariana tried and failed to keep annoyance from her voice.

"Oh, no! That is, I did not mean you are not important, your Highness," Olivia stuttered. How to properly speak with royalty had not been a topic of study during her training, and that formal training had been cut short by the forces of Acedor attacking Lord Salva. "Quite the opposite. You should be protected by a *real* wizard! I am still only a student," she opened her hand, and displayed the feeble fireball that was all she could conjure without relying on her special technique of drawing magical fire with her other hand. "If you were faced with a threat from a real wizard, a powerful enemy wizard, the best I could do is hope they tripped over me on their way to destroy you."

"I am sure that is not-"

"It is!" Olivia insisted. "Madame Chu was rash to trust your life to me," she continued with bitterness. "I should be with her, or with Lord Salva or another real wizard, where I could learn. Your Highness, I fear the reason Madame Chu sent me here is not so much to offer my protection to you, but to keep *me* safely away from the fighting. I do not exaggerate when I tell you I will be unable to protect you against any serious threat. I do not yet have the skill, the knowledge, or the power."

"Well," Ariana replied automatically, while she thought of what to say. "Lord Salva thought I would be safest inside the royal palace, so perhaps you will not need to do anything other than," she waved a hand, trying to imagine what a young wizard like Olivia Dupres did with her time. "You could study all the scrolls you wished to in Lord Salva's tower. Oh!" She clapped her hands in delight. "And the royal library! It is the finest library in the world," she boasted proudly, knowing the monarchs of Indus and Ching-Do would dispute whose library contained a greater volume of important scrolls and books. "I could show you around the library, and you could look at anything you wish."

"Really?" For the first time, the idea of being stuck in Linden with the crown princess held hope of being something more than confinement. From what little she knew of royalty, she did not imagine they spent much time in libraries. Mostly, she thought, they had people to read dusty books and research arcane topics for them. "You enjoy reading?" She cringed as the words left her mouth unbidden.

"Oh yes," Ariana replied in seriousness, completely missing that the young wizard might have insulted her. "I love being in the library! I used to bring books and maps back to my study, to read about long-ago people and foreign lands, and imagine I was there. Koren and I-" She stopped, and a shadow fell across her face.

In spite of the great societal gulf between them, Olivia reached out to pat the princess's hand, and the future monarch squeeze her hand back as a tear rolled down Ariana's cheek. "I'm sure he will come back soon, your Highness," Olivia assured the princess softly.

"No, you're not," Ariana stifled a sob, wiping away tears with the sleeve of her dress, not caring about the impropriety of the action. "No one is. Not even Lord Salva, is he? He *hopes* to find Koren somewhere in the wilderness, because Koren will not come back here on his own. Why should he? He thinks the Royal Army is hunting him as a criminal. He thinks *I* did nothing to protect him, that *my* government wishes to kill him or throw him in a dungeon."

"He will surely learn the truth, your Highness," Olivia offered, though the words sounded hollow even to her own ears.

"The truth?" Ariana laughed bitterly. "The truth, that he is a wizard, and his family would not have been banished from their home, that his parents would not have *abandoned* him," she pounded her fists on her thighs, "if the Wizards Council had seen to their responsibilities properly? And that the reason he worked as a servant, rather being granted the knighthood he deserved, is that we could not trust him with the truth about himself? Oh, yes, when Koren learns that, he will surely be *happy* to come back to Linden, and all will be forgiven!"

Olivia sat in stunned silence for only a moment, for Madame Chu had told her all about the unfortunate Koren Bladewell, and had told her what to say if, when, the princess raised the subject. "Lord Salva will take full responsibility, he had sworn it. I do believe that when Koren learns the full truth, that everything Lord Salva did as to protect Koren, I-" she paused, then sighed. She could not simply parrot the words Madame Chu had given her, they were empty. What Ariana needed was not false words of assurance; she only needed someone to listen. "The truth is, your Highness, I do not know Koren Bladewell. I never met him, and I cannot imagine what he has been through. Lord Mwazo believes an immensely powerful wizard such as Koren appearing now is no coincidence; that the spirits must have anticipated our hour of great need and given Koren the power he needs to defeat our enemy. If that is true, then whatever path Koren has taken and all the bad things that have befallen him along the way, they are his fate. Lord Salva," she smiled at the memory of Paedris and Cecil arguing about the very concept of 'fate'. "He does not put so much faith in mystical notions such as 'fate'. He told me his faith is in Koren himself. Paedris believes in the end, Koren will swallow his anger and do what is right, because of the essential goodness inside him. Lord Salva is a great and wise master of wizardry, Highness, I know of no wizard of such power. If Paedris trusts in Koren, then I do also."

Ariana looked away, out the window. "My fear is that Koren may come back to Linden, he may even save us all. But he will not come back to *me*," she buried her face in her hands and sobbed.

To that, Olivia had no answer, she did not know what to say, what anyone could say. So, she sat in silence, giving the young princess time to compose herself. It was several minutes before Ariana wiped away her tears, sniffed and sat upright. "I do feel safer having a wizard as my bodyguard."

"Highness, I really am not ready to be your bodyguard," Olivia said while looking out the carriage to avoid the princess's eyes. "Against a skilled assassin, I could not protect you."

"Madame Chu thinks you are ready," Ariana replied, though her voice did not sound entirely convinced. "Besides," she brightened, "Lord Salva placed magical wards around the palace. No enemy can get past the wards to hurt me!"

Paedris had explained the operation of those wards to Olivia. She as yet lacked the technique and power to establish or even renew such wards, but she now understood how to check they were in place and working correctly. Paedris had expressed confidence the wards would have sufficient strength to last months without being reinforced by a wizard, and he was supremely confident it would take a very masterful enemy wizard to disable or slip past the wards.

While the court wizard had boasted of the wards to the crown princess, he had also explained to Olivia the limitations of the magical wards; what they could *not* do. In truth, the wards did not cover the entire palace, for that elaborate and sometimes opulent structure was simply too large, with too many windows and doors. The wards guarded only the private family residence and a few public rooms, when Ariana went outside of that limited area, she would be vulnerable as if the wards did not exist. The wards could not stop an assassin's arrow from flying through a window, nor deflect magical fire cast by an enemy wizard. That last danger was unlikely, for unseen secret wards protected all of the royal castle, no enemy wizard could use magic within those walls without raising an alarm, and any hostile wizard approaching the royal palace would certainly use magic for guidance to their target.

Most importantly, Paedris had told Olivia with grave emphasis, all the wards in the palace did were prevent an enemy from gaining entry to the building. The wards sensed if a person was not authorized to be within their confines, but if the princess were betrayed, a traitorous guard could sneak an enemy assassin past the wards. Only those people most trusted could be allowed within the warded part of the palace.

That was the part of acting as Ariana's bodyguard that most worried Olivia; she had not spent much time around the royal palace, and she lacked the magical skill to detect deception and hostile intent in people around her. If the crown princess were attacked inside the palace, it would be by betrayal, and Olivia feared she could do little to prevent that.

.

"Whoa!" Bjorn demanded. "Slow down there, you young fool. I know you are eager to get to Linden, but if you make this a race, you will lose."

Despite his foul mood, Koren had to laugh, though he laughed *at* his companion and not with him. "Lose? To you? Would you like to see who can get to that-"

"Not to me, you idiot. You will lose a race against this mountain, if you try running down this trail," Bjorn pointed to the rough track they were following, it could barely be called a trail. Even sure-footed mountain goats trod warily on the track, as it was narrow and covered with smooth stones and loose shale. Bjorn's boots skidded while he spoke, he waved his arms and teetered out over the edge of a ledge higher than he was tall. If he tumbled over the ledge, he would survive the short fall, but he would not survive subsequently skidding farther down the hill out of control and into the deep gully below. Pulling himself back away from the ledge, he shook a fist angrily at Koren. "I nearly just fell, and I am placing every footstep carefully."

"Don't you know, Bjorn," Koren jested disdainfully at the older man, as Koren danced along the precipice of the ledge, showing off his unnatural ability to balance on the balls of his feet. "I'm a wizard! We can walk easily on the slightest surface," he boasted, recalling how Lord Salva had strode along a stone ledge at Duke Yarron's castle, when Koren first met that wizard. At the time, Paedris had carried a tray of pastries with one hand, barely using his other hand to steady himself against the castle wall. That feat had amazed Koren at the time, now that memory only made him more angry. Koren had nearly fallen to his death off that roof, all because he had not been trained to use the innate wizardly abilities that he did not even know he had! Paedris could have told him, could even have instructed him how to walk easily along a ledge that nearly caused Koren's heart to seize from panic. Instead, Paedris and all the other wizards had kept the truth to themselves, lied to Koren, and-

Koren's own arms flailed wildly as he overcorrected from his feet skidding on loose stones and in desperation, he flung himself away from the ledge, crashing painfully onto stones with his belly. "Oof, I, help!" He shouted when the smoother stones beneath him rolled as his momentum propelled him backward, his boots frantically scattering stones in an attempt to prevent his sliding over the ledge. His heart leapt into his throat as his boots flapped uselessly in empty air, and-

Bjorn grasped one of Koren's hands in both of his own, falling without dignity on his backside. "Ah! Oh, that hurts," Bjorn grunted from a sharp pain to his tailbone. While Koren got gingerly to his feet and checked nothing was broken, Bjorn rolled to one side, mouth open, unable to breathe for a moment.

"Are you hurt, Bjorn?" Koren bit one of his knuckles in anguish that he might have injured his friend.

"Only my pride, and my backside will be sore for a fortnight. Help me up, please." With Koren's assistance, Bjorn stood and walked stiffly, assuring himself he could walk normally if not without pain. "Ah," he rubbed his aching tailbone, and kicked over the ledge the particular stone he guessed had caused his injury. With a miniature mock bow, he addressed Koren. "You were bragging about your supernatural balance, oh master wizard?" Bjorn was not smiling.

Koren looked down at his own dusty and torn pants, at the dots of blood where he had scuffed his knees. With a sheepish grin, he admitted "Perhaps I need a bit of practice before I can fly."

"Ha!" Koren looked so thoroughly embarrassed that Bjorn chuckled despite his anger. "If you ever do try flying, warn me first so I don't leap out into a canyon to stop you, eh?"

"I promise," Koren said seriously. "Bjorn, I am sorry. You can lead the way, please. I am not quite," he glanced sideways over the ledge and into the gulf beyond, "*that* eager to get to Linden."

CHAPTER TWO

"Halt," Regin Falco commanded the guards as they tramped down a corridor under the royal palace in Linden. "What is down here?" He pointed to a dark, narrow hallway that gradually sloped down and curved to the right. The entrance to the hallway was barred by a gate of heavy ironwork, mostly simple vertical bars, but with intricate scrollwork in the center. Looking more closely at the scrollwork, Regin considered with a frown that the four holes arranged in a square likely used to hold a royal crest attached to the gate.

A crest of the Falco family, for this part of the palace was old enough to have been built before the Trehaymes took over the throne of Tarador. Seeing the missing crest and imagining his family's symbol that had once been there made Duke Falco's grind his teeth briefly, then he shook his head and concentrated on his purpose that morning.

The light from his lantern shown between the iron bars, illuminating a layer of dust on the stone floor of the hallway, or, Regin realized, it was actually a tunnel. Dust along both sides of the tunnel floor was darker and dotted with splotches, as water condensed on the rough bricks of the tunnel walls and roof and slowly dripped down to the floor. Other than the splotches of moisture, the dust was undisturbed. No one had been into the tunnel in a long time.

"Down there, Your Grace?" One of the guards replied, expressing mild surprise. "It is access to the, the-"

Another guard spoke. "To the water system, Your Grace. There is a pipe underground, I believe it cuts directly under our feet, carrying clean water from the cistern atop the east tower."

"Ah," Regin nodded. Clean, fresh water from a fast-running stream coming from the royal forest north of Linden was brought to the castle through an aqueduct, then pumped by windmills up to the cistern at one of the highest points of the castle hill. Water flowed out of the cistern to various points around the castle, providing drinking water. The Falco's home castle in Burwyck province had a similar system, although there Regin had installed two additional cisterns with enough capacity to store water for six months. If anyone ever laid siege to the Falcos in their home, the ducal family would not run out of water, for they could also collect rainwater from the roof. In Linden, Regin thought with disdain, the royals could not hold out nearly as long against a siege. The difference was the royal residence in Linden was a palace, dedicated to pleasure and the affairs of state rather than to defense. If Regin sat on the throne, there would be many changes in Linden, and seeing to the security of the palace would be among the first of those changes. "Open this gate."

"We can't, Your Grace," the first guard looked stricken. "Only the chief of the palace guard has those keys."

Regin inspected the gate itself. It was heavy, and although it had been painted regularly enough for layers of paint to build up in corners, dots of rust marred the surface around the critical hinges. Streaks of rust ran down from the bottom hinge. "You have been in there?"

"I have, Your Grace," answered the second guard. Anticipating Duke Falco's next question, the man stepped forward. "The water system is inspected once each year, in summer when the royal family is at the summer palace, and the cistern can be drained for patching and cleaning."

Regin nodded, for much heavy work was done around his own ducal castle during the summer. "This year?"

"Your Grace," the man's cheeks reddened, "I am afraid to say that as the princess was at the summer palace only briefly and her mother remained here, we did not have the opportunity to perform the usual-"

Regin spun toward the guards with anger. "Do you mean to tell me the girl who is both crown princess and Regent is on her way here at this very moment, and the security of these lower passages has not been reviewed in over a year, though Tarador has been invaded and our armies have only recently stemmed the enemy's advance??"

The guards looked at each other. "I will bring the chief guard immediately, Your Grace," one of them stammered and ran off, his boots slapping on the hard floor.

The chief guard resentfully came to the tunnel entrance, then gave the keys to Duke Falco, grumbling that the guards had better things to do. For the remainder of the day, Regin and a rotating pair of guards inspected all the tunnels, with the duke impressing the guard force by his diligence. Thick spider webs, tunnel floors slick and stinking with muck from dripping water, narrow passages where the Duke needed to squeeze through by himself, nothing deterred the man who ruled Burwyck province. Exhausted guards returning from exploring the lower tunnels reported the duke was tireless in his effort to secure the palace before his future daughter-in-law arrived. And they reported the duke did find issues which needed to be attended to; rusted locks, bars where the metal had corroded away from the stone and mortar it was fastened to, even one alarming instance of a gate with one set of hinges loose from its mounting. The chief guard hastened to make repairs, though some repairs required the services of the Royal Army engineers, making them unhappy also. He muttered to himself that Duke Falco was making a huge fuss about nothing, that while security of the lower tunnels might be less than perfect under the palace, access to the other ends of the tunnels was assuredly secure. How, the chief guard asked aloud to no one, could an enemy agent get into the palace through a water aqueduct? Impossible! Even if, in the extremely unlikely event an assassin could get *into* an aqueduct, the man or woman would be trapped in there, for the heavy iron covers were fastened and locked from the *outside*. The enemy would be trapped and drown, or die of exposure in the cold water. Impossible, the chief guard muttered as he shook his head. The only benefit to the duke poking around in the warren of tunnels under the palace was it kept the damned man from making trouble elsewhere!

"Your Grace, if you will allow me past you, I can-"

"Nonsense," Regin told the man coldly, refusing to move aside to let the guard squeeze past him in the narrow tunnel. "You think me fragile, spoiled and useless because I am a duke? In my home keep, I personally oversee security arrangements *twice* a year, and I do not miss a single nook of my castle." What he said was true, because Regin did not trust anyone with his life, a lesson he learned from his father. And a lesson Regin had painfully been taught by his younger brother, who twice attempted to have Regin killed while they were boys. Their father had laughed at the younger boy's first clumsy attempt at assassination, and only sent Regin's brother away the second time because the foolish boy had involved a rival ducal family. Murder within the Falco royal family could be forgiven if it was done for the reason of grasping for power, but stupidity and embarrassing the Falcos could not be tolerated. Thus, Regin's younger brother had been sent on an 'educational' journey that eventually took him all the way to the Indus Empire where he remained, acting as the Falco's trade representative in that far-away land. The two brothers exchanged letters once or twice a year, without any trace of familial affection. Both brothers preferred their relationship to be strictly business; their business ties meant they needed each other and that need kept them both alive.

The duke held his lantern in front of him, peering down the tunnel to see the low-ceilinged chamber where the tunnel ended. The brick roof of the aqueduct ran along the floor of the chamber, and there was a round iron cover over an opening on top of the aqueduct. "Ah!" Regin pretended to slip on the wet and somewhat slimy floor of the tunnel. "Stay here," he turned to the nearest guard and jabbed a finger at the floor. "I don't need you clumsy oafs falling and knocking me over."

"But, Your Grace, we are responsible for inspecting the-"

"Which you were not doing at all until I forced you to get off your lazy behinds!" Regin retorted vehemently. "The crown princess is my future daughter-in-law and *I* am taking responsibility for her safety while she graciously offers me hospitality in the royal palace. Now, stay here while I check the lock on this cover. When I am done, you two blind idiots can fumble around uselessly as you wish but until then, stay *out* of my way," Duke Falco demanded with a sneer. The play-acting came easy to him, it was how he treated the guards at his own castle in Burwyck, except for a very trusted few who had earned his grudging respect and trust over the years.

"Yes, Your Grace," the guard agreed reluctantly, and remained in place while the duke made his way down the sloping tunnel, holding a lantern with one hand and using the other hand to steady himself on the slick floor.

Regin made a show of slipping on the floor than was really only damp from moisture seeping between the bricks of the tunnel roof, scraping his boot heels to the side and grunting in mock frustration. When the guards did come down the tunnel to inspect the security of the aqueduct cover, he wanted them to move slowly, to delay them looking at the lock mechanism.

The circular iron cover had a simple bar across it, holding it in place, and a lock on one end of the bar. Tampering with the lock would achieve nothing, for even if the lock were not there at all, the bar was still under two hoops and anyone on the other side of the cover had no way to slide the bar aside. Regin stood huddled over the lock, pretending he was looking at it closely, keeping his body between the two iron hoops and the pair of guards who were holding their lanterns stretched out in front of them to better see what the duke was doing. Working quickly and with shaking hands, Regin pulled from inside his jacket a vial given to him by an agent of the enemy. "The lock is rusted, this is disgraceful," he remarked as he removed the stopper from the glass vial and poured out the clear liquid in four places; where the bases of the iron hoops met the stone they were set into. The liquid dried rapidly, in seconds the surface appeared no more damp than anything in the underground chamber. Dismayed, Regin caught a whiff of an acrid smell but that, too, was quickly gone, lost in the overall mildewed odor of the tunnels. Satisfied he had performed his task as part of the bargain with Acedor, and with hands shaking from fear, he walked back up the tunnel, this time not having to pretend his unsteadiness. "Well?" He demanded. "Get on with it, you lazy slugs! I don't have all day!"

Regin allowed himself a smile, concealed in the darkness, as the two unfortunate guards skidded down the tunnel to peer at and pour oil into the rusty lock. The men only gave the iron cover, bar and hoops a brief glance before hurrying back to the duke. "It is done, Your Grace. Thank you for noting the rust on the lock, we will mention it to the royal engineers."

"Mmm," Regin grunted haughtily, and groaned to himself. He had been working for hours in damp, unpleasant, slimy tunnels just to drip the contents of the vial on that particular area. Now he must continue to uselessly wander the warren of tunnels for another hour, at least, while his fine boots became crusted with dried muck and his stomach grumbled with hunger.

No, he told himself. Additional time spent in the tunnels was not useless, far from it. By laboriously inspecting *all* the access points below the palace, he would throw suspicion away from himself if anything unusual and unfortunate were to happen in one of the tunnels.

Trust no one, Regin reminded himself. One thing he was certain of was that the enemy, above all, could not be trusted.

"Do you know what they did to me?" Koren asked. "All of it?"

"As you only recently told me your real name, I do not really know anything about you, *Koren*," Bjorn emphasized the last word. "So, no, I don't know your story, because you haven't told me. Or you haven't told me the truth, or all of it."

"If you did know, you would understand," Koren answered defensively.

"Koren," the former King's Guard said with a sigh, "I pledged to follow you to the end of your journey, whatever that is, but I wish you paused to put some thought into exactly *what* you plan to do once we reach Linden. You told me the Royal Army has orders to kill you, what makes you think Linden is the place you should go? It seems to me you should be running in the other direction."

"No!" Koren said vehemently. "No more running," he shook his head with fierce determination. "I've been running away from my problems for too long. My father told me," he stopped as a lump formed in his throat. "My father," he took a sip from his water flask, "told me never to mope around and feel sorry for myself, that someone out there," he waved to the mountains towering around them, "has it worse than you. I haven't been feeling sorry for myself, at least," he thought back to when he tried and failed to throw himself over the side of the *Lady Hildegard* when he thought his jinx curse had followed him to sea and was going to sink the ship. He had to admit, he had been feeling plenty miserably sorry for himself before he worked up the courage to jump over the side. "At least, I stop when I realize that I am feeling sorry for myself. I'm not guilty of that, but I also have not been standing up for myself."

"Koren, you didn't know that you are a wizard," Bjorn reminded him gently.

"I'm not talking about that. I should be a knight. Twice over! *Three times*!" He shouted, shaking a fist at the sky.

"A knight?" Bjorn worked to keep the skepticism from his face. Judging by Koren's expression, Bjorn was not successful.

"I saved the life of the princess, did you know that? I saved her life three times in one morning." He told the story to Bjorn, who listened with amazement, so much that he needed to look down at where he placed his feet as they walked, lest his attention wander and he fell over the edge.

"Koren, I had not heard that story. Well, hmm, maybe part of it. My mind was often much addled by drink back then, you remember, so I don't recall much of the tales I heard. If I did hear such a tale, I would have thought it no more than idle tavern gossip. Truthfully, if I didn't know you, I would not believe it. It happened just like you said?" The idea of a boy rescuing the crown princess from a giant bear, a raging river and a pack of bandits was ridiculous, except Koren was no ordinary boy. He was a wizard. According to the dwarf woman Frieda, Koren must be an extraordinarily powerful wizard.

After a pause to consider seriously whether he had embellished a story that needed no exaggeration, Koren nodded. "Just like I said."

"Well," Bjorn let out a breath. "That is surely quite a thing you did. A knighthood would not be out of the question, certainly," Bjorn mused, although thinking to himself that if Koren had been wearing the uniform of the Royal Army or the King's Guard, what the boy did that morning might simply be considered doing his duty. "But I do not think you would get *three* knighthoods for saving her three times. It was, after all, part of the same event-"

"No, Bjorn. You don't understand. Saving her that morning was *one* thing I did. You heard about the Cornerstone being found?"

"Aye, that I did hear about. Everyone heard about that. Why, I got a free drink the night that news reached the town where I was staying, the tavern keeper was so happy to hear about it." For a moment, Bjorn thought blissfully back to that free drink, the mellow whiskey hitting his tongue, the warm sensation of- he shook his head angrily. No. He did not drink any longer, and did not want to think fondly in any way of those days. Drinking had cost him his family, his health and his pride.

"The story you heard was that the princess herself found the Cornerstone?" Koren asked with a neutral expression.

Bjorn looked to the sky, pulling to the surface a dim memory. "Yes, yes, that is what we heard. She is a clever girl, our princess," he smiled. "Though now I suppose we have to call her the Regent, which seems a crazy notion to m-"

"It wasn't Ariana who found the Cornerstone," Koren interrupted, lifting his head with pride. "I did it, All by myself. *I* did it! Her mother and the wizard persuaded me we needed to let people think it was Ariana's doing, because that would strengthen her position against the Regency Council. Or something like that," Koren was now bitter about agreeing to keep silent about that lie.

"*You* found the Cornerstone?" Bjorn's voice carried no trace of disbelief, he was beyond that. Nothing the young wizard had done could surprise Bjorn Jihnsson any longer. "The princess took credit for it herself?" If true, that would surprise Bjorn. Though, he admitted to himself, it had been a long time since he last saw the princess with his own eyes. The girl had grown up surrounded by war and strife and the Regency Council's political machinations to control her. A young woman who faced those threats every day could become very practical about bolstering her own power.

"No. Or," he recalled, "she told me she didn't want to take credit for it, that I should have been given, *something* for it. Maybe that was another lie," he choked on the word. A powerful wizard lying to Koren made him angry, but Koren had never been anything but a servant to the court wizard. Certainly, Ariana was his princess and future sovereign, but she had also been his friend. Or she had pretended to be. Why else had she invited him to read books and study maps of exotic lands with her? As princess, she gained nothing from spending time with the wizard's servant boy, so had she truly been his friend back then? Or, Koren dared not hope, more than a friend?

No.

It didn't matter. That was all behind him now, all behind both of them now. Ariana was, to everyone's astonishment, Regent of the land. And more astonishing, she was engaged to be married to, of all people, Kyre Falco. Most astonishing of all, Koren himself was a *wizard*!

He admitted to himself that, regarding the crown princess, he did not know what to think. His quarrel was not with her, even if she had known all along that Koren was a wizard. If Lord Salva had advised Regent Carlana Trehayme that the secret had to be kept from Koren, then perhaps Ariana had not been told. Or, she had been told, and all the time they had spent together had not been about friendship at all; it had been the future queen's attempt to curry favor with a future wizard.

Koren did not know what to think, other than that while Lord Salva's betrayal made him angry, a betrayal by Ariana would cut him deeply. The thought was too sad to bear.

"Koren? Koren!" Bjorn interrupted the boy's daydreaming.

"Hmm? Sorry, I was, thinking."

"You were thinking that you should have been knighted for finding the Lost Cornerstone?" Bjorn asked knowingly. "I have to agree with you there. Koren, you gave the entire realm hope again! I overheard Royal Army soldiers talking, they were telling each other that now we have the Cornerstone again, we can defeat Acedor. The legend of the Cornerstone may only be a story, I don't know, but while it was missing, many people never truly believed in their hearts that Acedor could be destroyed, that we could ever end this war. You gave us hope! You!" He stared at the boy in wonderment. Not only was the boy secretly, unknowingly a wizard, he had been at the very heart of critical events in Tarador. That could not all be a coincidence, and Bjorn had to ask himself whether his own part in Koren's life was also not any kind of coincidence. Bjorn had been there when King Adric Trehayme died and Ariana became queen-in-waiting. Two people who had been present during events that shaped the current realm of Tarador, brought together without previously knowing or even having heard of each other. That could not be a coincidence, could it?

"I should be a knight for that! Or at least," Koren threw up his hands, "a medal, or something. Some gold coins would have been nice."

"Gold coins are always nice," Bjorn agreed. "So, that's two times you should have been knighted. First, for saving the princess, then for finding the Cornerstone. What's the third time? You said you should have been knighted three times."

Koren realized he did not actually know the criteria for granting knighthoods. He supposed someone needed to perform a spectacular act of bravery, or do something especially, vitally helpful to the kingdom. But for all he really knew, a princess could grant a knighthood to someone who served her a particularly tasty bowl of soup. The ways of royalty were, after all, a mystery to Koren. "Oh, that. When Lord Salva was attacked by enemy wizards and the Royal Army was stuck on the wrong side of the river, I went to find the wizard and help him. He was trapped in a ruined keep and the enemy-"

"Koren?"

"Yes?"

"Could you tell me the details later, when we're not clinging to the side of a cliff?" Bjorn suggested. They were not exactly on the side of a cliff, but the seldom-used track they had been following had almost disappeared, and they were having to hold onto roots, shrubs and rocks to stop themselves from falling. Ahead perhaps a quarter mile, the land opened and there was a nice flat trail to walk on, until they reached that blessed spot Bjorn was watching where he placed every footstep.

"That's a good idea," Koren agreed, and they didn't speak until they could walk normally again. Once they did not need all their concentration to avoid falling to their deaths, Koren told Bjorn about how he had killed an enemy wizard with an arrow, and how he had barely escaped after sending Lord Salva safely away on Koren's own horse.

Bjorn remained silent, so Koren told him everything, all the way to when they met again so unexpectedly.

"You saved the life of Lord Salva, and you expected a knighthood for that?" Bjorn asked when Koren was done telling his tale.

"Yes!" Koren said with indignation. Well-deserved indignation, he thought. "Instead, the Royal Army wanted me arrested as a deserter."

"That was not their fault, as far as the Army knew, you *were* a deserter. I'm sure if you had stayed in Linden, it would all have been cleared up soon enough. The Royal Army can be a big clumsy bureaucracy, but they are not in the habit of punishing people who act with courage. Hmm." Bjorn scratched his beard. "Koren, have you ever considered that, you being a wizard and all, that the things you did; saving the princess, finding the Cornerstone, rescuing Lord Salva, are merely what is expected of a wizard? That maybe you weren't granted a knighthood because, well, you just did what wizards are supposed to do as part of their duty?"

It was good that Koren was walking on flat ground at the time, because his feet wobbled. "What?" He asked, thunderstruck. "I didn't deserve any honors, because I acted as a wizard should, even though I had *no* idea I was a wizard?"

Bjorn made an exaggerated shrug. "I never said life was fair, Koren. And I was only guessing, no, I was throwing out crazy ideas. No less crazy that a wizard who doesn't know he's a wizard," he added under his breath.

"They lied to me about being a wizard, then acted like I knew all about it?" Koren's face turned red.

"Koren, I don't know why they would have lied to you, there doesn't seem to be any point to it, if you ask me. Maybe if I were a wizard, a properly trained wizard, that is," he hastened to add, "it would all make sense. But they must have planned to tell you the truth at some point."

"Why bother?" Koren demanded, fuming mad. "When it is so much easier to continue lying to the stupid farm boy!"

"Because," Bjorn said gently, "eventually, it would *not* be easy to continue the lie. You discovered the truth, and you didn't even talk with a wizard."

"Frieda knows about wizardry," Koren objected.

"I'm not talking about Frieda," Bjorn explained. He reached in his pack and pulled out a honey-soaked cake they had bought from the dwarves. Breaking the cake with his hands, he gave half to Koren. They had hard bread, hard cheese, dried strips of meat for their long journey, and a few small apples. The food in their packs was not sufficient for walking all the way to Linden, for if they had to walk the entire way, Winter would be upon them before they reached the capital of Tarador. "I'm talking about what you've seen with your own eyes. You have unnatural fighting skill. Even as a boy, before Lord Salva supposedly cast a spell on you, when you shot an arrow, you never missed. Never?"

"Never," Koren agreed. He did not like where the conversation was going.

"You said the bear that attacked Ariana was thrown backward when you held out your hand, without even touching it. When you fought those two enemy wizards to rescue Lord Salva, you shot one with an arrow, and the other wizard threw a fireball at you, but the fire flowed around you."

"It did, and I thought that was Lord Salva's doing!" Koren defended himself.

"Was Lord Salva there when the flaming bomb from that pirate ship missed you, and missed your ship entirely? Koren, the sailors on that ship suspected you are a wizard, the ship's captain certainly knew something was odd about you."

"And I didn't," Koren's shoulders slumped. "Damn it all, I am an idiot. You are right, Bjorn, I should have known."

"You're not idiot, but, perhaps you are not as aware of yourself as you could be. Whether you met Frieda or not, eventually, likely soon enough, you would have seen the truth. It couldn't be hidden forever. Lord Salva deceived you, for whatever reason I cannot guess, but the court wizard is not stupid. He must have known you would realize the truth, so he must have planned to tell you at some point."

The next morning, cranky, exhausted and sore, Regin was up before sunrise, early enough that chief guard Captain Temmas was not yet in his office when the duke arrived. Temmas was warned by his people, and hurried up to his office, still buckling on chainmail as he came though the outer door. Palace servants, not even the head of the entire guard force, did not keep a duke waiting, especially when that duke was a guest of the princess in the palace. As a sign of each man's irritation with the other and mutual lack of sleep, the exchange of pleasantries was brief. Within minutes, Temmas had assigned a pair of guards to accompany Duke Falco to inspect the second and third floors of the palace, and the duke left with two very unhappy guards.

By late afternoon, having taken only a brief luncheon break, Regin declared he was satisfied with security in the residence area of the palace. While the crown princess remained within the residence, she would be safe as she could be without restricting her movements to an impractical level. The unfortunate pair of guards were warily pleased to hear the duke's praise of security measures within the residence. "But," Regin glowered, "all that is well and fine, until the princess leaves the residence, as she must in performance of her duties. While I would prefer the mother of my future grandchild treat her own safety as her paramount concern, I fear," he faked a dismayed smile, "she is far too conscientious about her duties to hide inside the residence. Her devotion to duty is a blessing to Tarador, and a burden for us, eh?" He said with a wink.

The guards, weary from tramping all throughout the residence and being on their best, most formal behavior around the duke, were taken in by Falco's apparent offer of comradeship. "Yes, Your Grace, it is a trying task."

"Hmmm," Regin pretended to consider where to go next. "Oh, blast it," he threw up his hands in a show of frustration, "the public areas of the palace are too extensive to cover in one day," he looked out a window to judge the position of the sun. "Tell me this; if the princess were threatened while she is in a public area, for example during an audience in the great hall, where would she be taken for safety?"

The guards shared a look of mild surprise. Surely the duke already knew the answer to his own question? "To the Citadel, Your Grace."

"Ah," Regin nodded slowly. "Of course." He pretended to consider for a moment, then, "let us go there."

"Your Grace," a guard said with a pained expression, "we are not allowed to open the inner door of the Citadel unless-"

"Unless the door is opened to admit a royal person who needs to be brought within the Citadel for protection. Tell me, if an enemy threat was imminent, where would I be directed to go?"

"The Citadel, Your Grace."

"Clearly, then, I am authorized to access the inner door," Regin noted, his expression again unfriendly.

As a credit to their training, the guards sent a request back to Captain Temmas, who quickly granted permission for the duke to enter the inner Citadel, accompanied by the guards. The two men feared the duke would want to poke around every nook and cranny of the Citadel tower, but to their surprise, Falco seemed satisfied merely to go through the heavy iron-clad door and ascend the first flight of stairs. "Oh," he rubbed one knee with an exaggerated grimace, "all this tramping around is making an old battlefield injury flare up on me. I am no longer young like the two of you. Go," he waved a hand dismissively, "look around the upper levels, I will remain here."

Without questioning the duke, the two guards scurried off up the stairs, eager to finish the task and hopeful the duke's weariness meant the aging royal would soon give up for the day. When they returned, they found Falco standing beside the heavy door, tapping a foot impatiently. The duke insisted on swinging the door closed behind them by himself. "Uh," Falco grunted, "this door is impressively sturdy." He needed to lean backward and use his weight to get the door moving on its well-oiled hinges. After the door closed with a solid 'thunk', Regin rapped his knuckles on it appreciatively. "Well, in a crisis, I could do worse than to be secured behind such a substantial fortification." His experienced eyes took in the massive stones in which the door was set, with the hinges on the inside. Once the door was barred from within, there was no way to get it open from outside.

"We will be certain to get Your Grace to safety is needed," a guard bowed slightly to the duke.

"Hmmm," Regin grunted. In a crisis, the very last place he wanted to be was inside the Citadel with the princess. "That is enough for today, I am famished."

The knees of both guards sagged ever so slightly with relief. They had escorted Duke Falco long past the scheduled end of their duty shift, not daring to mention that detail to one of the most powerful men in the realm. The prospect of leaving the duke after walking back to the residence with him was tantalizing, and monopolized the attention of the guards as Falco intended. With thoughts taking off boots to rest their aching feet, food and possibly a well-deserved mug of beer dancing in their minds, the two guards could perhaps be forgiven for not noticing that Duke Falco's jacket was fastened a bit tighter, as if he no longer had a package hidden inside the jacket.

Like a dog with a tasty bone, Koren could not let the subject drop. He was obsessed with understanding all the misfortunes that had happened to him, so he continued the discussion as soon as they resumed walking after an uncomfortable night sleeping in a forest. "That all makes sense, and it's a nice happy story, Bjorn, but tell me this: why, then, does the Royal Army have orders to kill me?"

"How do you know they do?"

"I," Koren halted in his tracks again. "I overheard soldiers, no. I overheard stablehands talking, one of them said the army had orders to kill the wizard's servant, because they thought I was responsible for an attack on the princess."

"Mmm," Bjorn grunted. "You didn't hear it direct from a soldier, then, nor did you see their written orders? Koren, what you heard was a rumor, and rumors spread far and fast when they are sensational. People who like to gossip know to embellish the facts, to make a better story. You won't know the truth until you ask a real soldier about it."

"And if the soldier responds by killing me?"

"Um, good point. If, when, we meet soldiers, I will approach them to ask about it. You can stay back until we know the full truth of the situation. Oh," a thought hit Bjorn as he saw the crestfallen expression on Koren's face. "Well, I've gone and done it, then. You were all filled with righteous indignation, ready to march into Linden and take vengeance on those who wronged you. And now you're feeling let down?"

"Yes!" Koren admitted. "Even, even if," he balled up his fists, "Lord Salva planned to tell me the truth eventually, he and the whole Wizards' Council were supposed to tell me I am a wizard a long time ago! I should be training properly now, and, and my parents should be alive and swimming in gold coins! Nothing that has happened changes that fact."

"Aye," Bjorn could not argue with that point. "You have the right of it there. Lord Salva does have much explaining to do. I just do not think your best approach is to storm into Linden intending to beat the truth out of the wizard. We don't even know if he is in Linden," Bjorn chided his young companion, "and as you keep complaining to me, you don't know how to use magic!"

Koren made an angry, dismissive gesture and resumed walking down the trail. Bjorn was right, his enraged daydreams of storming into Linden and making people pay for how they mistreated him, were nothing but an immature boyish fantasy. Koren's father had taught not to wallow in self-pity, and Koren now saw how difficult it was to avoid feeling sorry for himself. It was difficult, because first he had to admit to himself what he was doing. Taking vengeance on Paedris would not bring his parents back. He could not bring his parents back, nothing could. What, then, did Koren truly want?

The truth. The whole truth, all of it.

He would confront the wizard, hear the truth, and then he would decide what to do next.

That was the right thing to do, he knew it then.

It just did not *feel* as good as the idea of making the court wizard, and everyone who had wronged him, beg for forgiveness. Damn it, Koren told himself bitterly. Why did doing the right thing feel so drearily *dull*, while imagining doing the wrong thing felt so deliciously satisfying?

Later that morning Bjorn called a halt. "Koren, wait."

"Why?" Since Bjorn's relentless logic popped the bubble on Koren's savory dream of revenge, the two had not spoken for hours. Koren was lost in his own thoughts, mostly kicking himself for not realizing the truth by himself, much earlier. How could he have been such a fool? Giant bears were not frightened away by unarmed boys! He should have known right then that something was very wrong with what he thought he knew about himself.

"We should have met someone by now," Bjorn announced with concern. For the past hour, they had been walking down what could almost have passed for a road in the dwarf lands. While they saw many footprints, belonging to dwarves, ponies and horses, even the occasional flock of goats, the land they walked through was utterly empty. By going back up the mountains and detouring north toward Westerholm before once again going south toward Tarador, they had hoped to slip around the invading orc army in the flatlands below. Bjorn expected to encounter dwarves coming up through the passes for the security of their mountain strongholds, or elements of the dwarven army marching down to fight the orcs. Instead, they had not seen a single person. The signs of heavy traffic having already gone up the mountain worried Bjorn, who pointed to wispy columns of smoke in the valley below. They could not yet see the valley, for a ridge of foothills blocked their view, but the entire area was covered with a low-lying haze of smoke. Was the smoke from dwarves burning supplies they could not move, to deny those supplies to the orcs? Or were the orcs already in control of the valley, and burning farms and buildings from the hateful spite that was the nature of orcs?

Koren was startled out of his reverie. "You're right. I didn't think of it, sorry."

"I've been thinking it, ever since we reached this road. My expectation was that we would find slow going down the road, with all the dwarves moving their families and livestock up the road against us. That we haven't seen anyone at all is worrisome."

"What should we do?"

Bjorn considered for a full minute before he spoke. "If the orcs are in the valley already, they are likely to send a patrol up this road, hoping to find and kill stragglers among those fleeing from them. I say we get off this road," he looked around. The land was mostly low scrub brush, dotted with groves of pine trees. There were no trails other than the sort of road they traveled, the only other paths appeared to have been created by wild animals. Bjorn walked forward, then off the road to examine a faint trail. "This is a deer print, and I think that print is from a goat. We need to get to the crest of those foothills, see what lays ahead in that valley, before we decide what to do. Koren, keep off this deer track for now, if orcs do come up this road, we don't want them seeing our boot prints near the road." He looked back at the road, the surface was so trampled down that signs of their walking down would only be noticed by someone looking carefully, and not by orcs running in haste after easy prey. Or so he hoped.

The plan was that once they skirted around the invading host of orcs, Koren wanted to find his horse first, though Bjorn had warned the boy that finding one horse in the vast land between them and the border of Tarador would be nearly impossible. They had no idea where the retreating dwarves had taken the horses from that stable, Bjorn reminded the distraught young man. Koren needed to be prepared to purchase the first horse they found available, and be satisfied with that for their journey to Linden. "Thunderbolt found me alone in the wilderness once," Koren shot back when Bjorn reminded him one too many times that finding one horse in the chaos of an invasion was unlikely, perhaps even impossible, and certainly foolhardy. "He came all the way from," Koren paused, for he didn't actually know how Thunderbolt found him, or how far the horse had traveled on his own to get there. "From a great distance, anyway."

"Good," Bjorn brightened. "That settles it, then. Problem solved."

"What?" Koren stared at the former King's Guard. "How is that?"

"Well," Bjorn shaded his eyes to study the smoke haze that lay beyond the last ridge they were approaching. "The horse found *you* once, he will find you again, if it's meant to be."

That idea brought Koren to a halt. Walking while thinking did not seem like one of his capabilities that day. "You think, you think Thunderbolt found me because I'm a wizard, that, somehow I called out to him?"

"I don't know the ways of wizards," Bjorn stated truthfully, knowing Koren was also entirely ignorant about how wizardry worked. "Something made that horse come straight to you in that wilderness, where even you didn't know where you were." Bjorn's intention had simply been to allow Koren to think he had to allow the spirits to determine whether, when and how he was reunited with his horse, so the boy would forget the idea of running around a battle zone in a vain attempt to find one particular animal. But now that Bjorn really thought about it, the idea of a magical bond between Koren and the horse was not only possible, it was the only explanation. Bjorn also stopped walking to ponder that thought. "Koren, if the spirits want you to find your horse, I suspect they will guide Thunderbolt to you. If the spirits do not will it, you and I could wander this area until even you are old and gray, and never find that horse."

Koren did not like the idea of *not* trying to find Thunderbolt. There was a saying he had learned as a boy; the spirits help those who help themselves. Maybe that expression did not apply to wizards, who had the ability to bend the energy of the spirit world to their own will. "Hmmm," he grunted.

"What?"

"Oh," Koren hadn't realized he had said anything aloud. "Perhaps what I am supposed to do is will the spirits to bring Thunderbolt to me. *Safely* to me," he added hastily, lest the spirits misunderstand him. An amateur wizard trying to make the spirits do his bidding might only make them angry, and mischievous spirits did not do anyone good.

"That's the spirit!" Bjorn exclaimed, then, "No pun intended."

Koren began walking up the rocky ridge again, distracted by his thoughts. "I wish I knew how to make the spirits do what I want!"

"How did you do it the first time, when Thunderbolt found you?"

"I didn't *do* anything!" Koren gritted his teeth in frustration. "I didn't let myself even think about Thunderbolt, or anything I enjoyed about my old life in Linden. It was too painful, and thinking about it did me no good."

"Well then, maybe trying *not* to think about it is what you are supposed to do?" Bjorn guessed unhelpfully.

"Arrgh!" Koren screamed, shaking his fist to the sky.

CHAPTER THREE

Lord Mwazo had to admit their journey down the river to the sea was physically comfortable, certainly sleeping the days and nights away on a real bed in the cabin of a riverboat was preferable to being jostled and jarred all day in a carriage on rough roads. The quiet and smooth ride of the boat, even the gentle rocking as the boat bobbed over small waves, had done wonders for Mwazo's constitution, by the time they reached the sea, he felt almost fully recovered. Even the food was good, though he did not wish to know how much the court wizard had paid for fresh, healthy food in the inflated wartime prices.

Lord Mwazo's discomfort was mental rather than physical. They had reached the seaport where the river met the vast ocean, and their idyllic days of lazily floating down the river were over. They must concentrate their full energies on the next step in their doomed and desperate journey, and Cecil had to push to the back of his mind the knowledge that he and Paedris would not be returning.

Despite the time of year and being on Tarador's southern coast, the early evening was damp and chilly; it had been drizzling all day and now the rain had settled into a dense, misty fog. Fine droplets collected on Lord Salva's beard and eyelashes, which he blinked away to run down his cheeks. The gloomy weather was exactly what he wanted, it kept people inside and prevented casual observers from identifying the two wizards who made their way through a tangle of side streets and back alleys near the docks. Both men wore cloaks and hoods, not unusual in the unpleasant weather and not attracting any attention. Weaving between mostly empty, discarded crates, old fishing traps and other junk cluttering the alleys, Paedris led the way to the side door of an inn close by the docks and produced a key from a pocket. The door was battered, with peeling paint, dents and marks that might have been caused by knives or even an axe. Paedris was not bothered, as this was known to be a rough section of the sea port and he had been there before. The lock mechanism, rusty on the outside, turned smoothly and silently, and the door hinges were well-oiled and made no sound. He had to push firmly on the door, for it was heavy, made of thick timbers. "Cecil?" Paedris gestured for his fellow wizard to enter. The room was used by those who wished to come and go without being seen by customers in the inn's front tavern, and Paedris had hired the room for the night. Or, someone had hired the room and procured the key for Paedris, as the wizard did not wish to deal directly with the innkeeper and her staff.

Lord Mwazo shuffled through the narrow alley to stand beside Paedris, and remained outside while he stuck his head through the doorway skeptically. "Here? You want us to meet potentially dangerous people here?"

"Are you afraid, Cecil?" Paedris was amused. "Of ruffians?" he teased, knowing his fellow wizard had no fear of common thieves.

"I'm afraid something living under the tables here will bite me." He peered dubiously at the rough and worn furniture in the room. "More likely something living *in* those chair cushions will bite."

"I can get a plain wooden chair for you," Paedris looked more closely at the chairs. In the dim light, he could not tell whether the pattern of the fabric was original, or the results of many mystery stains over too many years. "On second thought, I will get a wood chairs for myself also," he decided, wishing to avoid giving fleas an easy route into his robes.

"Then we need only fear poisoning from the food," Mwazo remarked dryly, wrinkling his nose at the scent coming from the inn kitchen's chimney.

Paedris smiled, light glinting off his teeth even in the gloom. "People do not come here to eat, Cecil. They come here to drink."

"They come here to *forget*, Paedris," he said as he took a step inside the room, and his boot squished on something he didn't want to think about. "I will want to forget this when we are done." He scraped the bottom of his boot on a broken crate in the alley and stepped inside. "Now?"

Paedris closed the door and wiggled the handle to assure it was locked behind them. The only other entrance was on the far wall, a door which opened to a hallway leading to the tavern's common room. That door was closed and, Paedris could tell with a rap of his knuckles, also thick and solid, though muffled sounds of shouting and laughter could be heard beyond the door. "Now, we wait. Let us push these," he pointed to the stained, overstuffed chairs, "aside and use these plain wood chairs, eh? Behind you, there should be, yes," he saw to his satisfaction, "a chilled bottle of wine and goblets. I am thirsty."

"You trust wine from this inn?"

"The owner of the inn is one of the most cunning smugglers in southern Tarador, she uses the inn as a front for her business. One of the items she smuggles is wine, and she is far more knowledgeable on the subject than the owner of a typical spirits shop."

"If you say so," Mwazo pulled the bottle from the bucket of ice and cold water. At least the wine was, as Paedris expected, chilled.

A few minutes later, having poured himself a second glass of the excellent wine, Mwazo thought that if Paedris was as right about other things as he had been about the wine, their evening might not turn out too badly.

Captain John Reed lifted his beer stein and pretended to drink from it for the umpteenth time. He had been sitting at a corner table of the tavern for over an hour, and the serving girl had taken away two full beer steins already. The girl had not commented on the sailor making a show of drinking without actually drinking, she had seen it before, it was none of her business, and the sailor tipped well. If other customers had been paying attention, they would have seen her pulling the tap of the beer cask behind the bar to fill a stein, and if they had been counting they had seen three beers delivered. They would have seen the serving girl taking away steins, but they would not have seen her pouring out the full stein into a drain when she was behind the bar.

Reed did not like meeting a potential customer in the back room of the inn, which was widely known to be a front for smugglers. Reed had not been above small-scale smuggling, especially earlier in his career at sea; the tariff laws from the many nations bordering the sea were so nonsensical and confusing that an honest merchant captain might become a smuggler without intending to, or even knowing. It was not the meeting place he objected to, it was the mystery surrounding his potential customer. An anonymous message had reached him that morning, requesting a meeting that evening, to discuss hiring his ship the *Lady Hildegard*. A few years ago, even last year, Reed would have dismissed any sketchy request; potential customers should come to the respectable inn where Reed maintained a room while ashore, or the customer could send a message out to the ship at anchor.

But now, Reed was desperate for business, like all the ship captains and owners in the port. After delivering most of her cargo at Gertaborg, the *Hildegard* had packed her holds less than a third full and set sail for Tarador's main seaport, hugging the coastline and taking advantage of unusually favorable winds. The ship's captain and crew would have preferred to wait at Gertaborg for a full cargo to haul, and a haul longer than a mere six day's sailing. No such cargo was offered, so Reed had taken aboard what he could get and hoped to find better fortune at Pernelleton, where most shipping merchants doing business in Tarador maintained offices.

Instead, to the great disappointment of captain and crew, they found the great harbor at Pernelleton crammed with ships riding idly at anchor, and no cargo going out. So many ships had been lost to pirates that insurance rates had shot sky-high, and no merchant could afford to transport goods by sea. The *Lady Hildegard* was the last merchant ship to enter the harbor, which is why she floated in an unfavorable anchorage nearly at the harbor's mouth, subject to wind and currents. Two warships of the Royal Navy had recently failed to return, and it was feared they had fallen victim to pirates of Acedor.

With no cargo being offered and none likely, the *Hildegard* was like the other unfortunate ships choking the harbor; some of those ships had been swinging on the end of their rusting anchor chains for nearly a year. Just last week, an abandoned hulk, stripped of everything useful including spars and topmasts, had taken on water from seams that had not been properly caulked in a year. As crews aboard other ships and crowds lining the harbor watched in either alarm or amusement, the old ship heeled over to starboard. As the harbormaster frantically sent out two boats to see if the hulk could be pumped out and refloated, people in the crowd took bets on whether the hulk would sink, and whether the boats rowing hard toward the abandoned ship would reach it before it slipped beneath the waves. The boats lost their race, although there was much shouting and arguing about the final outcome of bets, for the men rowing the boats had slowed as they judged they could do nothing to prevent the hulk from sinking, so why should they pull so hard on oars into a stiff breeze on a hot, sunny day?

Now the sunken ship was a navigation hazard in the crowded harbor, although the harbormaster had determined the deep water of the harbor allowed most ships to pass over the wreck without noticing. And, as the only ships coming into or out of the harbor were shallow-draft Navy vessels, one more wreck littering the bottom of the harbor was a problem for another day.

Captain Reed had talked, even pleaded, with the few merchants who still kept offices around the port. Give me a cargo, he said and offered the *Lady Hildegard* as collateral in lieu of insurance no one could afford to purchase. Sensibly, all the merchants had turned down his offer, reasoning that if Reed failed to deliver cargo, it would be due to his ship being seized or sunk by pirates. Reed had to admit he could not argue with that logic.

According to the merchant agents in the port, almost all cargo to and from Tarador was traveling overland, though that route was expensive, slow and carried its own risks. With the war boosting demand for almost all supplies, any ship successful in carrying cargo to Tarador could be assured of a handsome profit. The problem was, now even the great port at Gertaborg was nearly blockaded by pirates, so no cargo west of Gertaborg was moving by sea.

Reed had approached his dwindling crew with the proposition they weigh anchor and sail at best speed for Indus, hoping to find westbound cargo there. During the voyage, Reed could not afford to pay the crew, nor would there be assurance of pay when they reached the Indus Empire. Crew signing on for the outbound voyage would even need to pay for their own food during the passage. This announcement caused much grumbling and the loss of another dozen disheartened crewmen. To Captain Reed's surprise, enough crewmen from other ships offered to join the *Hildegard*'s run to Indus that he actually had to turn people away.

Then a second Royal Navy warship was declared overdue and presumed lost to enemy action, and Reed's new crew evaporated back into the taverns where they spent their days drinking away the last coins in their pockets.

Unless Reed could find paying work soon, he was facing the prospect of paying anchorage fees out of his own pocket. Most of the ships in the harbor were in debt to the harbormaster, some had run up fees so high, those ships had been abandoned by their owners and turned over to the port to manage. A petition to the harbormaster, seeking reduced fees during the pirate crisis, had been rejected despite the harbormaster's sympathy. Any reduction or waiver of fees would require approval by the Regent or crown princess or queen-in-waiting or whatever Ariana Trehayme's title was at the moment. As the young Regent was extremely busy pushing scattered remnants of the Acedoran army back across the River Fasse, relief from the Regent was unlikely.

That was why Captain Reed sat in the dark smoky tavern, pretending to drink one beer after another.

The front door of the tavern swung open, and Alfonze strode in, looking one way and the other as casually as he could manage, then went straight to Reed's table. "Two of them. Wearing cloaks and hoods, I couldn't see their faces."

Reed had ordered the trusted Alfonze to wait across the street at the end of the alley, to see who entered the inn's back room from the alley. "This fog is too thick," he looked out the still-open door, for the view through the tavern's filthy windows would appear foggy on a clear day. "You couldn't see faces anyway. Just the two?"

"Yes, both of them were men, by the way they walked. Sorry I can't tell you more."

Reed clapped his man on the back. "We are sailors, Alfonze, not spies." They sat quietly a few minutes until the clock struck seven in the evening, then Reed stood and brought his beer stein to the bar, placing it behind the counter to be emptied. In case the men he was meeting with had his own spy in the tavern, Reed walked with the unsteady gait of a man slightly drunk, bumping shoulders with Alfonze in the narrow hallway. At the door, Reed straightened and knocked.

"Come in," a voice called out.

"Captain Reed?" Paedris asked without stirring from his chair when the door opened.

"I am," Reed said cautiously, stopping just inside the doorway to allow his eyes to adjust to the dimness. The only light in the room came from a fire that had dwindled to one thin, flicking flame, and a candle that was too far away from the table to illuminate the two occupants. Reed could see two figures, one of whom had a hood draped over his head, concealing his face so all that could be seen was faint light glinting off his eyes. Knowing how that sort of meeting worked, he nodded for Alfonze to close the door behind them. "Who might you be?"

"A potential customer. I would not sit in those chairs if I were you," Paedris cautioned the merchant ship captain. He pointed to a pair of plain wood chairs, and the sailors sat cautiously, as if the chairs were about to collapse on them.

"Do you mind telling me what you want, since you won't tell me who you are?" Reed asked, growing in confidence.

"I want to hire your ship."

"To go where?"

"That will be revealed after we weigh anchor."

"In that case, you can't afford to hire my ship."

"We haven't discussed a price yet," Paedris expressed surprise.

"We don't need to. If the destination is so dangerous you can't discuss it," Reed's lips curled in a wry smile, "then you must think the odds are my ship won't be coming back."

Paedris was taken aback. He could not argue with the logic of the man's argument, but he had considered the possibility that no ship captain would accept a risky charter, and he had a plan. "I will buy your ship, then." Paedris offered.

Mwazo grabbed the other wizard's arm and pulled Paedris close to whisper "*Buy* his ship? We can't afford to buy a ship."

"*We* don't have to," Paedris patted his friend's hand. "The royal factor will buy it for us."

"You are sure of that?"

"I am sure that we have little choice." He raised his voice. "Your ship is the *Lady Hildegard*? She is in good condition?" Paedris had viewed the ship through a spyglass that morning; the *Hildegard* was riding at anchor near the mouth of the harbor. From shore, he could see her sails were neatly furled, her yardarms square, rigging taut and any painted areas freshly attended to. That only told him what his landlubber's eye could see of the ship's exterior, at a distance. Rumor in the port held the *Hildegard* was a good ship, well maintained by her remaining crew. Some sailors in the town, bitter about being stuck ashore with no prospects for paying work, laughed that the *Lady Hildegard* was too well maintained; that her crew were wasting their time as their ship slowly rotted at anchor from disuse.

"Good condition, aye," Reed sat up straighter in his chair as he spoke, throwing his shoulders back with pride. "She will have a mild coating of weed on her bottom by now, I'll not lie to you, but less than any other ship in the harbor." The ship's bottom had been thoroughly scraped in the South Isles before her last voyage, and Reed knew the other ships in the harbor had been swinging idly at anchor for months while barnacles, weeds and other denizens of the sea took root on their hulls."

"That is not good. We will need speed for our voyage," Paedris declared.

"This harbor has no careenage," Reed said, then at the potential customer's raised eyebrow, he explained. "A place where the ship can be run aground and heeled over so her bottom can be scraped. This is a good harbor because the water is deep. I need a shallow, sandy beach to careen the ship."

"Is there anything you can do here?" Paedris inquired, knowing nothing of ocean-going ships.

Reed rubbed the back of his neck. "I can heel her over somewhat in the harbor, get the sides near the waterline. Then we can pass a line under her bottom, work in front to back," he used landlubber terms for his customer. "That will remove the worst of it. Most of it." He was not looking forward to such a complicated operation. And his crew would not look forward to the hard work. On the other hand, he reflected, the hard work would keep the crew busy. And preparing the ship to go back to sea would be good for the crew's morale.

Maybe he should clean his ship's hull whether he reached a deal with the mysterious customer or not. A ship ready for sea at a moment's notice was likely to get any business available in the harbor, if there was any business available. Reed was still surprised by the wizard's offer. "You really want to buy my ship?"

"I am *willing* to buy your ship, since you refuse to charter her to me, under my terms. If she survives to return, then you can have her free and clear again, as your property."

Reed and Alfonze shared a look. While it sounded like a tremendously good deal on the surface, it was *too* good a deal. Both sailors knew such generous terms meant their customer did not expect the good ship to be coming back from wherever they wished to take her. Alfonze leaned toward his captain to speak quietly. "You've had the *Hildegard* for years, Captain. She's family to you. Would you really sell her?"

"You think she is happy laying at anchor, while her timbers slowly fall victim to dry rot? Better she goes out of this world doing the work she loves." Turning back to the customer, Reed asked for a price. The two men haggled while their companions sat silent, observing.

"I must say, Captain," Paedris softly hit the table with a fist in frustration. "You ask a very dear price for a ship with no other prospect of employment." He knew even the royal factor in the port had a limit to the amount of credit he could extend, for the finances of Tarador were already stretched to the limit by the war.

"And you, sir, offer salvage prices for a seaworthy ship."

"Her seaworthiness means nothing if she is fated to sink at anchor," Paedris noted.

"She will be at sea again soon enough, when this war is over," Reed answered hotly, insulted by the lowball offer for his beloved ship. "I'll not have you put her on the bottom of the ocean without just compensation."

"This war will end with our defeat," the other customer said in a low voice, speaking aloud for the first time, "if we fail in our mission."

That remark made Captain Reed lean forward and look more closely at the two customers. He gasped. "You are- you are Lord Salva! And you must be," he searched his memory for rumors he had heard since returning from the South Isles. With a snap of his fingers, he announced "Lord Mwazo," after seeing the dark skin of the other wizard's hands.

"You are remarkably casual about meeting a pair of powerful wizards," Paedris said unhappily.

"It is not every day the court wizard of Tarador asks for my help," Reed's bravado was belied by his body tensing in the chair. "Now I see why you wished to meet here."

"We require discretion," Paedris explained. "As my friend, as Lord Mwazo said, our mission is of the utmost importance."

"But the Royal Army has just won a tremendous victory," Reed protested. Rumor had it wizards were vital to Tarador's success in that battle, he would not insult the court wizard by mentioning that rumor.

Lord Salva shook his head sadly. "Only a temporary halt to the enemy's inevitable advance into Tarador, I fear. True victory in this war will not be achieved by the Royal Army." At his side, Lord Mwazo removed his hood and nodded. "There you have it, then," Paedris held his hands out in a gesture of supplication. "Lord Mwazo and I have a mission vital to the war effort, and it is possible your ship will not be returning."

"*Your* ship," Reed corrected the wizard. "She will be yours, if we can agree on a price." He leaned over and whispered something to Alfonze, and the two sailors had a quiet but animated discussion. "Lord Salva," Reed cleared his throat. "You say Tarador is in mortal danger?" That ran contrary to rumors in the port town, where confidence was finally returning after news of the smashing victory at the Kaltzen Pass. Many beached sailors were beginning to hope of going to sea again, though knowing it might still take much time before merchants were willing to risk their cargoes in waters still menaced by pirates. A victory on land did not always imply success at sea.

"Yes. Tarador, the *world*, has never been in greater danger than now," Paedris hoped the vehemence of his words would help persuade the reluctant sea captain to part with his precious ship. "Do you think Lord Mwazo and I would undertake a hazardous journey, if we were not truly desperate? This is our last hope, for survival of Tarador."

"You are a businessman, Captain Reed," Mwazo leaned forward, jutting out his chin. "Think on this: if we purchase your good ship, and Lord Salva and I succeed, you will have coins in your pocket and can buy a new ship. If you refuse to sell your ship and we cannot continue our journey, *all* the ships in the harbor will be worth nothing because Tarador will fall. Viewed purely as a business proposition, if you prefer, you have nothing to lose and everything to gain by dealing with us."

"Aha," Reed was not yet convinced. "The coins you pay for my ship will not buy a new ship for me if you succeed, for restoring seagoing commerce will cause prices to increase. And a dead man cannot spend coins, no matter how heavily they lay in his pockets. Please tell me, Your Lordships, what will happen to us if we do not agree to your terms?"

Paedris sat back in his chair, beginning to relax. Captain Reed would not have asked that question, unless he had made up his mind what to do. Mwazo rubbed a thumb on the table, in a gesture the two wizards had planned. "We will choose another ship. A ship not as good as yours, not as swift. Our mission will be placed at risk, and Tarador will be less likely to survive. And your pockets will be lighter, while your ship swings idly at anchor."

"No, Lord Salva, I meant," he pointed a finger to his chest, then Alfonze. "What will happen to *us* if we refuse to sell our ship to you?"

"Oh," Paedris sometimes forgot that most people he dealt with were not wizards. "You will, *forget* this conversation," he said simply, with a nod to Cecil. "You must understand, we cannot risk the enemy learning we intend to journey by sea, so your memories will be adjusted. It is painless and will not damage you permanently, I assure you."

"Such assurance is not necessary, Paedris," Mwazo declared quietly. "Captain Reed has decided to sell his ship to us, and not only as a business transaction. He wants to make a difference in the war."

"How do you know that?" Reed demanded.

"Because," Paedris noted the captain did not deny what Mwazo had said, "we are after all, wizards, you know."

The negotiation went on for only another quarter hour before wizards and merchant captain agreed on a price for the ship, most of the sticking points were about what items could be taken off the ship, and what items needed to remain aboard for the voyage. Storm canvas and anchors could be removed, to lighten the ship. Reed was free to sell such unneeded equipment separately from the price of the ship, to sweeten the deal for him.

"We are agreed then," Paedris expressed relief.

"Yes," Reed nodded. "Lord Salva, I suggest you come aboard the, *your*, ship in the morning, where we can discuss details."

"Details? What, details such as?"

"For one, master wizard, you now have a ship." Reed looked to Alfonze and the two experienced sailors shared a smile. "You will need a *crew*."

After the sailors left the room, the two wizards sat silently for a moment, each lost in his own thoughts. Paedris slowly sipped wine while he wondered and worried about Madame Chu, who was slipping across the Fasse into enemy territory again to stir up trouble. She had barely recovered from her ordeal of lending Paedris her power to pull down the Gates of the Mountains, and Paedris had wanted Wing to accompany the crown princess back to the capital city, where Wing would hopefully be far from the fighting and relatively safe. Instead, because she knew that with Paedris and Cecil headed for the sea, she was the most powerful wizard available to the Royal Army, she was placing herself in great danger. And Paedris felt his heart going with her. While they had recovered in the Royal Army hospital tent near the Kaltzen Pass, the two wizards had time to speak privately, a rare opportunity they each had been seeking since fate had brought them back together. Words were whispered, fingers lingered interlaced as they held hands across the space between their hospital cots. Promises were made, promises neither of them expected to be kept, because keeping such promises required a hope for the future they were both too wise to indulge in.

"You are thinking of Wing," Cecil said quietly, refilling his friend's wine goblet.

Paedris looked at the other wizard sharply. "You were reading my-"

"No," Cecil replied with a shrug.

"Oh," Paedris felt shame he had accused Cecil of invading his privacy without permission. "Am I that obvious?"

"No one gets that look on their face unless they are thinking of someone they love very much," Cecil stated softly. "Paedris, is it wise to, to-" he searched for a kind way to speak his mind.

"To think of her, to dream a life with Wing, when neither of us expect to live long enough to see each other again? Yes, Cecil. *Especially* now, it is important to imagine a better future, to give us hope." He raised his wine glass for a toast. "To Wing, wherever she is now."

Cecil raised his glass and drank, thinking to himself that Paedris could contact Madame Chu if he wished, although doing so took considerable energy, and the two of them might want privacy.

He drained the last of the small wine bottle into his own goblet and swirled the liquid as he had seen Paedris do. Lord Mwazo was not a wine expert like his friend, but he knew what he liked, and the wine was excellent. Perhaps Lord Salva was right. Perhaps, now, with defeat almost certain and death inevitable, now was the best of all times to enjoy and appreciate the pleasures of life. Wine. Friendship. Love. Even a love doomed by circumstance.

Paedris returned the discussion to a less intimate subject. "Tell me, Cecil, how were you able to sway the good captain's mind so quickly? I did not detect a spell being cast. Are my powers slipping?" He asked only half-jokingly.

"Your powers are unmatched, but I did nothing, I didn't have to. Captain Reed is a man of honor; he fears for Tarador and wishes to do something other than watch his ship rot at anchor. Paedris," Cecil said with a faraway look as he sipped the last drops of wine, "did we just buy a ship?"

"Yes," Paedris enjoyed a chance to smile. "I think we did. I intended no more than a charter, but as we both know this will be a one-way voyage for the ship, I feel better being honest about it. Besides, legally *we* are not buying anything. The royal government is purchasing the *Lady Hildegard*, so she will technically be owned by the sovereign."

"Interesting," Cecil chuckled. "Princess Ariana bought a ship she will never see."

CHAPTER FOUR

Captain Reed sent a boat to collect the two wizards, for he trusted the men he hand-picked to row the boat, and did not want rumors of wizards coming aboard his ship. If the wizards hired a boat from the port, they would certainly be recognized, for the disguises they chose were laughable. Reed arranged for his boat to meet the wizards at an empty warehouse that stood atop pilings reaching out over the harbor. The boat went under the warehouse, where the two wizards were able to walk down stairs and board the boat unseen. With the port languishing dormant for months, any activity was sure to attract attention, and the boat picking up two people and rowing hard for the *Hildegard* had many people on shore peering through glasses to see what was going on. As the pair of wizards had donned hooded cloaks when they climbed unsteadily into the boat, the curiosity of people ashore would have to remain unsatisfied.

Reed should not have been surprised that both wizards climbed nimbly up the ropes to the ship's deck, although neither of them appeared to have enjoyed the boat's passage across waves that were being tossed by a freshening wind blowing straight from the sea. "Are you well, Lord Salva?" Reed asked while suppressing the grin he was feeling inside.

"I have never enjoyed sea voyages," Paedris admitted, breathing deeply to quell his rebellious stomach. Though there were spells and potions to cope with seasickness, Paedris did not wish to appear so weak as to need magical assistance simply to travel out into the harbor. He looked over Reed's shoulder to the open sea beyond the harbor's mouth, where foaming whitecaps were crashing against each other. "I will be fine. Where can we talk, Captain?"

"Come to the, well, I guess now it is *your* cabin," that time Reed did allow himself a grin. He led the wizards below deck to the owner's cabin, which was located in the stern next to his own cabin. As it had been many years since the *Lady Hildegard* had an owner aboard who was not also her captain, the owner's cabin had long been converted into two smaller cabins for senior ship's officers. Reed had the cabin's partitions torn out to restore the space to its original spaciousness, which still felt cramped to the wizards. The cabin did have a skylight to let sunlight and a fresh breeze into the enclosed space, and windows spanned the rear wall. The tall Lord Mwazo had to be careful not to knock his head on a large wooden beam that cut across the cabins' ceiling, but otherwise he was pleased enough with the cabin. After all, he and Paedris did not intend to be aboard the ship for a long voyage.

Sitting down at a table, Reed poured wine for the wizards. "Your Lordships, we can speak safely here. You now own the ship," he patted a chest pocket, in which he had the official papers that had been delivered only shortly before the wizards boarded the ship's boat. How the wizards had gotten the official royal factor to move so quickly must have been magic, or a miracle. It was only within the past hour that the *Lady Hildegard* officially belonged to the royal government; a late-night message from Paedris to the royal factor in the port town had been returned with a disbelieving note. Even considering the bargain price of the ship, the royal factor was flabbergasted he was being asked to use precious wartime royal treasury funds to buy a merchant ship, when the harbor was fairly choked with ships slowly rotting because ships were useless during the piracy crisis.

Lord Salva's reply note, written early that morning in language more polite than he wanted, made it clear the royal factor was not being requested to purchase a ship, he was being *ordered* to purchase a ship, and if the man wished to discuss the matter further with the immensely powerful wizard he should take a boat out to the *Lady Hildegard* and continue the conversation face to face.

The factor's next note stated funds from the royal treasury were being made available immediately, and ownership of the *Hildegard* would be transferred to the royal government by the end of the morning. And that it was not necessary for the court wizard to trouble himself thinking about the royal factor at all. Please.

"Where are we bound for?" Reed asked over a sip of wine. Drinking wine so early was unusual, but so was the situation. Offering tea to the wizards would not do for such a special occasion. "I must know in order to staff and provision the ship."

"Have you guessed?" Paedris asked while sipping the surprisingly good wine.

"Guessed? Why would you want me to guess?" Reed did not understand the point of the master wizard's question.

The sailor Alfonze tilted his head and had a thoughtful expression, so Paedris gestured for him to speak. "Because if we can guess the wizards' intentions, others who are less friendly can also guess where you are going?"

Mwazo pointed to Alfonze with grim satisfaction. "Correct. Keeping secrecy about our mission is almost more important than the mission itself. The enemy must not know our plans."

"Er," Paedris stared at his friend. "The mission itself *is* rather important."

"Yes, but, Paedris," Mwazo gently chided the court wizard, "if this boat sinks with us aboard, or we die along the way, other wizards could attempt to fulfill our mission after us. But if the enemy learns of our plans, of the enemy's vulnerability, they will be alerted and we can accomplish nothing."

"Oh," Lord Salva's cheeks reddened. "You make a very good point, as always. Lord Mwazo is right, Captain Reed."

"Very well," the captain nodded unhappily. He and his crew were sailors, not spies. Their knowledge was of wind and sea, not intrigue. "You wish me to guess where you want us to take the ship; I believe it is fairly obvious. The two of you need to go somewhere across the sea, perhaps to obtain assistance from other wizards in those lands? To do that, you need to run through the pirate blockade. And the only reason to risk running the blockade is to gain swift passage to lands across the sea."

Paedris shared a happy look with Cecil. "It is that obvious?"

"Yes," Reed nodded. "I must tell you, rumors are already flying around the port that this ship intends to run through the line of pirate ships out there," he gestured toward the open sea out the back windows of the ship. "Anyone in shore, with a glass or bare eyes, can see we are mending sails and scraping her bottom as best we can. Once we offload cargo to lighten ship, even a fool could tell what we have planned."

"Excellent. Captain Reed, please do whatever you can to feed that rumor. We do plan to run the blockade, as you say, but our destination is not across the sea. It is westward along this coast. Your mission will be to put us ashore in Acedor."

Both sailors gasped. "*Acedor?*" Alfonze asked, thunderstruck. "Are you completely mad?"

"Forgive my first mate's language, Your Lordships, but his sentiment is true," Reed stated softly. "Going to Acedor, particularly by sea, is certain suicide. For yourselves, and for this ship and crew."

"Nonetheless, that is our destination," Paedris declared. "We have a ship, Captain Reed, and if this crew cannot carry us to Acedor, then we will endeavor to find sailors willing to take the risk. We will not think less of you or any of your fine crew if you refuse this voyage, the risk is as extreme as you say. However, I believe that with careful planning, and," he winked slowly, "some measure of assistance from magical elements, we can be successful. By 'successful', I include the safe return of your crew. If that can be accomplished, after Lord Mwazo and I are ashore."

Captain and first mate looked at each other, eyes wide open in disbelief and dismay. "I can say, Lord Salva," Reed remarked dryly, "you certainly have everyone on shore, and my crew, fooled with your true intentions. If the enemy is similarly deceived, then," he bit his lower lip, "it might, it just might be possible to do as you ask. The pirate blockade will not be expecting us to sail *west* from this harbor. Where," he paused to clear the table and unroll a map, "do you wish to be put ashore?"

Cecil and Paedris looked at each other in mild dismay. "We were hoping," Paedris explained, "that you could suggest where best for us to go ashore."

"Me?" Reed's eyebrows flew upward.

"You are an experienced sea captain," Cecil observed.

"Experienced, aye," Reed snorted, "and if you wish the wisdom of my experience, you will forget this entire foolhardy notion. However," he took a deep breath, "as that is unlikely, can you give me a rough idea of what area of the coast you wish to land? Acedor," he waved a hand over the map, "has a coastline stretching hundreds of miles, even before the peninsula turns to the north."

"We wish to go ashore in this general area," Paedris tapped with a finger to indicate the spot on the map spread across the table.

"*Here?*" Captain Reed asked in quiet disbelief, and made a show of putting his face close to the map to make absolutely certain he did not mistake where the wizards wished to be put ashore. "Your Lordships, that is the absolutely worst stretch of coast to go ashore. This entire area is sheer cliffs down to the water, with jagged rocks offshore. Would it not be better for us to put you ashore here," he pointed to an area closer to the border of Tarador, "or even here, where the coast turns north? The currents there are unfavorable," he frowned, "and the weather can be unpredictable, especially at this time of year." The more he thought of attempting to sail north along the western coast of Acedor, the less he liked the idea. He had only ever been there once, when he served as a young lieutenant in the Royal Navy, and his ship had been battered by a powerful storm that swept in from the northwest overnight. He recalled vividly that terrifying night and the next day, as the storm had pushed his ship toward the coast of Acedor. To risk death at sea, or enslavement and eventual death in Acedor, was no choice at all. Reed's ship had survived due to extraordinary efforts by captain and crew, and not a little bit of luck. Of the eleven Royal Navy ships caught in that storm, two had foundered and sunk, with another ship smashed to bits against the shore. Those few sailors who survived to stagger onto land likely wished they had died at sea with their fellows. No, Reed did not like the idea of sailing up Acedor's wind-swept west coast, but the wizards had asked his opinion and he owed them honesty. "The west coast here has many rivers where we could send a boat in at night, set you ashore well inland. It would not be easy, we would have to evade patrols-"

"No," Paedris declared flatly. "We must be here," he jabbed a finger on the map. "Our destination lies inland, and we must shorten our journey. To walk even a short distance inside Acedor is perilous."

"Very well," Reed considered the map. He knew the wizards' plan now; they were going to the capital of Acedor. They were going to challenge the demon at the heart of their ancient enemy. "The difficulty, then, is I know of only one place where it is practical to land a boat along this coastline, one place where there is a break in the cliffs."

"The great ancient harbor of Talannon, which the enemy now calls Tokmanto?" Paedris nodded knowingly. "That is what we expected, and feared. I hoped you would know of a better place, but we must go ashore, and if Tokmanto is the only place that is possible, then that is where we must go."

Reed liked the idea of taking his ship into Tokmanto even less than he wished to sail up Acedor's west coast. "Lord Salva, surely you do realize this fine harbor is the main port for pirates of Acedor? There must be a dozen pirate ships based at Tokmanto."

"Two dozen," Mwazo corrected the merchant captain. "Twenty eight, at last count. Although that information may be outdated. We can obtain an exact count when we are closer."

"Two dozen? Oh, well then, that is *much* better," Reed exclaimed with a weary look to Alfonze, who nodded silently.

"Captain," Paedris understood the man's skepticism, and he needed the experienced captain to devote his full attention to the problem at hand. "We appreciate the difficulties in going ashore there. Allow me to explain. To journey deep into the interior of Acedor, we must go ashore as close to the ancient capital city as possible. That leaves out any place east of the Garligan river. As you mentioned, West of the Garligan the coast is all high cliffs with large rocks offshore; no ship can get close to the shore, and boats would require a miracle not to be smashed to bits against the cliffs. The only break in the cliffs is at Tokmanto, cliffs at the head of the harbor there are lower, with many breaks for roads and trails we can use to gain access to the interior of Acedor. We simply do not have time to go ashore at a more distant point and walk the remainder of the way. I know it is difficult, however-"

"No, Lord Salva," Reed boldly interrupted the master wizard. "It is not difficult. It is *impossible*. I need to, Alfonze, hand me that cask of ship's biscuit."

Alfonze lifted the cask of hard-baked biscuits, basic rations no sailor enjoyed but were used to stretch fresh food supplies during long voyages. Even when freshly baked, the biscuits were tough and impossible to chew unless dipped in tea, coffee or even water. That particular cask of biscuits had traveled from Tarador to the South Isles and back in the bottom of the *Lady Hildegard's* hold and, now opened, was used by the crew only as bait for fishing over the side. Even the fish did not care for the biscuits, except for the occasional fat and juice weevil eating its way through a biscuit.

Captain Reed lifted the lid off the cask, selected a handful of biscuits and tapped them on the rim of the cask to knock loose any weevils close to the surface of a biscuit. "Here," he said, "I will use these biscuits to make a map of the cliffs." He piled up biscuits on the table, making an approximation of the seacoast around Tokmanto harbor more accurate than he thought possible. "This is the harbor."

"Yes, I see that," Paedris admitted, impressed. Reed had made the biscuit cliffs lower at the closed, northern end of the great arc of the harbor.

"Good. Here," he brushed a crawling weevil off the table and placed another row of biscuits, "is the offshore reef that protects the harbor from storm surges. That is why our ancestors favored Talannon as their main seaport. There are only two gaps in the reef, here," he pointed to the center of the harbor's mouth. "And here," he made another gap in the biscuit reef close to the western shore. "The main channel is patrolled by at least two ships, or it was the last time I visited Tokmanto during my Royal Navy service. Two swift rowing ships, able to make way against wind or tide, guard the main channel. When pirate ships are not moving in or out, a heavy chain is stretched across the gap, from here, to here," he indicated the two ends of the gap which formed the main channel. "Rumor has it the reef has been dying because the harbor water is filthy, and the channel was grown wider over the years, but it is still blocked by the chain."

Paedris scratched his beard and looked at Cecil. "What do you think, Lord Mwazo? Could we snap this chain?"

"We?" Cecil asked, surprised. "There is no 'we' in that regard, Paedris, my powers lay in other directions."

"I suppose, if the chain were not too thick, and too deep under the water, I could break it," Paedris mused. "But I would need to be close, and we would lose all surprise. The enemy would instantly know a powerful wizard was breaking into the harbor, and-"

"Lord Salva," Reed wished to avoid useless speculation. "I am sure your powers could sweep away any chain. It makes no difference; even if the chain were not there either because you broke it, or it was open to allow pirates ships access to the harbor, we cannot use the main channel. It has been well known since my days in the Royal Navy, the only way into that main channel is with a squadron of ships, with four ships engaging the guard ships to clear a path for the others. Even then, it is nearly impossible, that is why the Royal Navy never tried such an attack. When the tide is going in or out, there is a powerful current through the main channel," Reed explained, realizing with a start that he was repeating the words spoken by the captain of the ship he had served aboard many years ago. "The prevailing wind there is onshore; that is fairly good for getting into the harbor on an incoming tide; if the tide is flowing out, no amount of wind can get a sailing ship in through that gap against the force of water. The problem is, if the tide is going in and with an onshore breeze, any attacking ships will be trapped in the harbor until the wind dies and the tide slackens. That is too long for our ships to be at the mercy of swift pirate ships rowed by slaves. No, the only way to attack that harbor through the main channel is at slack tide, quickly in and quickly out before the tide turns against you. You have to use sweeps," he saw the wizards did not understand so he explained. "Sweeps are long oars used by large ships like the *Hildegard*. Depending on the wind, you row either on the way in or the way out, unfortunately it is most likely a ship would need to row on the way out, against the prevailing winds. This is all an academic exercise anyway," he mused as he brushed another escaped weevil off the table. "That plan was designed to be used by a squadron of the Royal Navy, and even their commanders thought it suicidal. The enemy knows they are most vulnerable at slack tide, so they always have the chain stretched across the main channel then, and an extra guard ship on patrol, day or night. We have one ship. There is no way for us to deal with two or more guard ships. Ah," he waved a hand in disgust. "It doesn't matter anyway. Even if there was a way for this big ship to get into Tokmanto harbor, we could never hope to get her out."

"Captain," Paedris stared at the map, looking up at Reed through his eyebrows. "As I now own this ship, her safe return is not a priority. She need only get us *into* the harbor."

"And my crew?" Reed clamped down a flare of anger.

"I have an idea about that, which may also help provide cover for Lord Mwazo and I to go ashore unseen." Paedris explained, then he and Reed argued back and forth until the captain nodded.

"That might, just *might* work. I think this old girl," he rapped knuckles on the great wooden beam stretching across the cabin above his head, "would like that." As a sailor, Reed had come to think of his ship as a living thing. He knew that was not true, but it *felt* true, and he could not deny the ship was more than stout timbers and towering masts.

"Very well, Lord Salva, we can refine your plan later. At the moment, we still are faced with the fact that there is no way for this ship to run the gauntlet into that harbor."

"I can see the problem," Paedris expressed his dismay, not having expected the sailing part of his desperate mission to the greatest difficulty. "As we cannot use the main channel, what about the other gap in the reef, over here?" He tapped his finger at the biscuit reef, pulling his hand away as a weevil crawled out of a crushed biscuit that was part of the modelled 'reef'.

"No," Reed squashed another crawling weevil with a thumb. He really needed to dump that barrel of old biscuits overboard, they were now half biscuit and half weevil. "This ship draws too much water. Even pirate ships cannot use that break in the reef except at high tide. Years ago, Acedor sank several ships in that gap to prevent our Royal Navy using it to gain access to the harbor. Perhaps there is a way into the harbor, but I do not know it."

"Captain," Alfonze spoke for the first time. "How many times were you at Tokmanto in the Navy?"

"Once," Reed shrugged. "Twice, if you count one evening sailing west and the morning sailing back east, and praying the whole time the enemy ships would not come out of the harbor to challenge us. Why? You are familiar with this place?" He asked, surprised. He knew Alfonze had never served in the Taradoran Royal Navy nor any other naval force; the man had been aboard merchant ships since he was a boy as his father been a captain.

"No. But Jofer knows it like the back of his hand. He served in the blockading squadron for over two years. He still speaks of it." Complaining was a form of speech, Alfonze told himself, because complaining is about all Old Jofer ever did about anything. Whenever he spoke about his years with the Royal Navy squadron block assigned to blockading Tokmanto and bottling up the pirate ships in their harbor, Jofer complained. He complained about the boredom, the lack of fresh food, the infrequent messages from home, but mostly about the endless, relentless, suffocating boredom. Day after day of sailing back and forth, east then west across the harbor entrance, no matter what the weather. When the wind blew strongly toward the shore, the Royal Navy ships were pushed toward the deadly reef that protected the harbor. The usual response of sailing ships was to stand farther out from a lee shore, lest they run aground. But with swift pirate ships poised to exploit any opportunity to sneak out of the harbor, and those shallow-draft ships rowed by slaves and not caring about the direction of the wind, the blockading squadron had to risk hugging the reef. More than one Royal Navy ship had run aground and had its bottom torn out on the jagged reef, with crews of other ships watching helplessly, and pirates sweeping in to kill or capture survivors. After that, when the Royal Navy pursued a pirate ship, they had to wonder if the slaves cruelly chained to the oars were former shipmates.

"Jofer?" Reed thought he had not heard Alfonze correctly. Though Jofer had served aboard Reed's ships for five years, the old man never been popular with his shipmates, not being known either as a skilled sailor or a hard worker. Jofer did the work he was ordered to do, no more, and without enthusiasm. When the *Lady Hildegard* reached her final port after Gertaborg and Captain Reed had paid off most of the crew as there appeared to be no prospects for cargo to carry, Jofer had remained aboard the ship the ship even though Reed had hinted he would not be sorry to see the man go. Reed had been planning not to sign Jofer for another voyage, and he wanted to avoid an awkward confrontation. Hearing that old Jofer might actually be useful, that Reed may need the lazy crewman, did not make the captain happy.

"Who is Jofer?" Cecil asked.

"One of my best crewmen," Reed rolled his eyes in disgust.

"Ah," Paedris understood. "Yet, of all the people aboard, he has the most extensive knowledge of Tokmanto? Surely there must be someone else in the port you could consult?"

Alfonze gritted his teeth. "Not likely. The Navy has mostly pulled back to harbors east of us, so few of their sailors are here now. And the Royal Navy has not blockaded Tokmanto in, what?" He looked to Reed.

"Twenty years, maybe longer?" The captain guessed. "Even in my day, we dared not challenge the pirates in their lair. Alfonze, you may be right that Jofer is the only person who knows those waters, but I wish it were someone other than him."

"Can we trust this man?"

Reed looked to Alfonze. Reed had known Jofer for more years, but there was always a distance between captain and crew. Because Alfonze lived below decks with the crew, he likely knew the man better. Alfonze hated being put on the spot. "Jofer does love good gossip, that's for certain. Yet," he stared at the skylight, where white clouds were highlighted in the sunlight. "If you ask whether I think he would betray us," he shook his head, "no. Jofer can be lazy and tiresome, but he is unfailingly loyal to his shipmates."

Cecil made an almost imperceptible shrug. "That's good enough for me." There were magical means of ensuring a person kept secrets, if needed.

Reed called a crewman into the cabin and ordered him to send for Jofer, hoping the man had not already drunk his daily ration of rum. Of all Jofer's bad qualities, he was not a drunkard, but with the ship slowly rotting at anchor, many of the remaining crew had become bored and looked for rum to past the time.

Jofer came into the cabin, bowing and pressing a fist to his forehead as a gesture of respect when he saw the wizards. "Your Lordships," the man was trembling slightly.

Cecil took pity on him. "Jofer, Captain Reed informs us that you are the most experienced sailor aboard the *Lady Hildegard*."

Jofer looked up to meet the tall wizard's eyes, his hands still shaking slightly. "That I am," he said warily. He did not know if by 'experienced' the wizard was simply using a kindly word for 'old'.

"In this case, it is your knowledge of Tokmanto that we seek," Cecil continued.

"Tok-" Jofer swallowed hard, coughing. "Begging your pardon, Your Lordship, but I have not been there in many year." His expression turned thoughtful. "The Royal Navy has not been there in many a year, me thinks. Captain, you may have been with the last squadron to sail past that nest of snakes, and that was before we met. The Captain here could tell you more recent news of Tokmanto, but I don't see how as that could be useful to you."

"Aye, Jofer, it has been a long time, too long, since the Royal Navy ruled the seas and kept that nest of snakes trapped at Tokmanto. You served with the blockading squadron when the pirates of Acedor dared not challenge us upon the seas," he fed the man's ego, knowing that would make the old sailor more at ease and cooperative.

"We did make those pirates fear us," Jofer stood up straight and puffed out his chest with pride. Then his shoulder sagged. "But the Royal Navy has fallen on hard times, and can't even protect their own ships. I can't tell you anything about what ships the enemy has at Tokmanto now. I've heard rumors, of course, and I like gossip as much as the next man," his eyes briefly twinkled, "but I know not to put any stock in unfounded rumors."

"Neither wind nor tide will have changed since you last were there?" Paedris spoke to the old sailor for the first time.

Jofer appeared surprised by the question. "I suppose not, Your Lordship. What is it you wish to know?"

Captain Reed explained the situation, and their problem. To his amazement, light came into Jofer's eyes and the man smacked a fist into his palm. "You mean to attack the pirates in their lair?" He grinned with fierce enjoyment at that thought. "Oh, the old girl would like that, wouldn't she?" Reaching up to touch the wood beam, he patted it affectionately. "Slowly fading away of dry rot at anchor is no fate for a fine ship like our *Lady*."

"Yes, Jofer, we do mean to hit the pirates where they least expect it. The question is, *how* to do that," Reed ground his teeth. "I am not as familiar as you with Tokmanto, but I do not see any way for the *Lady* to gain entrance to the harbor. We are too slow to storm the entrance, even if we strip the ship of everything not needed for a one-way voyage. Even at night, I cannot think of a way to get us close enough, quickly enough, to race through the gap. The guard ships would be on us before we could get through the reef."

"Aye," Jofer tugged at his beard. "It is a puzzle, for certain." He stepped forward to gaze at the map, recalling the years he had served aboard ships of the blockading squadron, sailing back and forth, east to west and back again across the mouth of the harbor, in good weather and bad. For a long minute, his fingers traced long-forgotten contours of the land, his lips moving silently as he recalled ships and shipmates long scattered to the winds. "There is a strong onshore wind most days," he looked up at Reed. "It picks up mid-mornings, and slackens off toward evening. We could not count on a favorable wind to get us close to the reef during the night. Unless," he turned to Cecil, "Your Lordships could arrange a strong nighttime wind for us?"

"Your captain asked us for such a favor. Unfortunately, the answer is no. To conjure up a wind strong enough to move this ship swiftly would attract attention from wizards of the enemy. Worse, it would alert the enemy to our presence, which we cannot risk. No," Paedris looked wistfully at the map, thinking of the havoc he could wreak if he were not under restrictions of secrecy. "There are subtle tricks we can play with the weather, if given time for preparation, and favorable conditions. Summoning a wind where one is normally absent is not within our powers on this voyage."

"Hmm." Jofer stared at the map again. "Captain Reed is right, there is no way for a single ship to force the harbor entrance. When I was with the blockading squadron, the admiral considered going in with a half dozen, or maybe it was eight ships, to hit the pirates. Winer was coming on, and none of us could bear the thought of another cold, dreary season sailing back and forth across the entrance to the damned harbor." Jofer blanched at realizing he used bad language in front of two wizards. "Begging your pardon, Your Lordships."

"I would use harsher language to describe what the ancient harbor of Talannon has become, but 'damn' will do nicely for now," Cecil replied. "Go on, please."

"Uh, oh, yes," Jofer was flustered. He had rarely met wizards, and never met wizards who acted like regular people. "The admiral had a scheme to, as I said, send in eight ships. Four ships to tangle with the guard ship, and four loaded with extra sailors to land at the docks. We planned to knock holes in the bottom of all the ships at the docks, then burn the ships and the dockyards. That would have set them back years. Ships can be repaired, but not without dockyards. They would have had to construct new dockyards, and bring in all new spars, timbers, sailcloth, everything. The admiral's hope was that winter, he could pull most of the blockading squadron back into port, rebuild our strength. Our ships were getting worn out from beating back and forth all day, every day, month after month, you see."

"Why didn't the admiral launch the attack?" Paedris asked intently.

"Too difficult," Jofer shook his head slowly and sadly. His ship had been assigned to assault the docks, and he had known that he and many of his shipmates would likely die in Acedor, far from home. Of those who were not killed, many of them would become slaves and wish they had died. Despite that terrible knowledge, Jofer and his fellows had been eager for a fight, anything to break the suffocating monotony of the endless blockade. "The evil one," he made a hex sign in the air with his fingers to ward off the demon, "must have sensed we were planning something, or their sailors simply used common sense and knew we would be desperate enough to try an attack before winter. Our attack was planned for a moonless night, on the slack tide, but three days before we could strike, more than a thousand enemy soldiers marched down from the hills to reinforce the port. Two guard ships became four, and our chance was lost. It was a cruelly bitter pill to swallow. The enemy kept up their vigilance until the winter storms began rolling in, and our squadron had to pull away from the coast lest we be dashed upon the reefs. When the relief squadron arrived in midwinter, it had four fewer ships, and three years later, the Royal Navy ceased the blockade. We missed our opportunity then, and that's a pity. Aye, we would have lost ships, and good sailors, but how many have we lost since then? And for what? Nothing! Now those pirates rule the seas, and our own Navy fears to set out from port. Ha!" He almost spat in disgust, holding himself back because of the wizards. "I'd barely call what we have now a 'Navy'. Many a good shipmate of mine now sleeps beneath the waves, or died chained to the oars of a pirate ship." He used the back of a sleeve wipe away tears. "Better I had died burning out that nest of pirates, I tell you."

Jofer's vehement anger was a revelation to Reed, who had only ever seen the man moping around on deck, or slacking off, or engaged in idle gossip. Maybe all the man needed was a cause to believe in, to know his life had purpose. Reed had been planning to leave Jofer on shore when the *Hildegard* set sail, now he was reconsidering. If the man could be relied on, then his knowledge of Tokmanto harbor might be a useful, even vital, asset.

"There is, there is," Jofer's voice trailed off as his mind was flooded with memories. With a fingertip, he traced the outline of Tokmanto harbor on the map, and when he spoke again, it was barely above a whisper. "There is one possibility." He looked up to meet Reed's eye. "Before the admiral decided to storm the harbor entrance by force, there was another plan. My captain thought we should have tried it, and so did I. More's the pity we never did. See this headland here," he pointed to the western arm of the harbor. "The reef doesn't extend onto shore, instead there are jagged rocks. The cliffs there go straight up, most of those rocks in the water broke off the cliffs over the ages. The channel between the cliff and the rocks is narrow, and you have to know those waters, but it can be done if the ship doesn't draw too much water. There are submerged rocks that could rip out a ship's bottom if she's not lucky. A pirate ship slipped through our blockade one night, coming into the harbor. It ran through that channel, one of our ships gave chase but had to break away."

"It struck a rock?" Alfonze guessed.

"No, it turned away before then," Jofer explained. "The enemy has catapults atop the cliffs, they can throw bombs of burning oil down on any ship trying to run that channel; our ship couldn't risk going right under those cliffs. Our ship found one thing that was very interesting to the admiral; there is a strong current running eastward along that headland. Once the pirate ship caught that current, they raised oars and were carried along swiftly."

"Why does that matter?" Paedris asked from ignorance.

"Because," that brought a smile to Jofer's face. "The admiral was thinking we wouldn't need an onshore breeze to carry us into the harbor if we can get into that current. We could attack at night, when the wind dies. All we would need to do is wait for a good, thick fog so those catapults on the cliffs above can't see us, and we ride that current right on into the enemy's very lap," he balled up his fists in delight at that thought.

"Mmmm," Reed murmured, unconvinced. He looked to Alfonze, who nodded.

"Jofer," Alfonze pointed to the map, running a fingertip from the narrow channel under the cliffs to the wide-open harbor beyond. "The current must fall off when the channel opens into the bay here. On a night of fog, there will be little wind. Once a ship comes out into the bay and loses the current, it will be adrift and easy prey for the pirate guard ships."

"No," Jofer jabbed the map excitedly. "You see here, this gap in the hills beyond the harbor, above the cliffs?" He indicated a spot several miles from the harbor. "Most nights, there is a wind blowing down this gap in the evening. My captain told me when the sun goes down, the air cools, and well," he was embarrassed by such an absurd notion, "the air get heavier, and it rushes down this gap into the harbor."

"The air gets heavy?" Alfonze's skepticism was clear.

"It's true!" Jofer insisted. "The locals even have a name for that wind, although, I can't think of it right now. Anyways, a ship coming out into the harbor, if everything is timed just right, could pick up that wind as it leaves the current here. It's true!" He scrunched up his face at seeing the expression Alfonze was giving him. "We even tested it once, the admiral did, I mean. He sent a boat through on a foggy night, just one boat with a dozen men. The boat went through the channel, picked up that wind I talked about, but the wind was late that night. By the time the boat caught the wind, the fog was lifting, and one of the guard ships spotted our boat. The boat tried to make it back over the reef, it was a shallow-draft boat and the surf was gentle that night. But," he closed his eyes sadly, "they didn't make it. The boat got hung up on the reef, then turned turtle. Fortunately for those wretches, they were all bashed against the reef and drowned. A better fate for them than becoming slaves on a pirate ship."

Reed could only imagine that terrible sight. "The admiral never tried that again?"

"One of the men aboard that lost boat was the admiral's son," Jofer explained.

"Oh," Reed looked away.

"The admiral, and my captain, were fairly sure the pirates never knew how our boat got into the harbor. They likely thought it floated in over the reef at high tide, then got trapped. For a fortnight, the pirates doubled the number of guard ships at night, but they never did anything about stretching a chain across that channel under the cliffs."

"There was no chain in that channel when I was there, years later." Captain Reed mused while rubbing his chin. "One of our ships did approach those cliffs, just to tweak the enemy's noses, until the catapults on the cliff top came close to hitting the ship. I remember seeing fishing boats in that area," he fought to bring long-unused memories to the surface of his mind. "Jofer, thank you, that is interesting. Your Lordships," he turned to the wizards, "I do not see how this helps us. The current is reliable, but we would need to catch that evening wind at the right moment. And I do not think you can have us linger just over the horizon for weeks while we wait for a heavy fog to roll in."

"No, we cannot wait," Paedris stated. He hunched forward over the table, taking in the map's intricate details. "Captain, if you can get this good ship into that channel at night, and take advantage of a fortuitous current and wind, then I," he grinned broadly, "will provide the fog."

CHAPTER FIVE

Olivia groaned and tugged at the collar of her formal scarlet robes, reaching behind her neck to undo one button that had been choking her. The morning had been dull and tedious and boring, and Olivia could not believe she had gotten stuck with the duty of being Ariana's supernatural bodyguard. Everything the young princess did at the palace was dull and formal and uninteresting, even the changing of the guard ceremony caused Olivia to stifle a yawn, as she had already seen that daily ceremony many times from across the courtyard. Being beside the dais where the princess stood was no more interesting.

At least now, Olivia told herself, she was not stuck shadowing Ariana's every move. In her role as Regent, the crown princess would be spending the rest of the morning and most of the afternoon catching up on the frustrating but necessary paperwork of the realm. While Ariana was trapped in an office reviewing accounts and other pressing yet mundane matters of state, Olivia would finally be free to inspect the magical wards Paedris had placed around entrances to the royal residence, and using her senses to pry for any hidden dangers. During their long journey back from the mountains, Olivia had pleaded to ride ahead on a swift horse, so she could inspect the security of the palace before the princess arrived, but Ariana had insisted Olivia remain with the royal carriage. There were hundreds of royal guards at the palace, Ariana reasoned, and wizards had exhaustively combed the palace for threats less than a month ago. How could the enemy have snuck someone inside the palace, past all the guards and magical wards, in so short a time? Especially while the enemy had been concentrating all their efforts on forcing a crossing of the River Fasse and smashing through the Royal Army?

Olivia admitted Ariana's logic sounded correct, and she had no argument against it, but she still *felt* it was wrong in a way she could not explain. Her uneasy feeling was not a magical sense, for she had not yet mastered that ability of listening to the faintly whispered, maddeningly vague warnings from the spirit world. Such warnings were all too easily corrupted by a skilled enemy, so that Madame Chu and other master wizards had cautioned Olivia against relying on the spirit world providing her advanced notice of impending disasters. No, the feeling Olivia had was entirely of the real physical world, and she could not shake it.

Walking down an elaborate hallway of the palace's second level, she took deep breaths, forcing herself to relax. She was being overcautious, she told herself. It was early afternoon of a bright, sunny day and the princess was in her office surrounded by guards and courtiers. Olivia would have been happier for the future monarch to be within the bounds of the royal residence part of the palace, within the protection of magical wards to warn of intruders. Still, any attempt on the life of the princess would likely come after darkness, and at that time, Ariana Trehayme would be tucked away inside the residence. Olivia needed to tour the halls of the palace for the next several hours, keeping her senses open to the subtle vibrations of dark magic. After a light dinner, she would rest so she could remain awake throughout the night, keeping watch against supernatural threats as only a wizard could.

Thinking of dinner caused her stomach to grumble and made her regret skipping a meal at mid-day. She thought longingly of the afternoon tea the princess would be enjoying as that girl endured the grind of dealing with the hundreds of people who urgently needed the Regent's attention over the coming days. Olivia actually smiled, considering that staying awake to patrol the palace all night was preferable to-

What was that? Her reverie was broken by shouts coming from the broad set of stairs leading to the first level of the palace. As she broke into a run, the shouting was accompanied by the clashing of swords and screams of men dying!

Cully Runnet had been walking across the inner courtyard of the palace, hurrying as best he could without calling attention to himself, and skirting the walls to stay in the shadows. As he had come directly from working in the royal stables and was not as clean as he could be, he was not supposed to be so close to the palace. The official rules stated servants were to be dressed in a 'presentable fashion' while crossing the inner courtyard, but going all the way from the stables to the royal hospital was *such* a long and convoluted way around, unless you took a shortcut through the inner courtyard. Cully and many other servants had used the shortcut often while the crown princess had been away from the palace, and that day he justified using the shortcut one more time because the princess having just returned meant he had extra work. A frightening lot of extra work that had gotten him up well before the sun rose over the hills east of Linden, and would have him busy long after the sun set and the only light was provided by torches and lanterns.

He had picked up his pace when a pair of guards looked at him unhappily and one of the guards made a shooing motion for Cully to get out of the courtyard. Perhaps the princess herself was coming into the inner courtyard at any moment, Cully thought with alarm, nearly tripping on uneven cobblestones in his haste.

Suddenly propriety was forgotten and the guards had better things to occupy their attention when an alarm bell sounded, followed immediately by trumpets. The guards needed only to draw their swords and cinch their chainmail armor tighter, for they were already where they were supposed to be during an emergency. Cully was nowhere close to his assigned station, which was at the south entrance to the royal hospital. By the time he got there, the emergency could be over, and servants were not supposed to racing around the castle grounds willy-nilly while guards were engaged in the serious task of securing the castle against enemies. Doors and gates throughout the castle's myriad buildings and surrounding walls would be closed and barred, Cully knew his path toward the hospital would be blocked shortly.

No matter, like all servants who worked within the castle walls, he had been trained what to do when caught away from his post in an emergency, and he had practiced his assigned task at least once a month during surprise drills. He was to stand by the nearest fire brigade box, ready to use the buckets and bins of sand within to contain any fire. There was a fire box to his left across the courtyard from the Citadel tower and he lost no time in running to it, all concerns about his dirty clothing forgotten. The distinctive dark green box with a bright red lid was of course unlocked for quick access and Cully swung the lid up to pull out six buckets, setting them on the cobblestones for ready use. Two of the buckets he filled his sand as he had been trained to do, then he stood still, his neck on a swivel side to side trying to see what was going on. The two guards were apprehensively holding their swords and looking around. Could this be another unscheduled drill, Cully asked himself? Surely the captain of the guard would not wish to disturb the princess so soon after she returned from a tiring journey? Unless, unless, Cully asked himself, the captain of the guard wished to demonstrate to the princess how diligent he had been in keeping up training standards while she had been away?

Except, it did not feel like a drill. There was far too much panicked shouting, and the guards racing atop the fortified walls were stumbling over each other in their haste.

He looked across the inner courtyard to the hulking tower of the Citadel, seeing iron shutters being pulled shut over the lower windows and arrows poking through slits in the thick, dark stone walls. Everyone in Linden knew the crown princess had just returned from crushing the enemy in battle, so what could possibly be the threat?

Having taken the stairs in three unnaturally long strides, Olivia flew around the corner, even her incredible wizardly sense of balance challenged as her shoes slid across the slick polished floors of the palace. She came around the corner into a scene of utter chaos.

An enemy assassin, distinctively swathed head to toe in the magic-enhanced cloth that could have been black or gray or brown and made the evil being's outline difficult to see at a glance, was racing down the corridor toward her! At the far end of the corridor, two guards were already down and the two guards running after the assassin would never catch their swift foe. Olivia heard herself shout a warning as she crashed painfully into the far wall, a sharp pain jarring her shoulder and she knocked a precious painting to swung against the wall.

What should she do? Behind her around the corner, broad stairs led up to the second level of the palace where the structure was more extensive and an assassin could find many places to hide. She could not allow the assassin past her.

Between her and the assassin were only three guards armed with swords, no match for the enemy figure who moved with such speed. As Olivia braced herself and watched helplessly, the assassin threw a dagger which caught one guard full in the chest, ducked under a second guard's sword and ran halfway up a wall, vaulting and somersaulting to strike the third guard in the back with a knife.

With the three guards scattered and harmless behind him, the assassin crouched to regain his footing, smoothly kicking one leg off a wall for balance and launched himself straight at the young wizard. Olivia's heart fluttered as she swallowed hard to calm herself and concentrate on pulling power from the spirit realm. Standing straight and defiant, with one hand conjured forth a flicker of flame, and teased it into a flaming ball with-

The ball of magical fire blinked out, as Olivia had to duck aside and use one hand to fend off a dagger thrown by the assassin. Mindful that the weapons of an enemy assassin were almost certainly dipped in deadly poison, she did not attempt to catch the dagger by the hilt for to do so was too dangerous. The heel of her hand deflected the dagger's hilt away from her to send the weapon clattering to the floor and spinning away down the hallway behind her. There being no time to create a fireball, she faced the skilled enemy without any weapons to defend herself. The man was running full speed at her, knowing his life depended on closing the distance before the wizard could summon magic in her defense, and already reaching for another dagger.

And the unexpected happened.

A door opened along the wall between Olivia and the assassin, and into the hallway stepped Charl Fusting. The fussy royal chief of protocol was carrying a valuable ancient teapot and two delicate cups on a heavy silver tray, bringing it out of storage to serve afternoon tea for the crown princess. When he entered the hallway, Fusting wore an expression of extreme annoyance, prepared to disapprove of whatever noisy and unnecessary nonsense was going on in the serene halls of the royal palace. In a flash, the man's face twisted into a mask of fear and horror at the scene of guards down on the floor, an assassin racing toward him and a terrified young wizard struggling to conjure magical fire.

The assassin did not bother to give Charl Fusting more than a glance, having sized up the man as no threat in an instant. While Olivia staggered backward, one arm slipping along the wall to prevent herself from falling over backward and the other arm stretched over her head in a feeble attempt to call forth wizard fire, the assassin pulled another throwing dagger from his belt and drew it back to throw.

Charl Fusting was no solider, no guard, never trained in any kind of combat. He abhorred violence as something less refined cretins resorted to, when they could not settle their differences with reasoned discussion like civilized people. The scene in the hallway of the royal palace, however, with blood smeared in the floors and walls and precious paintings knocked off their hooks to be dashed onto the hard floor, spurred him to action before he could consider his recklessness. Not knowing what else to do, with an undignified frightened shriek he heaved the tray upward, sending the teapot and cups nearly to the ceiling. The heavy silver tray, now relieved of its easily breakable burden, was grasped on one end with two hands and swung with all the force of righteous indignation Fusting could muster to batter the amazed assassin straight in the face!

The stunned enemy's head was flung backward and his feet slid out in front of him, throwing dagger lost to tumble through the air and embed itself in the center of a painting of King Elbard the Second, slashing the face of that mostly unloved and forgotten monarch. The force of impact caused Fusting to lose the tray and fall backward through the still-open doorway, his own feet flying up in the air and his head coming down to crack on the wooden floor of the cutlery storage room.

Though stunned more by the unexpected nature of the attack than by impact of the silver tray, the assassin recovered instantly, a hand reaching back to draw another throwing dagger from his belt even as he tumbled head over heels backwards through the air. One outstretched hand broke his fall and the assassin somersaulted back onto his feet, one eye clouded by blood from his broken nose. He scrambled forward, regaining momentum in an unnaturally rapid fashion and hurled the dagger at the young wizard.

Olivia had seen the foolishly heroic act of Charl Fusting though her mind had not the time to process it. The chief of protocol's reflexive attack had slowed the assassin for only the blink of an eye and Olivia realized she could either continue gathering a fireball that required use of both her hands, or she could try to catch the spinning dagger hurtling toward her. Without time to think she lifted her feet off the floor to fall, twisting herself to the side so the razor-sharp dagger sliced through one sleeve of her robes as she clumsily tossed the half-formed ball of wizard fire down the hallway. Even as the ball of fire left her hands she knew it would miss the assassin who was even then dashing aside to avoid the deadly fire.

And, just then the assassin lost his footing as the delicate ancient teapot and pair of cups crashed to the floor and shattered at his feet, making him skid on the fine porcelain. A cry escaped his lips, the first sound the assassin had made, as he lurched out of control into the path of the fireball. Sizzling flame caught his left side, burning through his magically-enhanced clothing. The enemy went down and curled into a ball, screaming in agony as the fire from the spirit world ate into his mortal form.

Exhausted, dizzy and off-balance, Olivia fell backwards to thump her backside painfully on the hard floor. Astonished, she watched as the partly-charred assassin tried to rise to his feet though one side of his face was horribly burned, strips of crisped skin hanging away from bone. Without taking time to stand, she held her hands out to draw another fireball with strength she did not have. Somehow, the assassin got to one knee and fumbled for a throwing dagger, glaring hatred at Olivia with his one good eye. In a panic, she scrambled backwards to get away, not hearing the sounds of boots thudding on the floor behind her as royal guards ran down the stairs three at a time and around the corner. The presence of the guards was not noticed by her until a pair of spears flashed past her toward the assassin, one spear being knocked aside and the other embedding itself in the enemy's belly. Even a steel-tipped spear sticking through him did not fully stop the assassin, who ignored the injury and drew back an arm to throw his poison-tipped dagger.

What did finally stop the assassin was a pair of spears being run through him with the weight of onrushing guards behind the weapons; so hard did the guards stab the enemy that they tumbled over the prone body and fell headlong, grinding along the polished floor in their chainmail shirts. More guards ran to stand between the young wizard and the now-motionless enemy, brandishing swords, spears and axes.

"Are you injured, Madame Dupres?" A guard asked her, his eyes darting rapidly between the wizard and the charred and smoking body of the assassin.

"I," she slumped against the wall and took a breath. "No, I don't think so." A sleeve of her robe was sliced cleanly and pulling aside the rent fabric revealed her arm was thankfully unmarked. She knew how to deal with poison but doing so would weaken her and slow her ability to protect the princess. "That was," Olivia gasped, pushing herself onto her knees and using one hand on the wall to steady herself, "too *easy*," she realized with a shock. She had barely escaped the brief fight against a single assassin with her own life, yet even so, she knew there was something wrong, very wrong. Somehow, the assassin had gained entrance to the palace, most likely through the tunnels beneath the old structure, for the enemy had come racing up from the lower level of the residence. It made no sense that the enemy would risk attacking the crown princess in the heart of the palace during daylight, but send only one assassin. Even had the skilled enemy killed Olivia, he would have had to cut his way through dozens of guards before reaching the princess, and with the alarm sounded, more guards were pouring into the residence to defend the princess. "Where is the princess now?" She demanded.

"Her Highness is safe now, Your Ladyship," another guard grunted as he also staggered to his feet, holding a shaking sword toward the prone body of the assassin.

"Where is she?"

The guard blinked. "Safe. She has been-"

"*Where* is Ariana?" Olivia shouted as she took hold of the man's leather vest and shook him until his head rattled.

"They took her to, to the Citadel. The tower, my Lady," the guard sputtered. "You should be caref-"

The man never finished the thought as he fell when Olivia let go of his vest and with a bound, she was around the corner then racing up the broad stairs. Was she already too late, she asked herself in terror?

For too many days after attaching the magical device to the back of the door to the inner Citadel, Regin fretted his treason would be discovered, enduring one sleepless night after another. To avoid the risk of being brought to the Citadel during an attack, he had risen early the day after the princess arrived, to ride out into the countryside. His intention had been to stay away from the palace as much as possible until the enemy acted against Ariana, but he could only make excuses so many days in a row before the princess and her damned chancellor became suspicious and he needed to remain close to the castle so he could act swiftly during an emergency. Thus, he was riding almost aimlessly across the countryside several miles from the castle that rose on the hill above Linden, pretending to be scouting fields and forests for a hunt the next spring, when one his own guards shouted. "Your Grace! Look!"

Regin turned in the saddle as he pulled his horse's reins to face the castle. Large yellow flags of alarm were being hoisted atop the castle's battlements, and yellow-colored smoke was rising from signal fires. The code yellow meant the castle was under attack from within. At first, Duke Falco's heart soared with joy and anticipation. The enemy had struck quickly. Which meant, Regin realized with fear, the enemy must have been near or possibly already even within the castle walls while he had been poking around lonely, dark corners of the palace. The thought he might have nearly encountered an agent of the enemy made him shudder until he shook off the momentary weakness. Sitting straighter in the saddle, he shaded his eyes with a hand and made a show of peering at the signals above the castle. This was his time to act, and he had nearly ridden too far from the castle, but then he had not been expecting the enemy to strike so soon after the princess arrived.

Regin had carefully planned what he would do, so at that moment he needed merely to follow his plan rather than adapting to circumstances. The signals sent up by the castle guard force meant the enemy was loose within the walls and Regin knew the crown princess would soon be no more, if she were not dead already. This was the opportunity he had waited and planned for., With the girl who was both Regent and crown princess dead, Regin Falco as the only member of the Regency Council in Linden, would take responsibility for the reins of government. The guards and members of the royal court within the walls and the Royal Army garrison stationed outside the walls would be in shock following Ariana's death, craving leadership that Regin would be more than happy to provide. He needed to get to the castle while the situation inside was in chaos, before other people in authority like Chancellor Kallron could seize the mechanisms of power.

Just then, as he forced himself not to smile in exultation, Duke Falco had a terrible, gut-wrenching thought. "My son!" Regin cried out in anguish that was not a show for the benefit of his guards. While he had expected and been waiting, hoping, for the yellow flags to signify the enemy was acting against Ariana, he felt a stab of panic in his chest when he realized he did not really know full extent of the enemy's plans. His eldest son was recovering at the royal hospital within the stout castle walls! Until that moment, Regin thought he knew his feelings toward Kyre, a son and heir who had proven himself disloyal to the Falcos legacy and to his father personally. Now, facing the possibility that Kyre's life was at risk because of Regin's treasonous actions, the Falco duke's throat choked with panic. "My son is at the castle!" Kyre had acted disloyally, but Kyre was still a young boy, Regin reminded himself, and young men often acted rashly in the manner of youth. In the recent battle against the enemy, Kyre had acted with courage and good judgment and in that moment, Regin felt deep, utter shame. "We ride!" He ordered with a roar, spurring his horse to race across a farmer's field and jump a fence ahead of his frantic escort.

"NO!" Olivia screamed as a royal guard reached for the handle to the Citadel's inner door, two other guard having already turned the keys to the heavy locks. The guard holding the handle was slow to respond, focused on his one vital task of opening the door so the princess could be safely whisked into the most secure part of the palace. The man turned toward Olivia to see what the commotion was but as the young wizard did not know his name, he did not understand she addressed her warning to him. In horror, Olivia realized that as the man turned toward her, the momentum of his arm was automatically pushing the door open.

She had no time. The young wizard had raced toward the Citadel as fast as she could, shouting warnings that fell on deaf ears in the loud confusion of the guards rushing the crown princess to the safety of the Citadel as they were trained to do. There was no time to think, so she did the only thing she could do; fling herself through the air at the princess. Ariana's mouth opened in shock but before she could cry out, the young wizard collided with her, and both girls were knocked away from the doorway just as it exploded. Olivia's feet never touched the floor, the force of the explosion flung her through the air, her arms wrapped protectively around Ariana. All Olivia had time for was to flare her left palm open to shatter with magical power the heavy leaded glass window behind the princess. If Ariana's back had hit the window, she would have been seriously injured by jagged shards of thick glass or the metal crossbars. As it was, the window disintegrated outward and Olivia instinctively closed her eyes as she hurtled through into open air, clutching Tarador's future monarch in a fearful embrace.

Ariana thought her heart would stop. In one moment, she went from being hustled along hallways of the palace to being pushed through a window, and she tried to shout something to the wizard but no words came out. Wind rushed by her ears with such a roar she could not have heard herself if she had been able to speak.

Olivia could not fly. Even if she were a fully trained wizard, she would not be able to fly. She needed to, for although the Citadel section of the palace was surrounded by a moat on three sides, the window she had fallen through was directly above a gate and through the swirling flames roiling out the window behind them, she could see the drawbridge was still partly down! If they hit the sturdy drawbridge after falling three stories, both girls would be bashed senseless and likely killed. Without thinking what she was doing, Olivia *willed* herself to miss the drawbridge and she was rewarded by a hard shove against her back, knocking the breath out of her. Seeing she would fall into the moat, she let go of the princess and pushed the other girl away. Ariana hit the water with her backside first while Olivia awkwardly windmilled her arms to avoid hitting the water face-first as pushing the princess away had thrown Olivia terribly off balance. There was wrenching pain as she fell into the water on her left side and her neck nearly snapped from the force of impact.

The two guards posted to stand watch by the east gate had received orders to go back through the gate and secure it behind them, leaving Cully Runnet all alone in the inner courtyard as far as he could see. Two other gates in view had also been closed and secured with an ominous clanging sound, sending a chill of panic up Cully's spine. Was he supposed to be there at all? The pair of guards had not gestured for him to come with them, but they had been busy and may have assumed Cully was someone else's responsibility. Suddenly frightened that he would get in trouble for doing something wrong, he looked up to guards on top of the castle's thick wall and weakly waved to them. They either ignored the servant boy, or shook their heads. Did that mean he should *not* move from where he was, or that he *should* move? He didn't know! Oh, why had he taken a shortcut through the inner courtyard, he lamented to himself.

If he did move away from the fire box, where would he go? All the gates he could see had been closed and he couldn't see himself simply going up to the heavy iron-clad gates and rapping on them with his knuckles. Where else? Across the inner courtyard there was the Citadel, but the solid iron gate there was closed, and the drawbridge that spanned the moat was just now being pulled up-

He was rocked back on his heels and nearly fell into the open firebox, catching himself by grabbing the side of the wood box and earning a splinter in his left thumb. A window on the fourth floor of the Citadel tower had exploded, a gout of angry orange flame shooting through the window into the air. The fire was incredible by itself, but what made Cully's mouth gape open in shock was the figures of two girls who were blown through the window just ahead of the flames! As the girls plummeted down, Cully realized with a shock that one of them was the crown princess, for he recognized the light blue dress she had worn while reviewing the changing of the guard ceremony that morning. Before he could wrest himself free of the fire box, he saw the girls were going to hit the drawbridge, when an unseen gust of wind that affected nothing else caught the two girls, and blew them just clear of the drawbridge. They hit the moat with a pair of splashes that threw water up onto the cobblestones of the courtyard.

Cully was up and running before he knew he had moved, his muddy shoes pounding on the cobblestones toward the moat. Though the fire had burned itself out after the initial explosion, burning pieces of wood from the window casing still floated down and worse, stones from around the window were tumbling to hit the water of the moat with tremendous splashes. As Cully ran, more stones began to fall as the structure grew weaker with the loss of each stone. He kept one terrified eye on the large lintel stone straddling the top of the window opening for if that shook loose, the impact might kill anyone in the moat below.

Again without thinking what he was doing, he reached the lip of the moat and, with only a glance at the water, flung himself over the edge. Two girls had fallen but only one was visible to Cully so he leaped in toward her. It was the girl with the light blue dress he believed was the princess. As he fell in feet-first, he could see the girl had her head above the water but her face and hair were so plastered with green algae he could not tell who she was, or even if she were a girl at all.

Hitting the water, he fanned out his arms to stop from plunging in too far, for he knew the water to be only a dozen feet deep, with sharp rocks at the bottom. After a dry summer, the level of water must have been shallower because one of his shoes hit something and he recoiled in fright. To his surprise, he bobbed to the surface right beside the girl, who was faintly gasping for air, her mouth opening and closing in spasms. "I've got you!" He assured the girl, wrapping an arm across her chest and realizing too late his forearm had touched where he shouldn't have touched any girl, let alone the future monarch of Tarador. He was about to babble an apology when a heavy stone fell into the water behind them and he wisely concentrated on swimming strongly away from the drawbridge, using one arm to hold the girl's head above the water and pulling hard against the murky water with the other arm. He feet kicked frantically as he mentally kicked himself for not taking his shoes off, the waterlogged leather was weighting him down and making him swim slower than he wanted.

In moments that felt like an eternity, Cully reached the lip of a pipe that carried water into the moat. The bottom of the pipe was slick with scum and algae, so he lifted one of the girl's hands- He lifted one of the princess's hands, for he now could see that underneath the streaks of algae was surely the crown princess, Regent and ruler of his nation. He lifted her left hand until her elbow was draped over the top of the pipe. "Can you hold on here, Your Highness?" He asked, the first words the servant boy had ever spoken directly to the princess.

She nodded once, her eyes unfocused. At Cully's intently questioning stare, she nodded again. "Yes," she managed to say.

"Who was with you?"

"What?"

"The girl!" He forgot all propriety and shook the princess. "The other girl who fell with you!"

"Oh. Olivia."

Olivia! Cully felt a shock. "Lady Doopers?" He released the princess and spun around, searching the surface of the moat for any sign of the young wizard. She had been wearing a red robe, he remembered. Nothing he could see was red, the water in the moat was dirty green or green algae. Where could she be? Taking a breath and ducking his head under the water, he opened his eyes to see that he could see almost nothing.

The wizard could not have gone far from where she had fallen into the water, and that was near the drawbridge. Back above the water, he swam to the drawbridge, took a deep breath and dove down, down as far as he could, nearly bumping his head on a sharp rock at the bottom. Nothing! He could barely see his hand in front of his face, and was about to go up to breathe when his right hand brushed against something soft that was not a rock.

Then a hand grasped his forearm! With a mixture of embarrassment and panic, he felt along an arm and then reached down for a leg. Her soaked, billowing robe was in his way and he was beginning to feel an urgent need for air when his hands felt her foot and a stone. One of her feet was wedged between a rock on the bottom of the moat and a stone that had fallen from the crumbling window frame.

With no way to communicate, Cully knelt on the sharp rocks, cradled his hands under the stone, and lifted. The stone did not budge as it too, was wedged solidly against the rocks. His lungs begged for air and there was a roaring in his ears but the girl's hand on his shoulder squeezed him only weakly. He could not fail her. Shifting his knees to get better leverage, sharp rocks sliced into his knees and shins. He ignored that pain, interlaced his fingers, and *lifted* with all his might, feeling something pop in his lower back.

The stone shifted, and the girl pulled her foot free. The hand let go of his shoulder and Cully wasted no time pulling for the surface himself, coming above the algae-slick surface of the moat to gasp raggedly. Next to him, the young wizard was doing the same, her face nearly blue. Somehow, with strength he did not know he had, Cully took hold of her right arm and pulled her toward the side of the moat. As his fingers touched the rough stone, he turned back to see normal color returning to her skin. "Hold on-"

His own head was bashed against the side of the moat as three large stones fell into the water, throwing up a violent wave. Pain exploded in his head then he felt nothing as he blacked out, slipping beneath the surface.

Ariana clung to the slimy pipe, regaining strength as she was again able to breathe regularly. She heard splashing behind her and turned around to see the boy towing Olivia toward the wall of the moat. The wizard did not look good, she was not able to help the boy pull her toward the wall and as her fingers touched, three stones fell with a tremendous splash and the boy's head was battered against the rock wall of the moat. He spun toward Ariana, face bloody, then lost his grip on the wizard and fell backwards with a grunt, disappearing beneath the mats of sticky green algae. "No!" Ariana tried to shout, only to have her words choked off by a coughing fit. Still coughing uncontrollably, she let go of the pipe and pulled herself along the wall stone by stone, trying to reach Olivia before the wizard went under the water again. Awkwardly, the princess grasped the wizard by the first thing she could reach; the girl's blonde hair.

"Ow!" Olivia gasped, which Ariana took as a good sign the wizard was regaining her wits. The princess got a good grip on Olivia's robe and struggled to hold both of their faces above the water, her other fingers kept slipping on the stones of the moat.

"Help," the words threw Ariana into another convulsion of coughing. Where were her guards? Where was *anyone*? The crown princess and a wizard were blown through a window into a moat, and their only rescue was a servant boy? "Help!" She shouted without choking.

There was the sound of boots pounding on cobblestones and the faces of two men appeared atop the moat wall, staring down at her. There was a flash of relief on their faces when they saw she was not dead below the water. "Your Highness!

"The boy! Help that boy first," she insisted, gesturing with what strength she possessed.

"But Your Highness," the two guards hesitated.

"That is an order!" She demanded as she glared at the men, and to the credit of the royal guard force there was no further hesitation. Both men kicked off their boots, having discarded their helmets, sword belts and chain mail armor during their headlong race across the courtyard. Without another word, they leapt into the water, one on either side of the servant boy who was floating facedown. One of them rolled Cully over, and the boy spat up water when the guard squeezed his chest. Then, orders or not, the other guard swam over to Ariana to see to her safety. "Hold Lady Dupres, please, I don't have the strength," Ariana admitted, and was relieved when the guard put an arm under the wizard's back, holding her up.

Cully was choking up water, Olivia was nodding and waved appreciation as she recovered her strength, and Ariana clung to the moat wall, fearfully looking up at the crumbling stones around where the window used to be in the Citadel. "We should move away from the drawbridge," the princess suggested, and led the way, half swimming and half clinging to the slick stones. Moments later, the faces of more guards appeared above the moat, and ropes were lowered down.

Cully was barely aware of being lifted out of the moat and half carried, half dragged across the courtyard and into a storeroom. A guard shook him gently and gave him a canteen of water to drink, though Cully took a mouthful and searched for a place to rinse his mouth out. In a panic, he tried to hold the water in as he could not possibly spit on the floor in front of the crown princess!

Except that was exactly what the crown princess was doing with the water from her own canteen. "Oooh, I do *not* want to know what is in my mouth," Ariana spat repeatedly to clear the nasty taste of algae and other things. Seeing Cully's distress, she smiled. "Rinse out your mouth, kind sir, I would not wish you to fall ill by swallowing that moat water."

"I already," Cully nodded to guard who took pity on him and gave him an empty bucket to spit in, "swallowed too much." His face went white again as he remembered who he had spoken too. "I mean, Your Highness," he bowed deeply, which threw him into a coughing fit that brought him to his knees and brought more water spewing from his mouth. "Sorry."

Ariana had no time to reply, for the storeroom door swung open to admit the chief of the palace guard. The man secured the door behind him and dropped to one knee, taking off his helmet. "Your Highness," he said as tears streamed down his face, "I have failed you."

"As I am alive," Ariana pulled algae-matted hair away from her face, "your guards have not failed me, Captain Temmas. What happened?"

Temmas almost reluctantly regained his feet. "It appears there was some sort of device behind the door leading to the most secure area of the Citadel, Your Highness. I would appreciate anything *you* can tell me about the incident, for none of the guards who were with you survived. How did you survive?"

"Olivia threw me out a window," Ariana covered her mouth and laughed, she couldn't help herself despite the serious situation.

"I didn't *throw* you," Olivia protested and had to laugh also. "I fell out the window too, if you remember."

Temmas looked at the storeroom ceiling, a questioning look on his face. "Your Ladyship," he addressed the wizard, "that window is directly above the drawbridge, how did you not strike the bridge when you fell?"

"I saw that!" Cully exclaimed, forgetting the high-ranking people he was speaking to. "The wind blew you aside, but," he shuddered and fearfully glanced at the young lady wizard, "that wasn't wind, was it?"

"No, it wasn't wind. It was *magic*," Olivia explained. "Captain Temmas, how did that assassin get inside the palace?" She stamped a foot.

"Lady Dupres," Temmas stammered, "we do not know as yet. It appears the assassin came from beneath the palace, we are searching the tunnels now. What I do not understand is what the enemy hoped to gain, surely the assassin must have known he could not get past all our guards, to the princess. Why did the assassin attack in broad daylight? Surely if he had waited for nightfall-"

"Waiting for the cover of night would have gained him nothing," Olivia replied. "You have just as many guards on duty in the palace after sunset?"

"More," Temmas assured the wizard.

Olivia nodded. "Then the assassin would have just as much opposition to get past, and at night the princess would be behind wards in the residence, where no assassin could hope to catch her unawares. By attacking in daylight while she was receiving visitors in her office, the princess was more vulnerable than if she were in the residence," Olivia mused, partly to herself. "Captain Temmas, what is your procedure if the royals are threatened while in their offices?"

Horrified understanding dawned on the chief guard's face. "We bring the princess to the Citadel," he answered in a hoarse whisper. His shoulders slumped. "Lady Dupres, it is your belief the assassin's true purpose was for Princess Ariana to be brought to the Citadel?"

"Who knows your procedures?"

"Too many people know. Such knowledge would not be difficult to obtain," Temmas mused. "It is standard procedure for the guard force, even the servants," he glanced at Cully with irritation, "know it. We train for it often. The Citadel had been used for the purpose of safeguarding the royal family since ancient times, it is no secret. So," the man pulled at his beard in fierce concentration, "the enemy's *intention* was for Ariana to go into the Citadel. That means the enemy had prior access to the inner chamber of the Citadel, even though access there is restricted to only the most trusted members of the guard force. I will need to question each one of-"

"It was magic, Captain," Olivia stated with a shake of her head. "None of your guards could have been responsible. I felt the presence of dark magic, just before a guard opened the door. I shouted to stop him, but it was too late. That is why I took you out through the window, Your Highness," she automatically bent a knee as a curtsey toward the future monarch. "It was the only way to protect you."

"I thank you, Lady Dupres," Ariana said with a frown, wishing the wizard would use her first name. She resented the distance forced between them by formality and tradition.

"The question then is, *how?*" Temmas growled. "How did the enemy get a magical weapon into the Citadel?"

"To answer that question, you will need a wizard," Olivia answered wearily while wiping her dirty hands on her even filthier robes. "I must go to the Citadel first, to learn what I can there." No! She thought. What was needed was a real, fully-trained wizard, as Olivia had been insisting while everyone ignored her.

The chief guard blanched at the idea of the young wizard wandering around the palace. He would need to assign guards to protect her, that would hurt his force's ability to scour the large building from top to bottom against the possibility of more assassins lurking in wait. "Please, Lady Dupres, remain here a while longer, as this is the *only* room in the palace I can be certain of to be safe at the moment," the man said with a pleading expression. "First, my people are sweeping the residence, for Her Highness cannot spend the night here in a storeroom," he grimaced.

While the princess, wizard and chief guard had been talking, Cully had been shuffling his feet, edging toward the door. When his hand touched the door handle, the princess spun toward him. "Where are you going, Mister, um," she was embarrassed that she did not know the servant boy's name. One of his parents worked in the royal hospital, she vaguely remembered.

He dropped to one knee and stared at the floor, his cheeks red and not only from the blood still trickling from the cut on his forehead. "Cully Runnet, Your Highness. I need to go, my station during emergencies is at the hospital. Or," he recalled that the gates to the inner courtyard were closed and barred, "with the fire brigade."

"Yes," Captain Temmas brusquely dismissed him with a wave of a hand, "report to the guards outside. Highness-"

"*No.*" Ariana glared at her chief of the palace guard. "This boy saved my life. I was drowning, and where were your guards then?"

The chief guard's face grew white as blood drained into his boots. "We, the gates to the inner courtyard were locked, Highness. It took, too long, for us to get the gates open," he gave an explanation that he knew was an excuse for an inexcusable failure. He looked down at the floor of the storeroom. "I have no excuse, Highness. You may have my resignation-"

"I do not want your resignation, Temmas," Ariana cut off the man's tortured words. "I want answers. And I want you to *fix* the *problem*. Our security has been breached and that is your responsibility."

"Certainly, Highness," Temmas shuddered with relief. Working to fix a problem was something tangible, something he could focus on.

"Well?" Ariana demanded.

"Highness?" Temmas expressed his confusion.

"You can't oversee palace security from this storeroom!" The princess chided.

"Oh," he dipped one knee then rose to full height, adjusting his sword belt. "Certainly. Now that I know you are safe here, for now, I will search the palace top to bottom, I fear there may be more nasty surprises." He shuddered. If the Citadel was not secure, no place within the palace could be trusted. At least he could be sure the humble storeroom had not been booby-trapped. The princess would have to remain there until the palace had been thoroughly scoured for enemy agents and devices. Temmas opened the door, nodded to the guards outside, and stepped through.

Cully moved to follow, but Ariana had other ideas. "Mister Runnet, a moment, please."

"Your Highness?" The servant boy's lower lip trembled fearfully. He had touched the crown princess in the process of rescuing her, and he did not know how much trouble he might be in. Surely even the royals would make allowances for the circumstances? "I am terribly sorry that-"

"You have nothing to be sorry about, Cully Runnet," Ariana stood in her most regal pose. "Kneel," she ordered the boy. To the guard on her right, she held out a hand. "Your sword, please."

"Highness?" The guard blanched, not understanding.

The wizard understood clearly, and she was alarmed. "Princess Ariana," Olivia spoke sharply. "May I speak with you, privately? *Now*?"

Ariana froze, then turned toward the wizard with irritation. "What is it?"

"Please," Olivia nodded toward a back corner of the storeroom. "It is important, and it *cannot* wait."

"Oh," Ariana threw up a hand in exasperation. "Very well. Stay here," she gestured to Cully, then, seeing the boy's confusion, she added, "you may stand up." The crown princess stomped off to a dark corner of the storeroom, and when the wizard joined her, hissed "What is so important?"

"What were you about to do, Highness?" Olivia asked, knowing full well what the future queen of Tarador had in mind.

Ariana's jaw set. "I am going to do something I should have done, for someone else, some time ago."

"Cully Runnet is not Koren Bladewell."

"Yes, thank you," Ariana's tone contained no thankfulness. "He is not Koren, and he will receive far more than Koren ever did, though Koren deserved *so* much more." At that, a tear rolled down her cheek unbidden. Putting a fist to her mouth, she stifled a sob.

The gulf of formality and station between them made it awkward for Olivia, so rather than offering the grief-stricken girl an embrace, she took Ariana's hand in hers, and squeezed in a gesture she hoped conveyed comfort. "Koren did, does, deserve much more. But, Highness, if you give this boy honors for saving you, for saving us, will it not seem suspicious that you did not give such honors to Koren?"

"As if that matters now," Ariana pulled her hand away and used it to wipe away tears. "With Koren wandering the wilderness all alone, or wherever he is," she could no longer contain her emotions, and slumped against a stack of crates, softly crying.

Still hesitant to be familiar with the princess, Olivia reached out to touch the other girl's shoulders. "Did, do you love him?"

"No," Ariana's eyes welled with tears. "How could I love him? I didn't even know who he is. *He* didn't know. Koren saved my life, he brought the Cornerstone back to us, he saved Lord Salva's life, and I rewarded him by making him fear for his own life."

"You did not do that, Your Highness."

Ariana shook her head angrily. "I am the heir to the throne. Tarador is *my* realm, what happens here is *my* responsibility."

"Your mother was Regent-"

"She is not Regent now! I can't help Koren, I can't fix all my mistakes. He probably hates me-"

"I'm sure that is not true."

"How could he not hate me? I cheated him out of the honors he deserved, and my Royal Army hunted him like a common criminal. Still hunts him today, because Lord Salva tells me that is necessary."

"It is, Your Highness," Olivia winced at how empty her words sounded even to herself.

"Lady Dupres," Ariana's tone was icy. She wiped tears away with a filthy sleeve of her dress and stood up straight. "It was advice from wizards that got us into this mess. Koren would not have run away if my mother had not taken Lord Salva's advice. It was *wizards* who failed him. Please do not tell me now that you and your fellow wizards know what is best for Koren Bladewell, or that you care about him. Lord Salva sees Koren only as a tool, a weapon. They don't care about *him*."

Olivia knew that was absolutely far from the truth, and she also knew anything she could say would only make the princess more angry, so she took one step back and simply nodded. "As you wish, Highness. I must admit, nothing you do here now could make the situation worse for Koren. If you want to reward that boy, could I offer him my thanks also? He saved my life also. My foot was wedged under a stone, I would have drowned soon if he had not reached me. He nearly died saving me."

Cully had remained kneeling on the floor, trembling slightly and trying to tilt his head so the blood seeping down from his forehead stayed out of his eyes. In a far corner of the storeroom, the Regent of Tarador and a powerful wizard were arguing about something, and Cully feared that though they spoke too softly for him to hear, they had to be talking about him. What would be the punishment for a lowly servant boy who touched both a crown princess and a wizard? A young lady wizard? He could only imagine, and his fears nearly ran away with him. It was all he could do not to burst to his feet and rush out the door. The discussion apparently ended, both regal girls returned to the front of the storeroom. The wizard still looked unhappy and the eyes of the princess were red from crying, but she appeared- happy? Cully did not know what to make of that. Why was the princess happy, when she had barely escaped another attempt on her life?

"Your sword," Ariana held out a hand, and this time the guard did not hesitate. The man went down on one knee and surrendered his sword to his Regent, pommel held out first.

Ariana took the sword, nearly dropping it as the weight of the weapon surprised her. She fumbled awkwardly, her turn to be embarrassed. The delicate fencing weapons she used in her all-too-infrequent sparring sessions with the royal weapons master were light and well balanced compared to the heavy battering sword carried by the royal guard force. When she feared she would clumsily cut the servant boy's ear off, she took hold of the sword with both hands and carefully placed it on Cully's right shoulder, the blade trembling slightly. "Cully Runnet, for service above and beyond the call of duty, for saving the life of your crown princess *and* a wizard in service to Tarador," she grunted slightly in a fashion not befitting a princess, as she slowly swung the sword to thump harder than she wanted onto Cully's left shoulder. "I knight thee *Sir* Cully Runnet."

"Si-" Cully's head reeled in disbelief. "M- me? But, but I can't-"

"Sir Runnet," Ariana's amusement shone on her face though she tried and failed to scowl at the boy. "Are you questioning your future queen?"

"That would not be good," Olivia played along. "A knight of the realm owes absolute loyalty to his ruler."

"No!" Cully blanched and wavered on his knees, needing a hand on the floor to steady himself. "I mean, Your Highness, I," he stammered and lost his voice.

Ariana dragged the tip of the sword across the floor and held out the pommel to the guard, who returned it easily to his scabbard. "Rise, Sir Runnet," she gestured dramatically.

Cully staggered to his feet. "I'm, Your Highness, I am truly a *knight*?"

"Yes, you are, Sir Runnet," Olivia assured him, placing a steadying hand on his shoulder to prevent the stunned boy from falling over.

"Now, Sir Runnet," Ariana's expression turned serious again. "Report to the royal hospital to have that cut on your forehead attended to. Guard," she ordered the man whose name she could not recall, "see that Sir Runnet reaches the hospital without interference."

"Your Highness," Cully had tears freely streaming down his face and he made no attempt to wipe them away with the dirty sleeve of his shirt. "Thank you."

"Sir Runnet, you may thank us," Ariana used the royal 'we', "by serving us faithfully as a knight of the realm. *After* you see the doctors, and after you are properly trained to your service."

Cully needed a guard's help to stand. The man guided him out the door with a gentle hand on Cully's shoulder. Outside in the inner courtyard, the servant boy had to pause to bend over, hands on knees and take deep breaths. "I've never been a *knight* before," he explained to the guard, feeling foolish even as he said the words.

"Nor have I, Sir Runnet," the guard smiled, and it was a genuine smile. The servant boy, former servant boy, had saved the life of the crown princess and a wizard. Awarding a knighthood to the boy was as it should be according to the rules the guard lived by, and it made him hopeful he might someday be rewarded if he performed with distinction.

"Oh. Yes. Sorry," Cully stood back up, and squared his shoulders. He was a knight of the realm now, *Sir* Runnet. He could not slump when he stood. He needed to hold himself tall and proud. Whatever else knights did was still a mystery to him, but he did know knights carried themselves with dignity. He looked around the courtyard. Thin, gray smoke was curling up from the shattered window of the Citadel tower, and several blocks of stone were teetering precariously, threatening to fall into the moat. The drawbridge was now fully retracted, and all the lower windows had heavy iron shutters closed and barred across the openings. He looked the other way, to the fire brigade box, to the six buckets he had pulled out to sit on the cobblestones. The buckets were still there, unused. Someone else, he realized with a start, would be putting the buckets back when the emergency was over. He would no longer be standing by a fire box during drills, nor working in the stables, nor splitting or hauling firewood. He would not be a servant at all. He would not be one of the servants. His shoulders did slump slightly when he considered that all his friends were servants, and now there would be a vast gulf between them and Sir Cully Runnet. That thought made him sad.

Then he thought of how proud his parents would be to learn their son, who had caused them a fair share of trouble over the years, was now a knight. A *knight*! "Which way," he looked around, embarrassed, "to the hospital?"

CHAPTER SIX

Departing the harbor was far more complicated that Paedris expected; it had been many years since he had taken a sea voyage. The ship was prepared with the small crew waiting for Captain Reed's order to set sail at any moment. Supplies were tucked away below decks, the ship's bottom had been scraped of weeds and algae and barnacles as much as was possible without beaching the ship, and the sails furled on the yardarms were new or freshly patched. The wind appeared to Paedris to be favorable at times and he eagerly anticipated getting underway, but the sailors always felt something was not right. The wind was blowing from the wrong direction, or the wind could not be trusted to last more than a few hours which would leave the ship becalmed off the rocks at the harbor entrance. Or the wind was good but the tide was coming in. The sailors of the *Lady Hildegard* reminded Paedris of the people who farmed his land; they also were almost never happy about the weather. It either rained too much or not enough, Spring came too early or too late, the first frost arrived before the harvest was in or the late summer heat lingered too long after the crops were in. When there was a rare year when every condition was perfect and a bumper crop was harvested, all the surrounding farms also had grain bins overflowing at harvest time and prices were low. Also, a near-perfect growing season was not to be trusted, according to the farmers, because that meant Fate was toying with them and the following years were sure to be disastrous. Paedris could sympathize with the people whose livelihoods depended on things they could not control such as weather. He had less patience with experienced sailors who could not seem to get their ship to sail!

"Captain Reed," Paedris walked to the rail where the ship's master stood, on the third morning the ship had swung idly at anchor despite being entirely ready for sea. "Surely this fine breeze will carry us out of the harbor this morning?" He tilted his head back to looked at the sky, and the wind playfully stirred his beard.

Reed also looked up, although rather than staring ignorantly at the pretty white clouds, he noted the type of cloud in each layer of the sky, and how the breeze made the ends of lines sway on the topmast. To his satisfaction, the lines were swaying more than they had been early that morning, as were the telltale ribbons attached to the shrouds leading down to the deck. "Not at the moment, Master Wizard, for the tide is still coming in and would be against us." he looked down and pointed at a piece of wood floating in the lee of the ship. The waterlogged stick was bobbing along steadily, moving past the ship and into the harbor.

"Ah, the damned tide again," Paedris muttered unhappily.

"Fear not, Lord Salva," Reed chuckled. "Slack tide is in two hours, and we should cast off from the buoy then. The afternoon breeze here is typically onshore, but with this wind from the east, we will clear the harbor well before we must begin beating back and forth."

"Beating?"

"Tacking," Reed explained to the landlubber wizard. "Sailing to port then to starboard, into the wind," he motioned with one hand to illustrate. "Come evening, we will pick up a breeze from the land and it will carry us over the horizon, where we can pick up the Easterlies."

"Easter-" The wizard repeated without understanding.

"This time of year, the prevailing wind is from the east, or east-southeast, and will carry us toward Acedor. Unless," he bowed in an audaciously bold manner, "your Lordship would care to conjure up a more reliable, favorable wind for us?"

"No," Paedris took the captain's jest in good humor. "Getting underway later this morning will be sufficient."

Reed looked at the telltales lazily flopping in the inconsistent breeze. "We will get her out today. It may, Lord Salva, require us hiring boats to tow her out toward the harbor entrance. These hills," he gestured left and right to the rolling but tall hills that ringed the harbor, "block the wind and make it swirl unpredictably at times."

"Boats?" Paedris asked, not understanding.

"Yes. If I had a full crew, we could man the sweeps ourselves; even then I would want the security of boats to keep us off those rocks," he pointed to the western shore of the harbor, where dark rocks stood half submerged.

"Boats rowed by mere men can pull this ship?" Cecil asked incredulously. He knew, because he had seen with his own eyes, that the *Lady Hildegard* had been lightened by removing anything not needed for her voyage of hopefully less than a month. She carried no anchors or chain, no heavy storm canvas, and only minimal provisions for the crew. What weight she carried was tucked away in the lower hold where it acted as ballast. The ship probably had never been so light since she was launched. But still, Cecil had to think the ship still weighed many, many tons!

"Certainly," Reed nodded. "I have been in difficult, awkward anchorages where the only way out, short of a miraculous offshore wind, is to use boats to tow an anchor farther out from the harbor. Drop the second anchor there, haul up your first anchor, then use the windlass to pull the ship up to the second anchor. Use the boat again to tow the first anchor out farther, and" the captain shrugged, "repeat."

Cecil looked at Paedris, eyes wide in disbelief. "That seems to be, rather a lot of work."

"A sailor's life can be a hard one, aye," Reed agreed with a touch of pride. "But, we have our tricks to make things easier. If this breeze freshens as I expect, boats will not be needed." He raised an eyebrow.

Paedris caught the man's meaning. "Yes, if you need to hire boats, do so and I will see they are paid. I wish to get underway *today*," he stated flatly, not adding that he had really wanted to get underway two days ago.

Within the hour, the two wizards could see and hear increased activity aboard their ship. Orders were shouted, feet pounded on the deck and men ran up from the lower decks to tend the sails. Paedris and Cecil left their cabins and went topside to view the excitement.

"It's almost slack tide," Captain Reed explained with a broad grin, "and the wind has picked up nicely and is now blowing due east; we will not need boats to tow us out today! We'll be unmooring soon. Gentlemen," he gestured for the two wizards to stand by the windward rail, "you are of course welcome to enjoy the sights, but please stay out of the crew's way. That is partly for your own safety, and mostly because we are shorthanded and the crew are hard pressed to fulfill their duties."

"Oh, um, certainly," Paedris shuffled his feet awkwardly step aside, nearly tripping into Cecil as the two men back up toward the rail. "You look happy, Captain," Paedris observed. To date, Captain Reed had shown two expressions: concern and anger, or perhaps concern and frustration. Mostly concern.

"I am!" Reed clapped his hands. "I'm going back to sea! I am a sailor, Lord Salva, Lord Mwazo; it's in my blood, it calls to me. The sea is where I belong. Until you two came along, I despaired of ever feeling the deck move beneath my feet, except to ride at anchor."

"You enjoy this?" Cecil's skeptical tone was enhanced by the ship suddenly heeling over slightly as unfurled sails filled and caught the wind.

"To be master of my own ship, that is, I mean," Reed added with an anxious look to Paedris.

"We know what you mean, Captain Reed. The crown princess may own these timbers," he stomped a boot on the well-worn planks of the deck for emphasis, "but at sea, you are master of this vessel."

"Yes, thank you," Reed was relieved. "To be underway, feeling her sails catch the wind and her slip across the waves," he closed his eyes for a moment. "It is the greatest feeling for a sailor. Now, if you will excuse me, your Lordships," he said without a trace of sarcasm, "I must lend a hand. The crew will think me out of practice, it is time to show them I can still handle a line."

The two wizards stood by the rail, with their backs to the wind, enjoying the cooling breeze and the crew charged to and fro in seemingly chaotic disorganization. Unlike almost every ship Paedris had been aboard, the crew of the *Hildegard* appeared to be universally happy to go about their duties, each man knowing what to do and anticipating the next order. Orders were still shouted, because traditions needed to be kept, and simply out of long habit. In response to shouted orders that were usually unnecessary, the crew laughed, and sang songs in unison as they readied their ship for an ocean voyage.

From the rail, Paedris could see similar activity aboard four other ships in the harbor. At the instructions of the court wizard, the royal factor in the port had hired four other vessels to set sail at the same time as the *Lady Hildegard.* Across the harbor, long-unused sails were being loosened and shaken out. Unlike the *Hildegard,* the four other ships had not been stripped of everything nonessential to speed their passage, and they had only been hired for a fortnight. Not being as ready for sea as the *Hildegard,* the four other ships were slower to slip from their moorings, gathered speed less quickly and were generally sloppy about putting to sea. By the time the *Hildegard* cleared the hills at the harbor entrance and the ship heeled over from the wind, with the water churning to white foam at her bow, the last of the four ships behind her was still unfurling canvas on her mizzenmast.

Even a landlubber like Paedris could appreciate how efficiently the *Hildegard*'s crew got their ship moving, and how their ship responded to the stronger wind outside the harbor entrance by fairly flying across the waves. Paedris could not fault the other four ships for being slower; most of those ships had crews hired only for the fortnight and were not used to that particular ship and to working with each other. Perhaps the slow response of those vessels was not entirely due to clumsiness by the crews; the captains of those ships knew their part in the operation was to act as bait for pirates, while the swifter *Hildegard* raced to escape through the pirate blockade of the port. Any pirate would note how high the fast-sailing *Hildegard* rode in the water and would conclude that ship was lightly loaded, while the other four ships were not only slow by comparison, but riding low enough in the water to signal they carried heavy cargo that would be very tempting to any pirate.

What the pirates could not know was the four decoy ships carried only a cargo of sandbags and water casks, and when the decoy ships were pursued by pirates they would dump that worthless burden overboard and race back to the safety of the harbor. Whether the decoy ships ventured beyond the harbor for the full duration of their contract, or only one day, made no difference as long as they drew the attention of pirates away from the *Lady Hildegard*.

"Ah," said the sailor named Alfonze as he approached the two wizards, although Alfonze was busy coiling a line and securing it for later use, rather than watching the sights. "I see our friends in the Navy have decided to join the fun," he pointed to the inner harbor, where a pair of ships were shaking out their sails.

Even to the inexperienced eyes of the wizards, the two Royal Navy ships were different from the five merchant vessels also making their way out of the harbor. The merchant ships had stout hulls designed for carrying cargo, and square sails that were easier for a small crew to handle. The Navy ships were narrow to speed their passage through the water, and the sails were rigged fore and aft to sail better into the wind. Navy ships had another advantage which explained why they had no need to rush when the merchant ships had slipped their moorings; the Navy ships had large crews not only for fighting, but also for manning banks of oars. Water churned on both sides of the Navy ships as their crews rowed them out to the middle of the harbor, where the surrounding hills sloped down and the water was exposed to the full force of the midday breeze. As Paedris and Cecil watched, the Navy ships set their sails and oars were raised out of the water to be stowed. The pair of warships overtook one, then two, then four merchant ships, leaving only the *Hildegard* unescorted.

The plan was not for Tarador's Royal Navy to challenge the pirates offshore, although the naval commander was spoiling for a chance to fight. The mission of the two warships was merely to make any pirates think the convoy of four heavily-laden merchant ships were valuable enough to be given a Royal Navy escort; valuable enough to attract the full attention of any pirate ships in the vicinity.

As the wizards watched and the *Hildegard*'s deck heeled over from the stiffening wind, the last of the trailing merchant ships cleared the harbor and joined the other three to set course southeast, while the *Hildegard* skipped across the waves heading due south. The Navy ships took up position to seaward of their four charges, hovering near them like sheepdogs herding a plodding flock.

All went well for the *Lady Hildegard* until midafternoon, when three sails were sighted to the east, slightly closer to land. Through a spyglass, the two wizards could see the strange sails were triangular. They had to be pirates, for the only Royal Navy ships in the area were plainly in view to the northeast, and no fishing vessels had been foolish enough to venture more than half a league from the harbor since the pirates took control of the sea lanes.

"I don't suppose either of your Lordships would care to go aloft?" Captain Reed looked meaningfully to the crow's nest of the mainmast. Although he had spoken in jest, a part of him hoped one of the wizards would accept the offer, or challenge, and climb to where they could see better.

"No, I would not," Lord Mwazo answered emphatically. Like almost all wizards, he was blessed with an uncanny sense of balance. He also had a good sense of self-preservation, and no desire to climb to the top of a swaying mast.

"I can see perfectly well from here, thank you very much for your kind offer," Paedris replied with a tight smile.

"You can see the sails of those three ships we know of," Reed pressed his two passengers. "If others are over the horizon from our view here on the deck," he looked aloft again to emphasize the advantage of altitude, "they might be visible to a person higher above the waves."

Paedris shaded his eyes and squinted up at the crow's nest, which was moving to and fro wildly enough in the building seas that it made the wizard slightly queasy just to think of the poor sailor up there. "And that is why you have wisely posted a lookout, eh?"

Reed bit his tongue, knowing it was useless and might even be dangerous to argue with a powerful wizard. With ordinary men, he could taunt their manhood, imply they were afraid to go aloft, but if his two passengers were merely ordinary men, he would not care for them to act as lookouts.

"Do they see us?" Cecil asked.

"Certainly," Reed nodded grimly. "Our masts are taller; they see us before we see them. Unless our lookouts get lucky·and we strike topsails just in time."

Paedris looked up to study the canvas high above his head, seeing the material stretched and filled by the wind. "Should we do that now?"

Reed shook his head. "No, there's no point to-"

"We don't *know* they've seen us," Paedris protested. "If you-"

Cecil touched his friend's shoulder. "Lord Salva, just as you and I are masters of wizardry, Captain Reed knows his ship and the arcane arts of seamanship. Allow the man to do the job you hired him for."

Paedris cringed slightly and made a very short bow to Reed, then straightened. "My apologies, Captain. Do as you think best."

Whatever Reed planned to say next was swept away by a cry from the lookout. "One of those ships is coming about, heading straight for us!"

"Damn," Reed cursed. "We-"

"And there's two more ships with them. Only one coming our way," the lookout called out to be heard, as his voice was partly carried away by the wind.

"Well, that's done for. Blast!" Reed shouted. "I was hoping they would all go for the decoy convoy."

"What now?" Cecil asked with a calmness that surprised himself.

Reed "Now? Now, we do exactly what we are doing already; we keep on this course."

"And when the enemy gets closer?" Paedris inquired.

"Then?" Reed shrugged. "That depends on a great number of things. Chiefly, what the enemy does. If they mean to take us, we turn to run more to the west; with these sails we are best sailing with the wind. If the wind shifts direction, or slackens as it can do in the afternoon hours in this area, we could be in trouble," he said the last with a raised eyebrow. Surely two powerful wizards would not allow the ship to be taken with them aboard.

The two wizards shared a look, then Paedris shuffled his feet uncomfortably. "I'm sure we are keeping you from your duties, Captain Reed."

Reed's irritation with his passengers was soon pushed to the back of his mind, as he had more immediate things to occupy his full attention. Climbing to the crow's nest, he assured himself only one enemy ship was sailing in his direction, the others had taken the bait and were racing after the convoy. To his satisfaction and mild surprise, he saw the two Royal Navy ships were remaining with the merchant ships rather than charging out to meet the pirates. Earlier attempts at escorted convoys had inevitably resulted in Royal Navy ships breaking away from the convoy to tangle with pirate ships, leaving the merchant ships easy prey for other pirates. Perhaps Lord Salva's harsh words to the Navy captains had served to focus those ship on their assigned duty rather than seeking glory or revenge.

Still, Reed thought to himself with a bitter smile, he would wait to see what the Navy ships did when the pirates were close enough to attack. Would those two captains maintain their discipline when pirates sailed close enough to shout taunts across the water?

Reed handed the spyglass back to the lookout and slipped easily over the side of the crow's nest, forgoing the shrouds to slide down a line hand over hand, with the line clamped between his boot soles to slow the descent. Ultimately, what the Navy escorts did with the convoy was not his problem, and hopefully he would be over the horizon and out of view by the time the pirates reached the decoy merchant ships. Until, and unless, he survived to return to Tarador, the only view he would have of the upcoming convoy battle would be smoke wafting into the sky, and he would not know which ships were on fire.

"Alfonze!" He shouted as his boots touched the deck, wincing in pain from the rope burn to his left calf. Skylarking by sliding down a line was for the young, and he was out of practice. Reed gathered the leaders among the small crew. "We need to shift cargo," he explained. "We're lightly loaded and she's too heavy toward the bow, she's digging into the waves. You know what this will be like," he searched the crew's faces and could see people groaning inwardly. They did know what it would be like. Back-breaking work shifting the cargo around then adjusting sails as the captain experimented to determine the arrangement for best speed. "I know I can count on you," he said with a meaningful gaze toward the pirate ship whose hull was now over the horizon and closing on the *Hildegard*.

Three hours later, after much frustrating trial and error, Reed was satisfied with the way his ship was responding, and the crew agreed their *Lady* was now moving much more gracefully over the waves. To test the ship's ability to run straight downwind, Reed ordered a turn due west and held it only long enough to be satisfied he knew how the *Hildegard* sailed on that course, then returned heading west southwest. If he did need to run downwind, he did not want the pirates to know what his ship was capable of.

"Your Lordships," he nodded to the wizards who had come back on deck, "the pirate ship will be within hailing distance well before nightfall. They have the weather gage, so," he halted at the utterly blank looks from the two master wizards. "The pirate ship is approaching us from the direction of the wind," he explained patiently and illustrated the action with his hands playing the part of the two ships. "He can sail downwind to intercept us, but we cannot catch him."

"That is due to the shape of his sail?" Cecil asked insightfully.

"Partly," Reed agreed then hurried to finish his thought before the wizards could delay him with amateurish questions. "Mostly it is because with our sails," he gestured above his head, "we cannot point as well into the wind. Your Lordships, I must ask what you intend to do, if the pirates engage us."

"I will not allow us to be captured," Paedris answered with a frown. "Nor allow this ship to be sunk," he raised his eyebrows to emphasize how obvious that last statement was. "You mentioned we might turn and run to the west?"

"We might do that, aye, that is no surety we will escape that way. I expect the wind to fall off in the evening. Lord Salva, that pirate ship is faster than the *Hildegard* in all points of wind, except in heavy seas. Do not trust to our escape, if the pirates wish to take this ship, they will attack."

"And we will defend ourselves, if we are forced to, and only if we must. Can your crew put up enough of a fight to discourage an attempt to board us?"

Reed blinked incredulously. Biting his tongue to hold back a smart remark, he reminded himself the wizards had no practical knowledge of fighting at sea, or of anything to do with seamanship. "That is difficult at the best of times. With our reduced crew complement, that would be impossible, I fear."

Paedris rubbed his beard while he stared at the approaching pirate ship, which was now close enough for his keen eyes to discern individual pirates standing at the bow. A glint of light flashed from the other ship. "They have a spyglass," he muttered. "It is good we are not wearing our confounded robes, Cecil, or they would know we are wizards."

"Or priests," Cecil responded, amused.

Paedris turned his attention back to the ship's master. "Captain, when that ship comes alongside to board us, I could set her sail ablaze."

"That action would be more helpful at a distance, your Lordship," Reed remarked. "For boarding, the pirates will likely trust to oars rather than their sail."

"Hmmm," Paedris was surprised and dismayed to hear that. "I can only throw wizard fire a limited distance, and into the wind?" He squinted and judged the strength of the breeze by ribbons attached to his ship's shrouds. "Perhaps a hundred yards? It will be less effective the farther I have to cast the fire."

Reed was impressed. "A hundred yards will do nicely, my Lord! Even if you do not burn their ship, you will certainly discourage them from trying to board us."

"Yes," Paedris said unhappily. "That will discourage them from boarding us. But it will *encourage* them to follow us. Any ship of Tarador carrying a wizard of power would be of great interest to the enemy; certainly any pirates in thrall to the enemy would have orders to track such a ship. Our mission requires the utmost secrecy, we cannot afford to have a pirate ship trailing us. No, if I am forced to act, I must sink that ship, and to be sure of doing that, it must come uncomfortably close."

"That would be dangerous to us, and I do not need to remind you why," Reed hinted darkly. "The enemy can hurl flaming darts from a considerable distance, this past Spring we were attacked by pirates and were very fortunate to escape with our lives. If we had not-"

"Yes, Captain," Paedris cut the man off from what the wizard assumed wrongly would be an irrelevant recount of a previous battle. "If the enemy fires upon us, we must endure it until they are close enough for me to be sure of destroying their ship."

Reed, knowing the discussion was over and he had been dismissed, bowed curtly and strode to the ship's wheel.

Paedris nodded his head to the side, wishing Cecil to follow him farther away from the crew, where they could speak privately. "Before I am backed into a corner and must do something showy and dramatic," the court wizard said with a sour expression, "is there anything you could do, to discourage that pirate captain from pursuing us?"

"What do you have in mind?"

"It would probably be useless to attempt sowing fear into the hearts of those pirates; they will fear the demon above all. No, I was thinking you could subtly remind those pirates that their fellows are pursuing a fair more tempting prize closer to shore," he narrowed his eyes and peered toward the horizon, where only the topmast of one merchant ship could be seen, along with the triangular sails of four pirate ships bearing down on the decoy force.

"Ah, I should sow greed rather than fear," Cecil smiled tightly. He rubbed a finger against his cheek while he thought. "I could try, Paedris. It would be helpful if the pirates thought this ship a difficult quarry to catch, so they could do the work of persuading themselves for me."

It was Lord Salva's turn to smile, and his was broad. "Use the enemy's weakness against them?"

"Just so."

"I will request Captain Reed to turn the ship-"

Cecil caught his friend's arm. "Paedris, wait. I will send forth my senses first, to judge our chances of success."

"Agreed," Paedris said, and helped the tall, thin wizard to sit so he could concentrate.

Cecil gathered himself, calming the clamor of his inner thoughts and reaching into the spirit world for power. Gently, subtly, he sent the faintest wisp of his consciousness on a thin, ephemeral tendril reaching out toward the enemy. Unaware of wind or wave as he sought the minds aboard the pirate ship, he used only the bare minimum or power to-

And he recoiled in shock, gasping as his eyes flew open. "Paedris! I can do nothing. There is a wizard aboard that ship!"

"A *wizard?*" Paedris gasped a whisper. "How could-" he stopped himself. No, a wizard aboard a pirate ship did not necessarily mean the enemy knew of their secret mission. "Did you get a sense of-"

"Not a wizard of your power, Paedris," Cecil anticipated his friend's question. "But, powerful enough. I cannot attempt to influence their minds without first acting on that wizard, and I judge," he sat up straighter to look over the rail, "that will take too long." The pirate ship was close enough to see men on her deck shaking their fists at the *Hildegard*.

"Ah," Paedris sighed deeply in frustration. "A wizard is a complication which could be fatal to our mission."

"Even if you sink that ship," Cecil held his hands palms upward.

"Yes," Paedris snorted. "That wizard would live long enough to signal his dark master that wizards of Tarador are at sea. Even his death would be like ringing a bell."

"What can we do, then?"

"I will inform Captain Reed it is time to run straight away, or play whatever other card he has up his sleeve."

"And I? Is there anything I can do?"

Paedris took a moment to think. "Cecil, you can pray for our deliverance."

Reed played his only card. He turned to run more with the wind, and ordered his crew to scramble aloft to lay on additional sail until it seemed like even the crew's dirty laundry was being tied to a mast. The *Lady Hildegard* surged forward, helped by another strenuous effort by her crew to shift cargo below decks. "This is the best she can do, Lord Mwazo," Reed said with a nod of his head rather than a bow that he did not have time for. The other wizard had gone below to rest, preserving his power for the coming conflict.

"I have never been aboard a ship so swift," Cecil replied truthfully, though as he had no way of knowing the ship's exact speed, he could perhaps be forgiven any exaggeration. "How long now?" He knew Paedris would appreciate a quarter hours' notice before he was needed on deck.

"Half a glass?" Reed guessed. "It depends on how eager those pirates are to grapple with us before dark. They could take to their oars and be upon us quickly, if they- what?" He was startled by what he saw.

The pirate ship had turned, swinging her bow around to run perpendicular to the wind. Reed feared the enemy was moving to get in front of his ship, but the enemy continued to turn until they were sailing northeast, exposing their stern to the *Hildegard*. On the aft deck of the pirate ship, a half dozen pirates were jeering and shouting at Reed, their words carried away by the wind. He did not need to hear the words to understand their meaning, then one pirate added emphasis to his jeers by bending over and pulling his pants, to show his bare buttocks to the fleeing merchant ship.

Embarrassed for his honored guest, Reed turned to apologize to Lord Mwazo when that wizard smiled. "Well, I suppose if you don't have anything to show in the *front-*"

Reed guffawed at the unexpected remark, and in an instant, every sailor in earshot was doubled over with convulsions of laughter. There was a sound of boots pounding on a ladder and the court wizard appeared on deck, looking around in astonishment. "What did I miss?"

"Apparently there was nothing to see," Cecil choked laughing at his own joke. "That is the point," he slapped Reed's shoulder for emphasis, and the captain grinned.

Recovering his wits, Reed pointed to the swiftly receding pirate ship. "My guess is when they saw how high we are riding in the water, they judged us not worth the fight. Not when our decoy force is still so tempting."

"You are certain?" Paedris asked, fearful of getting his hopes up.

"Certain? At sea, I can be *certain* of nothing. I judge the enemy would not be showing their stern to us now, if they still intend to engage us in battle. We are safe enough for now, Lord Salva. By nightfall I expect us to be over the horizon, out of the sea lanes, and once under cover of darkness we will turn westward toward Acedor, where no one will expect us to be. Alfonze!" He roared. "We should lighten sail before this wind carries away a mast."

CHAPTER SEVEN

Regin Falco swept into the room, not waiting to be formally announced. Upon reaching the castle the day of the attempted assassination, he had found the drawbridges up and the gates shut and barred, even to him. No amount of bellowed threats had persuaded the castle guards to give him entrance, though they had reported there was no apparent danger at the royal hospital. Hearing that his son had not been harmed made Regin shudder with relief, momentarily swaying in the saddle and accepting a steadying hand from one of his escorts. Then, after he demanded to know what had happened, he received a great shock; princess Ariana had been attacked but was alive. *Alive*! He could not believe it, and this time he nearly fell out of his saddle. Instead of racing back to the castle to take command in the chaos and begin to cement his power, he was faced with the very real prospect of his entire plan having failed and his treason discovered.

Regin Falco had become duke of Burwyck province due to fortunate order of birth and having survived his younger brother's attempts to kill him. He had remained his position because he thought quickly and decisively, and that is what he did then. His near-swoon in the saddle was, he explained with false embarrassment, due to his great relief that his Regent and future daughter in law had survived. The words and actions of Duke Falco at the moment of receiving word that the princess had survived would be inquired about and reported, Regin knew, if not to Ariana herself then certainly to her very shrewd and capable chancellor.

That was why as soon as Regin was allowed into the castle, with the immediate crisis over, he went directly to the crown princess rather than to see his son. Before Ariana could speak, the duke of Burwyck province dropped to one knee and gazed down at his well-polished boots. "Your Highness, I have failed you. I cannot ask for forgiveness."

Ariana was taken aback, both by the duke's unexpected arrival and by what he said. She had been writing a letter to a baroness who wished to meet with the crown princess and now would have to wait until the palace was declared fully secured. "What? Your Grace, what do you mean?" She was automatically suspicious about anything Regin Falco said.

Not looking up to meet her eyes, the duke spoke and his voice was truly miserable. "Captain Temmas told me about the attempt on your life, Highness. Before you arrived, I inspected the palace for security risks, including the Citadel, and the lower tunnels. I am worthless! The assassin gained entry to the palace through an aqueduct, after I made the guards carefully inspect all the locks on those gates!"

"Duke Falco," she looked to her chancellor, having no idea what to say in response. "Captain Temmas is still investigating how the enemy got inside the palace, and if you insisted on assuring the locks were in working order," she waved a hand unsurely, "that could only have made the enemy's task more difficult."

"I thank you for your kind words, Highness, but I failed nonetheless. Princess Ariana," he glanced up to meet her gaze. "Your family and mine have had our differences over the years. We are now at war, in a desperate battle for the survival of our entire nation. My duty is to do everything within my power to assist you in winning this war. You are my Regent, and my future daughter in law. I will not accept risks to your safety, but I failed you."

With the duke gazing back down at his boots, Chancellor Kallron raised his hands palms upward to the crown princess, not knowing how she should respond. One thing he did know was the Falcos in general and Regin in particular were not to be trusted, but the duke had made a very good point. The man was determined, even obsessed, with his son marrying Ariana and the next heir to the throne being Regin's grandchild. It made perfect sense that Duke Falco wished absolute assurance that Ariana survive to inherit the throne, marry Kyre Falco and have a baby. After that baby was born, of course, Kallron knew the future Queen Ariana would have to watch her back whenever the duke was around, but until a Falco-Trehayme baby was born? No, Gustov Kallron could not think of any reason Regin Falco would wish or allow harm to the crown princess. He knew Duke Falco had been inspecting security of the palace and in the surrounding castle, and at the time Kallron had been mildly irritated about the interference. The chancellor had allowed the duke's poking into every nook and cranny of the palace because doing so had kept Regin busy enough he had not time to bother the palace staff other than the guard force. And, also, Kallron had allowed it because the palace security needed to be reviewed anyway prior to Ariana's return, and a fresh set of eyes never hurt. Thus, he did not object to or question Duke Falco's apparently heartfelt apology.

"Duke Falco, we," Ariana replied using the royal 'we', "do not blame you for missing signs of supernatural intrusion into the palace. Lady Dupres is even now searching the palace for magical devices of harmful intent." Harmful intent. Such a soft-sounding phrase to speak of such evil. "You could not have seen a device created from dark magic. Perhaps," she could not believe she was hearing herself offering praise to a Falco. "Your efforts are responsible, in some way, for the attempt on my life having failed?" She forced herself to smile, and when Duke Falco lifted his head, the anguish on his face was evident. After all, as a duke he would also have been escorted to the Citadel if he had been in the palace when the enemy attacked, it was the duke's good luck that he had been out riding in the countryside at the time. Why did she feel the need to comfort her enemy? She did not know, but she felt it was the right thing to do under the circumstances. Maybe, just maybe, the long enmity between the Trehaymes and the Falcos could begin to be broken, even if just a tiny bit.

"Thank you for your kind words, Highness," Regin breathed a sigh of relief. "What can I do to help? Command me, and it shall be done."

"I," she looked to her chancellor for guidance.

"Please, Duke Falco," Kallron spoke, "you can best help by continuing your efforts to rally the Regency Council behind the princess. We have a long struggle and many battles ahead of us, before the enemy is forced to give up hope of owning territory on our side of the border. Princess Ariana has won a smashing victory against the enemy, now some of the Council may be tempted to relax their support, to squabble amongst themselves, to resent the funds and troops they provide to assist the Royal Army. Now is not the time for our focus to waver."

"Yes," Falco agreed grimly, rising to his feet. "It will be done."

"Your Grace?" Ariana added. "There is one other thing you may do, for us. Your heir acted bravely and was injured in the battle at the Gates. We would appreciate it if you could do what you can to raise his spirits, to ensure his swift recovery. We could," words failed her. In spite of his words pledging eternal loyalty to her, Kyre Falco was her enemy and always would be. Why did she care that he not suffer permanent effects from his wounds? "We could use brave leaders like Kyre on our side."

At dinner that night, a feast delayed by the necessity for Captain Reed to assure his ship was properly rigged to run in darkness, the two wizards relaxed with Reed, Alfonze and Jofer. A bottle of wine provided by the court wizard made its way around the table, and Paedris found himself having to make an effort at conversation to keep the weary men around the table from falling asleep in their soup bowls. "Captain Reed, you mentioned today that this ship encountered pirates earlier this year, when you were coming from the South Isles? How did you survive?" In truth, Paedris had no great curiosity about what he expected to be a boastful tale of Reed's superior seamanship, ship-handling skills and cleverness, he was only trying to be a polite guest at the captain's table.

As his captain was chewing on a mouthful of tough ship's biscuit, Alfonze answered simply. "Magic," he said while spooning soup into his mouth.

"Aye," Jofer agreed, and made a protective hex sign on his forehead. "Meaning no offense to you of course, your Lordships," he was quick to add. "That there was dark magic," he shuddered as he spoke.

Reed swallowed his soup. "Not dark. It saved our lives, didn't it?"

"Aye," muttered those men who had been part of the *Hildegard*'s crew back then, what seemed so long ago.

Paedris froze in place, soup spoon halfway to his lips. The motion of the ship caused the soup to slosh off the spoon back into the bowl unnoticed. "What do you mean by 'magic'?" When he first heard the word he thought Alfonze spoke in jest, or referred to some silly talisman the superstitious crew believed had magical powers. When Jofer remarked the magic had been dark, Paedris for some reason felt a chill on the back of his neck.

"Captain?" Alfonze looked to the ship's master. "You spoke to the boy, afterward."

"What boy?" Paedris demanded with a vehemence that startled the sailors.

Reed set his spoon on the table. "I suppose there is no harm in telling you now. We had a boy in our crew, he came aboard at Tarador, before set sail for the South Isles. He-"

Paedris reached to his right and took Reed's forearm in a grip so powerful, the captain feared the two bones there would break. "What was his name?" Paedris half stood from his chair.

"Lord Salva," Reed pleaded in a strangled voice.

"Paedris, you are hurting the man," Cecil chided gently, tugging the other wizard's hand away from the ship's master.

"Oh," Paedris looked at his hand and released the captain. He addressed Alfonze and Jofer curtly. "Leave us. And close the door."

The two sailors did not argue, so fearsome was the expression the court wizard's face. After Alfonze closed the door behind him, Reed stood and used a hook to close the skylight, explaining "The crew at the wheel can hear everything through that skylight. Lord Salva, what is so important about this boy?"

"What was his name?" Paedris repeated. "And when did he come aboard?"

"His called himself Kedrun."

"No surname?"

"Many people who choose a life at sea go by one name, which might not be the name they were given at birth," Reed shrugged. "Some people go to sea to escape something on land. I'll not have a known criminal aboard my ship, but if someone chooses not to reveal his past, I ask only that he work hard and learn seamanship. This Kedrun joined us in late Spring, I can check the logs for the date if that would help you. He was young, fourteen, fifteen, maybe? Dark curly hair, and he was a landsman; he knew nothing of ships, sails, knots, nothing. We took him aboard partly for his skill as a cook, he told me his previous master liked spicy foods from, er," he suddenly remembered that court wizard was not from Tarador, but Reed did not know Lord Salva's homeland. "From Stade, perhaps? He was a good cook, exceptional, truly, the crew treasured him."

"Kedrun," Paedris breathed, and slumped in his chair. "This ship? *This* very ship," he excitedly jabbed a finger at the deck beneath his chair, "not another you commanded?"

"Yes, truly," Reed was mystified why a powerful wizard was so concerned about a mere boy. Unless- Reed sucked in a breath.

"Captain," Cecil spoke quietly with a glance toward the skylight. "You had best tell us the whole story."

With a slightly shaking hand, Reed poured himself a goblet of wine and took a mouthful before he plunged forward with the tale. The odd and unbelievable tale of Kedrun, the boy who had a potentially dangerous magic spell cast upon him by a wizard. While he told the story, he kept his gaze fixated on the wine goblet and avoided the intense eyes of Lord Salva. Kedrun had told of a wizard casting a spell on him, unwanted and without Kedrun's knowledge. Was Lord Salva's interest in the boy because the court wizard was outraged at the unlawful actions of a fellow wizard?

Or because the very wizard from Stade who cast the spell on young Kedrun, was now sitting at Captain Reed's table?

Reed finished telling all he knew, he had surprisingly been interrupted only once, and that by Lord Mwazo. Lord Salva sat silently while Reed spun his tale, the court wizard seeming to fix his gaze on a flickering lantern hanging from a peg on the opposite wall. The three sat in uncomfortable silence, each lost in his own thoughts and listening to the groaning and creaking of the ship's hull as it bobbed on the waves. Finally, Paedris cleared his throat and reached for the wine bottle, disappointed to find only a splash was left. "Captain Reed, you have no idea where this Kedrun boy went after he left your ship at Gertaborg?"

"No, my Lord," Reed replied truthfully. "If he took my advice, as he assured me he would, he was going upriver. Then," Reed shrugged. "To the dwarf homelands, however he could. With the war on, I could not give him advice on how best to get there; I imagine some roads are jammed with traffic, and others left to bandits."

"*This* ship. This very ship," Paedris whispered to himself.

Reed took that as a cue, and an opportunity, to make his way out of the cabin. "If you esteemed gentlemen will excuse me, I must go on deck to see to the sails."

"Certainly, Captain Reed," Cecil said dismissively, distracted by his thoughts. When Reed closed the cabin door behind him, the dark-skinned wizard from a land even more distant than Estada rose and selected a bottle of wine from a cabinet. That bottle was not chilled from having been lowered on a line into the water, but Cecil preferred red wine at a warm temperature anyway. And right then, he thought Paedris simply needed wine in his goblet, regardless of type temperature. "Drink this," Cecil held up the goblet for his mesmerized friend, and gently shook his shoulder.

"Eh? Oh, thank you." The goblet was only halfway to his lips when Paedris paused. "This ship. This same ship! Cecil, surely that cannot be a coincidence, that we hire the very vessel Koren used to escape from Tarador?"

"You are certain this boy 'Kedrun' is really Koren Bladewell?"

"Who else could it be?" Paedris raised eyebrows in disbelief.

"I agree wholeheartedly," Cecil hastened to assure his fellow wizard.

"You are our lore master, Mwazo, what could this mean?"

"Lore?" Cecil poured wine for himself, swirled it in his goblet, then took a sip to test the new bottle. He nodded approvingly. "This is not necessarily a matter of lore."

"Cecil-"

"I know what you are asking. Think on this. Koren returned from the South Isles because the *Lady Hildegard* was swift enough to carry Koren past a pirate blockade-"

"With Koren's help," Paedris added with irritation.

"Yes, then the *Hildegard* survived sailing from Gertaborg without Koren, and you purchased her because she is the swiftest and best-maintained ship in the harbor. Both Koren, and we, require a swift ship, so that part requires no coincidence."

"Is that what you truly believe?"

"No. My intention was to remind you that not everything in this world requires magical intervention by the spirits. However," he took a swig of wine and smacked his lips in appreciation, "even the skeptic in me finds it difficult to believe this ship was available to us, now, purely by coincidence. Also, Paedris?"

"Yes?"

"Koren Bladewell coming back into Tarador at this time can also not be coincidence. Just when our need is most dire, he comes back to us."

"Except he did *not* come back to us! He is," Paedris pounded the table with a fist, "wandering the wilderness, and we know not where!"

"We do know where he is going," Cecil chided gently. "He seeks a dwarf wizard. We need only to look at a map, to see the best route from Gertaborg to the dwarf lands."

"No," Paedris shook his head. He rose and rummaged through the captain's chart locker to find the map he needed. Almost all the maps showed seacoasts, of course, as ships did not travel inland. Finally, near the bottom, he found a tightly-rolled old map of Tarador and the surrounding nations. Being careful not to damage the fragile old parchment, he unrolled the map and placed it on the table, using discarded soup bowls to weight down the edges. "Look here," he jabbed a finger at the great port of Gertaborg. "From Gertaborg, Koren almost certainly traveled up the river. My guess is he wished to avoid crossing into Tarador on a major road, so," his lips pursed in a grimace, "he could have crossed anywhere. None of that matters. I know when Thunderbolt, his horse," he reminded Mwazo, "jumped the fence and ran away, the wind was from the northeast. Koren must have already been over the border and inside Tarador. The problem for us is that area is thinly populated with few roads, it is too close to the orc strongholds in the northern mountains," he shuddered slightly thinking of Koren Bladewell wandering alone across northeastern Tarador.

"Paedris, Koren seeks a dwarf wizard. We do not need to search all of northeastern Tarador, we can concentrate on the places he could have crossed into the dwarf homeland. Those cannot be many? I heard the dwarves have effectively sealed their borders to outsiders."

"Yes. Cecil, we can do nothing from here. Shomas and Captain Raddick are already searching for him, and now we know they are in the right place!" He clapped his fellow wizard on the back with a smile. "I begin to have hope again!"

Cecil Mwazo forced a smile, while inwardly he felt a chill of fear. Most dwarf wizards would be with their army. To meet such a wizard, Koren would need to expose himself to danger at the front lines.

Paedris stood staring at his wine glass, contemplating whether he could have another sip. "We know one thing for certain, Cecil. Koren has *not* yet found a dwarf wizard to speak with, or we would have been notified immediately."

Regin Falco left his hasty audience with the crown princess with his jaw set in fearful anger. After a brief visit to Kyre in the hospital, he returned to his fine apartments in the royal palace and removed his jacket. Flinging the garment on a desk, and poured himself a glass of whiskey, downing half the liquid in one gulp. Almost he reached for the bell cord to summon his advisor Niles Forne before remembering he could not discuss the issue, this one all-important, all-consuming issue, with Forne. His chief advisor was an amoral, scheming, sneaky, underhanded devious genius who had carried out many acts that even Regin considered unsavory, and had proposed other schemes Regin had rejected as going too far beyond the pale. But Niles Forne was at heart a Taradoran patriot and would never support Regin's latest move to regain the throne for the Falco family. Would never allow it! In spite of his long, loyal service to the Falcos, and his family line's service in the duchy before him, Forne would be horrified to learn his duke had joined forces with Tarador's ancient enemy.

In a rage, Regin swallowed the rest of the whiskey, then threw the heavy glass into the empty fireplace, nearly catching a shard in the face as it exploded back at him. Loudly, he cursed himself for his foolishness and weakness and immediately there was a pounding on the door. "Do you need help, my Lord?" The muffled voice of a guard called to him.

"I am fine!" Regin wished the glass had cut him so he could feel pain at his own stupidity and weakness. "Stay out," he ordered. The servants could clean up the mess later, and he cared not if any of those wretched underlings cut themselves. He reached for the whiskey, stared at the bottle, then slammed it down on the table. This was not the time to appear drunk or in any way compromised within the halls of the royal palace.

Damn it! He had risked everything, *everything*, to do as the enemy asked. He had done exactly as the enemy requested, no, ordered him to do, and the enemy had *failed*! That evening, he should be pretending to mourn for the princess while consolidating his grip on power, rather than fearing that young wizard brat would discover his treasonous part in the assassination attempt.

Stupid! He had been stupid, foolish, an idiot to trust the enemy. Worse, he had been a traitor to align himself and the house of Falco with Acedor. Now he was trapped, with no way to back out of his deal with the evil that was the power behind Acedor. From within the royal palace, he could not even communicate with the wizard that was his only link to the enemy. With magical wards around the palace, and a young wizard who had proved much more capable that Regin expected, the enemy dared not contact Regin within the walls of the palace. He would need to make up an excuse to go to the Falco mansion in the city of Linden, outside the gates. He would need to be in the mansion overnight, for the enemy only spoke with him in the darkest of nights. How to do that? With the attempt on the life of Tarador's Regent, palace security would want all royal and important persons within the castle walls where it is easier to ensure their safety. He would need a very good excuse to stay a night in the Falco mansion, and he did not have any excuse at all. He sat down heavily in a chair, burying his face in his hands. If he did go to his mansion, a contingent of royal guards would insist on accompanying him, so he would have no peace there at all. He needed to know soon, he needed to understand what to do next, and if anything-

No, he slowly realized. He did *not* need to act quickly. If the enemy required him to act further, then the damned enemy could figure out a way to get word to him! Surely with the forces of Acedor still east of the River Fasse and a massive army poised on the western shore, the princess would be going back out to accompany the Royal Army on some ill-advised and ultimately doomed campaign. Regin had already heard rumors of the princess planning to return to the field soon, after assuring her position as Regent was secure within the Council, and after gaining promises of additional funds and troops from the seven dukes and duchesses. With the great victories of the past month, Ariana had to be supremely hopeful of getting whatever she wanted from the Council.

Yes, Regin decided. What he could do, what he needed to do, was exactly what Chancellor Kallron requested! He would do his utmost to secure the full support of the Council for Ariana. The sooner she had such support, the sooner she would be away from the safety of the palace. Traveling in the field, even with an army surrounding her, Ariana would be more vulnerable than she was behind the thick walls of the palace. It was extremely unlikely Regin could bring magical devices inside the palace a second time, not with that damned blonde girl wizard watching everything like a hawk.

Satisfied he had a solution to his immediate problem, he picked up the whiskey bottle again, then set it down. No, he was a duke, and now at least a grudgingly trusted member of the royal household. Why should he drink alone in his apartments? He would take his dinner in the great hall, at the head of the table, where everyone could see his great concern for the safety of the crown princess. A hearty dinner, with food and wine provided by the Trehaymes, when he could discuss grand strategy of war with Niles Forne. That was what he needed that evening.

As to what to do about his larger problem, of having betrayed Tarador and his own family for absolutely no gain, he could worry about that later. "Guard!" He shouted. Someone needed to come in and clean up the shattered pieces of the glass, it would not do to have the duke's fine boots crunching on glass shards as he dressed for dinner.

Olivia was not able to get into the Citadel for two days after the explosion, the Royal Army engineers feared the internal structure of the tower had been seriously weakened and they thought the third floor might collapse onto the second. It took one day to carefully clean up debris and inspect the damage, then another day to shore up the third floor with heavy wood beams. By the afternoon of the third day, with the royal engineers still fretting that stones might fall away from where the window used to be, Olivia stomped a foot on the entrance to the Citadel's third floor. "Sir, I must get closer to where the explosion happened," she explained to the man in charge of the engineering team. "With every hour's delay, the signature of dark magic fades and soon I will not be able to understand anything about the nature of the device that, as you tell me, nearly toppled this most secure tower!"

The man's face turned red, then white as he wavered between irritation at the young wizard rushing what was a very delicate operation, and fear that she had spoken the truth. The Citadel had stood for centuries as the ultimate safehold for the royal family within the palace, yet a single explosive device had significantly compromised the integrity of the tower. The royal engineers were dismayed and ashamed to see how weak the tower truly was, and they were frantically working around the clock to understand how they could make it strong as its ancient reputation held it to be. "Lady Dupres, there is still danger."

"Your people are in there," she took a step forward and craned her neck around the man to get a better view down the hallway.

"My people know the risks, and frankly," he lowered his voice, "all our lives do not add up to the value of the only wizard in the castle. If you are injured, or lost," he looked away, "then who will protect the princess?"

Ariana knew the man was attempting to make her feel guilty about wanting to risk herself, and she was not falling for his ploy. "The best way for me to protect Princess Ariana is to learn what I can about the device that was used, and who placed it there. The agent of the enemy could still be among us!"

"That," he hesitated, "is a good point to consider, certainly." If an enemy agent had placed additional devices of dark magic around the palace, he absolutely needed to know about that. "Could, perhaps, my people bring some of the debris out to you, here, rather than you placing your Ladyship at risk-"

"*Mister* Crawley," she protested and moved forward slowly, forcing the hapless man to step back. "I am a wizard. If the floor collapsed on me suddenly, I can fly out the window to safety." For a change, Olivia could let a silly and annoying notion about wizards work in her favor.

Crawley sputtered, then nodded and stepped aside. He had been about to remark that if wizards truly could fly, then why had Lady Dupres fallen into the moat with the princess, but he held his tongue. Rumor held that only magic could explain how the two girls had managed to avoid fatally striking the half-open drawbridge on their plunge into the moat, so if the wizard were injured in the unsteady structure, or even twisted an ankle on the wobbly floor, he knew the blame would fall on him. On the other hand, if the wizard found something that prevented another attack on the princess, that could only be good for Tarador, the Royal Army and Crawley himself. "Very well, Lady Dupres, I am sure a wizard can best trust her own judgment. Please, do be careful?"

Olivia was bitterly disappointed and frustrated to leave the Citadel half a glass later, knowing little more than she did before she risked life and limb by making her way through the hastily-installed supports to the yawning, charred gap where the explosive had detonated. Mr. Crawley the engineer had not been overcautious as Olivia supposed, the third floor of the tower was indeed alarmingly shaky. To get close enough for her still-developing wizard senses to reach into the spirit world and detect anything useful, she had been forced to clamber among temporary scaffolding that bridged out into where the unfortunate door had been.

One thing she knew was she had been just in time to save Ariana's life, and that throwing the princess out the window truly had been the only way to save both their lives. Holding out her palm to shatter the window before Ariana was smashed against it had also protected them from the full force of the explosion, an unintended benefit of the spell she had instinctively cast in a split second. If she had not acted as she did, both she and Ariana would have been incinerated in the furnace-like heat of the explosion, likely after their bodies were crushed by flying pieces of the heavy steel-clad door to which the explosive had been attached. That was the fate of all the guards who had been protecting Ariana when the device exploded, the engineers were still engaged in the sickening task of picking up burned, crushed parts of the guards tangled in the debris on the first level.

Olivia was not sure how to feel about knowing she had done the only thing that could have saved the princess. Should she be happy that her actions had been correct? Or should she be terrified how close she come to death? No, not mere death, she faced death every day. She should be terrified how close she had come to disaster for Tarador, for the entire free world. Perhaps a combination of happiness and terror was appropriate, along with one other emotion; anger!

Lord Salva and the other fully-trained, fully capable adult members of the Wizard's Council should never have placed Olivia in the position of being Ariana's guardian. A half-trained young wizard who had barely glimpsed the potential of her power had no business being the sole, or even primary guarantor of Tarador's future monarch. She felt like sending a scathing message to Lord Salva right that very minute. Except she did not know how to send messages through the spirit world, having not yet been given that training. Which was exactly why she should not have been thrust into a responsibility that would be a challenge even for an adult wizard!

"What did you learn, my Lady?" Crawley asked, once they were safely out of the danger zone, on the solid floor of the palace outside the Citadel.

She shook her head and suppressed a shudder. "I learned the enemy wished to be certain the princess did not survive the explosion, that is why it was so powerful."

"The device sensed the presence of the princess?" Crawley guessed.

"No. There are such spells, and the enemy is capable of infusing a device with such power. But those seeker spells are," she used a work non-wizards could understand, "noisy. I would have sensed such a spell from inside the palace proper. My guess is the device was set to explode when that door was opened."

Crawley's mouth gaped open. "The door to the inner Citadel is to be opened only in the presence of the royals," his expression was deeply troubled.

"Exactly," she agreed. "The enemy somehow placed a device of dark and powerful magic in the most secure part of the palace, they knew the procedures of the guard force. They knew the guards were trained not to open that door until the princess was there and ready to be brought within the sanctum. I do not know which is worse; that the enemy smuggled dark magic inside the Citadel, or that they knew how the guards would respond."

Crawley appeared puzzled. "The guards told me they opened that door, to inspect the inner Citadel, only days ago. In fact," he tapped a finger on his chin, "Duke Falco insisted the guards open the door for him, so he could verify the condition of the Citadel. Why did the door not explode then?" What Crawley thought and did not say was the door exploding the and killing the duke rather than threatening the life of the princess would have been preferable. Even desirable, to remove Duke Falco from the great game of Taradoran politics. While he would have been sorry if guards were killed, Crawley would not shed any tears for Regin Falco.

"That is a good question," Olivia admitted. The assassin had gained entrance to the palace through an aqueduct, by forcing open a cover held in place by weakened rings. Duke Falco had been in the tunnels also, could he have- No, Olivia pushed the thought from her mind. Sowing fear and suspicion among the powerful of Tarador was exactly what the enemy wanted. The idea of Duke Falco having set the assassination in motion was ridiculous; where could the duke have gotten such powerful dark magic? "Once set in place," she explained, "the device could have been set to remain dormant for a set number of days, and the date of the princess returning to the palace was no great secret. Once the device became active, it would explode the next time the door was opened. A wizard should have inspected the Citadel, only through magical means could a device of dark magic have been detected," she declared, having no confidence that she could have found the device even if she had inspected the Citadel. Madame Chu certainly would have seen the danger, but that powerful wizard from Ching-Do was in the field with the Royal Army, leaving Olivia to perform a vital task she was not trained or ready for. She shook her head wearily. There would be many more sleepless nights protecting the princess, and days spent tramping about the corridors of the palace, her senses open to listen for signs of magical intrusion.

CHAPTER EIGHT

"Captain," Shomas said quietly, though less quietly than he intended, for he had almost run to catch up to the army captain, and the wizards was a bit out of breath. "I don't wish to alarm you-"

"But you're going to anyway," Raddick looked around instinctively, seeing no obvious danger in the thick woods of the foothills they were climbing.

"Er, yes," Shomas' face turned even more red, nearly matching the color of his beard. "There is a band of orcs behind us, to the south."

"How close?" Raddick turned to peer through the trees to the south, in the direction they had come. Seeing their captain reach for his bow, the army troop fanned out silently and without needing orders. They had all seen signs orcs had recently been in the area they were traveling through, even glimpsed roving bands of orcs from afar. The army troop was less than twenty soldiers, a number intended to move quickly and quietly, to perform their mission with little fuss and return across the border of Tarador. In any major battle, they would be hopelessly outnumbered.

"A league, perhaps a bit more?" Shomas answered. "I have been trying to locate them exactly but, alas, that is not my best skill as a wizard. They have been getting closer, I fear they are tracking us."

Raddick muttered a curse under his breath. He was in a bad position to flee from pursuit. Because they were headed up into the very rough terrain of the mountains, they had no horses, not even a pony or donkey to carry provisions. Everyone, even the wizard, was weighted down by a pack. Any escape would require running uphill, for that morning they had seen a large group of orcs downhill to the southeast and they dared not go in that direction. Lord Feany was a master wizard but, the man freely admitted, not very handy in a fight. He could not cast a fireball and his skill with nature could at best only slow down a large party of the enemy. If he were forced to use destructive magic, the effort would drain his energy so much he would be unable to walk.

"Thomas," Raddick called out, ordering the man to him. "Take the pack from Lord Feany and distribute his things."

"Captain, there is no need-" Shomas began to protest.

"Forgive me, Lord Feany, but there is every need. We must move with speed, and orcs are tireless in pursuit, it might be days before we can rest. Please, use your energy to conceal our movements if that is possible."

Shomas shrugged and held his hands out to the sides in chagrin. "That, too, is not my best skill with magic," he said with regret that he had volunteered for a dangerous mission so far from the borders of Tarador. The unique skills of Paedris and Cecil may be urgently needed elsewhere, but if Shomas were to fall victim to orc arrows and Koren Bladewell were lost as a result, in the end it would not matter what Lords Salva and Mwazo had done.

The first night after the pirate ship had given up chasing the *Hildegard*, the weather turned foul, with gusty winds out of the northwest and driving rain. Captain Reed was forced to sail in a more southerly direction, standing out farther to sea and delaying their planned turn toward the west. The following two days held much the same, although the *Hildegard* was able to make some progress in a westerly direction, and Reed was satisfied that no pirate ships were likely to lay across their path.

Overnight, the wind veered so it was coming from the northeast, and that morning dawned to a partly blue sky dotted with clouds rather than the low, solid overcast they had been enduring. With the wind now favoring her, the *Lady Hildegard* heeled over moderately and the crew quickly found the point of sail where their ship was most happy.

They glided on, hour after hour in the steady breeze, the crew hardly needing to touch a sheet or guide the great wheel. It was so pleasant, so favorable, so unusual that the crew began to mutter amongst themselves. Began to cast sidelong glances at the two wizards who sat by the rail, engrossed in reading or merely enjoying the ship's progress. Finally, Captain Reed, concerned that talk by the crew was becoming uncomfortable, with some men making hex signs to protect themselves, left the wheel and approached the two wizards. Lord Salva was engrossed in reading a battered leather-bound book, while Lord Mwazo had set his own book on his lap and was gazing out to sea. "Your Lordships?"

"Eh?" Paedris was startled, seeming just then to remember he was on a ship instead of back in the library of his tower at the royal castle. "Oh, hello, Captain," he greeted the man with a smile. While the ship had struggled with foul weather, the captain had been up on deck most of the time, so the wizards had taken meals in their own cabin and had not the chance to speak with the ship's master.

"I trust you are enjoying this pleasant day?" Reed asked with a strained smile.

"Yes, very much so," Paedris replied, and Cecil nodded agreement. "My compliments to your crew, why, I barely feel the ship moving beneath us! If only every day at sea were like this, I would travel more often." Paedris had struggled to sleep and eat during the heavy weather, wishing he could easily perform a spell upon himself to sooth his unsettled stomach.

"Er, yes," Reed stared off to the horizon above the wizards' heads, then at his shoes. "About that. Your Lordships, while we appreciate, very much appreciate," he stumbled over the words, "this fine weather. The crew feels it is unnatural, and that no good can come of it."

"What?" Paedris looked at Reed as if the man had grown an extra head.

Cecil chuckled softly, understanding the captain's meaning. "Paedris, the crew believes this favorable weather is our doing."

"It's not?" Reed expressed surprise.

"No," Cecil shook his head. "It is certainly not anything *I* did," he declared with a quizzical look toward Paedris.

"Don't look at me!" The court wizard protested.

"Good," Cecil exhaled, relieved.

"I would have told you if I were to, attempt something so foolish."

"I hope so," Cecil replied with a tilt of his head. More than once during the time the two wizards had known each other, he had to restrain the more aggressive instincts of the court wizard. "Captain Reed, it would take extraordinary effort, certainly beyond my ability, to conjure up such favorable weather over so long a time. As Lord Salva has explained, we dare not use magic of any significant power, lest we attract the enemy's attention. There are certain, subtle ways to influence the forces of air or sea, but they take time and are not so dramatic as," he gestured to the blue sky dotted with fluffy white clouds, "this."

Reed scratched his beard. "Hmm. Perhaps it is best the crew thinks our two wizards did bring us this weather, to protect us and speed our passage."

Cecil shared an uncomfortable look with Paedris. "Captain, we think it is not wise to mislead people about wizardry; this is how the public gets silly, superstitious notions that wizards can turn people into frogs-"

"Although such notions can be useful at times," Paedris interjected.

"Quite so. Just because neither of us caused the winds to blow in a particular fashion, that does not mean the spirits did not do so on their own. That would be an omen that the spirits favor our mission, hmmm?"

Reed pursed his lips. "Would that be another superstition, Lord Mwazo?"

"No. The spirits often act in ways we do not understand, and they mostly act without our knowledge. Even the most powerful wizards can only bend the spirits to their will for a tiny fraction of time."

"It would be good for the crew to know the spirits favor us," Reed flashed an unconvincing smile. "Very well, I will tell them. Thank you, your Lordships." With a curt bow, he strode across the deck back toward the wheel.

"Cecil," Paedris whispered to avoid being overheard. "Why did you let the man think the spirits granted us this fine weather?" He asked, mildly annoyed.

"Because we don't know they didn't," Cecil replied with a raised eyebrow. "You told me it cannot be a coincidence that we find ourselves on the very ship that brought Koren Bladewell back to Tarador. Now we find winds speeding our passage toward our destination."

"Ha!" Paedris grimaced. "That could also mean the spirits know we are heading toward our doom, and they wish to be rid of us sooner."

"Paedris," Cecil sighed, "why must you look on the dark side of everything?"

"Because my experience tells me that is usually correct?"

As Koren and Bjorn climbed toward the north side of the ridge that was the local summit of the last foothill, the going became harder as the land rose steeply. While the towering mountains now behind them were mostly bare rock on their upper slopes and scrub brush at lower elevations, the foothills tended to be thickly forested, which made for slower progress as they had determined to stay off any well-traveled roads or trails. Bjorn had wanted to go a longer way to the south where a meadow went up and over the ridge crest, arguing they could see the meadow was relatively easy terrain to cross. Koren had insisted they go the shortest route, straight ahead, and though he now regretted it, he didn't admit it and Bjorn was tactful enough not to say anything. Even when to climb the last hundred yards, they had to hold onto tree branches tangled with vines having sharp thorns. "Ah! Damn it!" Koren pulled back his hand and sucked on a thumb bloody from being stuck deep by a thorn.

"I thought wizards could see the future, and avoid being pricked by thorns," Bjorn teased to lighten the moment.

"If I could see the future, I would have agreed to walk up through that meadow like you wanted," Koren lamented. "We should-Shhh!" He held up a hand for silence. The breeze had shifted, and now that it was blowing from the south, it was bringing sounds toward them.

Bjorn stood still, calming his labored breathing. "I don't hear anything," he said quietly.

"*I* do," Koren declared, pointing to his left ear. "Wizard hearing, remember," he explained, only half joking.

"What do you hear, Oh Great Lord Bladewell?" Bjorn retorted before getting the sinking feeling that, sooner or later, Koren would be addressed as 'Lord Bladewell' by everyone, and it would not be any kind of a joke.

"There is," Koren stood still, listening intently. Did wizards have extra sharp hearing? Probably, and at the moment Koren wished he knew how to make his own hearing sharper. "There's some sort of, I think, fighting. I can hear lots of shouting."

"Who? Who is shouting?" Bjorn asked anxiously.

"I can't understand any words, it's, it's a jumble. Too many shouting at once."

"Orcs? Do any of them sound like orcs?"

"I've never met an orc," Koren admitted with dismay. "What do they sound like?"

"Their language is harsh. I used to speak it, at one time," Bjorn strained his throat to utter a few words of orc speech. "That's all I remember. Koren-"

"I know. If it's orcs, we run. But, Bjorn, if it's dwarves, and they need our help-"

"And if we *can* help. If there's a hundred orcs against a dozen dwarves, the two of us can't do anything but get ourselves killed. Unless you can do some sort of wizard thing?" Bjorn added hopefully, then regretted saying it. He might only have given Koren a terribly bad idea.

Koren held out his right hand, palm upward, and tried to conjure a fireball. Nothing happened, not even when he closed his eyes, concentrated intently and pleaded with the spirits. Demanding the spirits do as he wished also did nothing. "No," Koren said, disgusted with himself. Then he pulled the long bow out of its sling, bent it to the ground and fitted the string. "I do have a full quiver of arrows, and one thing I know for certain is that I never miss."

With a grim nod of agreement, Bjorn gripped the hilt of his sword. While he also carried a bow, his skills were pitiful compared to Koren. In a fight, Bjorn's best way to be useful was to close with the enemy and attack with his sword. The two climbed the last few yards up the ridge, Koren cursing himself not waiting to ready his bow until he finished the climb, as he needed both hands. He paused a second to sling the strung bow over one shoulder, he heaved himself up to clear the ridge.

Orcs. It was orcs, Koren could see them even through the trees. It was his first view of orcs, and the sight made him stand still, mouth agape. Not quite agape, for his lower lip quivered slightly from fear. Orcs. He had heard so many tales of mankind's worst and most ancient enemy, the foul orcs of the mountains. Shorter than men, orcs were about the height of dwarves, although orcs tended toward being skinny rather than broad and sturdy like dwarves. Koren had read some speculation that the almost gaunt appearance of orcs was caused by a poor diet, lack of abundant food in their mountain lairs, and lack of basic hygiene. Mothers in Tarador urged their children to wash themselves, especially to wash their hands before eating, by telling children they did not want to be sickly like filthy orcs.

From the distance, even Koren's sharp eyes could barely see the faces of the orcs, and most of the enemy wore helmets with grotesque, hideous masks. They reminded Koren of the men of Acedor he had seen that fateful morning in the sleepy village of Longshire, when a line of the enemy had stepped forward from the treeline, and the peace of a Spring morning was shattered.

They saw orcs, but, to Koren's great surprise, the orcs were not fighting dwarves, they were fighting a group of men. Not just men, from their tunics Koren could clearly see these were soldiers of the Taradoran Royal Army. Taking in the scene quickly, he estimated eight men, two of them laying on the ground already wounded, besieged by more than twice as many orcs. Pulling the bow from his shoulder, he reached back for an arrow though they were yet too far away.

Bjorn gripped his arm. "Koren, wait. Those are Royal Army soldiers. If they do have orders to kill you, is it wise to help them? There are likely many more orcs coming, we could quickly be surrounded and overwhelmed."

Koren tugged away from Bjorn, breaking the man's grip angrily. He took a step forward. And stopped. Bjorn was right. What obligation did he have to the Royal Army, or even the entire realm of Tarador? None, he had none.

What he did have was a conscience. Orcs were the enemy of all mankind, not only those of a particular nation. He had an obligation to defend the helpless against the cruelty of orcs. "Bjorn, neither of us can stand here and do nothing. If it comes to it, you do the talking. My name is Kedrun, right?"

"Right," then Bjorn grabbed the strap of Koren's quiver of arrows. "Wait! You are a wizard, and we need wizards in this war far more than we need men like me, or even a half dozen soldiers," he gestured with his sword toward the cluster of men besieged. They were now standing back to back in a circle, with the two wounded men on the ground inside the circle. As he spoke, one man was hit in the chest by an arrow, his chain mail protecting him from death but the impact making him stagger. "If needs be, you run, save yourself so you can learn true wizardry. One of you is worth a hundred, nay, a thousand soldiers. Promise me!" Bjorn tugged on the strap, making Koren turn to face him.

Koren did not like the idea of running again, from anything. A part of him wanted to tell Bjorn he had no right making demands of him, yet another, smarter part of him saw the common sense of Bjorn's words. Koren nodded, then when Bjorn tugged on the strap again, he spoke. "Yes! All right, yes! I will run like a coward and save myself if it comes to that. Will that make you happy?"

"No," Bjorn replied as he released the strap. "But if I die today and you later avenge me by burning the enemy with wizard fire? Aye, that will make me happy."

"Pray that never happens," Koren swallowed hard, fearing he would never create more than a feeble flame above his open palm.

They ran down the hillside, leaping over fallen logs and rocks, stumbling through underbrush. Koren halted and jumped atop a flat rock when a tiny voice in his head told him the distance was now within his range. Bjorn continued on down the hill, running pell-mell with a sword in one hand and a dagger in the other. When he saw the first orc's head fly back as the creature was struck dead in the eye by an arrow, he shouted a challenge, and the startled orcs turned to see one man racing toward them. That gave the besieged Royal Army soldiers a momentary respite, and they pressed the advantage as more arrows thudded into the orcs.

When Koren jumped onto the rock, surveying the scene to choose targets, he breathed deeply to slow his pulse. A shaking hand, the royal weapons master had told him, could throw off his aim, and although Koren never had missed yet, it was good advice.

What made Koren's pulse flutter was not the run down the hill, nor the prospect of battle, but fear. Fear not for himself, but that his reliable, perfect skill with a bow was now something he recognized as part of his wizard skill. His only useful wizard skill, the one unnatural ability he had command over, if he still had even that. He could not create spells, make potions or conjure a fireball, would his skill with a bow fail him now that he knew it was a gift from the spirits? The spirits had not answered his call, his desperate pleas, his demands nor his futile offers to bargain with them. Would they now refuse to help guide his aim with a bow?

There was nothing he could do but try, to fit arrow to bowstring and do what he had done since he was a little boy, shooting at targets on his family's farm with a toy bow his mother had made for him. Koren sighted on one orc who wielded an evil-looking axe and was battering the sword of a tall Royal Army soldier. He waited for the indescribable inner feeling that *now* was the exact perfect time to release the arrow, his stomach churning that the feeling would never come to him.

The arrow flew before he realized what had happened. Rather than reaching back for another arrow while the first was in flight, he slumped, his knees weak with relief. The spirits had not abandoned him. Straightening as he saw the first arrow bury itself in the eye socket of the orc he had targeted, he pulled another arrow out of the quiver and fitted it to the bowstring, trying to think of what he had done to bend the spirits to his will.

No.

Thinking is what he needed *not* to do. He needed to do as he had always done, before he knew his incredible ability with a bow came from magic. He needed to let it happen, trust in himself and the spirits. The third arrow was ready and aimed while the second was still in flight, and Koren had the feeling he was an observer outside his own body. Knowing it came from magic made his shooting seem more remarkable, not less. He also found the confidence to do things he had not dared try before, such as shooting at a target before he could clearly see it. With his third arrow, he aimed at an orc who was behind a soldier from Koren's point of view, and as the arrow flew Koren had a shock that he had shot the arrow at the soldier's head! Koren opened his mouth to shout a warning when the orc's axe swung downward and the soldier parried the axe with a sword, the motion driving the soldier almost to his knees. Just as the soldier slumped, the arrow flew in, the bottom feathers of the arrow brushing the top of the man's helmet and burying itself in the forehead of the orc, who was flung backward, struck instantly dead.

Six arrow flew and six orcs died before the enemy saw their danger. The moment when the surviving orcs turned to look up the hill toward Koren, Bjorn crashed into an orc, knocking aside the creature's axe and stabbing it in the belly with a dagger. Kicking the orc away, Bjorn backed up to join the circle of soldiers, whose leader screamed defiance and ordered a charge! The circle broke, soldiers advancing toward the now-hesitant orcs.

Orcs were fierce fighters, but their cruelty in battle was matched only by their boastful cowardice. Seeing a seventh member of their group felled by yet another arrow shot from an unreachable distance, and with disciplined soldiers of Tarador now running toward rather than away from them, the orcs broke by unspoken agreement. As one, they turned and ran away, their short legs carrying them leaping over forest clutter with surprising speed.

"Let them go!" The leader of the soldiers ordered. "Reform the line! Protect the wounded!"

"Cap-" Koren froze, startled and dismayed to recognize the leader of the soldiers. "Captain Raddick, Sir," Koren acknowledged the man with a salute he did not know was proper or not. Raddick thought him a deserter and danger, perhaps an enemy of Tarador, was a salute warranted?

Raddick gave him an answer by returning the salute, though the gesture made the man freeze in open-mouthed astonishment. "Koren? Master Bladewell? What are- How are you *here*?"

"What are *you* doing here?" Koren was just as surprised.

"Was that you with the arrows?" Raddick looked around at dead orcs sprawled on the forest floor.

"Oh, um, yes," Koren agreed, embarrassed though he knew not why.

Koren stood on the balls of his feet, prepared to run for his life, when Captain Raddick did the last thing Koren expected. The man went down on one knee. "Master Bladewell, we have been seeking you. Thank the spirits we found you alive! Lord Feany feared he would die before finding you in the wilderness, but *you* have found us. And," Raddick stood and wiped his bloody sword on a cloth he pulled from his belt, "saved us also."

"Lord Feany?" Koren had almost turned around when Raddick said 'Master Bladewell', assuming the man was speaking to someone behind Koren before understanding that *he* was now 'Master Bladewell'. "Shomas was with you?"

"He came with us," Raddick explained, striding over to one of the wounded men laying on the ground. "I hope he is still with us, he was gravely wounded when the orcs hunted us down and attacked. We carried him until we could run no more, and made our stand here." He knelt by a large man who did not wear a Royal Army tunic, and Koren flung his bow aside in his haste to join the army captain.

It was Shomas Feany! The usually jolly wizard's face was the color of cold ashes, and blood soaked his plain brown shirt and vest, with blood also seeping from a deep gash to his upper left arm. Blood had saturated the crude bandage and was dripping onto the ground. "Shomas!" Koren cried as he crashed to his knees, taking the wizard's uninjured right hand in both of his own. His heart soared when the wizard squeezed back, though the pressure was weak.

"Koren?" Shomas stirred weakly, one eye fluttering open. "Is that you, boy? Good lad, always a good lad."

"It's me, Lord Feany," Koren assured the man, squeezing his hand hard as if that could cause life to flow into the wounded wizard.

The wizard's one open eye gazed up, unfocused, to the tree canopy above. "Are we back in Linden already? So pretty here, so peaceful."

"Yes," Koren replied with tears in his eyes, flowing freely down his cheeks to drip onto the wounded man's chest. "We're in the royal gardens, don't you see? Would you like me to fetch a honeycake from the kitchens? You did love those honeycakes."

"Honey. Cake." Shomas' lips twisted in a happy smile and his eyelid closed.

"Those honeycakes are good. I'll fetch them. Would you like tea? Shomas?" In a panic because the wizard was no longer squeezing his hand, Koren asked "Shomas? No!"

Raddick gripped Koren's shoulder. "He's gone, Master Bladewell. It was too late, no one could do anything for him."

"He *can't* be gone!" Koren protested even as he knew the awful truth.

"Koren," Bjorn spoke. "Let him go, give him peace now."

"Aye," Raddick agreed. "He died happily, for he knew you are safe, Master Bladewell. I wish to be so happy, when the time comes for me."

In horrified disbelief, Koren rose to his feet, stumbling backward. Staring at the wizard who had passed, he was motionless. Then, remembering where he was and his own peril, he stood three strides backward, never taking his eyes off Raddick, even when he bent to retrieve his bow. "Shomas was here looking for me? You were all looking for me?"

"Yes," Raddick replied.

"You have orders to kill me?" Koren asked with a meaningful look to Bjorn. If Koren needed to run, he hoped the other man could assist even briefly, by distracting the Royal Army soldiers.

"Kill? Koren- Master Bladewell," Raddick bowed from the waist. "My orders are to *rescue* you, even if it costs my life and those of all my men. I was charged with this duty by Lord Salva and Regent Ariana themselves."

"You are not here to kill me?" Koren asked warily.

"No," Raddick insisted with a shake of his head. "I do not know how you heard that, but the army does have orders to kill you, *only* if you have been captured by the enemy and there is no other way to prevent the enemy from gaining access to your power."

"What? Access to my- what?" Koren whispered back.

"Lord Salva explained it to me," Raddick spoke slowly and surely, being careful to remember what the master wizard had told him. He didn't like speaking about it in the open, but by now, all of his soldiers knew what was supposed to be a secret. "Just as one wizard can lend power to another, a master wizard can *take* power from another, unwillingly, and use that power for his purposes. Koren, if the enemy, the demon, were to capture you, it could pull power from you, and destroy Tarador. Destroy the *world*. Lord Salva told me the power inside you is immense, unfathomable even by himself. Someday you will have control of your power and then you can protect yourself. You could even destroy the enemy yourself," Raddick's wide-open eyes reflect his incredulity at that statement. "Until you have mastery of the power within you, you are vulnerable, a tool to be used by the enemy. My mission here is to bring you home, bring you to safety, so you can be trained. Lord Bladewell, the court wizard and the Regent impressed this upon me most urgently: without you at our side, Tarador has no true hope for victory in this war. If you were in the grasp of the enemy, there is no hope for this world. The demon will use your power to break the barrier between this world and the underworld, releasing a demon host to consume us all, forever."

"I-" Koren did not know what to say.

"That is why Lord Salva could not tell you the truth," Raddick continued. "He feared that if you knew you are a wizard, you would be tempted to use your power and harm yourself, or at least reveal your power to the enemy."

"Paedris lied to *protect* me?" Koren could not believe it.

"Shomas intended to tell you the whole story, but, yes, the truth of it is the wizards lied to protect you. It's a hard thing to hear, I know, but there it is. You must come with me, now. Those orcs will be back, with others. They have already killed most of my men, and one wizard."

"We cannot leave Lord Feany here," Bjorn argued before Koren had to. "He is a master wizard, from a foreign land, come to aid Tarador. To leave his body for orcs to toy with, and carrion-eaters to consume, is beneath our honor as a nation."

Raddick scuffed the ground with a boot heel. "The soil here is rocky and we have no shovels, no picks to dig with. We have no time," the army captain declared. "Those orcs will be back with more, they-" he halted as they all heard a harsh, guttural cry echoing through the forest. "We may already be too late. Master Bladewell, Mr. Jihnsson, we had twice our numbers yesterday, half of my men are already laying unburied behind us. It pains me to leave them, as it pains me to leave these two, but we must. My orders are to find Koren and bring him safely back to Linden, *at all costs*. Those were Lord Salva's exact words to me. If you," he looked at Koren, "can summon wizard fire to cremate these men, then we will-"

"Ha!" Koren laughed bitterly. "Captain Raddick, what you have seen of my wizard ability is all I can command. I am an excellent archer, that is all. I have no more ability to pull fire from the spirit world than I can fly to Linden."

"That is," Raddick searched for a tactful word, "unfortunate."

"Could we make a fire?" Bjorn asked. He had been digging at the ground with his own boot and he was forced to agree with Raddick that digging graves there was impractical. So was carrying the bodies elsewhere; Raddick's men were exhausted and Lord Feany was too heavy for one man to carry far. "An ordinary, unmagical funeral pyre? There is plenty of wood around here," he kicked a log for emphasis. That log was damp with moss, but late in the season, the woods were dry even though it had rained the previous night.

Raddick's hand clasped and unclasped the hilt of his sword as he decided. The idea of leaving behind the bodies of men who had sacrifice their lives for Tarador did not sit well with him. Pausing to listen, he did not hear any more orc battle cries. "Very well. Gather wood, and-" He was interrupted by another blood-curdling, guttural sound as orcs called for their fellows to join the hunt. There was an answering cry, both too near for comfort. "No!" Raddick shouted in alarm. "Run now! Run for your lives!"

CHAPTER NINE

Paedris and Cecil staggered at the same time, falling to their knees in their cabin aboard *the Lady Hildegard*. "Shomas," Paedris announced as he breathed deeply, fighting nausea that threatened to overwhelm him.

Cecil nodded, putting his head between his knees and gulping air slowly and evenly. "Oh, Shomas. What a good friend you were. Paedris-"

"I know," the court wizard replied, anguish evident in his voice. "We will mourn our friend in due time. For now, we must go on."

"How can we?" Lord Mwazo pushed himself to his feet, and helped Paedris stand. "Shomas is dead, and he had not yet found Koren. If we cannot bring Koren back, this," he waved a hand to encompass the desolate land around them, "is all for nothing."

"We will go on because there is nothing else we can do," Paedris chided gently. "We are committed here, we can do nothing to help Raddick find Koren."

"We don't know whether Captain Raddick is still alive!"

"We do not, neither do we know he is dead. We do know Koren is not dead, for we certainly would have felt that. We must continue onward, and have faith, until we have reason to believe our hopes are for nothing."

Cecil nodded after a moment. "You know I hate it when you are right, Paedris."

"Would you prefer I was wrong?"

"Not in this instance, no. Ah, Shomas being gone from us is a bitter pill."

"Come," Paedris clapped his friend on the back. "When we return to Linden, we will have an epic feast in his honor, and stuff ourselves until we burst."

"Yes," Cecil agreed, though he knew the two of them would never again see the city of Linden, nor ever again eat anything resembling a feast.

"Master Bladewell-" Raddick began to say when Koren spun angrily toward him.

"Stop calling me that! Call me Koren. I'm not a 'Master' anything." Koren knew he was acting like a pouting child but he didn't care, he was sick of how the army captain looked at him. He saw the man's slightly awed and distinctly fearful expressions, and he knew none of it was justified. "I'm *not* a wizard! Look," he held out a hand, palm open, and willed fire to appear in his hand, knowing it would not happen. It didn't. There was no spinning ball of magical fire, not even a slightly warm pink fog.

"I, don't see anything," Raddick's face reddened with embarrassment, though whether he was embarrassed for himself or for the young wizard, was not clear.

"Exactly!" Koren whispered. "There's nothing to see, because I can't do it! Ask me to shoot the feathers off a bird in the air," he pointed to a sparrow flying overhead, "I can do it every time. There isn't any other magical thing I can do. Call me whatever you call a master of archery, but don't call me Master anything, because I'm not any kind of a wizard."

"You have incredible sight and hearing," Bjorn noted unhelpfully.

"I'm younger than you," Koren retorted with a bit of spite, instantly regretting the hurtful comment. "I'm sorry, Bjorn, I didn't mean that. What I meant is, I don't know if my eyesight is because I'm a wizard, or because I'm young. When I was aboard the ship, the captain always selected younger sailors and lookouts."

"Ship? What ship?" Raddick asked, staring at Koren in wonder. What else did Raddick not know about the young wizard's recent adventures?

"It's a long story, for another time," Bjorn waved a hand dismissively. "Koren, you can create a fireball with magic, I've seen you do it," he insisted.

"When was this?" Raddick asked eagerly.

"Once!" Koren shot back at Bjorn. "I did it *once*. I have no idea who I did it then, and I have only been able to make even the most feeble flame appear a few other times."

"Ah," Raddick nodded happily. "You can do it, then. Lord Salva told me you will be a powerful wizard, and I believe him. Lord Feany intended to instruct you while we traveled-"

"He's dead!" Koren threw up his hands. "Shomas is dead, and now no one can help me, can they? The Wizards' Council was supposed to have begun my training years ago, but they didn't and now everyone expects me to save the world? The whole world, by myself? I can't do it. Whoever you hope I am," he jabbed a finger toward Raddick, "I'm not that hero. Leave me alone, damn you!" Fuming, Koren stomped off, then began running up the slope, leaping from stone to stone on the exposed ground.

"Thomas," Raddick ordered a soldier, "go after him! We cannot let him-"

"Leave him be," Bjorn advised with a hand on the captain's forearm. "He needs to be by himself a while and think. He won't run off, where would he go?" Bjorn made a sweeping gesture toward the tall mountain peaks all around them. "He is a wizard, as you say, maybe even a powerful one," Bjorn could not keep the skepticism from his voice. "Think on this; a few months ago, he was a servant who thought his parents abandoned him because he caused too much trouble. Now you tell him *he* will be responsible for destroying Acedor, and saving the world? He's just a boy, Captain Raddick," Bjorn pointed up the hill, where Koren was already slowing, no longer racing from rock to rock. "Give him time to take it all in."

"We don't have time," Raddick frowned, but gestured for Thomas to remain where he was. "He doesn't have time. I am sorry if he finds the truth difficult to understand, but I can't change the truth. If he had not run away from the castle, he wouldn't be having-"

"From what I have heard, fools in the Royal Army caused Koren to run away, fearful of his life, because they falsely called him a deserter" Bjorn stepped closer to he and Raddick were almost nose to nose. Bjorn was not in the army, nor any longer part of the King's Guard. Raddick had no authority over him, and Bjorn was angry enough not to care what Raddick thought. "When I met Koren, he was seeking a dwarf wizard to remove a spell Lord Salva had cast upon him unwillingly. Shortly after, the lad learned his parents had *not* abandoned him, they were killed by a bandit. I helped him track down and kill that bandit." Bjorn took a step backward, holding up his hands in a peaceful gesture. "I costs you nothing to give the boy time to think, we will be traveling these mountains many days, I think, before we can turn south toward Tarador. It will gain us much if, when he finally reaches a wizard who can help him, he has accepted the part he is fated to play in this war."

Raddick was silent, his pride hurt by Bjorn's defiance, and worried he would look weak in front of his men. Then, Raddick realized he had taken time to think, exactly what Bjorn wanted for Koren. The former King's Guard was right, it cost Raddick nothing to leave the boy alone for a while. The army captain nodded assent. "Very well. No one has ever told me I had to save the whole world, I suppose young Master Bladewell has a lot to consider."

"It would be helpful to call him simply 'Koren'. He can be Master, even Lord Bladewell when he's ready. Right now, he wants to be accepted by you and your men, not treated as an oddity."

"Sound advice," Raddick looked toward his men, who acknowledged their captain's unspoken order. "Now, Bjorn, what is this about his parents being killed by a bandit?"

Half an hour later, Raddick held a hand over his face, shaking his head in stunned amazement. "In the short span of time you have known him, Koren learned," he took the hand away from his eyes to avoid tripping on a rock, and counted on his fingers. "That his parents did not abandon him. That they were instead killed by bandits. That, rather than him being a dangerous jinx, he is a *wizard*?"

Bjorn tried to grin at the absurd situation but found his could not find any amusement in the boy's pain. "Aye. Then you tell him the Royal Army is ordered to protect him rather than kill him. And that Lord Salva lied to Koren to save the boy's life. Oh, and, of course there is the little detail that he is our only hope to defeat a demon army and save the world. That is six rather jarring revelations in a short time."

"I can see why you asked me to give him time alone to think," Raddick looked ahead to where Koren was trudging with determination up the mountainside, a hundred or so yards ahead. The boy had slowed to match the army troop's pace and they gave him privacy. Whenever Koren walked sideways as the trail took a switchback to climb a particularly steep section of the mountain, Raddick could see the young wizard's lips move and his hands gesturing as he talked to himself.

"Everything that boy thought he knew, he was wrong about. If you told him the sun would now rise in the west beginning tomorrow morning, he might think nothing of it."

Raddick walked beside Bjorn silently for a while, each man lost in his own thoughts. Finally, when they reached the top of a rise and realized it was only a false summit which had hidden the real ridgetop from view, Raddick halted to drink from his water flask.

"A copper coin for your thoughts," Bjorn offered.

Raddick watched Koren continue up the hill in front of them, the boy silhouetted against the low afternoon sun. "I was thinking many of us ask our children to grow up too quickly. Koren had responsibilities on his parents' farm, yet he could still enjoy a normal childhood. Suddenly, he had to become a man on his own, to survive. Now he must save us all, if Lord Salva is to be believed. Our princess rules the land at her tender age, and she never really had time for to be girl. It is so for many royal children, they are used as pawns in their parents' game of power, and those who stand to inherit must watch their backs lest their younger siblings change the order of succession. Children born in less fortunate circumstances are often sent away to train in apprenticeships as soon as they can work."

"You have children?" Bjorn asked quietly.

"A son and a daughter. My son already wants to join the army, though at ten he can barely lift a sword." Thinking of his children made Raddick sad, then he pushed aside thoughts of anything but his immediate mission. "Night will be coming soon, and that looks like rain," he gestured to clouds building in the north. "We cannot risk a fire, and being exposed on this mountain is no way to spend a night, if we are to resume a brisk pace in the morning. Thomas! Take Lem and scout ahead for shelter, let the wizard join you if he wishes. Oh, and remember to call him Koren."

The two soldiers called Lem and Thomas, unburdened by their packs that were now carried by the others, quickly caught up to Koren, who had not been paying attention to anything behind him. "Ho, there, Koren!" Thomas called out.

"Oh. Hello," Koren said warily. He struggled to recall the man's name. "Thomas?"

Thomas paused beside the young wizard. "We're scouting for shelter to spend the night, Captain thinks rain is coming. I don't suppose you know any place 'round here with soft beds and good beer?"

The remark made Koren smile. That and not being formally called 'Master Bladewell'. "Would you settle for a bed of dried grass and moss, and cold water from a mountain stream?"

Thomas shrugged. "Better than many nights I've spent in the army. Will you help us? Three pairs of eyes are better than two."

Koren thought the man had made a joke about his unnaturally keen wizard sense of sight, and stiffened. "Even a wizard can't see what isn't there," he looked around at the exposed landscape of rock, low-growing shrubs and clusters of stunted, wind-swept trees.

"Ah," Thomas waved a hand and lowered his voice. "I don't know if this wizard talk is real, or a bunch of nonsense," he looked Koren up and down skeptically. "You're a master with a bow, that's for certain, but as to the rest of it?" He held his palms upward. "You find us someplace on this mountain to keep us dry tonight, and I'll say you're a true wizard."

Koren grinned. "I'll take that challenge."

Thomas and Koren strode on ahead, while Lem scouted to the right of them. "So, what's it like, being a wizard and all?" Thomas finally asked the question that had been burning inside him. He had been told their mission was to rescue Koren Bladewell the wizard's servant, but until Raddick spoke after the death of Lord Feany, none of the soldiers had known that Koren himself was a wizard.

"I don't know. Really," he added as Thomas looked at him skeptically, thinking the boy didn't want to talk about it. "Really! I didn't even know I am a wizard until I got up in these mountains. I haven't been trained at all, I don't know how to *do* anything, not yet."

"Captain said something about us needing you to save all of Tarador?" Thomas asked with a raised eyebrow.

"I don't know anything about that," Koren said truthfully. He hoped that was a great exaggeration by Paedris, intended to spur Raddick's search for the young, untrained wizard. Koren could hardly believe he was a wizard, certainly he could not be the most powerful wizard in the world. It couldn't be true, could it?

Koren wasn't the one who found the overhanging rock ledges to shelter under, that was Lem, and Koren felt better that their shelter for the night was not provided by his dubious wizard skill. Lem, an expert woodsman whose father was organized hunts for royalty, knew to look for a particular type of shrub which took root in the thin soil that was washed down by rain to gather in crevices and under ledges. He called out to Thomas and Koren, and soon the remainder of the troop was stashing their packs and thin bedrolls under overhanging rock. The cavern under one ledge extended deep and tall enough to almost be considered a cave, and because it faced north up the mountainside, Raddick risked allowing a fire to heat water for tea once darkness fell and a steady drizzle began to fall. Food was still tough travel bread, hard cheese and dried meat and fruit, but holding a battered cup of hot tea made Koren feel less like the night on the mountain was less a desperate race for survival, and more like a hunting trip in the woods with good companions.

"Trade you," Thomas offered, plopping himself down on a flat rock next Koren near the back of the cavern. The wind sometimes caused smoke from the fire to swirl around the cavern, stinging Koren's eyes, but the fire of dried brush and lichen was so small he didn't mind.

"What you got?" Koren peered at the man's pack eagerly. The travel bread they had bought from dwarves was filling and easier to chew than the supplies carried by the Royal Army men, but it had an unfamiliar taste and Koren was anxious for a taste of home even if made his jaw sore. "I have plenty of this dwarven bread."

Thomas stuck out his tongue in disgust. "Sorry. There's nothing wrong with it, but the dwarves mix in mushrooms for flavor, and it tastes odd to me. Problem is, I spent almost a year up in the dwarf lands with a Royal Army patrol back when King Adric wanted us to push back the orcs together, and I ate too much of their travel bread that year. I see you have an apple, would you trade it for dried fruit?" He held up a cube of stuck-together mixed fruit.

"It's only a small apple, and it's got a bruise here," Koren said honestly.

Thomas handed him two cubes of dried fruit, and bit into the apple happily. "Ah, that's good. Not like apples from my home, can't expect that up here, I guess."

Koren bit into a cube of dried fruit, biting it in half with effort. He should have used a knife but didn't trust to use a sharp blade in the darkness of the cavern. The fruit, he guessed it was peaches and pears with something else mixed in, was leathery but sweet, and the cube had been dipped in honey before being wrapped in wax paper. He would eat the other half the next morning, then lick the rest of the honey off the waxed paper as he had been taught by soldiers who wasted nothing in the wilderness. "This is good," he mumbled over a mouthful. "Thomas," he asked quietly. "You've been in these mountains before? Do we have a chance to get out of here, back to Tarador?" Every time they tried to turn south to head for the border, they had found orcs already there. It seemed like their task was impossible, they needed to cross the lowlands to the south, but the army troop was forced to tramp slowly up and down mountains on foot, while the orc host had faster going in the lowlands. Koren, Raddick and his men were being forced in the wrong direction. If they were delayed too long, they would be trapped in the mountain strongholds of the dwarves by heavy winter snows.

"In these mountains? No, not here, I was stationed east and south of here, on the border of the orc dominion. What was the border, before, well, the orcs weren't so bold back then. Don't you worry none, lad," Thomas clapped him on the back. "The Captain knows what he's doing. I've served with him off and on for nigh on eight years now, he's gotten me out of scrapes worse than this."

Koren held his tongue and did not say that implied Captain Raddick had gotten Thomas *into* worse scrapes in the past. "Worse?"

"Well," Thomas took another bite of the apple, slurping so the juice didn't get wasted running down his chin, "not *much* worse." In the dim reddish firelight, he grinned. "Koren," his expression turned serious, "I'm sorry you were falsely accused as a deserter, when you were doing our job while the army dithered uselessly near Longshire."

"It's not your fault, Thomas," Koren's eyes grew moist at hearing the soldier's kind words.

The man tapped the castle and sword crest of the Royal Army on his tunic. "I'm part of the Royal Army. That means I share in the glory when we are victorious, *and* I share the responsibility when the army treats a courageous man shabbily. You can't have one without the other."

Koren's eyes did well with tears, he wiped away the tears with the back of a hand, and shook Thomas's offered hand. "Thank you."

"Thank *you*, lad. You acted to save the life of the court wizard, when my, *our*, army sat on their asses and protected themselves," Thomas looked at his boots in shame. "If you ever give up this wizarding foolishness, you might consider giving the Royal Army a try. We could use a man of fortitude and initiative like you. You did all that before you learned you are maybe a wizard, aye, that took some courage, there's no doubting that."

"Thank you, Thomas," Koren took a sip of tea. "I don't know that this wizarding thing will let me alone, whether I want it or not. It, it may be my fate, as Captain Raddick says."

"Don't you listen to this saving the world nonsense. I don't know what Lord Salva is thinking, nor the Regent herself, laying that weight on your shoulders," he shook his head sadly. "This war has been going on for a very long time, and, if it has come down to us needing one untrained wizard to pull us out of the fire, well, that's the failure of our society. We shouldn't have let it come to this at all. We've had generations, nay, hundreds of years when we could have dealt with the demon, and we always put it off for another year, another decade. *We* allowed this problem to fester unchecked. It is not the responsibility of your generation make up for the failures of the past, eh?"

"Someone has to," Koren muttered quietly to himself. He chewed the rough bread with no appetite, eating only because he knew he had to. Shomas Feany had died to bring Koren back to Tarador, and the kindly wizard's death might have been for nothing. Koren forced himself not to think of what orcs might have done to Shomas, though Raddick had assured Koren that orcs were very superstitious and would likely have burned the body, after casting hex signs and chanting whatever incantations they found comforting. Orcs would not have abused the body of the wizard, Raddick had explained, for they feared the ghost of Shomas haunting them afterward.

That was cold comfort as Koren sat by himself, mechanically eating bread while tears streamed down his cheeks.

After checking on the sentries he had posted, Raddick ducked under the overhang and took off his wet cloak, shaking it away from people, then stuffing the hood into a crack in the rock so it could drip dry. He sat down next to Bjorn and gratefully accepted a tin of thin tea.

"Fire's not causing us any problem?" Bjorn asked quietly.

"No," Raddick took too great a sip and nearly burned his tongue. If the tea was not strong it was at least hot, a virtue in the cool dampness of a mountain evening. "Any light would only be visible from straight up the mountain, I doubt orcs have climbed faster than we have. They don't have any reason to, there are plenty of spoils to steal or burn in the valley. No one can see far in this drizzle anyway. There's little wind and I'm glad of that, for the sentries."

"I can stand a watch," Bjorn offered.

"That's not necessary."

"Yes, it is. You have few men left and we are all tired. I have stood many a night watch in my time, Captain. I may not have wizard vision," he looked across the fire to Koren, "or even merely young eyes, but I can see well enough."

"I accept your offer. You can take the next watch, when Lem comes in." Raddick would rather have the unfamiliar man on watch in the evening, rather than in the wee morning hours when there was greatest risk of a sentry losing alertness or even falling asleep. Gesturing with his tin cup of tea toward Koren, he leaned toward Bjorn and lowered his voice. "It was not wise of me to tell our young wizard he must save the world, that is too much a burden for anyone."

Bjorn nodded. "Yes, but is it the truth? Is he our only hope?"

"Lord Feany thought so, or Lord Salva thought so and told our wizard. Ah, this is," Raddick squeezed a fist in anguish. "This is a terrible situation. I would rather have lost all my men, and myself, than Lord Feany. Shomas," he used the wizard's given name now the man was no longer with them to hear, "intended to explain the truth to Koren, speaking wizard to wizard. He was also going to begin the lad's training, help him understand and use his power. None of us are capable of doing that!"

"Lord Feany should have written instructions, perhaps, as insurance against his death."

"He told me that would not have worked, when I asked him for such," Raddick shook his head. "Apparently wizard training is not like instructions for constructing a wagon, it must be taught by a master wizard directly to an apprentice. Shomas said it is far too dangerous otherwise, Koren could kill himself, or us *and* himself, by toying with power he doesn't understand."

"Hmmm. He has been attempting to conjure fireballs, should I tell him not to do that?"

"That would be best, yes," Raddick said hastily, aghast at the idea the untrained boy had been playing with powerful magic. "He should wait until he has a wizard to instruct him properly."

"Do we have that much time?" Bjorn asked with weary frown.

"I don't see we have a choice. The boy can't use his power anyway, can he?"

"No, other than archery, and his skill with a sword," Bjorn declared. "One tiny fireball he created, that is all I have seen. Did Lord Salva truly say Koren must save the world? In those words?"

"No," Raddick admitted. "Not those particular words. And I do not think he meant for Koren to act alone."

Bjorn finished the last of his cooling tea, and reached for the pot to get another cup. "You should tell him that, then," he advised. "Right now, the lad is thinking he carries the weight of the world on his shoulders. It would be good for him to know he doesn't have to lift that burden all by himself."

Captain Reed could see a commotion near the port side of the bow, Alfonze was gesturing emphatically, engaged in an animated, whispered conversation with two other sailors. They seemed to be arguing about something, then the three of them stopped talking and stood still, listening intently. The spell was broken a moment later when all three turned toward the starboard side of the bow; even through the shrouding mist Reed could see their eyes were wide open. Alfonze pointed with a finger, ordering one man to hurry to report to the captain.

Walking quickly on feet padded by canvas slippers lest his feet make any sound on the deck, the sailor approached the *Lady Hildegard's* master. "Captain," the sailor said only when he was close enough to be heard in a whisper. "There's something out there. A ship, maybe," he added, feeling stupid as the words left his mouth. Of course it was a ship, what else could it be? Mermaids?

The sailors standing next to Reed overheard, and a murmur arose on the foredeck.

"Shhh!" Reed whispered harshly, making a slashing motion across his throat with one hand. He listened intently. The enveloping fog muffled all sounds. Barely, he could hear low, rolling breakers crashing against the unseen cliffs to port. A faint hiss to starboard announced languid swells lazily slapping against the starboard side, and he could hear the ship's timbers creaking gently without enthusiasm, as if the chilly unnatural fog were putting the ship's very bones to sleep. The ship's crew had done everything they could to make the ship's passage through the water absolutely silent. Extra sailcloth that was now not needed had been cut into strips and used to secure and pad anything that might bang against something else. Hammocks, rope, even spare clothing had all been tied around or stuffed between equipment that might make noise. Because, one way or another, this was the last voyage of the *Lady Hildegard*, Reed had instructed the sailmaker and his assistants to create padded slippers for the crew, even the captain was wearing canvas slippers rather than boots. The deck was liberally sprinkled with sand to prevent anyone from skidding, and everyone had been ordered to remain silent, unless requested to speak by a senior crewman.

With fog so thick the masts above their heads were lost in the mists, there was no lookout above, all the crew posted as lookouts were lining the bow rail as the *Hildegard* drifted along on the surging current. Everything possible had been done to make the ship utterly silent, yet Reed winced whenever a swell caused the ship to roll and her timbers creaked. The crew had used grease, even cooking oil that was no longer needed, and painted the lubricants in gaps between the great timbers of the ship. Still, the ship's structure groaned softly as it flexed, and neither Reed nor his dedicated crew could do anything to make the ship completely rigid. Captain Reed was certain no ship the size of the *Lady* had ever been made more quiet, and he took comfort in Lord Salva's assurances that the fog conjured by the master wizard muffled sounds like a thick pillow.

Reed shuddered slightly, as a tendril of unnatural mist curled around the back of his neck, the damp chilliness making him flinch. "I hear it also," he whispered back, and strode carefully across the deck to the tall, dark-skinned wizard. "Lord Mwazo, we hear-"

"I hear it too," Mwazo replied in a barely audible whisper, standing in the center of the bow, eyes closed. While Lord Salva was at the stern of the ship, in a deep trance as he struggled mightily to subtly extend his powers far from the ship, Lord Mwazo was using his own magical senses to prevent the ship from stumbling into the jagged, unseen rocks that were strewn across their path.

Cecil stood tall and silent, eyes closed, arms raised slightly to each side. In each hand, he held a string that ran back along the deck and down a hatch. When he sensed an obstacle to port, he moved his right arm forward, the string tugging on an indicator below the main deck. Down there, men stood ready at great oars called 'sweeps', a pair of them held out to each side. The sweeps themselves were well padded with sailcloth and old rope, and the crews moved slowly and carefully not to make any splash as the sweeps dipped into the water. The crew at each sweep walked their great oar along the side of the ship, lifting it slowly out of the water and letting water drip off before very carefully walking the sweep back and holding it ready for the next action. Thus far, the sweeps had threaded the *Hildegard* past numerous rocks more than halfway down the channel, but the narrowest part of the channel lay ahead.

"Two boats out there, both to starboard," Cecil whispered. "I can hear their crews talking and arguing, they do not like being out in this fog. We should glide right past them, as they are headed south while we go east, but-" He took a deep, calming breath and allowed his senses to *flow* outward. "There are two large rocks ahead to port. We will need to risk using the sweeps to steer around them. Captain, if the sweeps make any sound-"

"I know. Guide us, master wizard, and I will see we make no more noise than-" he had been about to say 'the grave' when he caught himself. Any mention of death would be a bad omen. "A mouse crossing a carpet," he finished.

Leaving the deck to Alfonze, though the first mate could do little to assure the ship didn't crash into the rocks ahead, Reed went below to supervise the sweeps. He did more than supervise, when the wizard tugged on the indicator to command the ship to starboard, Reed himself took the end of one sweep. Based on the position of the indicator, the wizard needed a substantial turn to avoid the rocks. "Gently, easy now," Reed ordered as he lowered the sweep into the water, then began walking it backward. "And up, slowly, slowly," he whispered. All four sweeps moved gently, carefully, one pair pulling the ship to the right, the other pair pushing the ship away from the left side. Twice, three, six times the sweeps went silently back and forth before the makeshift indicator attached to the ceiling went back to its neutral position. Reed left the sweep and stuck his head out the porthole, holding his breath. He could not hear anything, and to his chagrin realized he could not *know* anything as long as he was below the main deck. His ship was carried along the current while her captain was a mere passenger. Should he go back to the bow? No, that would only satisfy his own curiosity and show a lack of faith in Alfonze and the two wizards. The crew at the sweeps were heartened to see their captain with them, he needed to remain there until the danger was past.

"Cap'n," a sailor whispered harshly from another porthole. The man gestured forward to starboard and Reed peered out into the gloom.

Something was out there, something big and dark and dangerous. It was only a darker shadow in the enveloping gloom of the night fog, but it was there surely as if the night had been clear. A rock! A massive rock that threatened to tear the bottom out of his ship, leaving the crew to scramble into boats, to- To what? To row for their lives until they were inevitably chased down by the pirate guard ships, and then spend the rest of their short, miserable lives as slaves chained to an oar aboard a pirate ship? Better to go down with the ship, Reed thought to himself as his heart leapt into his throat while the dark rock drew closer. Going down with the ship is what Reed resolved to do, unless he saw a chance to kill a pirate before he died.

The rock now loomed above the ship, Reed imagined that without the interference of the fog, he could reach out and touch it. Had the wizard guided them too close to the rock? Did the wizard understand how deep the *Hildegard*'s keel lay beneath the waves, even unburdened by cargo? Reed knew he should trust Alfonze to advise the wizard, but he chafed to be on deck, having to will himself not to race up the ladder. At that point, there was nothing he could do but display false confidence in front of the crew.

Impossibly, miraculously, the ship glided past the rock, moving swiftly as the current was squeezed through the narrow passage between cliff and the offshore jumble of rocks. With Reed forcing himself to take even breaths, the slightly darker, indistinct blob of the rock fell astern and Reed joined the entire crew in an unspoken prayer of thankfulness. "Cap'n!" A sailor whispered from the hatch above. "Wizard wants you on deck."

Reed snapped a salute to the sweep crews, and those who had hands free returned the gesture. The *Lady Hildegard* was not a naval vessel, but many of the volunteer crew had served in the Royal Navy or the navies of allied lands, and Reed thought the grim nature of their current mission fully warranted a salute to his fine crew. Without haste that might create noise, he climbed the ladder through the hatch and strode to the bow, nodding to acknowledge the relieved grins of crewmen along the way. It was good for the crew to celebrate now, he considered, for they might all be dead within the hour. "That was too close for comfort, master wizard," Reed muttered, his continued tension overcoming his manners for a moment. "Ah, I beg your pardon, Your Lordship. We were all a bit frightened below decks. That rock looked close enough to touch."

"It couldn't be helped," Cecil replied with eyes closed, not breaking concentration. "I sensed rocks extending just below the surface to the side of one rock, so I steered us closer to the other. Sorry if you were-"

"You have no need to be sorry for anything, Lord Mwazo," Reed bowed slightly. "If my comfort is what I cared most about, I would never have chosen a life at sea." He laughed to ease nervous tension. "We're past those two big rocks," he remembered from the map that those two large rocks almost marked the inner end of the channel, with only a few widely-scattered rocks to avoid before the channel opened into the great bay of Tokmanto harbor. Sticking his head over the railing, he did not need to check the ship's progress against landmarks on the shore that was shrouded by fog, his long years at sea told him the water rushing past the ship was already slackening, and the ship slowing with it.

"Yes," Cecil acknowledged. "Beneath my feet I can feel the current dispersing around us, your eyes tell you the same?"

"They do," Reed agreed with worry. Already, the *Hildegard* was turning sideways to the current, as the rudder lost its effectiveness in the slower current. "Can I hope you and Lord Salva have another trick up your sleeves?"

"We do not have any other tricks to play. Lord Salva is growing weary and the spell is weakening, the fog will begin to lift soon." Cecil still had not opened his eyes, he dared not break his concentration until they were safely past the last of the rocks

"Weary?" Reed exclaimed in a voice louder than he intended. Of course the wizard was weary, enveloping half of Tokmanto harbor and the cliffs to the north must take tremendous effort. For three days, the *Hildegard* had lazily sailed back and forth just over the horizon, waiting for what the court wizard considered the correct weather conditions to create a fog without the enemy knowing it was an unnatural event. Conditions did not have to be perfect, merely good enough for fog to be possible. Above all, there needed to be little wind, and for the first two nights after they arrived off Tokmanto, the onshore breeze was blowing too hard for the wizard's liking. Each morning before the sun rose, the *Hildegard* added sail and raced south into the open ocean, straight away from the enemy harbor. Each night as the sun set, the ship crept closer to the harbor, making ready to dash in under cover of darkness. Captain Reed and his experienced crew of volunteers fretted all day, every day, as they lingered too closely to the pirates' lair. Even with sails furled and the Hildegard well over the horizon, beyond known routes used by pirate ships, there was still risk of discovery. Twice, Lord Salva had tested his ability to create fog without being detected by enemy wizards, declaring himself satisfied although dismayed by how much creating the spell drained his energy. The court wizard had slept past Noon after each time he attempted the spell. To maintain the spell for hours, and spread the fog widely around the ship, was almost more than Paedris could bear. When Reed had checked on the wizard as they approached the headland to enter the channel, the man's face had been ashen, his lips dry, his hands trembling. There would be a price to pay for it later, Reed feared, a terrible price.

And that severe effort would all be for nothing if the fog lifted while the *Hildegard* was drifting slowly on the slowing current. "Lord Mwazo, surely there is something you can do. For us to be caught now-"

"There is nothing I can do, and there is nothing any wizard need do now. What are your own senses telling you, Captain?"

Reed bit back a sarcastic reply, telling himself to trust the wizard once more. His feet told him the deck was swaying even more gently side to side now they were through the channel and into the open bay, where the ocean swells were dampened by the reef that formed the harbor's natural barrier. His ears told him nothing, even the few, faint sounds coming from the ship's creaking timbers was muffled. His eyes saw only gloomy mist in all directions. There nothing-

No! He felt the fog caressing his face and neck as he saw a particularly thick swirl of fog curling in front of him, around him. Reed took in a sharp breath while looking over the rail at the oily surface of the water. Other than the remains of swells rolling in from the open ocean beyond the rocks, the sea around the ship was flat calm, the heavy fog acting as a blanket. Then, he saw what the wizard meant, a ripple teasing the surface of the water. Then, another ripple, and the fog danced across the water. Turning his head, he felt a light puff of wind stir the droplets of water clinging to his beard. "I understand, master wizard. Alfonze!" He waved the first mate to him. "Raise sails and make ready. That night wind Jofer spoke of is indeed coming down that gap in the hills. It will blow this fog away as it reached the bay, we must take full advantage of it before it is too late!"

Using hand signals, Alfonze ordered the crew into action, and everyone moved silently, so different from the usual routine of orders shouted repeatedly from one man to another. Men climbed the rigging, shaking out sails, and soon Reed could see sails beginning to billow as the barest zephyr of a breeze wafted across the deck and built into a steady wind. Not yet enough wind to fill the sails, they were still mostly luffing, with the spars creaking against the masts. The *Lady Hildegard* began to respond to the increasing strength of the wind, gaining enough headway for steering control, then a gust caused a gap in the surrounding fog and the ship heeled over slightly as the sails caught the wind. Despite their discipline and the continued need for silence, a whispered cheer rose from deck to the topmast.

Cecil opened his eyes and slumped forward against the bow railing, his knees buckling. Reed caught the wizard, holding him up. "Steady, Lord Mwazo, easy."

"It is done," Cecil gasped. "We are past the last rock, wind and current are carrying us safely away."

"Has our presence been noticed?" Reed peered fearfully toward the shore, where glowing lights atop the cliffs were just becoming barely visible. The enemy lit watch fires above the cliffs at night. In the fog, the fires only blinded the enemy lookouts and made it easier for the crew of the *Hildegard* to judge their distance from shore. The ship was exactly where Reed had hoped to be, with the wind carrying her around the last inner headland of the bay, toward the docks where pirate ships were tied up for the night. If they could get around that headland before being detected, they would be too far inside the harbor for the guard ships to catch up with them. Or so Reed hoped. Now that he was able to judge the night wind, it was not nearly so strong as he wished, and that last headland would create a wind shadow, beyond which the *Hildegard*'s sails would go slack. He needed to change course to build up speed before rounding the headland. "Are you able to stand, master wizard?" he asked, and after Lord Mwazo nodded wearily, Reed waved a crewman over to help the wizard. "Quickly, prepare a boat for the wizards. Pass the word aft, I must tend to the wheel."

CHAPTER TEN

"No!" Reed cried out in anguish, and pointed back toward the ship. In the swirling current at the far end of the harbor near where the pirate ships were docked, the *Lady Hildegard* began to veer off course, the wind pushing her unguided hull toward a sandbar to the right of the docks. The sailors had allowed for some drift across the current, but movement of the water was swifter than expected, and as the ship sailed farther into harbor behind the headland, the breeze had less and less effect on the ship's progress. As her crestfallen former crew watched helplessly, their old ship presented her port quarter. "She's going to miss the docks!"

After the ship rounded the last headland and had built up good speed, Captain Reed had personally taken the wheel and steered straight for the largest of the two pirate docks. There was one pier extending out from the eastern shore where three pirate ships were docked, but Reed's target was the main pier and dockyard structures at the bottom of the bay. At first, steering of the ship had been guided by Lord Mwazo, as the patchy fog still made it impossible to see the shore clearly. Then the wizards had been hustled away into a boat rowed by four of the ship's strongest crewman, and Reed had been able to rely on his instincts, until the freshening wind began to tear rents in the fog and he could see the light of torches lining the docks ahead. At that point, Alfonze took most of the ship's crew away in boats, leaving only Reed and eight others to guide the *Hildegard* on her final voyage. They had steered the ship toward the docks, set the sails properly and lashed the wheel so the ship was making way directly toward her target.

With the pirates on the docks and aboard the two guard ships alerted to the totally unexpected danger, Reed had ordered his remaining crew into the last boat and they pulled with all their might for the east shore of the harbor. Behind them, the two guard ships were racing in after the *Hildegard* with all sails set and oars furiously churning the water on each side. The guard ships had been near the harbor entrance, becalmed and enveloped by fog when the *Hildegard* entered the open bay behind them. When the fog dissipated enough for the danger to be seen, the intruder ship was already past the headland and the pair of guard ships had no chance to catch her, but the guard ship captains knew the penalty for failure in Acedor, so they bellowed and cursed and whipped both their crew handling the sails and their slaves chained to the oars.

And now Reed's plan was all going to fall apart, for the unpredictable current was pulling the *Hildegard* off course! With the ship falling off toward the sandbar, Reed feared one of the guard ships would turn to chase his boat, if they spotted the small, dark craft in the patchy fog. "Pull, men, *pull!*" Reed shouted in alarm. Perhaps the *Hildegard* could still crash into one or two of the pirate ships that were frantically being cut loose from the docks or being readied for sea, but that left far too many swift and deadly enemy ships to chase Reed and his crew. Pointing toward a bank of fog laying low on the water, Reed exhorted his crew. "We must make for the-"

"Look!" A sailor interrupted, grasping his captain's arm. "Who is that?"

Across the water, a figure could be seen on the *Lady Hildegard*'s deck, holding onto the wheel. The figure swayed side to side violently as its arms sawed back and forth. "He's cutting the wheel loose!" Reed exclaimed in anger. "A pirate! He wants to make sure the *Hildegard* misses the docks completely! How did a pirate get aboard her so quickly? I wish we could-"

"Captain," it was the captain's turn to interrupt his man, as a cheer arose around the two of them. "That is no pirate."

Partly obscured by wisps of fog, the figure was spinning the great wheel, causing the *Hildegard* to turn back onto her intended course, now heading slightly to the left of the docks. The pressure of wind against her sails was giving her just enough headway to make the turn; the current would do the rest. When the upper sails luffed from lack of wind, the ship was running only on momentum, and the current was now pulling her along straight for the docks. On the docks, pirates shouted and screamed and shook their fists, even shooting arrows at the dark bulk of the merchant ship bearing inexorably down on them. "Who is that?" Reed questioned in amazement. "My glass! Give me my glass!" A sailor pulled the spyglass from a leather pouch slung over a shoulder and handed it to his captain. Reed extended the tube to its full length and put it to his eye, but darkness and remaining fog made it impossible to see who guided his former ship. "I can't tell who- Jofer?" Reed gasped in shock, realizing he had not seen the old codger since they left the *Hildegard*. "Jofer! Has anyone seen Jofer?" he shouted frantically, bobbing his head this way and that to scan the deck of their small boat. Reed had not seen Jofer since Alfonze departed with the other boats, and Reed had not personally counted heads as sailors scrambled down rope netting into those boats. He also had not seen Jofer while the much smaller crew set the *Lady Hildegard* on course for the docks and lashed the great wheel. The man could have hidden below deck, but for what insane purpose would he-

Just then, the thin fog parted momentarily and Reed caught a glimpse of the tiny dark figure still standing at the wheel as the *Hildegard* glided the last few yards and crashed into the outer docks, scattering and crushing pirate ships. Relentlessly, the great mass of the merchant ship snapped the docks before it like matchsticks, and pirate ships began sinking or being crushed under the onrushing ship, or both. The figure at the wheel staggered, holding the wheel with both hands in grim determination, though there was no longer any need or ability to steer the ship as her bow neared the dockyard buildings at the shore of the piers. Was Reed imagining what his eye saw through the spyglass? The figure staggered again, then held onto the wheel with one hand, while turning to face the ship's former crew in their little boat. With his right arm, the figure snapped a salute and held it as the deck beneath the man's feet splintered.

"That *is* Jofer," Reed whispered, and the whisper traveled from stern to stem of the boat. Reed lowered the glass, and returned the salute, a gesture picked up by every man not pulling on an oar with all his might. "Jofer. Who'd have thought it?" Reed wondered just as the *Lady Hildegard* rammed its bowsprit into a sturdy building atop a pier, and the building fell over onto the ship's deck.

The *Hildegard* erupted in a shocking explosion, sending burning debris and flaming oil high and wide. In moments, every pirate ship still docked and those few that had been cut loose were on fire, with flames raging across water and shore as burning gouts of oil fountained upward from the *Hildegard*'s hold.

Using his vessel as a fire ship had been Captain Reed's idea, thinking that a suitable end for his great *Lady*. No sad fate of rotting away at anchor for the *Hildegard*, her death had thoroughly destroyed the pirate base and almost all their ships. Her death had given her crew a fighting chance to get away, and struck a hard blow for the free world.

"Cap'n," a sailor clapped a hand on Reed's back, patting him gently. Seeing tears rolling free and unashamedly down his captain's face, the sailor remarked quietly "She was a good ship, she took care of us well right to the end."

"Aye," Reed rubbed away tears with the back of his hand. "She was a good ship, none finer I served aboard. I'm not sad for her, I grieve for old Jofer."

"Jofer got what he wanted, Captain," another sailor grunted between pulls at an oar. "He was sick, you see, and he also didn't want to waste away on land in some hospital. Or, knowing Jofer, in a tavern."

"I didn't know," Reed replied, ashamed of that.

"Not your fault, Captain. Jofer wanted it kept private. Huh," the sailor chuckled softly. "Old Jofer finally got what he always wanted; to be part of a true story as exciting as the lies he was fond of telling."

"That he is," Reed found himself smiling. "If we live to return home, I will tell the legend of Jofer in every tavern I visit. Now, men," he glanced at the two guard ships, which were still making swiftly for the docks, likely hoping to help extinguish the flames before they entirely consumed every ship, pier and building in the heart of Tokmanto harbor. Reed thought the errand of the guard ships to be foolish, he knew how much oil was now burning along that shore. Before they slipped anchor to put to sea, he had taken on barrels of flammable oil as ballast, the ship's only ballast. Working with Lord Salva, Alfonze had rigged the *Hildegard* so that when her bow crumpled, a timber would be forced backward to pierce a barrel of oil and tip over a lantern, setting the oil on fire. All the other barrels had their lids removed before Reed left the ship, making them veritable bombs. With all that oil floating on the water, and some barrels still exploding, Reed knew the pirates had no hope of stopping the flames before they burned themselves out. "Pull! Make for Alfonze, or we will not survive this night!"

"That's the signal," Alfonze announced with a wince at a sharp pain from a cut across his left forearm. The signal was a burning torch on a beach farther up the eastern shore, and it meant their true mission had been accomplished; the wizards were safely ashore and had not been seen by the enemy. The four men who had rowed the exhausted wizards to the beach were out in the bay somewhere, their small boat invisible in the misty darkness. Now, even if the entire crew was killed, the mission they had been hired to perform was completed successfully. "They'll meet up with us between the beach and the reef. Or they won't. Can anyone see the captain's boat?" Alfonse could not hold a glass steady with one hand, his left arm was too painful and shaky from being slashed by a pirate's sword.

While Captain Reed set the *Lady Hildegard* on course to crash into the docks, and a team of four sailors got the wizards safely ashore unseen, Alfonze had taken most of the crew on a raiding party in three boats. Along the eastern shore of the harbor was a pier with three pirate longships, a few buildings, and pens where slaves were kept. Those three ships could cut off the sailor's escape, so the mission for Alfonze had been to attack and sink two of the longships, or all three if it could not be helped. The three boats had reached the pier unnoticed, as the few pirates awake there assumed the guard ships would warn of any danger. Five unlucky pirates had their throats slit or swords run through their bellies before one pirate managed to shout an alarm. It was too late, for Alfonze and his men were chopping holes in the hulls of the two longships that were tied together, leaving the third for an escape attempt. Those two longships actually sank shortly before the *Hildegard* exploded, but a bank of fog across the middle of the bay prevented the main docks from seeing trouble to the east, and they had been entirely focused on the *Hildegard* looming toward them.

With two longships sunk at the pier and the other ship secured and being made ready, Alfonze had led a charge on the slave pens to release the wretches held captive there. Freed slaves could at least cause confusion amongst the pirates, but Alfonze hoped to find some captives healthy enough to help row the longship. He had lost four men in the fight, and had been disappointed to find only two dozen slaves huddled in the pen. But of the newly-freed slaves, all but five were capable of manning a longship's oars, and every one of them was tearfully eager to do what they could for the people who had given them freedom, short though that may be.

When the rowing benches were crewed by a mix of his own men and the freed slaves, Alfonze had ordered the longship's lateen sail hoisted, and he personally hacked away the lines tying the ship to the pier. With the sail catching wind blowing straight across the harbor and oars pulling, the longship was making encouraging progress toward the reef. The problem for Alfonze was; in which direction to steer? Captain Reed had instructed Alfonze that picking up the captain and his one boat full of men was less important than escaping with most of the crew, and Alfonze knew that was a very wise and practical decision. He also had no intention of following those orders unless he had no choice.

"I see them!" A sailor pointed along the spyglass he held. "They're between us and that guard ship!"

"Where?" Alfonze tried holding up a hand to shield his eyes from the yellow flames raging where the pirate docks used to be. "I can't see- is that them?" He thought he saw something bobbing in the water.

"Yes, that's them. That, that guard ship went right past them," the sailor added excitedly.

"We have a chance, then," Alfonze leaned on the tiller, turning the longship toward Reed's boat. "If those guard ships think we are pirates coming to help them, we just might make a success of this," he muttered to himself.

"If not?" The sailor helping him with the tiller asked under his breath.

"If not, then this is our last chance to see how a pirate ship fights another pirate ship."

"Captain," Alfonze tried to sit down hours later, before realizing his muscles were too stiff and sore to bend so much, even leaning on a railing made his legs scream in sharp agony. "The men cannot row another stroke, we are all exhausted." Lowering his voice, he bent to speak privately, or as privately as possible in the open deck of the longship. "The former slaves gave their all, I fear two of them will not live to see the dawn, but they were ill-treated before we released them. They all need rest, and more food than we have aboard." From the *Lady Hildegard*, her crew had brought casks of biscuit, dried soup and water, for they knew the water supply aboard a pirate ship of Acedor could not be trusted to be consumed. Water was not an immediate issue, a furious rain squall recently passing had filled several casks the sailors had scrubbed clean, but food had already been scarce before former slaves had swelled the number of mouths to feed. The *Hildegard*'s crew had no hope of acquiring more food other than fish until they could sail eastward along the coast back to Tarador, and the prevailing winds would propel the ship in the wrong direction. With its triangular lateen sail, the longship could point closer into the wind, but reaching safety would require many days of beating back and forth over the horizon from the coastline to remain concealed from pirate ships lurking closer to shore. To speed their progress by extending the oars and rowing would make their food supply problem worse; those manning the oars would need more food than sailors merely tending sails and the rudder.

"Aye," Reed gritted his teeth, shifting his weight from one side to the other as he sat on the rough wood bench at the ship's stern, holding the long tiller that was attached to the rudder post. He had taken several shifts at the oars and now he was shaking from exhaustion, and no amount of fidgeting on the seat found a comfortable position to sit.

Reed was already past the time his shift at the tiller was supposed to have ended, he had volunteered to remain steering the ship because feared he could not rise from the seat. Through rents in the clouds scudding low above the ship's lone mast, he could see the eastern sky becoming ever so slightly pink. "Belay the oars, give everyone rest. Sun will be up soon enough and we'll face the day then." Face their fate, Captain Reed said to himself. He was not optimistic.

Through the long night when no one aboard the longship got a wink of sleep, they had fearfully watched torches aboard two pirate ships hunting them, those pirates were no doubt mad as hornets and seeking blood. Only one torch was visible at the moment, but that was poor comfort to Reed and his crew. The other ship could have doused its torch, or be hidden behind a rain squall. Reed did not trust his luck enough to hope the second ship was over the horizon or had turned around to go back into the harbor. Their longship had not set course east after clearing the harbor entrance channel, instead they had taken advantage of a favorable though light breeze to sail straight away from land before turning east, Reed hoped that maneuver had surprised the pirate ships searching for him.

Daylight would bring no cover and no solace for the exhausted crew, Reed felt deep down they had pushed their luck as far as it could stretch and escaping the harbor was the last favor the fates would offer the former crew of the good ship *Lady Hildegard*. The prevailing wind along the coast blew toward the west as did the current, although the morning breeze had not yet made an appearance. Reed looked up to the single, triangular sail, luffing in the barest ghost of a breeze and the boom creaking against the mast.

"Aye, Cap'n," Alfonze acknowledged leaning against the rail to steady his aching legs and back. "There's kindling and oil aboard, when the sun is up we can get a fire going in the stove and heat soup for the crew?"

Reed nodded without making the effort to speak. He felt the tiller gently tugging under his arm and turned his head to feel the breeze ruffling his beard. Soon enough, the wind would pick up from the east, pushing the longship back toward the pirate harbor, and the pirates would bring fresh crews out to row against wind and current. With less than a full complement of rowers, and both former slaves and former men of the *Hildegard* unable to lift one of the great oars, Reed had no hope of surviving the day.

He smiled in spite of the dire circumstances. They had won a great victory, sneaking into the feared pirate harbor of Tokmanto, burning nearly every pirate ship there, destroying piers and dockyards, and most importantly setting the two wizards ashore without the enemy noticing in the chaos. Though their action that night would not break the pirate blockade of Tarador, Captain Reed and his brave people had hit the pirates hard in their own home, and perhaps gained a measure of revenge for the terrible crimes those pirates had committed on the high seas in the past year. If he died that day, he could take satisfaction that the pirates had to be burning up with rage to see their impenetrable harbor burned to uselessness.

Reed shifted on the seat again, trying to get comfortable when he realized the long tiller was pushing under his arm. He wiggled it gently, puzzled. With barely any wind, the longship made so little headway that he had been able to use only finger pressure on the tiller to keep the ship pointed in the right direction, and now the oars had been stowed, the ship was drifting listlessly on the current.

Except it wasn't. He looked up in surprise to see the sail flapping, the boom groaning against the mast, and his beard tickled as a freshening breeze wafted past. He pulled on the tiller, remembering that unlike the wheel on the *Hildegard*, a tiller is steered in the direction opposite where he wanted to go. With the longship pointed properly to catch the wind, the sail filled, the lines straining and creaking under the pressure. "Alfonze!" Reed called excitedly, pointing to the sail. "Let her out," he ordered, and Alfonze with two others adjusted the lines to let the boom swing over, catching more of the wind.

Reed looked toward the shore, still unseen just over the horizon. This unusual morning wind was coming from the northwest, and the longship was able to skip across the swells at a good clip, with the wind continuing to build. The motion of the ship heeling over awakened more of her exhausted crew, and they adjusted lines and shifted themselves and their meager supplies to the windward rail without needing to be ordered. Within a quarter hour, with the eastern sky becoming distinctly light as dawn approached, the longship had a wake boiling behind her and everyone who was not tending sails were stacked along with windward rail, their weight keeping the ship's long, narrow and shallow hull from heeling over too far. Reed and Alfonze, their desperate tiredness forgotten for the moment, discussed the finer points of handling the unfamiliar ship to get the best speed out of her. They experimented with trimming the sail while expressing disgust about its poor condition, and found that moving more of the crew aft made the ship happier and swifter across the wavetops. Reed found himself actually grinning as he saw the first orange light of the rising sun through gaps in the fleeting clouds.

"I thought the winds here came from the east?" Alfonze asked happily, looking behind the longship to where no pursuing pirate ships could be seen.

"They do!" Reed answered, wincing as his sore back tightened with a twinge of pain. A sore back he could live with and the pain no longer constantly bothered him, as he urged the wind to continue.

"Then the fates smile upon us this morning," Alfonze said before fearing he may have jinxed them by his eagerness.

"Fates?" Reed agreed, then frowned. "Hmmm."

"What is it, Captain?" Alfonze asked with concern.

"I wonder, Alfonze, if we owe this fortunate wind not to the fates, but to a wizard."

"A wizard? Oh," Alfonze felt his hair standing on end. "A wizard, eh?"

Lord Mwazo extended his senses slowly, carefully. Even through the cloud cover, he could feel the sun would soon rise above the horizon and indeed the thin clouds in the east were lighter in color. Since splashing ashore, the two wizards had climbed the hillside ringing the harbor, avoiding well-traveled roads and trails, striking out through rough country or following faint paths created by the goats and other wild animals who somehow managed to live in the inhospitable country. At first, the wizards cared about little else but speed and distance; getting as far from the harbor as quickly as possible. With the flaming chaos in the harbor fully occupying the attention of the pirates and soldiers of Acedor, no one was patrolling the lands away from the harbor. Other than the harbor facilities of Tokmanto, there was nothing of importance in the area, what had been fertile farmland before the arrival of the demon was now reduced to bare soil, scrub brush and huddled groves of sickly trees. With dawn fast approaching, Cecil needed to locate enemy patrols and outposts so they could avoid being caught out in the open. Though a quick check soon after setting their feet on solid ground determined no enemy wizards were in the area, at least a few were sure to arrive in reaction to the total destruction of the dockyard facilities, piers and almost all the pirate ships. Cecil and Paedris needed to find a route inland, that remained far away from any roads that would be traveled by enemy wizards on their rush to reach the harbor.

Cecil lay on dusty ground that, despite morning dew coating leaves of the trees above, smelled vaguely burnt. The acrid, unpleasant scent was an indication of how sickly the land of Acedor had become under dominion of the demon. With his eyes closed and Paedris laying still and quiet beside him, Mwazo subtly sent his presence through the spirit world, seeking signs of enemy soldiers and wizards. Sensing nothing in the immediate area, he searched farther in ever-widening circles until he found a group of mounted soldiers hurrying their horses down a road in the semi-darkness. That group of soldiers were headed toward Tokmanto, having received word of the attack there. Curious, Mwazo sent his consciousness along the road behind the soldiers, wondering where they had come from. Through the shadows of the spirit world, he passed by one, two, three outposts manned by soldiers, then saw another group hurrying along the road, this group of soldiers on horseback escorting two carriages that-

Cecil froze and carefully, slowly pulled himself back. There was a dark wizard in one of those carriages, and he dared not investigate more closely. He was certain the enemy wizard had not detected his presence, as the subtler forms of wizardry were poorly practiced by wizards of Acedor, and because Mwazo's brief glimpse had told him the enemy wizard was intensely focused on marshalling his dark powers for use at Tokmanto. The enemy had no way of knowing the attack there had been only a raid, never to be repeated, and the wizard was preparing to repel an invasion or fling back into the sea any soldiers of Tarador who dared set foot on lands under control of the demon.

Satisfied he knew where the enemy was located in the area and what path they should walk that day, Mwazo began the process of pulling himself out of the spirit world. As he came back to reality, he opened one eye to see Paedris laying flat on the ground a few feet from him. The other wizard was resting peacefully, keeping watch and making no disturbance that might distract his companion's search. Cecil smiled, thinking the formidable Lord Paedris don Salva looked deceptively angelic while resting, his face childlike and-

And, Cecil realized as his eyes narrowed with suspicion, Paedris' lips were moving silently and his fingertips were twitching. The movement was almost imperceptible, but the other wizard was clearly doing *something* when he had promised he would do *nothing* while Cecil sent his consciousness through the spirit world. What was Paedris doing? Cecil briefly dipped back into the spirit realm and-

Gasped. "Paedris!" He exclaimed, not worrying about being heard in the emptiness of the landscape.

"Huh?" Lord Salva's eyes snapped open. "What?"

"What? You know *what*? What are you doing? No, forget I asked that, I know what you are doing. What were you *thinking*?"

"Oh," Paedris was crestfallen, then sat up with a grin and a wink. "You saw that, eh? Damn it, Cecil, can I not hide anything from you?"

"You idiot," Cecil turned away in disgust, lest in his anger he say something regrettable. "The question is whether you can hide it from the enemy. The answer is no, you cannot. Why would you take such a risk? I know you are not so sentimental."

"I am also not so hard-hearted as to ignore sentiment," Paedris defended himself, then again smiled. "I do have a larger purpose to my actions. Cecil."

"Oh," Mwazo crossed his arms. "*This* I must hear. I am waiting." Inside, he was fuming. What he had caught Paedris doing was conjuring a wind from the northwest, using powerful and wide-spread magic to change the weather pattern. That unnatural wind would blow steadily for two days at least, speeding the passage of Captain Reed and his people back toward Tarador and relative safety.

"Yes, I am sentimental enough that I wish to aid Captain Reed. He and his sailors acted bravely, and their good ship sacrificed herself to give her crew a chance to live. We owe them, Cecil, I feel that strongly."

"Strongly enough to risk our vital mission?"

"My actions do not risk our mission, they aid us on our journey."

Mwazo did not bother to reply, his tilted head and rolled eyes speaking for him.

"Think on this, Cecil," Paedris continued. "The enemy will surely detect, by now surely has detected, that powerful wizardry has been used to create a wind to speed the escape of a pirate ship that was stolen from Tokmanto. The enemy knows our attack could only have been accomplished through use of wizardry, and that our attack was entirely successful; dockyards burned, ships sunk, slaves freed. So, a wizard of Tarador participated in the attack, and now an unnatural wind whisks a stolen ship away toward Tarador. The enemy could only conclude that the wizard who conducted the attack on Tokmanto is aboard that stolen longship, using magic to speed his escape. Thus," he made an exaggerated wink, "there is no reason for the enemy to search for, or suspect, a wizard within the borders of Acedor. We may stroll unhindered through this land, safe in the knowledge the enemy's focus is elsewhere."

"Hmm," Cecil grunted sourly, forced to concede Paedris was right. Wagging a finger, he scolded the court wizard. "Why didn't you tell me your plans?"

"Because," Paedris sighed. "We would waste precious time arguing about it, then you would be distracted with worry at a time when you needed to concentrate on your own search. It will not happen again," he cast his eyes downward sheepishly.

"Hmmmph. Until the next time, you mean."

"Oh, you do not keep secrets from me?" Paedris wagged a finger back, although he did it playfully.

"Let's not get into that now," Cecil said hurriedly. "We have many miles to walk today, we must get started. And, Paedris?"

"Yes?" The court wizard asked, hopeful any hard feelings were over.

"I agree we owe Captain Reed, and I am grateful you are able to help them. Just, don't do it again without asking me?"

Kyre dropped the wooden practice sword and picked up a real metal sword, fitting a bronze safety guard over it. The bronze sheath made the sword heavier and less well balanced, and it took more effort to handle it with finesse and accuracy, and those were all good things in practice. He had practice swords with a blunt tip and dull edges and those swords were used for practicing forms, training his muscles to act without thought, but that day what he wanted was effort, extra effort. He had felt weak laying in a hospital tent up near the Kaltzen Pass after the wizards brought down the Gates of the Mountains and the army of Acedor had been destroyed. He had felt weak during the long carriage ride back to Linden, and he had chafed at the forced inactivity while resting in the royal hospital. His wounds were fully recovered, he knew that and even the fussy doctors admitted as much. Now he needed to recover his lost strength and stamina, and a hard session working with heavy swords in the sparring ring was just what he needed. His guards had offered to spar with him but he knew they would hold back for fear of embarrassing him, and anyway he knew he was not ready to spar against an opponent. So he thumped the leather and canvas practice targets by himself, and later he would hike and run out into the countryside rather than riding a horse.

Grunting with effort and dripping with sweat, he was disgusted to see his sword hand was struggling just to maintain a firm grip. He was not wearing a glove or using the sticky rosin substance provided in the sparring arena, because he wanted his hands and forearm to become strong enough to securely hold a sweat or blood-soaked sword hilt. He had learned that in battle, weapons are often coated with sweat, or blood, or merely wet from rain. He should not plan on having proper gloves, he could not even count on using his own sword or bow in battle. The greatest lesson Kyre had learned about combat is that it was complete, utter chaos and that anything could happen. His injury had been caused by a wizard, and none of his time in a sparring ring had trained him to fight a wizard.

"Watch your footwork," called a voice behind him.

"Sire," Kyre turned quickly and used the sword to salute his father. "Forgive me, I did not know you were here," he said in a formal fashion devoid of familial warmth.

"I arrived only a moment ago, but long enough to see you dragging your back foot," Regin said without a smile. "An enemy would exploit such a weakness."

Kyre nodded stiffly. Many sons would think their father too harsh, while knowing the father acted out of concern for the son's well-being. Kyre no longer entertained such illusions, knowing his father reproached him from disappointment rather than any sense of protection. "In the sparring ring, or a duel, yes. In real battle, I have found there is little time for studying an enemy's footwork," he said to remind his father that he was no longer the pampered eldest child. He had been in desperate battles that stretched over days, and he had faced an enemy wizard when he thought he would die.

Regin nodded without speaking, understanding his son's meaning. Kyre had seen combat, had nearly died. Regin remembered the first time he had fought a real battle and how that had changed him. He had a scar across his left shoulder from an orc's axe, a wound that still ached when before a rainstorm.

Father and son spoke awkwardly for a while, until Kyre put away his sword and picked up a bow for archery practice. His arms were trembling from exertion and that was the perfect time to test his skill with a bow, for in battle he would need to shoot arrows whether his arms had strength or not. "Father, I heard you inspected the palace before the princess arrived. I thank you for that. She has many enemies, we must protect her."

"I failed," Regin replied stiffly, not wishing to address the subject.

"You did your best, Madame Dupres told me only a wizard could have noticed the danger." Kyre paused from shooting arrows and turned to look at his father. "Did I tell you I swore an oath to protect Ariana? It was after the battle at the Gates, when I was in a hospital cot. Before Lord Salva pulled down the Gates I thought our princess was weak for allowing the enemy across the river to spite Duchess Rochambeau's vote against her in the Council, but Ariana was not weak, she was very clever."

"She is a clever girl," Regin said through clenched teeth. "Mind your aim," he pointed to the archery target, "you are pulling to the right." With that, the duke of Burwyck walked away, mindful not to stomp the ground in his anger. His eldest son and heir had pledged to protect the very girl who stood between Regin and the throne of Tarador! Regin needed somewhere quiet to think, and he knew just the place.

"My father seems," Kyre hesitated, realizing he was speaking of his family to a man who was only a guard. A trusted guard, a man Kyre had known for years, but the guard was not part of the Falco family. "Different," he finished the thought in as neutral a way he could.

The guard smiled to himself, knowing what his young charge had been about to say. "Your father's own guards have noticed a difference in him after your stirring victory at the Gates, Your Grace."

"It was not *my* victory, Jonas," Kyre protested from genuine modesty. "I never witnessed the final battle," he added, with genuine disappointment. "The truth is, if I had halted the enemy before the Gates, I would have ruined our Regent's careful plan."

"You did not know that, Your Grace. You acted bravely."

"And stupidly," Kyre said ruefully. "Jonas, if you are ever faced with a wizard, take my advice and run. That is what I should have done. My father's guards talk about him?"

"They talk to other guards," Jonas explained.

"I see," Kyre mused, wondering whether his guards talked about him. Of course they did, they must. "What do they say?"

"Only that," the guard looked away.

"Jonas, you may speak freely. Consider it an order," Kyre smiled, "if that helps."

"Yes, Your Grace. Your father is unhappy, distracted, he is often alone and he does not seek the counsel of Mister Forne. After the princess was nearly killed here in the palace, your father was very fearful, his guards thought him depressed."

"Did my father really inspect the palace before we returned from the Gates?"

"According to his guards, yes, he crawled in every nook and cranny. It was most tiring, from what I heard. The enemy assassin getting into the palace was not due to lack of effort by Duke Falco."

"Hmm," Kyre took the bronze sheath off his sword and placed it back on the rack. He was done with sword practice for the day, his arms shaking from the effort. "Yet, an enemy assassin did gain access to the palace. And a magical device was somehow planted in the Citadel."

"It is said your father apologized to the princess."

Kyre did not reply, his thoughts elsewhere. When his father spoke of how sorry he was about the attempt on Ariana's life, he had avoided Kyre's eyes, and his words had rung false to Kyre's ears. He knew his father, and he knew his father was lying about something, something important. Regin Falco played no games of small stakes, so whatever his father was hiding, it was something big.

It made no sense that his father would have somehow been involved in the assassination attempt, for Regin desired nothing more than to put a Falco on the throne of Tarador, and he needed Ariana and Kyre for that. Or, Kyre remembered sourly, Regin needed Ariana and one of his sons, not necessarily Kyre. When he first saw his father at the royal hospital, and Regin had talked of how proud he was about Kyre's bravery in battle, Kyre had sensed a hint that Regin Falco would have preferred Kyre to be a dead hero, so his more trustworthy younger brother Talen would be clear to marry Ariana.

Kyre slid his sword into its scabbard and decided he needed to get back into fighting condition sooner rather than later. "Jonas, tomorrow we will spar together."

"You feel ready for such exertion, Your Grace?"

"No, and that is the point. I *need* to be ready."

Regin Falco slowly ran his fingertips along the arm of the throne, a shiver of thrill traveling up his spine as he touched with his own hands the carved wood of the ancient chair, the surface worn smooth by centuries of royal hands both male and female. Yes, he thought, his expression darkening, the hands that had lawfully owned that chair had been both male and female, and there had been another, more important distinction. Those hands had belonged to the rightful rulers of Tarador, as well as more recently the usurper Trehaymes. The throne had belonged to the Falcos long before any unworthy Trehaymes sought to foul the throne by their presence. The throne had been stolen by the Trehaymes, who had schemed to keep it ever since. As current head the Falco line, the throne belonged to *him*, Regin thought as his fingertips pressed harder on the chair, his anger growing. When the Trehaymes stole the kingdom, they didn't even have the decency to use their own chair as the throne. No, decency was not a trait of the Trehaymes, and Regin knew they had kept the old throne as a symbol of legitimacy for their illegitimate rule.

"Your Grace?"

"What?" Regin spun to see who had intruded on his thoughts, holding behind him the hand that had been caressing the throne. "Yes?" He asked, straightening and throwing his head back haughtily, hoping to keep the guilt he felt from showing on his face. "Captain Temmas?"

The chief of the palace guard tilted his head questioningly as he kept his voice neutral. "May I help you, Your Grace?" Regin Falco was not supposed to be alone in the throne room, even though the duke had been invited to stay in the palace by the crown princess herself. While Temmas would not intentionally offend the powerful duke, Regin Falco had no authority over him. Temmas was motivated by a deep-seated mistrust of all Falcos, by disgust at the duke touching the royal throne, and most of all by something basic: he had seen the guilty expression on Regin's face as the man turned, and Temmas knew the man had been up to nothing good.

"No, I," Regin could not prevent a flash of irritation from flitting across his face and he knew Temmas saw it. Any time Duke Falco was questioned by an underling, he felt a flare of rage and this time his usual arrogance was intensified by guilt. Temmas was no fool, Regin knew that, yet he also knew the palace guard captain had no proof of wrong-doing. "I was only thinking," he tapped the throne lightly, "this throne will soon belong to my daughter-in-law, and someday by my heir's oldest child. My grandchild. It is a remarkable thing to think of, isn't it?"

"Er, yes, Your Grace," Temmas replied stiffly, not moving from where he stood. Regin Falco did not belong in the throne room by himself and certainly should not ever be standing on the dais, touching the throne itself. Captain Temmas was prepared to stand right there all day if necessary to make it awkward enough that the Duke took the hint and left. As a duke, Regin Falco could not be touched without his permission, or orders from the Regent, or very strong evidence of treasonous activity. To prove treason, Temmas had the two royal palace guards behind him, but he could not even prove Duke Falco's intent was treasonous, unless the mere fact of his being a Falco was sufficient. "The maids will be here shortly to polish the floors", he hinted, knowing that was a lie and knowing Regin Falco also knew it was a lie.

"Oh, yes, certainly," Regin tried to pass the moment off lightheartedly and failed miserably. "We must not keep *maids* waiting," he frowned haughtily. With a nod to the captain and the other guards, he stepped off the dais and walked toward the far door. "Good day to you, Captain."

Outside in the hallway, Regin continued on as if nothing had happened, striding purposefully up steps and continuing on up, up to the battlements that ringed the ancient castle. There, he dug his fingers into the old gray stone until his fingertips turned white and ached. He didn't mind the physical pain, it distracted him from the far worse pain of knowing all the lands he could see should be *his*.

Would be his, he told himself and pushed aside his nagging thought that he would be king in Tarador only as a vassal of Acedor. No matter, he lied to himself as he turned back to look over the roofs of the royal palace, a palace that had been built and paid for by Falcos. Regin's enemies would be vanquished, he would sit on the throne in Linden, and he would strive to ensure the best outcome for Tarador. The enemy's victory was certain, their forces overwhelming, and Regin Falco was, in fact, a patriot rather than a traitor. So deep was his need for self-delusion that he believed his own lies. Yes, he was a patriot, seeking to salvage what he could of Taradoran culture in the face of his country inevitably being conquered by Acedor. It was silly, deluded fools like Ariana and Paedris who were the real traitors, wasting the lives of brave soldiers in their desperate attempt to cling onto power until the last moment.

He was a patriot, Regin told himself. Sacrifices had to be made to secure any sort of future for Tarador, and there was one sacrifice Regin might need to make personally.

Kyre.

While he had been touching the throne that soon would be his, Regin reached the sad conclusion that his eldest son and heir would never accept his father on the throne, never accept the hard choices required to save some small part of Tarador from the coming invasion. Through long training and habit, Regin had become skilled at concealing his feelings, but his immediate family knew him too well. Kyre sensed something was wrong, knew his father was up to something. And his heir, despite everything Regin had done to bring the boy up right, was infatuated with the silly princess. Regin knew he would get no help from Kyre, that his own son would instead view his father as a traitor and do everything in his power to thwart Regin's plans.

If he had been thinking clearly, Regin might have stopped to wonder whether his cold-hearted calculation was due to influence from an enemy wizard, but the idea that he may be wrong never crossed his supremely arrogant mind.

It was unfortunate, it was tragic that such potential would be wasted, and Regin someday might shed a tear about it, but Kyre Falco might have to go.

The next evening, Jonas approached Kyre, who tilted his head quizzically at seeing the expression on the face of the man who was in charge of his personal guard force. "Your Grace," Jonas nodded his head to make the barest of bows, a gesture that did not bother the Falco heir. Kyre generally wished to dispense with formal greetings except for occasions which called for formality, and he especially did not want his personal guards bowing and scraping to him. That was something Duke Falco would never understand; Kyre trusted the guards with his very life, he needed them to know they were valued beyond the jobs they were paid for.

"Jonas, what is wrong?"

"Nothing is wrong, not least on paper. Your father has just ordered six of my men replaced with men from the Duke's own guard force."

"What? Why?" Kyre exploded.

"His Grace gave me the order directly. He feels that, considering the attempts on the life of the princess, he needs the most experienced men guarding the life of his heir."

"More experienced?"

"Aye, and I can't argue with that, Joss Haden himself is joining us, and I can't knock his experience." Haden had served the Falcos in a variety of roles for twenty years, and was widely rumored to have done unsavory things for the Duke. The man was well trusted by Regin Falco, extremely competent, and not trusted by almost anyone else. "The Duke assured me I am still in command of the force, but a man like Haden will not be happy about taking orders from the likes of me."

"We will see about this," Kyre buckled on his sword belt and began to pull on a formal tunic for an audience with his father.

"Er, Your Grace, your father expected you would seek to debate this with him, so he gave me a message for you. He is busy, there will be no debate, and you should be pleased that your father is so concerned about your well-being," Jonas smiled awkwardly, hating to be caught in a dispute between duke and heir.

Kyre paused, the tunic poised above his head. Disgusted, he flung it back over a chair. "When my father is in the mood to be stubborn, there is no moving him. I will wait until he is somewhat more willing to discuss the subject. Now, I *can* speak with Joss Haden, and I will. Where is the man?"

Kyre's interview with Joss Haden and the other five men his father had assigned went well on the face of it. Haden and the others were deferential, not insulted to be protecting the heir rather than the duke himself. They said all the right things to Kyre and Jonas, and swore to do their best to guard Kyre's life and obey the instructions of Jonas, and for a reason Kyre could not name, he did not trust any of them. In the end, he could not go against his father's wishes, so the six moved into the barracks with Kyre's other guards and began training with them. His vague feeling of unease was surely wrong, he told himself. His father valued Kyre as his heir, and needed Kyre to marry Ariana, despite the increasing tensions between father and son.

As long as Regin Falco needed him, Kyre decided with a shrug, he had nothing to fear.

Jonas made a full bow when ushered into the presence of Kyre's mother, the duchess Britta Falco. Kyre got annoyed when his personal guards gave formal gestures of respect to him except in special formal occasions, but the duke and duchess always expected deference. "Your Grace," Jonas bent at the waist and stood back up stiffly, waiting for the duchess to acknowledge him.

"Leave us," Britta ordered with a dismissive wave to her own pair of guards. The guards knew it was not proper for the duchess to be alone with a man, they also knew better than to argue with the formidable woman. "Jonas, come in please, sit down," she patted a chair adjacent to her.

Jonas sat down warily, almost not putting any of his weight on the chair's seat. "You wished to see me, Your Grace?"

"Technically, I ordered you here, but my wishes are the same as orders, so," she shrugged and Jason was surprised to see a twinkle in her eyes. He had spent little time with the duchess and had never had a private audience. Most of the time he was in her presence, he had merely escorted Kyre to visit his mother, and Jonas remained a discrete distance away. "We may have, no, we do have, a serious problem and I need your help."

"Your Grace?" Jonas did not know what to say. The duchess of Burwyck did not ask for help, she demanded her orders to be obeyed.

"Joss Haden," she explained simply.

"Ah," Jonas understood instantly. "He is a capable-"

"He is a dangerous snake," Britta interrupted. "I know this to be a fact, for Haden has performed discrete tasks for me in the past. The man is a deadly, dangerous tool, useful in the right hands. I do not want him anywhere near my son."

"Your husband the Duke told me he assigned Haden and the others to increase your son's security in these dangerous times," Jonas remarked, his words unconvincing even to himself.

"Joss Haden is not a shield to protect anyone, he is a dagger you point at an enemy's heart," Britta declared. "I do not know why the Duke has done this, but I can be certain it is to further an aim of my husband, and not for the benefit of my firstborn child."

Jonas said nothing, for anything he said might be considered treason.

Britta continued, in a soft voice that betrayed uncharacteristic vulnerability. "These past weeks, I do not know my husband. The Duke has changed and I do not know why. He has become unreadable, even to me. Jonas," she looked up sharply at the guard. "I fear my husband cares more for his own schemes than for the life of our son. Kyre is my son, my *child*," she dabbed at a tear forming in one eye and Jonas was nearly frozen in place to see such a display of emotion from the duchess. "The duke thinks of Kyre as an heir and a tool to grow the power of the Falcos, the fact that Kyre is also a person is an inconvenience to my husband. Tell me, you are sworn to protect my son's life above all?"

"Yes, Your Grace," Jonas replied, uncomfortable.

"The duke is of course your liege lord, but you are especially pledged to safeguard the life of my son, even at the cost of your own life?"

"Yes, Your Grace. My Lady, if I may speak freely?"

"That is why we are behind a closed door, Jonas."

"My men, and myself, need no oath to protect your son. He has demonstrated loyalty to us, we are all loyal to him, beyond the bonds of any oath. You can be certain any of my men would do their utmost for Kyre."

"I am pleased to hear that," Britta smiled, a gesture which quickly faded. "I wish you to keep this in mind, then. Do not trust Joss Haden and his fellows. He may be more a threat to my son than any orc or wizard of Acedor. If the time comes, promise me you will act accordingly."

Jonas slipped off the chair and went down on one knee. "My Lady, if I ever believe Haden is a threat to Kyre, I will not hesitate, nor will I need orders."

"Good," Britta said back slightly in her chair. "My son is fortunate indeed to have such loyal men surrounding him."

"If I may continue to speak freely, your son has loyal men because he is worthy of such devotion. He is a true credit to Burwyck," Jonas added, instantly fearing the duchess would interpret his remark as implying the Duke himself was less of a credit than his own son. Because that is exactly what Jonas thought.

"I hope," the duchess reached for her forgotten cup of tea, "Kyre lives long enough to demonstrate what he can do as duke of Burwyck."

Kyre had little time to fret about his new and untrusted guards, for the next morning, he accompanied his father and brother along with most of the ducal army of Burwyck, westward through the streets of Linden. Ahead of them with the Royal Army was a carriage where princess Ariana rode with her personal wizard and savior. And, just behind the royal carriage was the newest knight of Tarador, a Sir Cully Runnet, feeling quite foolish and out of place in his fine new clothes and clinging awkwardly to his horse's back. Cully was going to war, and for the first time in his life, he wished he could go back to a simple life of chopping wood and cleaning. He did not know, because he not been told and was too shy to ask, what the Royal Army would be doing once they met Grand General Magrane on the east bank of the River Fasse. Cully was hoping for a boring couple of months living in a tent, doing whatever newly-minted knights did, until the coming winter forced most of the army back into garrison posts until the snow melted.

Cully feared he might have already used up his entire lifetime of luck when he pulled two drowning girls out of a moat.

CHAPTER ELEVEN

Acting as the forward scout, Lem was well ahead of the party, moving from cover to cover where there was cover to be found. Coming down out of the mountains into the foothills, they were encountering more groves of trees, and the early Autumn shrubs and bushes were at their full height, allowing him to crouch down to move forward. Along the way, he picked scattered late-season berries to provide a sweet treat, a break from the hard travel bread and dried strips of salted meat the party had been relying on for food. Lem hoped to find wild game such as deer or the sure-footed sheep which inhabited the steep mountain slopes, but he had not seen even rabbits. It was as if the entire land knew orcs were approaching and had run to get away.

Lem heard a sound before he saw anything, and he froze, holding up a hand for the party to halt. Glancing behind him, he saw Captain Raddick acknowledge with a silent hand signal, and Lem dropped to the ground, inching forward through the tall grasses and scratchy shrubs of the meadow he was crossing. He couldn't see anything, not yet. All that morning, they had seen and even smelled smoke rising from the valley to the south and southwest. Seeing smoke in the southwest was especially troubling, for the border of Acedor lay only seventeen leagues to the west. The previous night, after an afternoon of rain, the party had finally begun to grow confident they had outpaced the invading orc host in the valley below, and could turn south to race across the valley and into the relative safety of Tarador. While the dwarves appeared to have abandoned the southern valley to the orcs, retreating to the security of their mountain strongholds, the duke of Winterthur was sure to have built up the strength of his army on his northern border. If the party could only link up with Winterthur's army, they could find safety and assistance.

Seeing smoke in the valley to the southwest had almost dashed the party's hopes. Had a second army of orcs or foul men invaded across the border from Acedor, to march east and meet the orc host that was burning and pillaging its way westward? If that were true, then the party's only slim and fading hope was to dash between the two enemy forces, or to be trapped in the dwarf homeland at least until the winter snows melted. By then, Raddick feared, there might no longer be a Tarador for them to go home to.

"What is it?" Bjorn whispered to Raddick.

"Lem heard something up ahead," Raddick explained.

"I heard something too," Koren whispered from beside Bjorn.

"From here?" Raddick looked at Koren sharply, then his expression softened. "Of course. What do you hear?"

"Voices?" Koren guessed, scrunching up his eyes to concentrate. "Just snatches of sound, when the wind is blowing in the right direction."

"Orcs?" Raddick demanded.

"I don't, I can't hear enough." Koren opened his eyes. "I don't think so." Now that he knew the harsh speech of orcs, he could identify it. Although he could not hear individual words and the voices were strained, it was not the throat-straining guttural language of orcs.

"Go on ahead, then," Raddick pointed toward where Lem's head was barely visible. "Get up there with Lem, he knows the hand signals to tell us what you hear." Raddick looked behind them with dismay. If orcs were coming up the hillside, the Royal Army party would need to retreat quickly. The mountainside above them grew increasingly exposed as trees dwindled and meadows gave way to bare rock. The army captain did not like the idea of relying on mere speed to escape from orcs. Living mostly in mountains like dwarves, orcs were sure-footed in hazardous terrain and their short legs could climb steep slopes faster than any man.

Without a word, Koren ducked low and followed the faint trail Lem had used, but he was less than halfway to the scout when the man rose to his knees and used both hands to flash a complicated signal to Raddick. Just then, a gust of wind brought clear fragments of voices to Koren's ears. "Dwarves," he breathed with relief.

Raddick came running with the others, and they approached Lem, crawling on hands and knees the final yards. "Dwarves, Captain," Lem reported, "several dozen at least."

Three dwarf soldiers, armed with axes and bows, lead the way, with families trudging along behind. Most of the dwarves were walking and were clearly weary, with no ponies and mules available to carry injured dwarves and supplies. Even the young and the old were weighted down with heavy packs, and some of the adults were carrying infants.

"Ohhhhh," Raddick sighed deeply, "this is not good." More dwarves were coming out of the tree line, pairs of soldiers flanking the column of civilians. From the battered helmets and chipped axe blades of the soldiers, and from their dirty and sometimes bloody clothing, they had already been in a battle, likely more than one. Raddick had no desire, and no *time*, to be burdened with guarding and caring for refugees. Yet, the dwarves must have news of events in the valley to the south, and he needed that information. "Koren," he whispered, "stand and call out to them, don't startle them." Raddick figured that Koren, being a boy, would be less threatening to the dwarves. He did not wish to alarm an armed group that had to already be on edge.

"Uh, hello?" Koren called out, gently waving both hands above his head.

"Halt! Who is that?" A dwarf soldier shaded his eyes with a hand, as the civilians all tensed to run, and the other soldiers unslung their bows.

"I'm Koren, Koren Bladewell," he said stupidly, realizing after he spoke that his name would mean nothing to the dwarves. "I'm a boy, from Tarador. We were up in the mountains when the orcs invaded, and we have been trying to get back to Tarador."

Arrows were pointed at his chest though Koren was not afraid. From that distance, he knew he could duck down before an arrow reached him, or he could draw his sword and cut an arrow out of the air. Several of the arrows were shaking as the tired arms of the soldiers felt the strain of holding back the heavy bowstring. "We?" The dwarf demanded. "Who is '*we*'? I see only one of you."

Slowly, with his hands held up in a peaceful gesture, Raddick stood. "I am Captain Arnse Raddick of the Royal Army of Tarador. As the boy said, we are trying to get back across the border into our own lands. We were caught in the mountains when the orc host swept through the valley. There are eight of us; me, the boy and six of my men. May I approach so we can talk?" Raddick made a show of dropping his bow and quiver on the ground and unbuckling his sword belt.

"You won't get back to Tarador going the way we came from," the dwarf said sourly, and spit on the ground. "Stay where you are, I will come to you. Kenwass," he ordered another dwarf, "get this lot moving again, we've no time to stand around."

The dwarf slung his bow but kept a hand on the hilt of his battleaxe as he climbed, until he reached Raddick. With an untrusting but not unfriendly eye, he took in the men with Raddick, and stuck out a hand for Raddick to shake. "Renhelm's my name," the dwarf said, "I'm a lieutenant, our captain was killed three, no, four days ago?" He shook his head sadly. "The days run together." The dwarf's eyes narrowed, looking more closely at Raddick's men. "What were you doing in our mountains?"

Raddick noted Renhelm had said '*our* mountains'. He decided the truth, at least part of the truth, would serve him best right then. "Looking for them," he pointed to Koren and Bjorn. "We heard they were up in your lands, but they found us first, then we were cut off by the orcs."

"What were the two of you doing in our land?" He directed the question to Bjorn, being the older of the two.

"We had been hunting bandits with a dwarf named Barlen," Bjorn explained, pretending to yawn as if the whole story now bored him. "This young idiot," he jerked a thumb at Koren, "well, let's just say there is a girl involved."

"She is *not* involved," Koren's face turned red as he misunderstood Bjorn's remark, and his reaction was more convincing than if he had caught onto Bjorn's play-acting. "She-"

"Save it," Bjorn chuckled with a disgusted wave of a hand, and a wink toward Renhelm.

The dwarf chuckled, and took his hand away from the axe hilt. "The young are foolish no matter where they came from. Fair enough. You wish to get back to Tarador, eh? You'll not get there by going down this hill, that's where we came from." As he told his tale, Raddick's men collected their belongings and followed the dwarf at the rear of the refugee column.

The story Renhelm told was sad and discouraging. He had been part of a cavalry troop, riding through the valley to warn of the invading host of orcs. Six days prior, they had been rounding up stragglers when they were ambushed by an advance force of orcs, this group having surprisingly come from the west. "They set upon us at night," Renhelm shook his head. "We are supposed to get warnings when the enemy crosses the border, there is a river running through a ravine that forms our border with Acedor. We have sentry posts all along the river, yet somehow the group that hit us snuck through. They have a wizard with them, that may explain it somewhat. Our captain rallied us and we pushed them back, aye," Renhelm smacked a fist into a palm, "they didn't expect us to fight back so fiercely. We cut a hole through their lines and got most of us out, then it was a desperate race to get away. Our captain reasoned we were too few to do much good roaming around the valley, and if the orcs were coming at us from both sides we were needed to reinforce our lines in the mountains. But the orcs were ahead of us, they cut or burned bridges and were waiting for us where the rivers could be forded. There was no choice, we had to abandoned our wagons, our mounts and most of our supplies and swim across. It's been a running fight since then, like I said, our captain was killed four days ago. Of the sixty who set out, there are twenty two remaining and not all of us able to wield an axe in combat. We picked up scattered groups of survivors, and," Renhelm shrugged, "we couldn't leave them."

Raddick's expression was sympathetic. "I had eighteen men when we came across the border. Now, I have these seven with me. Renhelm, how can I get to Tarador? My need is most urgent."

"Urgent, eh?" Renhelm asked with suspicion. "You found the boy, what does the girl have to do with it?"

Raddick's mind was quick and sharp and he had a ready reply. "Right now, I do not care about two young fools who think they are in love. I must return to my homeland; we are at war and that is where I belong, where my duty lies."

"Aye," Renhelm was satisfied with that answer. "I would seek to do the same if I were you. But, Captain, behind us in the valley, you will find only death. If you wish to do some good in this war, come with us to the fortress of Magross. That is where we are bound. There, I can slip responsibility for these refugees and rejoin a fighting unit. I fear you will be trapped in these mountains through the winter."

"That cannot be," Raddick's jaw set in determination. "We *must* return to Tarador, no matter the cost."

"The cost will be all your lives," Renhelm's grave expression invited no argument. "Captain, if you are determined to meet an unhappy end, then first help me get these civilians up to Magross. I'll not tell you our secret paths, but there is a deep and narrow ravine, part of it goes under the ground, that can bring you down almost to the base of the foothills. From there?" Renhelm shrugged with fatal resignation. "You will at least emerge behind the orc frontlines, and perhaps if you can remain concealed for a time, you might just live long enough to regret your decision."

Not knowing what else to do, Raddick nodded, turning back to his men and rolling his eyes wearily. Escorting civilian refugees was a familiar and unwelcome task for most soldiers. As they once again checked their gear and fell in with the dwarf guards on the rear of the column, Koren strode closer to Raddick. "Captain, the lives of your men are at risk because of me. It might be best for me to make the attempt to cross the border by myself. I could-"

"Master Bladewell," Raddick cut the boy off, speaking at first through clenched teeth. He had enough headaches without worrying about an adventurous, untrained young wizard. "While I appreciate your courage and concern for my men, you will *not* be running off by yourself, is that clear? *I* was given the duty to return you to Linden and I will not shirk my duty, nor will I fail. Remember Lord Salva's words; if you are captured by the enemy, all is lost. You see these refugees? They fear for their lives, but they think the greatest threat is a band of orcs on their trail. If they walk hard and are lucky, they might live to reach the safety of the fortress. But if you fall into the enemy's hands, these refugees, all of us, will be consumed by demon fire."

"Oh," Koren cast his eyes downward, chastened.

"Again, I do not question your courage. Because I also recall that following orders of a Royal Army captain is something you treat as a mere trifle," he forced a smile, "do not think of sneaking away from us at night. If need be, I can bind your hands an assign someone to watch you. Someone other than Bjorn, who seems to enable your adventurous spirit. Now, Koren Bladewell, promise me you will not run off. Promise you will not hinder me in my sacred duty, a duty given to me directly by our Regent."

"I promise," Koren still was looking at his boots. Looking up to meet Raddick's eyes, he added "I promise! Really! I," he swept a hand across the vista of forbidding mountains, "wouldn't know where to go anyway!"

Renhelm and Raddick wished to walk through the night, if that had been possible. Because they were tasked with herding along over a hundred refugees, and because it was too dangerous to walk through the tricky mountain paths in total darkness, they agreed to call a halt just after sunset. That far north, twilight lingered for nearly an hour, allowing time for finding or setting up shelters. Since they could not risk artificial light giving away their position, they did not allow torches or fires. A few of the refugees grumbled about the lack of hot food, but those malcontents were silenced by their fellows, who were grateful for the protection of soldiers. The civilians knew the sacrifices the dwarf army had already made for them, and knew the surviving soldiers would prefer to race ahead to the safety behind the thick, grim ancient stone walls of Magross.

Despite of most refugees expressing their gratitude, both Renhelm and Raddick chafed at how slowly the civilians were walking. Renhelm, concerned about how poorly the refugees climbed one moderate ridge on their journey, went so far as ordering the refugees drop anything not absolutely necessary, which caused arguments until Renhelm took the packs civilians were carrying one by one and rummaging through the contents himself, tossing out any items he considered to be not needed on the climb up to the fortress of Magross. In Renhelm's experienced opinion, that was almost everything. One dwarf argued when Renhelm tossed a pretty ceramic teapot onto a rock, shattering it. "That has been in my family for five generations!" The dwarf shouted angrily, needing to be restrained from striking the military leader.

"Aye, and if you wish there to be a sixth generation, you will toss aside anything that burdens you on this climb. You think these foothills are steep? Ha! You should see the *mountain* in front of us! The likes of you will be gasping for breath in the first hundred yards," he spat on the shattered teapot in disgust. Many mountain dwarves did not consider their cousins who lived in the relative flatlands of the valley just north of Tarador to be 'true' dwarves, even though the valley folk brought their livestock and harvested crops up to mountain villages for sale several times each year.

"Renhelm," Raddick whispered with a hand on the dwarf's arm, "a word, please."

When the dwarf stepped aside, he confronted Raddick. "This is no concern of yours."

"It is my concern, if arguments and discord slow us further. Most of these people are carrying oilcloth cloaks and extra blankets. It is, what, four days up to Magross?"

"Six or more, with us dragging this lot along," Renhelm grumbled sourly.

"The weather holds fine, and even up here will not likely snow so early," Raddick spoke from experience. "If these people wish to keep their precious possessions, tell them to wrap them in blankets and oilcloths to keep them dry, and we will stash everything under cover."

"Hmm," Renhelm considered the idea, not likely that a dwarf had to listen to a man from Tarador.

"And that means they will not be carrying heavy oilcloths and blankets they do not need," Raddick winked.

"Ah!" Renhelm chuckled. "Have it your way, but I want to get moving again in half a glass."

"Half a glass, no more," Raddick agreed, then hopped on a rock to be seen, and told the refugees what they needed to do to keep their precious possessions safe. Because one way or another, the civilians were not slowing down the entire column by dragging useless keepsakes with them, no matter the sentimental or monetary value. To the surprise of Renhelm but not Raddick, most people decided to keep their oilcloths in case of rain, and blankets to ward off nighttime cold, and discarded just about everything else.

Renhelm had to admit he was impressed. "You have a way with people," he offered as grudging praise to the Royal Army captain.

"Renhelm," Raddick replied with a sad shake of his head, "we in Tarador have all too much experience with moving frightened refugees," he said truthfully. He also said that because he wanted the dwarf leader to save face. It never paid to make enemies of allies, Tarador had enough enemies already.

"Aye," Renhelm puffed out his chest. "We have not suffered an invasion since, mmm, my great-great-grandfather's time? An invasion like this?" He pondered. "Never."

Raddick nodded, and waved for his men to resume climbing the ridge, prodding the refugees along. "That was a clever strategy by the enemy; they thrust into the lowlands between our peoples from east and west, cutting us off from each other. They knew your strategy would be to retreat up to your mountain strongholds as you have done since ancient times." Seeing as sideways look from Renhelm, Raddick added, "*Wisely* mustered your strength in mountain strongholds. The enemy knew the dukes in our northern provinces would not venture north of their borders to challenge the orcs. By invading and occupying only the lowland valleys, the orcs have effectively prevented our two peoples from aiding each other."

Renhelm considered that observation, scratching his beard. "Divide and conquer, eh? That is a good strategy. No such thought came from the mind of an orc!"

"I suspect the demon instructed the orcs to do its bidding," Raddick explained. "No matter. We are divided, now the enemy may conquer us each separately. Your ancient redoubts in the mountains are formidable, I know. I do not think even they will hold long after Tarador falls."

"This is *so* unfair," Olivia complained in shear exasperation, throwing up her hands. She knew her remark would be viewed by adults as overly dramatic and overly emotional, and typical of a young person who was not ready in terms of experience for adult responsibilities. Most people her age would be insulted by disparaging adult remarks about her lack of maturity, but to Olivia, such a response would not be an insult. It would be the whole point!

It *was* unfair. She was *not* ready for the crushing responsibility being dumped, being forced on her by wizards who should have been experienced and wise enough to know better. Olivia was in the very odd circumstance of arguing that she was indeed too young and inexperienced, too inadequately trained, too unready to be entrusted with such an important task. Most children her age were chafing at restrictions imposed on them by adults, and were eager to be treated as young adults rather than untrusted little girls and boys. "Go ahead," she said defiantly, jutting her chin forward, hands on her hips. "Say it. I'm a silly, weak little girl, and I should do as I'm told by the adults who know better."

"No," Madame Chu replied with a slight shake of her head and the barest of smiles. "You are not silly, or weak, or too immature for what we are asking you to do."

"But," Olivia's hands slipped and she pulled them back onto her hips. The master wizard had just thrown out Olivia's entire argument, and now she stood deflated. "But," she didn't know what to say. "I am *not* ready. You," having no idea where to take her argument, she crossed her arms silently and glared at Madame Chu.

"Olivia, you think we are giving you this responsibility because all the adult wizards have better things to do, and are desperately needed on the front lines of the battle? We," she caught herself, "*they*, are desperately needed, that is true. The enemy has more wizards arrayed against us than we can counter by sheer numbers, and the enemy trains their wizards only in the arts of destruction and deception. You know the enemy has more wizards than we because the demon *forces* power into its candidates. Anyone who shows the slightest ability to use magic is brought before the demon, so it can plant a spark of its essence inside them. Hundreds of candidates die in the process to create a single wizard and the demon does not care about the lives lost, it cares only for the destructive power at its command. The enemy has no wizards with the power to heal, none who are skilled in working with the natural world. Those few wizards we have who can wield magical fire are sorely needed on the front lines. We need *you* here."

"But," Olivia blinked back a tear. It was so frustrating, not being able to find the right words to make the master wizard see the truth that was right in front of her face. "Ariana is alive by the barest sliver of time. If I had been one second too late, if she had not been standing in front of that window-" Olivia shuddered. "If that servant boy had not been taking a shortcut through the courtyard at just the right time-"

"She *is* alive," Wing said gently.

"By luck!" Olivia protested. "I was nearly killed, very nearly killed by that assassin! An assassin with no magical powers, and I came within a hairsbreadth of being killed by a poisoned dagger. If that silly chief of protocol had not insisted the princess be served tea on a special, ancient tea set, I-"

"You were not killed, were you? That assassin was not totally without magical assistance; the enemy always equips his agents of evil with talismans and spells to enhance physical reactions, to block pain and fear, to remove all thought other than striking their targets. You are correct, Olivia, you were in very grave danger, more than you know. Yet," she smiled, "here you are. And the princess is alive and well to lead us today."

"By *luck*," Olivia insisted, arms across her chest, lower lip stuck out in defiance and dismay.

Madam Chu lowered her voice and glanced around to ensure no one could overhear her words. The four soldiers assigned to guard the master wizard knew when she wanted privacy and were standing a respectful distance away. One of them nodded when he met the wizard's eyes, gripping the hilt of his sword as if to say she could relax, for she was surrounded by the Royal Army. Wing flashed a brief smile back to the man, wishing to herself that she could feel safe enough to relax, but she could not. There were so many threats a dozen, or a hundred or more soldiers could not protect her from, no matter their fortitude and dedication. "For the past six days, we have been tracking a group of enemy wizards to the west of us. There are now a dozen of them, perhaps more," she bit her lower lip in concern. "We can't be certain of their exact numbers without giving away our own numbers, and our strength."

"They will attack us?" Olivia felt a chill despite the afternoon sunshine.

"Yes." Seeing Olivia's questioning, fearful look, Wing repeated the word, forcefully. "Yes. We know they will, we don't yet know when, or how. The unhappy truth is we cannot fight them with power against power. The enemy are concentrating their strength here to destroy our leadership with one blow, while our wizards are scattered across our frontier."

"Why?"

"Because the Royal Army of Tarador, even with help from allies," she gestured to the south, where the flag of the Indus Empire flew over an encampment holding almost a thousand soldiers from that distant land. "Cannot match the numbers the enemy has just across the river. Acedor's entire population is enslaved and dedicated to war, and their numbers are bolstered by orcs."

"We have the dwarves on our side," Oliva noted hopefully.

"We do," Wing flashed a sad smile. It was not the fault of Olivia that she did not know the full political situation; she was as yet too young to have learned everything an adult wizard had to know. "The dwarves are fully engaged in defending their own lands against the orcs. Because of the sacrifices the dwarves have made over centuries, the orc host we face across the River Fasse is much weaker than the full strength the orcs could throw at us. We have heard from our wizard counterparts amongst the dwarves; their army is hard-pressed and giving ground, retreating back through high mountain passes to their strongholds in the higher elevations. Even now, orcs are sweeping down from the north, crossing the border there and into Tarador's northern provinces."

"Can we stop them?"

"Yes," Wing sighed. "Part of the Royal Army is up north, fighting with the ducal armies to slow the orcs' advance, and working to evacuate civilians. Olivia, the enemy knows we will not stand by while orcs and foul men slaughter innocent people, so we must disperse our strength to protect Tarador's borders to the north, west and south. While we bleed away our strength all along our border," she stabbed the soil beneath her feet with her staff, "the enemy concentrates their strength to hit us with one massive blow. The demon cares only about crushing Tarador's army, and the easiest way to do that is to remove Ariana as our leader. Without her, the dukes and duchesses of Tarador's seven provinces would fall to fighting amongst themselves, and the Royal Army would be divided and weak."

"Then why," Olivia balled up her fists in anguish, "do you want *me* to protect her? If the princess is so important," she lowered her voice in response to Madame Chu waving her hands for quiet. "Why don't *you* guard her? She would be safe with you."

"She will be safe with you also. Your strength is greater than you know."

"Not great enough!" She pouted, crossing her arms and sticking out her lower lip. She was being childish and she knew it and she didn't care. She was still at least partly a child, though circumstances had forced her to grow up quickly, too quickly.

Madame Chu reminded herself to be patient with the trainee wizard. When Wing had been Olivia's age, she lived behind the walls of the wizard's compound on a hill overlooking the capital city of Ching-Do. She spent her days slowly and carefully learning the skills of wizardry in the ornate halls and lush gardens of the compound. Not until she had been five years older than Olivia had Wing ventured out into the countryside as an apprentice wizard, testing her skills in the real world, and making mistakes under the kind and watchful eye of a master wizard. Wing had been born in happier times, when wizards had been given proper time to learn their craft. Even one year ago, asking Olivia Dupres to assume adult responsibilities would have been unthinkable. Now, it was unavoidable. "Olivia, I am needed to the west, where we will fight those enemy wizards directly. You *cannot* come with us, it is much too dangerous."

"But-"

"You would only hinder us, and make one of us spend our energies protecting you rather than fighting the enemy. You don't want that, do you?" Wing added gently.

"No," Olivia's tone reflected her misery. "Madame Chu, I just feel so useless, babysitting the princess here in a camp with thousands of soldiers protecting us, while you fight. I could do so much more! I could learn *so* much if I were with you."

"I would not have time to instruct you," Wing laughed bitterly. "You will be doing much more than babysitting, as you call it. While I am away, there is something I need you to do-"

"Yes!" The young wizard exclaimed eagerly.

"You don't know it is yet," Wing allowed herself a ghost of a smile.

"I don't care. It has to be better than acting as a second shadow for the princess while she does," she waved a hand in disgust, "royal things." Since the assassination attempt at the palace, Olivia had been spending almost every waking moment with the young Regent, and seeing what Ariana Trehayme's days were like destroyed any illusions Olivia had about the life of a princess. While Olivia's own life as a wizard was occasionally as exciting as she expected, it wasn't exciting often enough, and it was not nearly as glamorous. In fact, it was disappointingly not glamorous at all. From what Olivia had seen, the life of the princess was certainly glamorous, with her opulent palace and carriages and an array of courtiers, but Ariana's life was surprisingly, insufferably *boring*. The poor girl spent most of her time reading dull messages and having mind-numbing discussions about crop yields and finances and relations with neighboring heads of state, and other things that made Olivia's head nod with oncoming sleep even in the mornings. From the expressions on the face of the princess and the little weary sighs she made when she thought no one could hear, Ariana also was crushingly bored with her twin responsibilities as crown princess and Regent. "If I have to sit beside the princess one more time, while she decides what sort of trinket is appropriate to give baroness so-and-so for her birthday, I am going to turn *someone* into a toad, and I don't care who it is!"

That time, Wing did not have to force herself to smile. "I am sure Ariana finds such trivial decisions just as tedious." Her expression turned serious again. "What I need you to do is dangerous, it may be very dangerous. It is also vital, so you should consider me entrusting you with this task to be a measure of my faith in you, your courage and your skills."

The master wizard's words chilled Olivia. Sitting next to the princess and being bored out of her mind was, she reflected, still better than being blown through a window and nearly drowned in the filthy water of a moat. What was the expression Olivia's mother used to say? Be careful what you wish for, because you just might get it. She swallowed, her mouth suddenly dry. "What do you need me to do?"

"Koren," Thomas whispered to the boy, with his hand over Koren's mouth to stifle a startled shout, "Captain wants you."

"Uh," Koren shook his sleep-befuddled head. "I'm up." That was an exaggeration, he was so tired after only four hours of sleep that he was barely aware of his own name.

"Good. Follow me." Keeping low and moving quietly in the faint predawn light, Thomas carefully led the way forward to where Raddick was huddled in a shallow hole behind a rock.

"Koren, one of the dwarf sentries thinks he heard something. I want you up there," he pointed to a slightly less dark area in the darkness, where the forested mountain ridge gave way to skyline. "You can move almost silently, I've seen that. Can you do it?"

"Yes, Captain." Koren had not been aware his movements were especially quiet, he had only been following the fieldcraft examples of Raddick's chosen men.

"It's probably only mountain sheep wandering in the darkness," Raddick squeezed Koren's shoulder with a grin. "Oh," he added, "and don't think of shooting one of those sheep for our breakfast, we can't have a whole flock of sheep making noise."

Koren moved from one rock to another, avoiding any dry vegetation that might snap under his feet. He knew to test the balance of a rock before putting his full weight on it, lest the rock slip and fall with a clatter. When he approached the lone dwarf sentry, his keen eyes caught the gleam of a razor-sharp arrow tip. He gave the pass signal; hooting like an owl twice, plus the hand signal for that day. The arrow lowered, and he could barely see the answering hand signal. He said nothing when he ducked down beside the dwarf, and the dwarf also did not speak. Using standard dwarf army hand gestures that

Koren had quickly learned the basics of, the dwarf indicated from which direction he had heard the sound.

Koren knew not to still his breathing completely for too long, as that would only make blood pound in his ears. He stilled himself, breathing evenly with a pause before exhaling. In the darkness, he closed his eyes, but heard nothing. After what he judged a full two minutes, he shook his head. The dwarf insisted he wait, gesturing emphatically.

Koren followed the dwarf's order, though he was not truly subject to orders from the dwarves. The sentry had sat long hours in the cold while Koren huddled asleep under a blanket, at least Koren could humor the sentry by remaining there a while longer, though his stomach was grumbling for breakfast. In the darkness, he put a hand to his mouth from embarrassment when his stomach squeaked loud enough for the dwarf to hear. Koren almost laughed, catching himself by biting the inside of his cheek. He would not shame his fellow-

What was that? Koren grasped the dwarf's arm and pointed with his other hand, his finger wavering one way then another as he located the source of the sound. There wasn't one source of sound, it was coming from several places in the darkness in front of him. Whatever was creating the sound, it was not close. Then there was a louder sound, like a rock being dislodged and falling onto another rock with a sharp 'clack'. The dwarf next to him nodded, he had heard that also.

Koren strained to hear more, wishing he could stand up from the cover the sentry had chosen, but he dared not. Orcs could see well in the dark, nearly as well as dwarves. Koren hoped even the night vision of dwarves was no match for his magical eyesight, but since he really didn't know how to use magic, perhaps his abilities were not as they should be? The sentry post was in a good spot, in a shallow depression where a great tree had fallen over, at the edge of the wooded patch where the group had rested for the night. The roots of the tree were sticking up out of the hole, and the sentry had cut branches to jam into crevices in the rotting wood of the roots, providing more cover. Koren nodded to himself in the darkness, admiring the dwarf's good thinking and experience. In the gentle early morning breeze, the branches swayed back and forth, their still-green leaves rustling softly. The swaying of the leaves would distract any watchful enemy eyes from Koren's own motion, if he moved carefully. Inching slowly, ever so slowly upward, Koren got his eyes and ears above the dead tree root in front of him. The sounds were louder now, still not distinct enough for him to tell what was causing the noise.

And, blast it! Behind him, the refugee camp was beginning to awaken, dwarves seeing the dim line of pink in the eastern sky that heralded the coming sunrise. They rose and began walking around on legs sore from climbing mountains for days, and stiff from sleeping on bare ground in the nighttime chill at altitude. He could hear stones being clumsily kicked in the darkness, and muffled curses, and the harsh whispers of soldiers telling the refugees to stay where they were and be silent. Koren knew the dwarves could not help making noise, no group of a hundred beings could move around and start their day in complete silence, but he gritted his teeth because the sounds from behind him were distracting him from listening to what was in front of him. If the 'threat' he was listening for was only mountain sheep, Koren was going to feel very-

Another clacking clatter of rock on rock followed by a dull thud, and, sending a chill up Koren's spine, a harsh curse word. Directly after, another thud, this time ending in a metallic ringing sound. Koren imagined what he had heard was someone tripping, causing rocks to scatter, the person falling down and shouting a curse. That last sound had to be a second person striking the first with the flat of a sword as punishment for making noise, with the sword blade ringing from the blow.

Beside him, the sentry's eyes were wide, the whites showing bright even before the false dawn of early morning. The dwarf leaned toward Koren. "That was no sheep nor goat," he stated the obvious.

No, it was not a sheep, nor anything that walked on four legs. Though whoever was out there unseen in the darkness had spoken only one word, and a short curse at that, Koren had no question what he had heard: an orc! Where there was one, there were sure to be more. Koren made the hand signal for orcs, waited for the sentry to acknowledge he understood the clumsy sign language, then the sentry slowly ducked down and crawled away to report. A minute later, Koren was joined by Renhelm and Raddick, with Koren pleased to hear the Royal Army captain made no more noise than the dwarf. Renhelm made a hand signal indicating he wished to talk, so Koren ducked down. "Orcs!" Koren spoke barely enough to be heard. "One at least for certain, likely two or more of them out there?"

"Where?" Renhelm asked, daring to look above the cluster of roots. The ground in front of the sentry post sloped downward and was bare of tree cover, that was why the sentry had chosen that particular spot. Down the mountain and a quarter mile away was another line of fir trees, a deeper black in the darkness.

"I can't see anything moving out in the open," Koren reported. "They must be in the cover of those trees?"

Renhelm chewed on his mustache while he thought. If he sent out scouts now, they would be caught in the open between the treelines when the sun rose. He tapped Raddick on the arm and the two soldiers crawled back away from the sentry post, to a dense grove of shrubs where they could talk. "We're in a tight spot here," Renhelm declared unhappily.

"Aye," Raddick agreed, glad for once that he was not in command, did not have the responsibility. The dwarf lieutenant faced an agonizing decision, if they had been detected by orcs during the night. He could attempt to slip away with a hundred refugees who were already desperately weary, knowing that would likely to be disastrous for everyone in the group. Or he could abandon most of the civilians, ordering them to scatter, and strive to break away with his soldiers in the confusion. That second plan was, Raddick knew, the only realistic chance of anyone reaching the safety of the Magross fortress. The cold logic of that second plan could not be argued with, but it did not set well with Raddick's heart, nor his soldier's sense of honor.

What mattered most was they did not *know* if their group had been seen or heard, although the continued clumsy movements of the civilians made Raddick wince and he knew sooner rather than later, any orcs within earshot would hear over a hundred dwarves making their way through the forest.

Raddick remained silent while his dwarf counterpart considered his options, but the Royal Army man watched the dwarf's eyes in the dim light. He saw Renhelm was watching the refugees stumble around in the predawn darkness, bumping against trees, dropping their packs, tripping over roots and rocks. Soldiers gestured frantically for everyone to remain still and be silent, but without lights, far too many of the dwarves did not get the message until too late. Raddick imagined he could see the wheels turning in Renhelm's mind, and he knew the terrible decision the dwarf was about to make.

"We don't know if the orcs have spotted us," Raddick whispered. "Not for certain."

Renhelm appeared startled that Raddick had spoken. "If they haven't yet, they will soon," he pointed toward the hazy triangle of light extending above the eastern horizon, visible through gaps in the trees. Then he looked up at the gently swaying fir trees, hearing the wind softly whistling through the needles. "I suppose we have to try," the dwarf said, his humble and uncertain words not conveying the courage it took to give voice to his decision.

"We could go back," Raddick used a thumb to indicate downhill to the southeast. "Stay in this tree cover until we get back to that stream, then climb the backside of this ridge? If the orcs stay west of the ridgeline, they won't see us." His weary mind struggled to recall details of the land they'd walked through early the previous evening, before setting up camp for the night in the welcoming grove of trees.

"Mm," Renhelm grunted. "*If.* Thank you, Captain. I'll have my men get the civilians on the move quietly as possible, will your people keep watch?"

"Agreed," Raddick nodded, and slipped away to give orders.

CHAPTER TWELVE

Koren's orders were to remain where he was, his impatiently grumbling stomach having to be satisfied with a bite of tough bread he dug out of his pack. Chewing on the bread and sipping from his water flask, he scanned the treeline across the open rock field, seeing more details as they morning sky brightened. The sun had not risen but the soft light of false dawn hung in the sky, and Koren knew this light heralded the true dawn in an hour. He kept his eyes slowly moving back and forth from one end of the treeline, looking for movement. His father had taught him while hunting that eyes were better at seeing movement than anything else, so Koren swept his eyes left to right and back again, knowing the orcs huddled under those fir trees were doing the same, looking for movement in his direction. He was confident the cover of branches moving in the morning breeze would fool the eyes of anyone looking toward him, although he moved as little and as slowly as he could.

He had not heard any more suspicious sounds, stilling his breathing regularly to listen for any sounds that did not belong on the mountainside. Either the enemy under those trees had settled in to wait for dawn, or, as Koren hoped, they had moved on. He did not bother indulging himself in the foolish hope that what he had heard was another group of lost dwarves rather than orcs.

He wished he did not hear any noise coming from behind him either, but that was not at all true. Every time there was a grunt or a conversation whispered too loudly or something dropped on the ground or a thump as someone bumped into a tree in the dark, Koren gritted his teeth. He knew his hearing was much more sensitive than that of an orc, and the orcs were far enough away that most sounds would not carry that far. He knew the increasing breeze stirring the trees and whistling through the fir trees covered up much of the noises made by the dwarves, but he also knew it was only a matter of time before someone shouted in pain as they bashed a knee on a rock, or dropped something noisy like a cooking pot. Or until a child cried. Even if by some miracle the civilians slipped away as Captain Raddick told Koren they hoped, the orcs in the woods across the rock-strewn open area could not fail to check the dark grove of trees where Koren was laying on his belly. No orc could fail to see the ground had been disturbed under the trees; they could not fail to understand a large party of dwarves had been there recently. And they would certainly follow the trampled underbrush.

Koren reached out and touched his bow for reassurance, then bit off another piece of the tough bread. He needed to refill his water flask at the first clean mountain stream he came across, the thought of cold fresh water making his parched mouth-

Movement! He saw something moving under the fir trees! This was no branch or bush swaying in the breeze, this was the dark shape of *something* moving under the dark trees. Koren was about to turn around to crawl back to report what he'd seen when he heard soft footfalls he recognized as belonging to Raddick. The Royal Army captain shook Koren's outstretched foot then eased himself up next to the young wizard. "Captain Sir, I saw something moving."

"Not an animal?" Raddick's tone held no hope that could be true.

"Taller, not as tall as a man. It was there only briefly, I- there's another one. Different place this time, I don't think it is the same one. Too far apart."

"The civilians need time to get away," Raddick's voice reflected his anguish.

"Sir," Koren decided it was time to be bold. "If I go up there," he pointed up the mountain, north of the fir trees where the orcs were hiding, "I could shoot down on them when they come out into this open area. If I can discourage them from coming under these trees-"

"Yes, then they won't see signs we camped here overnight." Raddick's stomach churned. His orders stated explicitly '*You shall take no risks with the safety of Koren Bladewell*' and in his career he had seldom been given orders that were so entirely clear. They were also not entirely realistic, for Raddick knew from experience that in the field, there was no such thing as *no* risk. The idea of sending Koren, alone or with soldiers, out from cover to put himself at risk by shooting at orcs was incredibly foolish.

But doing that might just be what Raddick needed to get himself out of a sticky dilemma. He needed to get away from Renhelm and the civilians. The refugees were a problem but they were not *his* problem. He was not a mercenary hiring his services to the highest bidder, he was a captain of the Royal Army and he followed orders rather than his own whims, even when following orders felt dishonorable or cowardly at times. "Wait here," he whispered to Koren, then slipped back toward where Renhelm was growing increasingly frustrated and anxious at the slow and clumsy pace of the civilians. Dwarf soldiers were rousting civilians who were still sleeping with a hand over their mouths and whispered warning. Civilians who were already awake and aware of their perilous situation muffled their fellows who were startled out of slumber without a soldier nearby. Parents stifled the cries of their children, even when mothers had tears streaming down their faces from being unable to comfort a child. Renhelm's soldiers were doing the best they could and the civilians were cooperating as best they could, but it wasn't enough. The ghostly white triangle light of false dawn was fading and the sky in that area was beginning to turn rosy pink as sunrise approached, too soon.

"We'll not be far enough from here by first light," Renhelm snorted, and wiped away a tear of his own.

"I have an idea about that. I propose to take my men up the mountain through these woods, then cut across the open area when we're high enough not to be seen by those orcs. We will work our way down, then my archers will hit them when the orcs come out from cover. We can pin them down for a while, discourage them from investigating these woods."

"The orcs will pursue you," Renhelm warned.

"I expect so," Raddick agreed, alarmed he could clearly see the dwarf's expression even under the trees. Dawn would be coming soon. "We can lead them away from you. Without being slowed down by civilians, I am confident we can stay ahead of orcs, and I will look for an opportunity to lose them higher up the mountain."

"You will make for Magross?" Renhelm asked, searching the man's eyes and knowing he was not being completely truthful about something.

"If we can, yes. Will you tell me how to find this secret ravine that leads to the valley?"

"I can't. It's a secret, I'd be committing treason by telling you. My plan was to blindfold you when we were close. It's well hidden," he shrugged, "I couldn't explain it even if I was allowed to."

Raddick gritted his teeth. "Magross, then," he lied, having no intention of being trapped in a dwarf fortress over the winter, perhaps longer.

"I can lead the way, Captain," Koren pointed to his eyes when Raddick had gathered his people. "I can see-"

Raddick held up a hand for silence. "Yes, you can see exceptionally well, and that means you might lead us through paths the rest of us cannot follow. Lem will lead," Raddick gestured for their lead scout to go ahead.

"Yes, Sir," Koren blushed in the dark, chagrinned because he knew Raddick was right. Koren's unnatural eyesight, hearing and sense of balance allowed him to move quickly and quietly in places where the others might stumble and trip over their own feet.

Bjorn tapped Koren's shoulder and whispered "You can lead me, my night eyes are not what they used to be."

Koren looked with guilt at the last civilian stragglers, seeing one elderly dwarf limping and leaning on a walking stick, shuffling along as best he could while one of Renhelm's soldiers urged the trailing group to move quickly. "We're not leaving the dwarves, are we?"

"Captain said we're to lead the orcs away from them," Bjorn replied. "Best thing for those dwarves is if the orcs never come into these woods and get on their trail."

"I know, but-"

"But nothing, young lad," Bjorn made a cutting motion with one hand. "You heard what the Captain said; Tarador needs you if we're to survive this war. How many lives will be lost if Tarador falls? More than the hundred here. That's what Captain Raddick needs to think about, you don't go making his task any harder."

"Yes, Bjorn," Koren forced himself to look away from the dwarves. He hoped he never needed to make such terrible decisions, and fearing he soon would.

Lem disappeared into the darkness and each soldier filed past Raddick, bouncing on their toes as the captain checked nothing each soldier carried would jingle or otherwise make a noise. Swords were cinched tightly in scabbards, with scabbards strapped across backs so they would not swing free or snag on underbrush. Arrows were tied together in their quivers, and all contents of packs had been hurriedly tucked into bedrolls. Such preparations made their weapons and other gear less available for ready use, but Raddick did not intend to engage in combat until he was ready. He would keep his promise to Renhelm to lead the orcs away from the refugees, but not at the cost of risking Koren's life, or risking the boy being captured.

Satisfied and proud that his people had all secured their gear, Raddick gave the hand signal to follow Lem. With one last look backward at the still-unruly gaggle of civilian dwarves retreating down the path they had so wearily ascended the evening before, Raddick turned to take up the rear, following Bjorn. He could not only see Bjorn, he could identify the man by his hair and the cap he wore. That told Raddick dawn was fast approaching, and they had no time to waste.

With Lem leading the way, they kept within the tree cover, even when the treeline bent in the wrong direction for a short distance. Raddick approved cutting through the open only where the trees dwindled away and low ground allowed the team to crouch down for the passage where they might otherwise be seen. Then it was back under the welcome cover of fir trees, a grove growing together so densely that it made for slow going. No matter, they only needed to climb another hundred yards before cresting a ridge, then they dared walk out in the open where rocks and low-growing shrubs clinging to crevices provided the only hiding places. From there, Raddick insisted on leading the way downward, approaching from above the grove of trees where the orcs were hidden.

By then, dawn was imminent, the sun not yet above the horizon though Raddick could clearly see individual trees in the grove in front of them. He halted and called Koren to him. The area offered poor cover, Raddick would not risk taking his people any farther down the mountainside. Behind them, it was more than a quarter mile up to the nearest tree cover. "Is this close enough?"

"Sir?" Koren asked, confused.

"Close enough for shooting," Raddick added, mildly exasperated. "Can you hit them from here?"

"Oh, yes, Sir. Unless they're down at the very bottom of that grove."

"We shall assume they are not," Raddick declared the discussion closed. He was taking as much risk as he was comfortable with, as much risk as he could justify to keep an escape route while keeping his promise to Renhelm. "Ready your bow," he whispered and gave the same order by hand signal to the others.

Bjorn took the arrows out of Koren's quiver, knowing the boy had carefully inspected each one the previous day. After laying the arrows on dry ground, he removed the dozen arrows from his own quiver and selected the six best, passing them to Koren. The boy sighted along each one and tested them for balance, keeping one eye on the treeline. Five were acceptable, so Bjorn added them to the row in front of himself. When it came time for battle, Bjorn's task would be to feed arrows to Koren quickly and smoothly so the young wizard could concentrate on choosing targets and aiming. To be ready, Bjorn took three arrows in his hands for he had seen the blinding speed Koren could shoot, one arrow being fitted to the bowstring while one was still in flight. "Ready?"

Koren answered with a curt nod, his focus on scanning the treeline. The position they had chosen was good for shooting once Koren stood, but less than ideal for keeping watch on the orcs. Raddick was not concerned, once the orcs came into the open Koren's extra sharp vision would not be needed.

Three other soldiers were ready as archers, though Raddick planned for them to only threaten the enemy, and be ready if the orcs were to charge at them. Unless the orcs came out of the trees near him, Raddick did not want to waste arrows at long range. From what Bjorn had told him, and what he had seen when Koren chased away the orcs while Shomas lay gravely injured, the arrows from Koren's bow alone should cause the orcs to flee back into the trees. Orcs could be-

Two orcs stepped out of the treeline together, crouching down and moving with a shuffling gait that looked awkward but did not hinder them. The two scouts hopped from one rock to another, using what cover they could find, shuffling along rocks and stepping over shrubs. It surprised Raddick as it always did when he saw how fluidly they moved for such sickly-looking creatures. These orcs wore leather vest made from the skin of unfortunate animals Raddick preferred not to think about, and his eye picked up a glint of reflection from otherwise rusted chainmail under their vests. The type of chainmail preferred by orcs was made of thicker, heavier and less finely-crafted metal than the type used by the Royal Army, but it was just as able to stop an arrowhead or to blunt a sword cut. Koren had been warned not to aim for the chests or bellies of orcs but the warning was not needed, the boy had replied he knew where to aim, and that he never missed.

Never.

If Raddick had concern that his little company relied on the skill of one boy, he did not give voice to his fears. The two scouts were joined by three other orcs, coming out of the treeline one by one, strung out in a line. The scouts were headed straight for the grove of trees where the dwarves had spent the night, though at an angle uphill. In Raddick's mind, that meant the orcs were simply scouting likely hiding places rather than being on the track of known prey, and for a tense moment he considered letting the orcs pass by, then discarded the idea. Once in the woods, the orcs would spread out and could hardly fail to see the trampled underbrush, broken branches and items inevitably left behind in the darkness by a large group of dwarves. If it were at all likely those orcs could pass on up the mountain without noticing the presence of dwarves, Raddick could consider his promise to Renhelm kept without putting his own people at risk. As it was not likely they could have such unhoped-for good luck that morning, Raddick sighed to himself and gave the signal to engage the enemy. Bjorn acknowledged Raddick's order and nudged Koren, who nodded without breaking concentration. In fact, though the boy smoothly rose to his knees behind the bush he used as cover, he kept the bowstring pulled back for a long moment. Too long.

Keeping behind cover, Raddick crawled to Koren and hissed urgently in the boy's ear. "Now?" The two scouts were uncomfortably close, and one of them stopped suddenly to sniff the air.

"Not yet." Koren replied with a frown.

"When?" Raddick was concerned by how long the boy had held back the heavy bowstring, although the young wizard's arm was not shaking at all. "How do you know when the time is right?"

"I don't know how I know. I just *know*," Koren's confidence was fading as he spoke. Now that he knew he was a wizard, he was always ready for the spirits to fail him, to ignore his needs, his silent pleas for help. He would know only when he never sensed the moment was right to release the arrow, and that would be too late. Raddick was right, the nearest of the orcs was too close already and sniffing the air suspiciously. The creature could not be detecting the scent of the Royal Army soldiers for the breeze was blowing across the mountainside, but the scent of over a hundred unwashed dwarves would be a powerful lure to a band of orc hunters seeking blood.

Koren pleaded with the spirits to aid him but they did not respond, if they heard him at all. Losing focus, Koren turned to look at Raddick, his eyes wide open with fear that he had failed them and all of Tarador. The captain kept his cool, merely gesturing for Koren to resume his duty. When Koren looked back, the closest orc was partially behind a tall, thin rock, so Koren switched aim to the last of the five and-

The bowstring twanged as the arrow flew. Koren had no time for register his shock before Bjorn slapped an arrow into his free hand and he automatically fitted it to the bowstring, pulling back smoothly and turning to the left, the second arrow launched into flight before Koren realized he had selected a target. By the time he had aimed at a third orc, the first arrow found its mark, hitting the orc's exposed neck with a sickening wet splat. The second target turned its head slightly in puzzlement at the odd sound when an arrow thudded right into its unprotected armpit and it fell backward with a strangled cry. The third orc was even less fortunate, the arrow aimed at it was flying directly at the stout leather vest and chainmail of its chest, when that orc dove for the ground in panic and the arrow instead hit it squarely in the forehead.

Bjorn's fingers trembled when he realized Koren had aimed not at the third orc's head, but where that orc's head *would be* when the arrow arrived. Such unnatural power was frightening, and Bjorn had to force his hands to still so he could place another arrow into Koren's waiting hand.

"Can you get him?" Raddick asked Koren as the captain pointed to one of the two surviving orcs, who had both ducked for cover at the sudden deaths of their three fellows. Both orcs howled, a terrible sound that sent chills up even Raddick's spine. They were calling other orcs, and the blood-curdling shrieks echoed off the mountainside.

"Not from here," Koren replied without explanation, "but," he released another arrow and was rewarded by a high-pitched wail. His quarry had been huddled behind a rock but one boot was showing, and that boot now had an arrow through from one side to another. The orc jerked, unable to pull the exposed foot behind cover because the arrow shaft was tangled in the branches of a stubborn shrub. Reaching down with both hands to grasp the boot was rewarded by yet another arrow slamming between the bones of one forearm, pinning that hand to the orc's shin. In agony, it rolled upward where a final arrow pierced the side of its skull, dropping it instantly dead.

Bjorn broke the momentary silence. "See, that's why *I* wear a helmet," he said without a trace of humor, but the unexpected remark and the release of tension caught the soldiers off guard, and they exploded with laughter.

"Helmet-" Raddick choked, his dry throat unprepared for hearty laughter.

"Well, it's true," Bjorn seemed surprised by the reaction to his offhand remark, then he too chuckled.

"Koren," Raddick brought himself back to the task at hand, which was the lone surviving orc, who ironically had been the closest. The creature was now running away, dashing from cover to cover and unleashing arrows of its own. The arrows were hurriedly aimed if aimed at all, though one came close enough to make Lem dive down for his life.

"I see it," Koren blinked to clear a tear of laughter from one eye. "This one is clever," he announced, worried. The orc was quick and skilled, it knew how to move through the terrain so there was almost no break in cover, no opportunity for Koren to get a clear shot.

"We can't let it get away," Raddick said with concern, for the creature was still howling for help, and faintly echoing answering cries were now coming from down the mountain. "Thomas, go to the right and cut it off from the treeline, we'll surround it if we have to."

"Can you hit it?" Raddick inquired of Koren, not liking to risk his people. The orc had arrows, and in close quarters orcs could be dangerous as a cornered snake. "Ah, this is impossible," he grimaced, judging he had asked too much even of a wizard archer. "If you can't-" He was interrupted when the creature's howl was abruptly cut off in mid-cry. It had dashed between two rocks and found an arrow waiting for it, an arrow that had plunged through its neck and wedged in the crevice of a rock, holding the dead orc upright as its dark red blood soaked the ground.

"The spirits say it is *not* impossible." Koren asked with a grin.

"No one likes a show-off," Raddick scolded while shaking a finger, but he could not hold back a relieved answering grin. "We're moving," he ordered simply, not needing to explain further. The soldiers gathered their arrows and secured the quivers tightly so they could move without making noise, and without a word, followed Raddick back up the way they had come down.

"It would be better for us to be back under cover of those woods," Bjorn suggested, nodding toward the grove of fir trees where they had spent the short, uncomfortable night. Before Raddick could answer, Bjorn spoke. "But we need the orcs to see us and follow us, if we are to keep your promise to the dwarves."

"Exactly," Raddick said simply. He pointed to the ridgeline above, while listening to the howls of orcs that were growing louder and closer. "I would like to be way up there when we allow them to see us, rather than down here."

"Agreed," Bjorn was already getting short of breath from the climb, and the mountainside was only getting steeper the higher they climbed.

By mid-morning, Bjorn was regretting Raddick's sense of honor. Not that he himself would have acted differently, but if their captain had been slightly less honorable about keeping their bargain with the dwarves, it might have saved Bjorn from a lot of serious trouble.

When the Royal Army party reached the ridgeline, with even young Koren huffing and puffing out of breath, they discovered there was another, higher and steeper ridge above, with only patchy groves of short fir trees for concealment. The situation was less than ideal, yet Raddick ordered the party to halt, exposed on the ridgeline, while the excited hunting cries of orcs grew ever more loud. To Raddick's great frustration, when a dozen orcs burst from the treeline, they were above where Koren had stood to shoot the scouting party, and the hunting party did at first not see the bodies of the dead scouts. The hunters were crossing the open area, headed directly for the grove of trees where they would surely see signs that dwarves had sent the previous night! Raddick could not shout for attention, that being too obvious an attempt get the hunters to chase them, but he did not know what else to do. The distance was much too far for an arrow to reach the hunters, and Raddick was at a loss for ideas when Lem reached inside his vest for a signaling mirror.

With that highly-polished disk of metal, he caught the light of the morning sun and flashed it toward the hunters, but the stupid creatures ignored him, their eyes on the ground looking for broken twigs and footprints. Several orcs were on their knees, noses snuffling the ground, when one of them saw light glinting off Lem's mirror and gave a warning cry. Almost at the same time, another orc spotted the bodies of the scouts, and immediately, the hunters began racing up the mountain toward the Royal Army party, leaping from rock to rock with alarming speed.

CHAPTER THIRTEEN

The wizard of Acedor shifted from his concealment under a thorny briar bush, a location chosen because even diligent patrols of the Taradoran Royal Army would be reluctant to go amongst the dense patch of briars. To have any chance of detecting the presence of the enemy wizard would require soldiers to go deep into the thicket, even crawling on hands and knees where the bushes grew so closely together even a small animal would have trouble wriggling its way into the maze. Or so it seemed. There truly was a thicket of briars in the low ground sloping down toward a muddy, overgrown creek, but the shrubs thinned out farther in as the briars grew under the shade of tall trees. To patrolling soldiers, the thicket appeared impenetrable because that is what the enemy wizard wished them to see. He had crawled along the creek bottom into the heart of the briars, and slowly and carefully woven a spell to discourage inquisitive soldiers. That particular spell was rather sophisticated and subtle for a wizard of Acedor, who as a group typically relied on raw destructive power and fear to do their dark master's bidding. To enhance the effect of the seldom-used spell, the wizard had cut briars from the heart of the thicket and placed them packed tightly together a few feet from the outer edge of the thorns, so hands reaching into the bushes to push aside branches would encounter thorns everywhere. Using cut briars was a trick that could work only for a few days, more than that and soldiers passing by would wonder why some of the briars had drooping, dead leaves. A few days was more than the wizard would need; he knew from listening to passing patrols that the Royal Army was scheduled to encamp in the area no more than two nights before packing up their tents and moving on to the west. Simple tricks like using cut branches as camouflage were necessary, for the wizard's skill in concealment was untested, and his ability to weave spells could fool only the eye, not a soldier's hands. A person seeing thickly tangled briars in front of his eyes, but whose hand passed through empty air, would know something was very wrong.

The wizard had endured four days of waiting in the briar patch, remaining still, not making any sound, ignoring biting insects and a chilly night of rain followed by blazing hot sun the following afternoon. He sipped water from a flask during the day, crawling on his belly down to the stream at night to refill the flask. For food, all he had were small, leathery and bitter-tasting loaves of bread that he moistened with water to chew, but he did not need much food and had little appetite. Food and water were requirements of the body because of the mortal body's weakness; his dark master had almost no use for such things and the wizard aspired to emulate the supremely powerful demon. Zeal to serve his master gave the wizard strength, that and hatred of the weak and pitiful enemies of Acedor.

Sensing his body's weakness, ashamed and disgusted by such mortal concerns, the wizard opened the flask and drank deeply of water. Looking at the sun, he judged it was still an hour before Noon and the day would be warm and sunny. With the prospect of the sun beating down on him all afternoon, he reluctantly took a small loaf of bread from his pack and set to eating it between sips of water, his jaw growing sore after only a few bites. After the sun set, he would need all his energy, for that very night he would strike.

"Good evening, Your Highness, Your Ladyship," a guard said as the crown princess and her wizard bodyguard passed through the temporary fence around the large tent reserved for the princess. The fence itself, consisting of ropes strung between posts set into the ground, was more for a show of royal dignity than for security. The fence had been set up to keep away annoying courtiers, who somehow managed to accompany the princess any time she left Linden. The real security for the princess was the troop of guards who patrolled the fence day and night, alert for intruders or anyone or any *thing* that should not be allowed in the presence of the girl who was both crown princess and Regent of Tarador. For that purpose, the fence was useful in providing a physical barrier inside which only a few people were authorized to be, and the guards knew all the people privileged to be on the list of visitors allowed to approach the tent.

"Good evening," Ariana replied, holding up a hand to stifle a yawn, her jaw stretching regardless of her effort. It had been a long day of meetings both consequential and mundane, vital meetings for planning the next move of the Royal Army, and tedious meetings to deal with internal politics of the realm. Even marching with the army, going west toward a battle that might very well be the final battle in the long war against Tarador's ancient enemy, Ariana still had to deal with petty jealousies and intrigues of the royal court.

Ertau instinctively hissed out of pure hatred before he could control his emotions, knowing his dark master would punish him for making a sound guards might overhear. The source of his rage was the witch coming out of the royal tent, the young witch's fair blonde hair glowing gold in the torchlight where the night breeze blew her hair out from under the hood of her cloak.

That witch needed to die, soon, and Ertau burned inside with a terrible fire to see her take her last breath. Olivia Dupres was not Ertau's target that night, but once he had performed the task assigned to him by the all-powerful demon, he would be free to expend his own considerable power and hatred in killing anyone he wished, anyone within his sight. All the adult wizards were away to the west in a vain attempt to match power with the overwhelming force of wizards Acedor had gathered to block the Royal Army's path. Those fourteen wizards, all masters of dark magic but none of them able to weave the more subtle forms of spells such as concealment, had not crossed the border and assembled merely to challenge the pitiful strength of Tarador in an outright physical contest. The fourteen wizards were together so they could combine their power and send it through the spirit world to Ertau. Alone, he could not hope to create and hold a spell of concealment strong enough, cunning enough, to slip him past the magical wards around the tent where the crown princess lay sleeping.

Ertau held his breath as the arrogant, *impertinent* young witch passed out through the ring of guards, on whatever errand took her away from the princess at that late hour. It may be expected the witch was too young to know she had no business challenging the dark master of Acedor, that the true and proper place of her and all her fellow wizards was to offer themselves and their service to the demon. It may be that her arrogance and ignorance was not her fault, that she was young and her mind had been poisoned by evil wizards of Tarador. Ertau had no patience with such soft thinking; the witch was an enemy of his dark master and she had to die, he would show no weakness of his own by showing her mercy.

The wizard of Acedor had planned to wait for the sky to cloud over and block the light of the quarter moon, but seeing the crown princess of his hated enemy nation was unprotected by magical means, he poised himself to move. Closing his eyes, he reached into the spirit world, feeling the connection to his fellow wizards, feeling the power they lent to him through the world unseen. Through that connection, he also clearly felt his fellow wizard's hatred and jealousy of himself, their desire for him to succeed was matched by their desire for him to die soon after. Ertau thought it very likely he would die that night, indeed he planned for it, hoped for it. There would be no skulking away for Ertau after the crown princess of Tarador lay dead and the house of Trehayme with her. He would fling aside the flaps of the tent with the blood of the princess darkening his hands, and he would send wizardly fire to destroy any and all who opposed him. Even a master wizard of Acedor could not stand alone against a host of Tarador, yet his hope was by standing his ground to fight, the young witch would bring herself to him where he could watch her die in terrible pain. Ertau's own death would follow within moments or minutes, and he would be released from the suffocating bonds of mortal life to join his demon master and claim his reward.

Ertau held his breath until the blonde-haired witch passed out of sight behind tents down the hill. The witch was skilled for one so young, he had not sensed even faint traces of magic emanating from her as he expected from a wizard not yet in full control of her powers, but he knew wizards of the enemy were trained first to control their power before they developed their full strength. That might explain, he thought as one corner of his lips curled up in a nasty smirk, why Acedor had a greater number of wizards, and more of those wizards were capable of pulling magical fire from the spirit world and casting it as a weapon.

Such speculation was idleness and useless, Ertau cursed himself as his lips pulled tight and he renewed his concentration. The spell of concealment was woven tightly around him, he could sense no flaws in the magical fabric. Slowly, he rose to his feet and carefully made his way up the hill, around tents and through the outer ring of guards. No one saw him, no one shouted an alarm. Patrolling guards walked right past him, guards holding stationary posts shifted from one foot to another as their feet ached in their boots. Ertau's heart was pounding in his chest, his eyes darting side to side and up and down. With the power of concealment protecting him from searching eyes, he only had to fear stepping on a twig to give himself away. The snapping of a twig. Or footprints in the straw strewn along the path leading to the front flap of the tent. Straw placed there to protect from mud and dust the hem of the fancy dresses worn by the princess as she walked along the well-trodden path from the camp to her great tent atop the hill. Ertau walked carefully, almost daring to smile to himself that the enemy had been very helpful to him that night. The hill where they set up the tent for their princess was in a meadow, with few twigs or branches dropped by the distant trees, and those few had been picked up to tidy up the camp, or to use for starting campfires. Any twigs left behind were easily seen even in the night, for the fenceposts surrounding the royal tent were all topped with burning torches, flooding the crest of the hill with yellow, flickering light. In that false daylight, the dark wizard placed his feet with care, avoiding the path to the front flap of the tent and instead coming from the east side. He paused to inspect again the strength and perfection of his concealment, feeling the security of the connection to his fellow wizards.

Now came the moment of greatest danger, for the royal tent was not protected only by a symbolic fence and guards armed with swords. Connecting the fenceposts in an invisible ring were wards placed by skilled wizards. These wards could not only sound an alarm if a person with harmful intent breached the fence, they could also paralyze an intruder with a powerful shock. Ertau gathered his strength and concentration, leaping over the fence so his feet cleared the top rope comfortably, and landed lightly inside the sanctum housing the princess.

He was in! No one had seen him, he had not made any sound, and the magical wards had not reacted at all. After he killed the princess, he could openly use his power to tear the wards asunder and strode boldly out into the camp, but for the moment he must put such thoughts aside.

He had a brief moment of alarm as two soldiers walked past him close enough to touch. Would they see the bent blades of dried grass where he had landed after vaulting over the fence? No, they were not looking down, they looked outward. The wards would warn them of anyone breaching the fence, the guards knew, for they had been told so by master wizards. The danger they watched for was outside the fence, a danger of an enemy coming in force to attack the princess. Knowing an assassin sneaking past the magical wards was impossible, they watched against the possibility of a small group of the enemy rushing the tent to overwhelm the guard force.

After the guards passed by, Ertau resumed his approach, crouching down next to a side flap of the tent. When he was certain none of the guards were looking in his direction, he quickly untied the flap and slithered inside, smoothing the fabric of the flap behind him.

Ertau stood, allowing himself to indulge in the weakness of a brief shudder. The princess was alone, he was certain of that. He had watched the royal tent for hours, counted people coming and going, and after the blonde witch left, only the princess remained within.

The interior of the tent was divided into rooms by thick curtains, and heavy rugs protected the delicate feet of the princess from the bare ground below. Ertau crept forward, sensing the weight of the poisoned dagger on his belt and disdaining the weapon, he had no need us such crude devices. Blades and poisons were for those without the ability to summon and control magic. Ertau planned to demonstrate to the princess the power of a wizard of Acedor, make her tremble with terror, before he killed her without soiling even his fingertips by touching her unworthy flesh.

The plush carpets would have muffled any sound, but Ertau's footsteps were unnaturally silent as he crept forward.

Madame Chu trembled from exhaustion, knowing she could not stop yet. Not now. On her own, she had wrapped herself in a cloak of concealment, pulling the spell around her like a soft blanket. With her fellow wizards still miles away, she had walked through forests, across fields and right through the picket lines of the enemy soldiers who guarded the wizards of Acedor. In their arrogance, they had not thought to search the area around them via magical means, although Wing thought their lack of vigilance was entirely understandable. More than understandable, she was counting on their lack of vigilance, and had gone to great troubles to convince her opponents that they had nothing immediately to fear from those who served Tarador.

The fourteen enemy wizards knew about the approach of five wizards who served Acedor, they even knew her name. The sheer number of five wizards against fourteen was not the only element in favor of the dark wizards, for those fourteen had been chosen not for skill or knowledge, but for pure, raw *power*. For the ability to conjure power from the spirit world and use to it for destruction. Of the five wizards who faced them that day, only Chu Wing could challenge their power one on one, and any fight would never be one against one. In a battle, Wing knew she would die, and she was prepared to sacrifice herself to save Ariana Trehayme and gain an advantage for Tarador.

Those wizards were standing in a circle, fourteen pairs of hands joined, lips moving silently as they murmured incantations of dark magic. They were standing in a shallow depression in the ground. Once, the area had been a farmer's field, but now the former healthy crops were dead, scorched, blackened. The soil was dead, poisoned by dark magic that hated living things. It would take years of gentle rainfall to leach poison out of the soil before even sickly weeds could grow there, and water in the wells would be unsafe to drink for many years after the field had become a meadow and sapling trees reached upward for the sun. To the south were the still-smoldering remnants of a house and barn, Wing hoped the family had fled as the enemy approached.

The wizards were accompanied by less than a hundred soldiers, according to the Royal Army scout force that had tracked the group of wizards after they crossed the River Fasse. The scouts had braved wizard fire and worse dark magic to keep General Magrane and Madame Chu informed of the enemy's whereabouts and intentions, but after it was clear the wizards were headed straight for the crown princess, Wing had requested Magrane to pull back the scouts. She and her fellow wizards could watch the enemy force well enough through magical means, it was not necessary for scouts to risk their lives. As she glided silently through the enemy camp, she could see with her own eyes there were far less than a hundred soldiers with the wizards, and many of the soldiers appeared to there as servants rather than for protection. Quite rightly, the powerful wizards of Acedor felt they had no need for clumsy mortals to protect them, and a larger force would only slow them down.

There was a last ring of soldiers who held torches, backs to the wizards, facing out to counter threats, but Wing slipped between a pair of soldiers with no more sign of her presence than a faint zephyr of a breeze on a soldier's dirty cheeks. The man did not react, and Wing continued until she was standing on the lip of the shallow vale, with the enemy wizards no more than a dozen yards away. Even through her skillful concealment, the enemy should have noticed her, but their full attention was elsewhere that night, and they paid no attention to their surroundings for they feared nothing in the mortal world.

Closing her eyes and opening her inner senses, Wing could feel the invisible cords of power that joined the fourteen wizards together, and a single strand reaching out through the spirit world to the east. Toward Ariana and Olivia. To Wing's senses, the night air fairly crackled and pulsed with awesome power, and she rocked back on her heels when she felt how much power the enemy was manipulating. It was more power than she had ever handled, more than she thought even Lord Salva could control, and his power was immensely impressive. Swaying on her feet, she regained her balance and stepped forward toward the ring of wizards, who were as yet unaware of her presence. Before Wing had cast a spell of concealment around herself, her fellow wizards had woven an illusion that at that very moment, was providing proof to the enemy that their powerful opponent Madame Chu was still miles away.

Slowly taking a deep breath, Wing lifted a foot and took a step forward, knowing she was committed, and that night could be her last.

Ertau extended his senses before quickly pulling them back, for they were not needed. Hearing alone was the only sense he needed, for the creaking of a chair on the other side of a curtain alerted him to the presence of his quarry, his prey. The chair creaked, and a shadow moved on the curtain as the leader of his enemy moved in her chair, her motions illustrated by the candles on the desk in front of her. He stepped around the curtain, his feet making absolutely no sound on the plush carpets. And he saw her. The Regent and crown princess, heir to the throne of Tarador and of the house Trehayme, was sitting on a chair at a portable desk, reading a scroll, her back to him. He could be on her in a flash, his dagger plunged into her back, the poisoned blade rotting her blood from within. It would be satisfying to watch his hated enemy writhing in uncontrollable agony as the poison worked its cruel havoc, watching her staring up at him helplessly. A hand crept to the hilt of the dagger, then he pulled his hand away.

No.

No dagger, no knife would be used that night. He was a wizard, he would use the power of the spirit world to kill Ariana Trehayme, and Tarador with her.

The princess moved suddenly, jerking her head up as if she had heard a sound, but Ertau knew his careful footsteps on the heavy carpets had not made any noise at all. He froze, then jerked backwards himself as the princess stood and turned to face him.

"*You!*" Ertau spat with a gasp.

"You were expecting the princess?" Olivia shed the auburn wig, shaking her own golden hair to fall onto her shoulders.

"You witch!"

"I am a *wizard*," Olivia corrected her evil enemy, though the bravado of her words was betrayed by her tremulous voice and shivering lips. Without another word for she feared her strength would fail, she squinted with concentration and summoned power to flare into a fireball above her right palm.

And the ball of magical fire was snuffed out with a contemptuous gesture by the wizard of Acedor, as he also held up a hand to conjure an invisible, vise-like hand around her throat. Another invisible hand pinned her right hand closed, and Olivia struggled to breathe. She could not even call out to the guards! "I, uh, I-" Invisible fingers dug into her windpipe, making her choke.

"What? What would you say to me, foul witch?" He spat in disgusted rage. "Save what little breath you have left. Soon you will pass into the unseen world, and my master will be waiting to claim your soul there in the endless darkness." He lifted a hand to strike the witch with the poisoned dagger, then halted with irritation as her lips moved and she struggled to say something. "What?" He demanded.

"I have-" Olivia's strangled throat could barely squeak out the words.

"You have what? You have to beg for your life?" Ertau laughed, enjoying a moment of pure, blissful cruelty. He may have failed that night, been tricked by the witch, and his dark master would not forgive his inexcusable failure, not after Ertau had been entrusted with the power of fourteen other wizards to ensure his success. If he were to die that night and be consumed by the demon, he wanted the witch to suffer before he did. He needed to hear her pathetically beg for her life, so he relaxed his iron-like magical grip for her to talk. "Speak, foul witch, before you die. What do you have?"

Even with an invisible vise no longer quite crushing her neck, Olivia could almost not make her throat move enough to choke out a breath, but even so she smiled as she uttered the words. "I have," she hiccupped in the barest of breath, "*this*," she said loud and clear enough for the evil enemy wizard to understand. And as the word left her lips, her eyes turned to the large ring on the middle finger of her left hand, while her thumb curled inward to touch the golden hoop there.

A lightning bolt leapt from the gemstone of the ring to strike the enemy in the chest, a lightning bolt that was surprisingly and disappointingly thin and watery and dull to Olivia's eye. When Madame Chu had explained the plan, Olivia had hoped and expected the ring to emit a searing fire. For a heart-stopping moment, she thought the tiny magical device had failed, as after his initial shock of fear, the enemy appeared unscathed by the lightning bolt's effect. Had Madame Chu underestimated their enemy?

The dark wizard smiled, a horrible sight. "Is that the best you can manage?" He hissed in anticipation of the savoring an even sweeter revenge than he had dreamed of. The witch had been about to die, now she would die knowing she had failed. Whatever her plan had been, her pitiful powers were no match for a true master wizard of Acedor. "Now you will-"

Ertau's smile vanished. He could not move. And then he realized with gut-wrenching horror what the witch had done to him. The lightning bolt from her ring was never intended to harm him. Its purpose was to hold him frozen, not only in place but in *time*. The words he had spoken had not reached the ear of the witch, who also appeared to be frozen in time, but Ertau knew that was because the entire world outside of his little bubble of existence was lost to him. He could not move, he could not act, he could-

He gasped and his blood turned to ice.

He could not break the connection to his fellow wizards.

Madame Chu felt the presence of the new magic spell before she saw the effect, and she knew the enemy wizards also had felt the spell approaching them. They must have sensed something strange, something unexpected, something *wrong*, through their connection with their fellow wizard to the east. From their startled expressions, Wing knew the enemy had sensed the danger and tried to react, but they were too late. Their connection through the spirit world could not be sundered in the mere blink of an eye; they were firmly tied to the assassin wizard and would not break that bond quickly enough to save themselves.

The fourteen wizards, still clutching each other's hands, had their contorted faces frozen in horror as they realized what was about to happen to them. What had already happened to them. They were frozen, suspended in time. Wing waited a breathless moment, not daring to move herself, before she was certain the spell had a firm hold on her enemy.

The time-freezing spell she had used was not well known even among master wizards, it was not widely taught, and appeared only in obscure scrolls and books about magic. The reason few wizards knew of the spell was the extreme danger it posed to the spell-caster. Many, even most, wizards who attempted to weave that spell found themselves trapped by their own creation and in need of skilled help to save themselves. The problem with any attempt at rescue is a wizard atempting to help one trapped within the spell could all too easily become trapped also. Wing herself had successfully cast that spell less than a dozen times before, and not recently. Ironically, the enemy sending power through the spirit world had made it easier for Wing to use the spell, and for the spell to hold long enough to doom the enemy.

She stepped forward, reaching between two wizards to lightly touch the undulating flow of power that was invisible to the untrained eye. She felt the power the wizards had pulled from the spirit world, surprised and alarmed by the awesome surge of power the enemy handled so casually. Within the magical lightning that bound the fourteen wizards together and to the assassin wizard, she sensed the deceptively weak force of the spell she had cast, a spell which was holding all fifteen affected wizards frozen in time. Holding her breath for fear she might also be pulled into her own spell's effect, she pulled power from the spirit world, unleashing a flare of force upon the real world.

Wing gasped, losing her concentration as the spirit power burst forth in a blaze of light. Around her, enemy soldiers shouted cries of alarm and her cloak of concealment vanished, swept away by the hellish power she had let loose. Squeezing her eyes shut, she pulled a barrier around her but it was too little, too late.

Olivia had fallen to the floor when the assassin wizard's grip on her had been broken, now she pushed herself to her knees, massaging her injured windpipe with one hand. The other hand she stretched out toward the frozen enemy, a tiny flicker of flame glowing there, ready to be pulled into a deadly fireball if the enemy so much as twitched. Madame Chu had warned her not to touch the enemy while he was trapped in time, and also not to attempt using magic on the evil man lest she too, become trapped and her fate entangled with his. Rising to her feet, she backed away, fascinated to watch the wizard of Acedor standing like a statue.

Madame Chu had also warned her the spell was dangerous, unpredictable, and its effect could be short-lived. Glancing at the ring on her finger now in fear, Olivia used the sleeve of her robe to pull the ring off and drop it into the carpeted floor, being careful not to touch the ring with her bare skin. Wondering what the master wizard had meant exactly by 'short-lived', Olivia backed up until she was behind the desk and used both hands to draw a fireball to spin above her right palm. If the spell suddenly broke and the enemy moved, she was not going to waste time.

Before she had the fireball teased into its full power, the body of the enemy glowed, first bright yellow then an intense blue-white heat that caused her to fling up her hands to protect her eyes, her fireball blinking out of existence. Even with eyes tightly shut behind both hands, the light made spots swim in her vision so that when the light snapped out, she had to blink several times before she could see anything other than ghosts of white fire dancing in her vision.

As her tender eyes took in the astonishing sight, the body of the wizard became a charcoal pillar of dust roughly the shape of the man, then the dust collapsed into a sooty pile on the carpet. And the enemy was gone.

"Ah!" Cecil Mwazo was struck by a wave of dizziness and his legs gave out beneath him. Unaware, he fell to the ground and skidded down the slope, pebbles spinning away as he tumbled out of control.

"Cecil!" Paedris shouted in panic, forgetting the need for them to be quiet in the heart of Acedor. "No!" The court wizard of Tarador raced down the slope after his friend, his own feet skidding on the dusty ground. The other wizard's eyes were again open in his own panic, arms flung out to halt his rolling down the slope. One arm got painfully wrapped under him and he stopped rolling over, but the energy of his momentum was transferred into him spinning on his backside, small stones rolling under him and his body digging furrows in the dusty soil. Heedless of the danger to himself, Paedris leaped for Cecil's outstretched hand, missed, and wrapped around a foot. That was good enough, except they both then slid down the slope, until one of Peadris' knees bashed into a rock and he ground to a halt.

"Oof," Cecil gasped, his chin hanging over the edge of the cliff. As he watched, rocks and pebbles and sand he had knocked off the slope spilled over the edge and tumbled out into space. Mesmerized, he watched one white stone arcing down, down, down to crack against rocks at the bottom of the cliff. That could have been me, he thought with an icy shudder, blinking away a tear induced by rocks scraped against his ribs.

"Are you all right?" Paedris asked, holding securely onto his friend's foot with both hands.

"I would not say *all* right," Lord Mwazo grunted, wiggling fingers and toes, assuring himself all major body parts were still working. "I can move. Let's get away from the edge of this cliff, it is making me nervous," he said as more pebbles tumbled over the edge. The two wizards helped each other to their knees, and on hands and knees, they endured a slow, undignified crawl back up to the narrow goat track they had been walking on when Cecil suddenly fell without warning.

Sitting on the goat track, legs braced to keep themselves from sliding back down the slope, Paedris offered a flask of water to his fellow wizard. "Drink this. Are you well?"

"Well enough," Cecil answered over a mouthful of water, feeling his tender ribs. He was bleeding in a few places, nothing particularly to worry about. He sat upright, scanning the sun-blasted hills around them. "Did anyone hear us, you think?"

Paedris considered the question. Other than the dust cloud from where the two wizards had nearly fallen over a cliff, nothing was moving. It was difficult to see in the light of the quarter moon even though the sky was cloudless, but the night air was still and he did not hear anything. No shouts of alarm. He did not see any torches carried by soldiers of the enemy, nor signal fires warning of intruders. "I believe we are safe for now. Cecil, what happened? I know you did not simply lose your footing in the darkness."

The other wizard laughed softly. "Your girlfriend is what happened."

"My girl-" His cheeks reddened even though they could hardly be seen in the thin, gray light of the moon. "Madame Chu is not my 'girlfriend'. She sent a message to you?" Paedris thought that odd, for Wing usually sent messages to him, and they had to be extremely careful while inside Acedor. Only messages of the most vital importance could justify the risk of the demon learning that wizards of Tarador were within its borders.

"I received a message, but not from Wing. Not directly," Cecil shook his head. "Paedris, the demon received a great shock, and I felt it." He had connected to the demon enough times through the spirit world that now he could not fully break the connection. It was only the faintest of impressions, a tickle at the back of his mind, usually something he could almost ignore. But the enormous, world-crushing power of the demon was always just at the edge of Cecil's consciousness. "Ten, or a dozen or more of the demon's most powerful wizards were suddenly snuffed out, burned from inside by fire from the spirit world."

"A dozen wizards killed all at once?" Paedris' mouth gaped open in astonishment. All the wizard on the side of Tarador did not possess the power to strike such a blow, not even if he had been with them.

"Yes. A dozen or more, you understand I could not get an exact count. The demon is hurt badly, enraged, frightened. This is the last thing it expected. I get the impression our enemy is also disappointed, as if it anticipated a great victory tonight, and all its plans have turned to dust. I can't imagine how, but," he smiled, his teeth shining even in the half moonlight. "For a dozen of the enemy's most powerful wizards to have been destroyed in one blow, Chu Wing *has* to be involved. No one else could do that."

"Yes," Paedris stared off into space with a look of wonder on his face. Wonderment, and pride. "No one else could," he added, and on his face appeared the goofy smile of a love-struck teenage boy. Chu Wing was not his girlfriend, although- His heart swelled when he thought of that wizard from the distant land of Ching-Do, and pride at her skill, courage and accomplishments was not the only feeling he had for her.

Cecil gritted his teeth as he felt his tender ribs, assuring himself nothing was broken. Carefully, he stood up. "Paedris, we must get moving. The enemy has been dealt a great defeat, and the demon is frightened. And it is angry. It will strike against Tarador sooner than the demon planned, and the blow will fall more heavily. I sense the demon has now lost patience for assassinations and tricks of wizardry, and now is the time to crush Tarador with the great host on this side of the border. The hammer will fall against the Royal Army, and it will fall sooner and heavier than it otherwise would have. Paedris, the death of those wizards has weakened the enemy measurably, but we are out of time. We must move now, swiftly and without pause."

Madame Chu had been propelled up and backwards by the eruption of power from the spirit world, protected only by the spell she had woven around herself at the last moment. The spell had offered only partial protection, she felt the skin on one side of her face was hot and painful as if she had suffered a terrible sunburn though it was the middle of the night. Over the general stench of burnt soot in the area, she sniffed the distinctive scent of singed hair. Her own, she realized as a scorched lock of her black hair snapped off in her hand. The hood of her cloak had shielded most of her hair from the brief and intense fire, yet she did not want to consider what had happened to her eyebrows, and the skin of her forehead was too sensitive for her to touch.

The ground all around her was blackened, clear even in the thin moonlight. As she pushed herself unsteadily to her feet, her hands left light-colored streaks on the ground, sweeping away the soot. Carefully placing one foot in front of the other, she walked back to see where the dark wizards had been. Nothing. Where they had been standing in a circle was nothing but sooty dust which stirred in the breeze, black wisps dancing in the darkness. The dark wizards were gone, utterly erased from the world of the real. Extending her senses for her eyes still swam with bright dots and her hearing was muffled, she could feel no trace of the wizards, not even an echo of their presence. They were gone.

What was that? Something loud enough for even Wing's abused ears to hear caught her attention and she turned to look behind her. Enemy soldiers, also shaking their heads to clear their rattled brains, were approaching her slowly, warily. They saw burned bodies of soldiers who had been too close to the wizards, and closer still were mounds of soot that once may have been soldiers. The approaching men had no idea what had happened, where their powerful wizards had gone, and who was the hooded figure standing before them, but they knew the figure did not belong there. One of the soldiers, running a hand across his face to wipe away gritty soot, shouted something at Wing, but she could not hear, the sound was so muffled.

The man raised his sword, shouting at soldiers to his left and right, urging them to charge forward with him. Wing tried to take a deep breath, her lungs feeling seared threw her into a fit of coughing. She had no strength for a fight against a squad or more of soldiers, and the only weapon she had brought with her was a dagger. Five soldiers screamed as one, their insults barely registering in her hearing. Two other soldiers remained behind, fitting arrows to bows. The soldiers of Acedor were bewildered and frightened by the loss of the wizards they had been entrusted to guard and they knew their dark master had no mercy for those who failed. Though the magical compulsion that had brought them across the border into Tarador had evaporated when the wizards were destroyed, they acted from long-standing habit when they ran toward the wizard of Tarador.

Holding her breath lest she launch into another uncontrollable series of hacking coughs that threatened to burst blood vessels in her eyes, Wing stood up straight and proud to face the enemy charge. Her body was weak, she knew that without any need to use her wizard senses. Her knees shook, her head throbbed with pain, and she could not remember ever feeling more hungry. Her use of power had drained her energy dangerously, even her wizard skills at fighting could not save her against a single enemy soldier right then.

She could not fight the men charging toward her, and she did not have time to fight them all anyway, for more foul men were already coming as they answered the shouted summons of their leader. So she did the only thing she could; she reached deep down into the spirit world, and pulled power from that unseen realm. Interlocking her fingers, she held her hands palms-outward, as fire flared into life in front of her hands. With a curse of defiance she heard mostly through her bones, she flung a thin stream of fire sweeping left to right across the enemy, burning through their ranks. In one moment, the soldiers went from charging her to rolling on the ground in agony, horribly burned by magical fire. The two archers and the men running toward her with swords were dead or dying, their muffled screams of agony registering even in her recovering ears.

Using every ounce of strength she had left to remain on her feet, she turned to face another group of soldiers who had come running to the aid of their fellows. Seeing the terrible fate of the soldiers Wing had incinerated, the enemy still alive halted, looking at each other fearfully. The enemy wizard who had just so easily killed a group of determined soldiers was now glaring at them, her face great and terrible in the moonlight.

It was too much. Released from the magical compulsion they had suffered under for years, their courage failed. First one, then all the soldiers turned and ran, flinging aside weapons, helmets and any other burden which might slow their escape.

Wing stood her ground until the last enemy soldier disappeared from view before allowing herself to fall to her knees, holding a hand to the scorched ground while she drew in breaths in between sharp coughs. The coughing, she knew, would not get better until she could get to a place where the air was not full of swirling soot particles. It was longer than she wanted, perhaps a quarter of an hour, before she could again stand. East. She needed to walk to the east, toward her fellow wizards who she knew were at that moment coming toward her as quickly as they could, riding heedlessly through the night. Trodding unsteadily across what used to be a farm field, she stopped to pick up a discarded sword. A blade of Acedor was not her weapon of choice, she felt tainted by even touching the hilt of such a crude and evil device.

As a weapon of war, the sword she held was crude. But, she had to admit, it made a fair cane for her to lean on as she limped her way to safety and freedom.

CHAPTER FOURTEEN

"Ah!" When Madame Chu killed the wizards of Acedor, Koren felt a wave of dizziness and fell backward, his arms flailing wildly to grasp onto anything but the ridge they were climbing was so steep, he was on the way down before he knew it.

"Got you!" Bjorn held onto a tough mountain shrub with one hand and the boy's jacket with the other, yanking forward and making Koren spin around to slam into the slope on his back. "Grab something," Bjorn grunted from the strain of holding the boy up with one hand. "You're falling!" He warned as Koren's own weight started him slipping out of the jacket.

"Yes, yes, I'm all right now," Koren said woozily while wrapping both arms around something.

"Koren, that's my boot you're hugging," Bjorn supressed a chuckle.

"Oh, sorry," he blinked, his vision returning to normal. First, he made sure his feet had firm purchase on a rock, then he let go of Bjorn's boot and took hold of shrub to pull himself upward. "I'm all right now, really."

"What happened?"

"I don't know," Koren said truthfully. "I got dizzy all of a sudden."

"Hungry?"

"No, I think it was a wizard thing. I've felt something like it before, when Paedris and the other wizards were testing me on top of his tower."

"This wasn't a test," Bjorn stated the obvious.

"No. I don't know what happened."

"It better not happen again until we get to the top," Bjorn fretted. They were climbing the last stretch up to the top of a ridge, where Raddick planned to stop for the night. It was too dangerous for the soldiers to be stumbling around in the dark, they were only climbing then because nightfall had caught them exposed halfway up the ridge. "Come on, then, you go ahead so if you get dizzy again, I can break your fall. Don't get dizzy if you can help it."

Koren didn't respond. How was he supposed to prevent himself from falling victim to something he didn't understand?

In the light of dawn the following morning, Raddick regretted his success in luring the orcs to chase him, for he feared becoming trapped. His plan had been to disappear behind the ridgeline, then go eastward and down before turning north again to resume climbing. That plan had been dashed when the party discovered a sheer cliff to the east, and they were forced to double back, losing precious ground and time as the orcs came upward with the skill of mountain goats. By the time the soldiers had laboriously climbed the steep second ridge, the orcs were far too close, and more orcs had come out of the treeline to join the pursuit. Raddick noted with dismay that the hunters had watched his team climb the steep ridge, learning what areas to avoid and the quickest route to the top. When the army troop reached the summit, only to see with a groan there was *another* ridge above them, Raddick called a halt for his people to rest shaking arms and legs. They waited longer than Raddick wished, but he had to wait, for his plan was for Koren to pick off one or two of the hunters as they climbed, forcing the others to retreat and wait for reinforcements.

"That's two," Bjorn said unnecessarily, as the second hunter hit by Koren tumbled down the steep ridge. "Can you hit that one?" He pointed to where an orc was huddled fearfully under an overhanging rock, clinging by its claws.

Koren frowned. All he could see of that orc was its hands, while all the other hunters had gone to ground, squeezing themselves into crevices or under rocks, not daring to move. Forcing the hunters to remain motionless gave the soldiers time to get away, but only until the orcs realized there was no one above to shoot deadly arrows. Every second the hunters delayed Koren, the much larger group of orcs below climbed ever closer. "I will try," Koren responded, and handed the arrow back to Bjorn.

"Something wrong with it?" The man asked, studying what looked to him like a perfectly good arrow.

"It's fine. It doesn't," Koren shrugged as an apology, "feel right." He selected another arrow from the row on the ground in front of him.

"You trust in those feelings of yours," Bjorn advised sagely.

"Right now," Koren admitted, "I feel like throwing down my weapons and running away crying like a little boy."

"Trust your feelings except *that* one," Bjorn wagged a finger.

Koren did not reply, instead focusing on the target even his keen eyes could almost not see. He aimed at the orc's exposed hands, but it did not feel right, and he had little hope of hitting something so small from such a distance, in the gusting winds blowing across the mountain slope. Closing his eyes, he muttered a silent plea to the spirits, receiving no answer. No answer, but there was a feeling, an almost imperceptible tingle at the back of his mind.

"Er, young master wizard," Bjorn whispered, "I don't wish to argue with the spirits, but you're aiming too high and too far to the left. Come right a-"

Koren released the arrow. It flew upward, wavering side to side as its flight was buffeted by the winds swirling up the slope. The untrained wizard and the former King's Guard watched the arrow drop below them and plunge downward, still flying too far to the left. The arrow seemed to stagger in the air, almost stopping before a gust of wind caught it and pushed right, right, right and down. "Not enough," Bjorn exhaled, disappointed as he saw it was going to miss the target.

Miss the target it did, the arrow disappeared from view well clear of the lucky orc clinging to the overhanging rock. A wail reached Bjorn's ears and, from where the arrow had gone out of view, the body of an orc rolled downward, tumbling over and over, picking up speed as it fell.

"Remind me never to argue with the spirits," Bjorn said, mouth agape in astonishment.

Koren merely grinned, and winked.

"Oh, shut up," Bjorn grumbled.

After Koren's arrow hit the unseen orc, Raddick ordered the party to move out, on up the next ridge. The slope there was less steep, the ground not entirely cluttered with rocks and the path was broad enough for people to walk beside each other. Raddick set a punishing pace, knowing the orcs hunting them would move quickly once they reached the top of the previous ridge. Though three of the hunters lay dead, there were at least twenty more orcs coming up the mountain, and they would not delay long once they saw no more arrows were raining down on them.

The pace of advance, the leg-burning climb and the thinner air on the mountain did not keep soldiers from whispering and looking suspiciously at Koren and grumbling, and a few hex signs were made with fingers to protect themselves.

After a while, Raddick had enough of the whispers. "Cease this foolishness! You are soldiers of Tarador, what is the matter with you?"

"Begging your pardon, Captain," Thomas spoke first, "but the boy's skill with a bow, it ain't natural, is all."

"No, it's not natural, because the boy is a wizatd. Now, move like we have blood-thirsty orcs on our tail," he was interrupted by a guttural howl from behind them, "because we do."

"How do you do it?" Lem asked Koren, intensely curious as they approached the crest of the latest ridge. "Hit a target you can't see? If you can't see it, how do you aim?"

"I don't know how I do it," Koren admitted. "The spirits knew that orc was there, even if I couldn't see it."

"The spirits knew it was there, but they didn't aim your bow," Lem insisted.

"They don't," Koren threw up his hands. "The spirits don't *tell* me where to aim, they don't speak to me at all," he complained. "I move the bow around until it, it just feels right. I can't explain it. And I release the bowstring when I feel that I should," he looked at the ground sheepishly.

"The wind blew that arrow all over the sky," Lem was not satisfied with an 'I don't know' answer from the young wizard. "You mean to tell me the spirits knew if you released the arrow at that precise moment, the winds would be blowing in just the right direction and force to bring it to the target? The spirits know the future?"

"Paedris- Lord Salva told me there is no past or future in the spirit world," Koren explained. To Lem's mildly disgusted look, he replied "That's what he told me, I'm not a master wizard!"

"I can't believe the spirits knew exactly how this wind," he tugged hair out of his eyes as a gust of wind twirled around them, "would move an arrow-"

"The boy bends the world to his will," Bjorn interrupted, tired of the constant questions. "The spirits know what he wishes, and they reshape the world however he wants. If the winds would not have guided that arrow to the target, the spirits made the winds do his bidding." Seeing Lem's surprise, Bjorn added "That is how it was explained to me by a dwarf woman who was servant to a master wizard."

Lem stared at Koren with astonishment, and not a little fear. "You bend the *world* to your will, and you are only an untrained wizard?"

"I haven't been trained," Koren protested, embarrassed. "I don't know how magic works, I only know how to do, the things I can do."

"Hmm," Lem unconsciously moved a step away from Koren. "If you can make the world do whatever you want and you haven't even been trained," he didn't finish the thought.

"Lord Salva needs us to prevent another invasion this autumn, so the enemy will be forced to wait through the winter," Ariana explained as she unrolled a large map on the table in her royal tent. In the soaking cold rains of late autumn in northern Tarador, roads would become impassable streaks of mud, rendering any large-scale movements by an army impossible. As the year wore on into winter, the muddy roads would freeze but ice and heavy snow would block roads just as effectively, and regular thaws made roads a sloppy mess. Not until the middle of spring would it be practical for the enemy to move an invasion force into northern Tarador, and that would give the beleagured nation time to rebuild defenses. Southern Tarador suffered somewhat less from snow and ice, but what fell as snow in the north fell as chilly rain in the south and made the roads just as bad. The true barrier to an invasion of southern Tarador was the terrain in that region; rugged mountains ran east-west with deep river valleys flowing north to south. To cross the rivers there, the enemy would have to build a bridge, and the Royal Army could easily prevent such an extensive effort.

"Where *is* Lord Salva?" Regin Falco inquired, and not for the first time. His question was not quite phrased as a demand, but it also lacked a bit of the deference owed to the young woman who was both crown princess and Regent.

That young woman ignored the tone of the duke who was her future father-in-law and, recently, a war counsellor. She found the man irritating but had to admit his strategic thinking was sound, even Grand General Magrane sought Duke Falco's advice occasionally. "That is not the subject of this discussion, Your Grace," she deflected the question yet again, and had a brief moment of satisfaction when she saw a vein throbbing on Regin's temple as he was frustrated once more. "Lord Salva is doing his part to secure allies in our fight-"

"*He* is greater than any ally we might persuade to fight on our side," Regin insisted. "Lord Salva should be here! We have too few wizards," he shuddered, remembering the overwhelming power the enemy had on their side of the river, including ranks of dark wizards. "Too many of our wizards and skilled in nothing but," he waved a hand dismissively, "reading fortunes and healing cuts."

"You would be thankful for our skill in the healing arts," Madame Chu said with icy calm, "if you suffer injury in battle."

"I am more likely to be cut with a sword in battle because Lord Salva is not here to fight by my side," Regin shot back.

"Enough!" Ariana threw up her hands. "This is what the enemy wants; for us to fight amongst ourselves. We are here to discuss ways to forestall an invasion, not," she glared at Duke Falco, "to debate the whereabouts of my court wizard. Paedris is on an errand with my blessing and full support, and there will be no more talk on that subject, is that clear?"

Regin Falco did not blush, because Falcos did not blush, or back down. They did, however, know to choose their battles. "Of course, Your Highness."

Ignoring the sulking duke, Ariana tapped the map with a fingernail. "General Magrane, could we take a substantial force across the river, to raid deep into Acedor? If we take control of enemy territory and destroy villages, crops and grain stores, the enemy would surely have to shift position to push us back, and we could then conduct a fighting retreat back across the river," she explained, proud of herself for developing the strategy. "By the time the enemy reorganized, it would be too late in the year for them to strike."

"Um, well, Your Highness," Magrane began, seeking a tactful way to let down his leader.

"It is a fine idea, Highness," Regin interrupted, "against any other enemy. Against Acedor, it would only hasten our doom. The demon cares nothing for the people under its dominion," Regin suppressed another shudder at having seen how cruelly the ruler of Acedor treated the unfortunate people under its control. "We could burn half the villages in Acedor, and the demon would not react except to take advantage of our having weakened our defenses east of the Fasse."

"Oh," Ariana stared at the map, crestfallen.

Magrane cleared his throat. "Duke Falco is correct, Highness. We cannot think of the demon the way we deal with other enemies."

"Very well," Ariana mentally switched gears to her second plan. "Madame Chu informed us the enemy has a major supply," she paused to recall the correct military term, "dump? Here, in this valley behind their lines north of us. Could we attack those supplies and destroy them? When Captain Raddick was tutoring me, I wished to know about tactics but he told me amateurs debate tactics, professionals discuss logistics. An army cannot move without supplies."

"I like it," Regin murmured with admiration. "The enemy knows they cannot rely on foraging for supplies here after they cross the river." At the direction of Magrane, almost all vital supplies of grain and other foodstuffs had been moved east away from the river valley. Ducal armies had orders and were prepared to burn anything useful to the enemy as they conducted a fighting retreat, depriving the invading forces of provisions to continue their advance. Any supplies the enemy needed during the invasion would have to be brought across the river and transported to the front lines. If an invasion happened anyway, Magrane planned to send fast-moving cavalry units to hit the enemy's supply wagons behind the lines, delaying the advance. That was a prudent plan, but it would be far better to keep the enemy west of the River Fasse.

"It is an excellent idea, Highness," Magrane agreed, "except-"

"It *is* an excellent idea," Regin did not allow the Royal Army commander to finish his thought. The more he considered the idea of attacking the enemy's supply dump, the more he liked it. Major units of the Royal Army would have to cross the River Fasse to make the raid successful, and the princess would almost certainly insist on leading the raid herself. That would make her vulnerable, especially if something, anything went wrong during the retreat.

Regin felt confident he could arrange for something to go wrong.

"We would need a flanking force to cross here," Regin gestured at the map, "to cover the raiding force. The enemy could not easily outflank us to the north, but we would need to pull the boats back east of the river, until they are needed to retrieve us following the raid." As he spoke, a part of him, a large part of him, wished he were truly planning for a successful raid rather than the betrayal and death of the crown princess. He was good at strategic planning, and he enjoyed it. Oh, if circumstances were different! Regin almost wished he did not know the overwhelming strength of the enemy, so he could plan a bold raid in blissful ignorance of the awful, inevitable truth that Tarador was doomed. To go out in a blaze of glory, fighting alongside brave men and women of Tarador, fighting his country's ancient enemy-

No. No, defeat was inevitable, he knew it in his heart. His action to betray the princess was not treason, he would be acting to salvage something recognizable from the destruction of Tarador. Regin Falco told himself he was acting out of patriotism, and after he sold that lie to himself, every step he took toward treason was easy.

"Duke Falco," Magrane held up a hand to interrupt. "Your Grace, your insight is welcome and your proposed tactics are sound, but I fear this task is beyond the abilities of the Royal Army at the present time." Crossing the river, conducting a large-scale raid and then safely retreating back across the river with the bulk of the raiding force intact would be a massive, complicated operation and Magrane's head ached just to think of planning the details. "The enemy knows the vital importance of that supply dump, and has stationed substantial forces to guard it. At great risk to herself, Madame Chu," he nodded

respectfully to the wizard, "has gathered valuable information about the strength and
disposition of enemy forces in that area. The enemy would have advantages of numbers,
terrain and supply lines."

Ariana grew increasingly unhappy and withdrawn as the commander of her Royal
Army and the Duke of Burwyck province argued about raiding the enemy supply dump.
For some reason she did not understand, Regin Falco insisted they had to take the risk of
sending the Royal Army deep into Acedor, though everything she had heard about Regin
was the man hated to take risks he could not control. Magrane remained steadfast and
calm in pointing out the flaws in Duke Falco's plan, and the discussion ended when
Ariana declared she must meet with her chancellor. Kallron did need to talk about some
boring matter of state that Ariana had been dreading, but anything had to be better than
being caught between two men who knew what they were talking about and loved to
argue.

"Madame Chu," General Magrane whispered as they exited the royal tent, keeping his
voice down to avoid Duke Falco overhearing him. "I wonder if you could spare a few
minutes of your time to speak with me?"

"Now?" Wing asked, slightly dismayed. She had much wizard business to attend to,
and military matters tended to bore her.

"Yes, now," Magrane lowered his eyelids and tilted his head to indicate the matter
was important and he needed to speak privately.

"Oh, certainly."

In Magrane's campaign tent, the floor of which was dirt and well-matted grass rather
than the carpets of the royal tent, he unrolled a map identical to the one the princess had
used.

Wing let out a heavy sigh. "General, did we not just spend an hour arguing uselessly
about this subject?"

"The subject, yes, but the time was not wasted." Magrane traced a finger along the
map, circling the valley the enemy had used to store mountains of supplies. According to
Wing who had 'flown' over the area while in the spirit world, crates and sacks of grain
and any number of other items vital to support a vast military force were heaped up in
piles under waterproof oilcloths, all down the valley floor. The location was well-
positioned to supply the two major encampments to the northeast and southeast along the
River Fasse. Roads fanned out from the valley both east and west, and Wing had seen a
steady stream of wagons moving east along the roads, bringing yet more vital materials
from within Acedor and from vassal states to the north and west who rendered tribute to
the demon. "My argument against Duke Falco's suggestion of a raid is based on the
strength of the enemy around their base of supplies, but perhaps I was hasty. Could you
get more current information about the area?" Magrane asked hopefully.

"No," Wing shook her head. "I was barely able to escape with my life the first time,
enemy wizards nearly trapped me within the spirit world there," she shivered slightly
recalling her fear at the time. "Now the enemy has cast spells to prevent anyone from
viewing this whole region," she swept her hand in a wide circle far from the target valley,
"through magical means. They are the same spells we use to conceal our numbers and
movements from the enemy."

"Then, unless we somehow discover the enemy has inexplicably left their major
source of supply unguarded, we lack the strength to attack there. As I argued with Duke
Falco, I- Damn, but that man is nearly as knowledgeable about military tactics as I am,

and he is damned accustomed to getting his way in everything! As we argued, I recalled something I learned while studying maps of Acedor when I was a mere foot soldier. This valley where the enemy has stored their supplies, it is dry now but it used to be a riverbed, did it not?"

It was Wing's turn to tilt her head. "General, I am from Ching-Do, half a world away from here. Why are you asking *me* about this?"

"I thought master wizards knew everything," he replied with a wink.

"That is a great exaggeration," she had to laugh. "However, in this case, I do know about the history of this area," she rolled her eyes without meaning to. Lord Mwazo took his reputation as chief lore master of the Wizards Council seriously, and that included endlessly lecturing his travel companions on matters of Acedor both important and trivial. The subject raised by Magrane was something Wing had mentally categorized as trivial, and she could not imagine why the commander of the Tarador Royal Army cared about such an unimportant matter. "Yes, the river you call Lillefasse used to flow through that valley, until roughly four hundred years ago. The river flowed through a gap, here, no, here," she jabbed a finger at the map. "There was a quake that caused a landslide, both sides of the gap fell in to block it. The river backed up to create this lake, but before it rose to the top of the dam, it found a new outflow down to the Fasse, here," she pointed to the northeast corner of the lake. "Lord Mwazo told me the landslide was partly caused by the demon having cut or burned away all the tree cover in the area, just as the demon has despoiled and poisoned most of Acedor."

"Yes, yes," Magrane did not need a lecture in proper land management techniques. "the Lillefasse now flows out through this channel to the northeast, but if the dam were breached?"

"It would resume its old channel, down to the southeast," Wing now understood why the general was interested in odd events in the history of Acedor. "General, the lake behind that dam is perhaps one hundred feet deep. Breaching that dam would cause a wave that would flood the valley below and sweep away much of the enemy's supplies."

"Yes it would," Magrane grinned and Wing was reminded of the predatory smile of a wolf on the hunt.

She considered the map. The lake was far enough north of the enemy's main camps that the Royal Army could cross the River Fasse unopposed, and march along the 'new' channel of the Lillefasse. A retreat could be conducted down the suddenly-dry channel to the northeast of what used to be a lake. Mountain ridges running west to east across the area would slow the enemy's ability to counterattack, leaving at least a possibility of the Royal Army getting back across the Fasse without a major engagement. "You have a plan to breach the dam? I assume your plan does not involve ten thousand men with shovels."

"My plan is to ask a master wizard for a plan."

"*What?*" Wing's face turned pale. "General Magrane, this is not a simple trick you are asking for."

"I know that. I also know wizards pulled down the Gates of the Mountains, and I would not have thought that possible until I saw it happen."

Wing cringed. Why did people not blessed with magical abilities think wizardry was so *simple*? "Collapsing the Gates was barely possible, even for Paedris, and he is not with us."

"Paedris told me to have full faith in your power, and he also told me that *you* should have faith in your own power."

"That is easy for him to say!"

"Madame Chu, I am not asking you to move a million tons of rock and soil by yourself. For now, I am only requesting you to look at the problem, to study it."

"Hmm," she sniffed unhappily. "You mean you wish me to examine the area through the spirit world."

"Can you do that?" Magrane asked in an even tone, not getting his hopes up yet.

"It *may* be possible," she closed her eyes to think. The dam was well north of the area covered by the spell cast by dark wizards, but that did not mean there were no other magical hazards around the dam. She would not only need to get in and out, she would need to do so without the enemy ever knowing she had any interest in the dam or the lake behind it. The enemy was not stupid, not stupid at all, the demon would instantly understand why a wizard of Tarador wished to inspect that lake and the vulnerable dam there.

"Time is critical," Magrane said unnecessarily.

Wing sighed, for she was already tired. "I will make the attempt tonight, for whatever it is worth. I make no promises, General!" She warned with a finger wagging to the old soldier.

Magrane made a short bow. "I promise not to question if you tell me it cannot be done. Is there anything I can do for you?"

"Stop dreaming up more things for me to do?"

The general had to chuckle at that. "I will consider your request. "Thank you."

She paused at the tent flap. "General, why did you not mention the idea of breaching the dam and flooding that valley, when we were with the princess and Duke Falco?"

"Two reasons," Magrane paused to soothe his parched throat with a tumbler of water. "Our Regent is wise beyond her years, but she can be excitable, and I do not wish her to become," he made a sour face, "*enthused* about a plan until I am certain it is practical. We do not have time to waste on plans that will never come to fruition."

Wing nodded agreement, the general was very sensible and knew how to handle his princess. "And the other reason?"

"I do not trust Regin Falco. Madame Chu, if we proceed as we discussed, I wish no one other than the princess and a few wizards to know of our true intentions. Everyone else may believe a fairy tale about a simple raid into Acedor to cut supply lines, or something like that."

"You do not trust him? Why? Even the princess seeks his counsel."

"I do not trust him for any reason other than that he is a Falco," Magrane made a cutting motion with one hand, declaring the matter closed. "The Falcos have for centuries been entirely focused on one goal; overthrowing the Trehaymes and putting a Falco on the throne of Tarador."

"Yes," Wing replied slowly, "Duke Falco has a plan to do that, and that plan requires Ariana living to become queen, marry Regin's son and produce an heir. He must also ensure there is a Tarador for Ariana to rule. I do not see his motivation could be against Ariana, or Tarador."

"On the face of it, that is true." Magrane agreed that Regin Falco, by all appearances, would benefit most through protecting the crown princess. But, there was something Magrane found odd, off, disturbing about the duke of Burwyck. Particularly recently, the duke sometimes had a faraway expression on his face when he thought no one was looking, and more than once Magrane had caught Falco looking at the princess with pure hatred. People who knew Regin best agreed something about him had changed recently, the Duke was different, that he did surprising things, actions that were out of character. A man who could not be trusted had become unpredictable, and that alarmed General Magrane. "Madame Chu, nothing is ever as it seems with this particular Duke Falco. I knew his father, he was a first-class schemer. Regin is far more clever, devious and dangerous. Humor an old man, please, and accept that we will not tell Regin Falco of our true plans. I will think of a suitable cover story for our raid, if needed."

CHAPTER FIFTEEN

At the crest of the ridge, Raddick's party was rewarded by the welcome sight of flatter ground, which drew a quiet, weary cheer from the soldiers. The land ahead of them was a wide, broad saddle between two ridges, and covered mostly with forest. Without a pause, Raddick lead the party between the trees which at first were clustered closely together and the ground littered with moss-covered logs. Going single-file, the party did the best they could to conceal their tracks, but moss slipped off rocks and logs when stepped on, and in many places there was no way between the trees without snapping dry branches. When they came to a stream, everyone drank as much as they wished and filled their water flasks quickly, with Raddick striding up the streambed where the trees did not form a barrier. Soon the trees became more sparse and the party was able to move more quickly, spurred onward by the hunting cries of orcs behind them.

"What's the plan now?" Bjorn asked as he caught up to Raddick.

"Plan?" Raddick replied with irritation. "I am not accustomed to questions from-"

"Yes, and I am not one of your soldiers, so, what is the plan? We well and truly have the orcs chasing us, so your promise to Renhelm is fulfilled. I assume you don't intend to take us up to the Magross fortress. I was there once, it's a formidable bastion, but the dwarves would likely insist we remain there, and overwintering in a dwarf fortress is no way to carry out your orders. You must have another plan. Is it too much to hope that you know this secret ravine leading back down to the valley?"

"I don't know it," Raddick admitted. "I've heard rumors about a secret path up the mountain, a series of caverns and ravines the dwarves have connected with tunnels, but Renhelm wouldn't give me even a hint."

"I thought as much," Bjorn stumbled over a log and Raddick steadied him from falling.

Raddick lowered his voice, relieved to have someone to unburden himself to. Bjorn Jihnsson had long experience in combat, and though he had served in the King's Guard instead of the Royal Army, Raddick considered the man a soldier. "The truth is, I am not certain where to go next. I am not familiar with these mountains, and the orcs are pursuing us closer than I expected. If we can lose them in these woods," he looked behind them with a frown at the trampled underbrush, broken branches, boot prints clearly outlined in mud and moss scraped off fallen logs.

"Unlikely," Bjorn declared.

"Aye. Do you have a suggestion?"

"Not really, not anything useful, except that if we keep climbing straight up this mountain, we risk coming to a cliff we can't climb."

"So, left or right?"

"Left is west, toward Acedor," Bjorn noted with a frown.

"The border is a considerable distance westward," Raddick replied. "But I don't like that idea. When we get up there," he pointed through the trees to an area where the continuous forest gave way to patchy groves of trees in an open rock field, "we stick to rock where we won't leave tracks, and we turn east."

"You've been in worse spots, surely?" Bjorn asked with a ghoulish grin.

"Worse for me?" Raddick mused. "Many times. Several, at least," he thought back, remembering moments in his life he had been almost as terrified as he was then. "Never with the future of Tarador depending on me succeeding."

"True," Bjorn agreed. Even when he had the sacred duty to protect the life of Tarador's king, the existence of the kingdom had never rested on the outcome. Bjorn knew that, for he had failed, King Adric Trehayme had died in battle, and still Tarador continued.

By what Raddick judged was two hours later, he began to hope they may have escaped the orcs. By walking on mostly flat rock without stepping on shrubs or muddy ground, they party had not left obvious tracks to lead the orcs eastward.

"Not that way," Koren spoke suddenly, having remained mostly quiet after he answered Lem's uncomfortable questions.

"Why?" Raddick asked in surprise. "You know these mountains?"

"No, I, I have a feeling about it."

The hair stood up on the back of Bjorn's neck and he came to a halt. "Is this a feeling from the spirits?"

"I don't know. I told you, the spirits don't talk to me. They don't tell me anything at all. Not directly."

"This feeling you have, it is like when you feel when to release a bowstring?"

"Sort of. Yes. Only this feels like we should *not* go that way, up there. It feels wrong."

"Captain," Bjorn said quietly, "if our young wizard has a bad feeling about-"

"I agree," Raddick did not need additional persuasion. "We go-"

"Look!" Thomas shouted, pointing up the mountainside.

Orcs. A party of orcs had come into view on the horizon, walking along a ridge crest. As the Royal Army soldiers watched fearfully, more and more orcs became visible. Many, many more orcs.

"How did they get ahead of us?" Thomas asked in a whisper.

"They didn't," Lem declared. "Those are not the orcs chasing us. That's no hunting party. That's an army. Two hundred?" He looked toward Raddick. "Or more?"

"Yes, damn it," the captain swore. "They must already have been on the mountain above us last night," he speculated with a chill creeping up his spine.

"I think they don't see us yet," Lem slowly stepped behind a tree trunk, peering around the rough bark up at the orcs.

"They will soon," Thomas looked around. "They're coming down here, and we can't stay in this little grove of trees. And we still have that hunting party tracking us." As he spoke, there was a howl from above, an orc standing with hands cupped around its mouth, crying out to the winds. That cry was answered by a muffled howl from down the mountain behind them.

Koren stopped, standing stock still. Bjorn grasped his shoulder and looked in the boy's eyes with dread resignation. "Another bad feeling?"

"No," Koren shook his head. "I hear something."

"Shh," Raddick ordered with a hand in the air, and the party halted. "What?"

"I don't know. Voices? The wind is blowing in the direction, so it carries the sound away," Koren explained.

"When you-" Raddick was interrupted by another howl from the orcs behind them. "We will go the edge of the clearing, then you listen again."

In front of them was no mere clearing where a few trees had fallen, it was a flat meadow between two arms of the mountain, more than half a mile across to the trees on the other side. Above those trees, the mountainside rose steeply to a rocky cliff, exposed to the winds. The ground in front of them was grasses and low shrubs, cut down the middle by a stream which formed a marsh. "Koren?" Raddick asked anxiously. If they were to cross the exposed ground, they could not hesitate long. Seeing the grasses waving in the wind, Raddick's experienced eyes imagined the best path across the open ground and did not like what he saw. The streambed was not deep enough for concealment, and slogging through the sticky mud and hummocks of the marsh would be slow going.

Koren held up a finger for silence, listening intently. The afternoon winds gusting across the mountain whistled in his ears, he tilted his head and cupped a hand to one ear to shelter that ear from the wind's roar. "It is voices," he announced uncertainly. "People talking, a lot of them."

"People?" Raddick asked, frustrated at the vague answer. "People like us, like dwarves, or like orcs?"

Koren closed his eyes. "Not orcs," he shook his head without opening his eyes. "Dwarves, maybe?" He was guessing. If not orcs, who else but dwarves could be in their mountains?

Thomas smacked a fist into his palm. "Dwarves would be welcome! If we have found one of their army patrols,"

"Don't get your hopes up," Raddick ordered, speaking more to himself than to Thomas. "You are sure?" He glared intently at Koren, not liking that he was entrusting decisions to a boy, a wizard who had no knowledge of wizardry.

Koren paused to listen again. "I am sure what I hear are not orcs."

"Do you have a feeling about it?" Bjorn asked.

"No. I, yes. I think this is the way we are supposed to go."

"The way *we* are supposed to go, or just you?" Raddick demanded, aware time was slipping away.

"I don't know!" Koren looked away, nearly in tears. "I'm telling you all I know."

They could argue all day and Raddick would have no better clue which way to go. Behind them and likely to the left were orcs. To the right, the meadow ended abruptly at what Raddick guessed was a cliff of unknown height. Spray thrown up by the stream tumbling down a waterfall told him that direction was not promising for an escape. "Right, then, we go forward. Quickly, no stopping until we reach the other side." His own water flask was half empty and though he did not know when next they would find fresh water, they could not stop at the stream, not even for a moment.

The party broke into a run, loping over the uneven grass with Bjorn struggling to keep up in the rear. "It *is* dwarves!" Koren said excitedly after a momentary stop. "A lot of them, and they're shouting something I can't understand."

"Go," Raddick slapped Koren on the back as he went past. "You can listen when we get to the trees."

They reached the edge of the marsh, trying to step across on hummocks, but the grassy mounds collapsed under their boots and the soldiers slipped off into the mud. Koren was following Lem, trying to keep away from the deepest parts of the mud, when something across the meadow caught his eye. "Look!"

It was a dwarf soldier, then two more. They stepped out from the trees, swords in one hand, shading their eyes from the sun with the other. At first, the dwarves held their swords out menacingly to Raddick's group, then turned to shout to someone behind them. Koren thought he saw the shoulders of the dwarves slump, then he realized with a shock why. "They're the *same* soldiers," he groaned.

"What soldiers?" Bjorn asked, peering at the three dwarves.

"The same ones we left behind," Koren explained as more armed dwarves stepped out from the trees. "Lieutenant Renhelm's group!"

"What!" Thomas exploded. "We have walked in a circle all morning?"

"No," Raddick said, spitting on the ground in disgust. "Not in a circle, but our paths have crossed again. And this time," he looked behind them with guilt, "we have lead the orcs right to them. Move! We must warn them."

Splashing through the marsh, Raddick and his people waved their arms to the dwarves, urging them back into the trees, but the dwarves were doing the same, animatedly waving Raddick to turn around. "Captain!" Koren caught snatches of what the dwarves were trying to say. "They want us to go back."

"I got that," Raddick nodded curtly. "They don't know about the orcs tracking us," which made him wonder; what danger was behind Renhelm's party?

When the Royal Army soldiers forded the stream and up out of the marsh on the other side, the dwarves gave up trying to warn them away, and one of them sheathed his sword and trotted out to meet them. "Captain Raddick, you must go back," the dwarf gasped breathlessly. "There is a band of orcs behind us, I fear our rear guard is already engaged."

Raddick groaned. "We have orcs behind us also, a substantial force."

The dwarf's knees almost buckled. "You must speak with Renhelm."

Renhelm was nearly at the edge of the woods when Raddick reached the treeline. "What are *you*-" the dwarf leader fumed, then stopped short of whatever he intended to say.

"We lead a hunting party of orcs on a merry chase after we left you, but then," Raddick judged the position of the sun, "two hours ago, we saw a larger group on a ridge above us. They must have already been on the mountain last night. We've been running from them, and now I've lead them right to you."

"You didn't know," Renhelm clapped a hand on Raddick's shoulder. "We have been tracked since mid-morning by what I estimate are twenty or more orcs. My rearguard is keeping them occupied, but we are running out of arrows, and they are too many," he sighed heavily. "Caught between hammer and anvil, we are. We'll have to make a stand here as best we can, the civilians can't move any faster and my people are exhausted. Captain, we made a bargain and you did your best to keep it, now I offer the same to you. Take your people north through the trees, there is a steep cliff you will have trouble with, but the orcs will be busy with us for a long while, and perhaps they won't notice where you have gone."

"No!" Koren spoke before Raddick. "We can't run away."

"You will go where I tell you," Raddick said coldly.

"I won't go," Koren crossed his arms defiantly. "It's not right."

"Koren," Bjorn stepped in between the army captain and the boy wizard, "none of us like to run away, not leaving defenseless people like this," he looked to the terrified refugees who were now streaming through the forest toward them. "Sometimes we have to-"

"Bjorn," Koren gritted his teeth. "It's not right. I feel it's not right. This is where I'm supposed to be, not running away."

"You *feel* it?" Raddick asked sharply.

"Yes! I feel it, like the way I know where to aim or when to release a bowstring."

Raddick and Bjorn looked at each other, torn. Raddick knew his orders, and allowing Koren to be trapped between two bands of orcs was not in keeping with those orders. "Koren did have a feeling earlier," Bjorn reminded, "before we saw that second group of orcs. He knew we shouldn't go that way."

"To remain here is madness," Raddick protested.

"And to flee, to hope the orcs forget about us, and to climb a cliff, likely in the darkness?" Bjorn asked. "The boy may be right. All our choices are bad ones, maybe making a stand here is the least bad. Go where you will, I will stay here with Koren. I, for one, have learned not to question the spirits, no matter how muddled their speech."

"Spirits?" Renhelm asked, confused.

"I will explain later," Raddick said, then stepped forward to whisper in Koren's ear. "You know I must not allow you to be captured."

"I know," Koren felt a lump in his throat. "The orcs may see to that."

The rearguard of the dwarves was rapidly losing ground as the superior numbers of the orcs began to outflank them, then the retreat came a disorganized rout as the dwarf archers shot their last arrows. Unable to do anything else useful, they ran, dodging arrows from the orcs, and moved along civilian stragglers as best they could, even picking up small children whose parents were exhausted and unable to continue carrying their burden.

As the refugees and Renhelm's soldiers ran on stumbling feet toward the meadow, three of Raddick's archers ran the other way, to engage the orcs. Faced with a new, fresh enemy whose arrows made the orcs pay for a lack of caution, the orcs halted their advance to consolidate their strung-out lines, and soon began to pour concentrated volleys of arrows back to the Royal Army soldiers. Thomas took an arrow to his belly that only dented his fine chainmail, but knocked the breath from his lungs and made him fall. Seeing that, the other two soldiers provided cover while Thomas limped backwards, unable to draw a bowstring. The orcs were still wary of their new enemy, and hung back so Thomas was able to reach the meadow with the help of his companions.

"I should have gone with them!" Koren protested.

"*You* are not going out of my sight," Raddick made a cutting motion with one hand, indicating the discussion was over. "Save your arrows," he ordered as the three soldiers he had sent into the forest emerged in retreat.

"Save them?" Koren could already see orcs rampaging through the woods, coming straight at him. "For what?"

"For a chance to do something other than a futile gesture," Raddick responded angrily. "If we are fated to die here today, the few arrows you carry will be of little use to us, unless we see an opportunity for them to make a great difference."

As the last civilian refugees straggled out of the forest, an orc army stepped out of the treeline on the other side of the meadow and advanced in well-disciplined rows, spreading out to prevent the dwarves from escaping north or south. Renhelm and Raddick got their soldiers into ranks but they were too few, and were trapped between an army of two hundred orcs advancing across the meadow, and a party of orc hunters coming up through the forest behind.

"Go back?" Raddick asked, not taking his eyes off the solid row of orcs that were splashing their way across the marsh and through the stream.

"No," Renhelm answered. "There're almost a sheer drop-off in that direction. Getting the civilians up there is when that orc hunting party caught us. If we run now, the orcs would catch us as we climbed down."

"We make a stand here, then," Raddick declared with a questioning look to Koren, who shook his head. If the boy had a feeling that this is where he was supposed to be, the spirits must want the young wizard dead.

Koren shuddered as the orc army halted fifty yards from him, shouted a terrible war cry as one, and thumped the flat of their battleaxes on their chests. The front rank of the orcs parted as a single orc, somewhat taller than typical for their kind and wearing a helmet with twisted horns sticking out to each side, stepped forward.

Koren felt cold all over. The orc with the grotesque helmet had its right hand stretched out, palm upward, and above that palm danced a ball of magical flame. He faced an orc wizard of unknown power! The wizard was looking toward Renhelm and Raddick rather than Koren, with the dwarf soldier shaking his axe and shouting something Koren's spinning mind did not hear. As the orc's lips twisted in a hideous smile and before Raddick could stop him, Koren's right hand whipped back to snatch an arrow, fit it to the bowstring, draw and fire. A second arrow was on its way as the first reached out for the orc wizard, and a third would have joined its fellows if Raddick had not grabbed Koren's shoulder and pulled him roughly aside.

Even with Koren using magical force to bend the heavy bow, the arrows had to follow a graceful arc rather than flying in a deadly straight line to cross the distance. A graceful arc and a time-consuming one that doomed the arrows, as a frantic shout of alarm sprung up along the orc front line. Before the wizard could take notice of his peril, the first arrow was diving to kill its prey. A desperate flick of the wizard's wrist as the creature threw himself to the side caused the arrow to miss, embedding itself in the neck of an orc to the wizard's left. Even having stumbled to the ground, the wizard easily deflected the second arrow's flight, knocking it to the ground to plunge uselessly into soft mud and disappear.

"Koren!" Raddick said angrily through gritted teeth. "You accomplished nothing but attracting that wizard's attention to you! Get behind me, you young idiot," he ordered as he tugged powerfully on the strap of the boy's arrow quiver, but Koren bent his neck and the strap slipped over his head, taking his helmet with it. With the strap suddenly no longer attached to the young wizard, Raddick fell backward to sprawl on the damp grass, rolling to one side and pushing himself upright, but he was too late. Koren had stepped forward.

The orc wizard did not know who was this remarkably skilled archer he faced, and the orc did not care other than making that archer the focus of his rage. The dwarf leader with his shouted insults was forgotten for the moment, the wizard shook off the hands of his own soldiers who helped him up from the ground, using a thrust from his palm to throw them angrily aside as they had witnessed the indignity and near-death he had suffered at the hands of an archer who appeared to be a mere boy. Summoning more power than he needed, the wizard spun a glaring fireball so large it scorched the skin of two orcs who were foolishly behind him, and with a scream of primal rage he cast the fireball across the meadow at the archer.

Koren had time only to regret how stupid he was when the fireball filled his vision. Instinctively, he ducked to one knee, closed his eyes and threw up a palm as he braced for searing death.

Behind Koren, Raddick had barely again stood up, his boots slipping to find purchase on the muddy grass when he saw the fireball coming at him for he was directly behind Koren. Raddick dived to one side, knowing the move was futile, so he was astonished when the glowing ball of deathfire *staggered* in the air and was violently shoved aside to splatter to the ground. The hellfire broke up as if it were liquid, deadly droplets splashing up as a fountain, burning and killing, scorching grasses and blasting craters in the muddy soil.

Incredulous to be alive, Koren fell back to thump his backside on the wet grass, stunned. How could he be alive? He hadn't *done* anything, not even had time to beg the spirits to aid him. A wailing to his right pulled him out of his momentary reverie and he looked to see the horror. The horror *he* had caused.

Though somehow he made the fireball miss him, it had found other victims. To his right, a dozen or more civilian dwarves who had sought the safety of being near the Royal Army captain, now lay dead or dying, terribly burned by the magical fire. While Koren sat frozen in shock, a dwarf woman, herself burned beyond recognition, tried to beat out the flames enveloping the child she had been holding, her own hands mere blackened stumps. Even as Koren's mouth struggled to speak and he scrambled to his feet, the woman collapsed on top of her child, both of them consumed by the fires of hell.

Koren took one step toward the dead dwarves, wanting nothing more than to take back what he had done, to go back in time and let the fireball consume him rather than killing so many innocents by saving himself. The bodies were already turning to ash, becoming dwarf-shaped piles of cinder on the ground. Another step was halted before he could lift a foot, knowing there was nothing he could do to help the dead.

He could not help those he had killed.

He could avenge them.

Slowly, he turned to look at the enemy wizard, who was staring at Koren in amazement and fear. Who was this unknown boy archer, and how had an unstoppable ball of magical fie been knocked aside? The orc wizard struggled to quell his shaking hands, concentrating all his energy to lift one hand above his head, willing another flame to dance in his palm. This flame wavered, flickering to reflect the shaken confidence of the wizard who conjured it into existence. The wizard redoubled his efforts, reaching into the shadow world for more power but then the fire snuffed out, because the wizard's will was replaced by stark terror at what he had seen. Across the meadow, the archer boy was staring straight at him, eyes narrowed, utterly focused on the orc magician, seeing right through him into his true essence. In that moment, the orc's connection to the shadow realm failed as he lost his entire sense of self.

Across the field, the archer boy's right hand was held out in front of him, and before that hand, a blazing white-hot sun sprang to life.

Raddick also saw to his astonishment the flame Koren had willed to appear, the light already blinding the Royal Army captain while the fire was still building in intensity. Mindfully of Shomas' warning that Koren could not use power without killing himself, Raddick leapt forward, his arms coming down to push the boy to the ground before the the he could kill himself and others around him by dangerously unskilled use of magic, but with the slightest gesture of two fingers on Koren's left hand, the Royal Army captain was launched twenty feet backwards to crash into Thomas. It was a gesture Koren was not even aware he had made, a use of power so small and insignificant it escaped his attention. He had needed to concentrate and Raddick sought to interrupt him, so the world had bent to Koren's unconscious will and thrown Raddick backwards with no more effort than the beating of a fly's wings in a thunderstorm.

"*NOOOOOOOOOOO!*" Koren howled out of control as he commanded the world, and the world bent to his will. From his right hand arose not a flickering flame, not a spinning ball of fire but a river of liquid fire, a torrent of flaming hell and he swept it across the ranks of assembled orcs, burning everything in its path. The orcs tried to scatter and run but there was no time, no place for safety as the blinding torrent of flame consumed all on the west side of the meadow, throwing up clouds of steam as the marsh in the center of the meadow cracked and burned. Wherever the flame touched the ground exploded upward, blasting a trench ten feet deep and three times as wide. Orc bodies instantly flashed into coal-black cinders and were flung high into the sky, parts of those creatures raining down even in the trees on the far side of the meadow. The only conscious impression Koren remembered was the wide-open mouth of the orc wizard as that being attempted a futile spell to ward off a power beyond comprehension. All the magical energy that wizard could muster was less than nothing to the raging river of flame that erased him from existence in a puff of smoke.

When his right hand had swept from one end of the orc line to the other and nothing there now existed, Koren's hand snapped closed into a fist, his knees gave out and he pitched forward onto the scorched grass.

Raddick lay dazed, shaking his head but otherwise unable to move. The only sound was the faint crackling of burning vegetation, and an odd crunching sound he realized with shock was the seared ground underneath where a marsh and a stream had been moments before. His eyes could barely see anything yet, for the flame that had erupted from Koren's hand had been as if the sun had touched the land. Blinking and shading his tender eyes, he perceived that where the stream had been were now only steam and black smoke, where the orc army had been, nothing but clouds of soot lazily dancing in the air. Flakes of soot hung suspended in the air, seeming to be as stunned into immobility as the men and dwarves who witnessed the cataclysmic event.

His ears ringing, Raddick pushed himself to his feet, pulling his sword from its scabbard and using the weapon to hold himself upright on legs like jelly. The air smelled like raw *power* and Raddick's mind struggled to understand what he was seeing, for he had seen nothing of the like in all his years of army service, and those years had witnessed several battles between wizards.

The orcs across the meadow were *gone*, not even lumps of ash remained where an army had stood. Of the orc wizard there was no sign, but- Raddick sucked in a sharp breath as he realized what he was seeing. Dull silver puddles were gently quivering in the breeze that was beginning to stir across the meadow, silver puddles quickly congealing because they had been axe heads and swords. The fire had melted the orcs' weapons, melted them so the metal ran like water, collecting in blasted craters and cracks in the blackened soil.

"Raddick!" The army captain had to turn around twice to understand where the call came from, and his flash-burned eyes still fought to focus as his eyes welled with protective tears. "Captain Raddick!"

It was Renhelm, leaning on his battleaxe as Raddick leaned on his sword. "Renhelm," Raddick answered weakly with a parched throat.

"What," the dwarf limped forward, gaining strength with each step, "was that?" He spoke to Raddick, but his eyes were locked on the prone form of the boy who had accompanied the Royal Army troop. "You brought a wizard with you?"

"Aye," Raddick worked his tongue to get enough moisture in his mouth to talk.

"Such power I have never seen, and from one so young," Renhelm marveled.

"Aye, he is young," Raddick's brain was slow, then he saw something that spurred him into action. Orcs. Koren had killed all the orcs on the west side of the meadow, hundreds of the foul creatures, but the band of orcs who had pursued Renhelm and the civilians up through the forest were regaining their wits and edging warily toward the dwarves. Even what Raddick's dazed mind estimated at only twenty orcs could overwhelm Renhelm's soldiers and the Royal Army troop, and as those orcs had been farther away from Koren, they were quicker to recover than the stunned dwarves. One orc had an arrow fitted to its bowstring and was blinking and shaking its head, seeking a target among the dwarves who were milling around aimlessly. "Renhelm!" Raddick pointed to the danger then had an idea, a desperate idea. "Help me!"

Raddick dashed on quaking legs to the prone form of Koren, kneeling to pull the boy's face out of the scorched grass. As Raddick rolled him over onto his back, the boy gasped and his eyelids opened briefly, then his head lolled to the side and his eyes closed. "Get him upright," Raddick instructed and with the dwarf leader's help, they got Koren upright, Raddick jamming Koren's helmet back on. The Royal Army captain dug into a pocket for a signaling mirror and squeezed it into Koren's open right hand. "Begone, foul orcs!" Raddick shouted from behind the boy, tilting the mirror to catch the bright sunshine and reflect it toward the orcs in the forest who were shifting from one foot to another, trying to work up the courage to attack.

Seeing light flare in the open hand of the boy wizard was enough, the quick blinding flash sending a shock of panic through the band of orcs for what else could the light be but another ball of magical fire? As one, the orcs cast aside their weapons and ran in sheer terror, screeching and wailing as they disappeared into the woods. "Begone!" Raddick roared before his strength failed him and he sank to his knees, Koren's limp body slumping to the ground with him.

"That was," Renhelm paused to catch his breath, "good thinking," he said with admiration. Then, his expression turned to accusation. "Why did you not tell us the boy is a wizard? And such a wizard! Where did he get such power?"

"Renhelm," Raddick leaned on his sword to stand, pulling the blade out of the blackened soil and wiping off the tip with his cloak before sheathing it properly. "Our purpose here is, or *was*, secret, I was not free to speak."

"The boy was your secret?"

"Aye," Raddick agreed, and shrugged as apology.

"Hmmm," Renhelm frowned unhappily, then nodded slowly. He understood the need for soldiers to keep secrets in order to carry out orders. He understood, though he didn't like it, and he suspected his counterpart from Tarador hadn't liked it either. "Well, it is no secret now. You are," he peered into the woods, where the fleeing orcs could not be seen, "still bound for Tarador?"

"Yes," Raddick replied wearily.

"You won't change your mind, I don't suppose? A wizard of his power could be useful up here in our mountains."

Raddick shook his head emphatically. "His power is needed urgently in Tarador, where the enemy is already across our frontier in great numbers. Renhelm, now you have seen the truth, will you aid my quest? You spoke of a hidden path down to the valley."

The dwarf shook his head sadly. "You can't get there from here, leastwise, not without crossing too much open ground, and these mountains are crawling with orcs. Hmm, there is," he tapped his chin while he thought. "There is another way down to the valley, it's not quite hidden but few people know of it. Captain, I must get these people to the fortress, but I can lend a guide to show you the way."

CHAPTER SIXTEEN

Cecil and Paedris were struck down at the same time, falling to their knees on the dusty trail in a forest of gnarled, stunted trees. Paedris slumped insensible to the ground, his face pressed into the dirt, breathing in dust that choked him. It was the dust in his nostrils making him sneeze uncontrollably that brought him back to awareness. All he could do was to roll onto one side, then painfully over onto his back where a sharp rock dug into his one shoulder blade, which he ignored. How long he lay like that he did not know, although the sun had not moved appreciably in the sky while he lay weak and unaware. Then a horrible thought struck him and he opened his eyes!

Lord Mwazo could not throw a powerful fireball, could barely summon a magical flame at all, but that wizard was much more sensitive to vibrations in the field of energy that formed the barrier between the world of the spirits and the world of the real. If Paedris had been knocked to his knees and rendered defenseless, Cecil would have been affected much more strongly, and be in serious danger.

Paedris, unable to stand yet, crawled on his knees to his fellow wizard, fearing that master of subtle magics might have choked to death in one of the pools of fine dust collected in what had been puddles. To his great relief, he found Cecil's head propped up by a tree root, with a gash on his forehead and a rivulet of blood seeping onto the ground. Touching the man's cheek, Paedris could feel the life force within was strong though Mwazo was deeply unconscious.

Feeling it more important to act correctly than quickly, Paedris took a minute to stand up and walk, waving his arms and feeling blood coming back into his limbs. When he could walk a few steps without spots swirling in his vision, he knelt beside his friend, rolling him off the tree root and settling him as comfortably as Paedris had the strength to manage. Closing his eyes, he lent energy to the other wizard, and Mwazo's eyes blinked.

"Oh," the man gasped, trying to push himself upright.

"Easy, easy," Paedris cautioned. "You had a terrible shock. We both did."

"Paedris," Cecil gasped, "I-" he was struck by a wave of nausea and fell to his hands and knees again. When he was able to think again, he understood his friend was holding onto his shoulders, preventing him from pitching face-forward into the burnt-dry dirt.

"Cecil, up, come sit here," Paedris helped the other wizard half walk and half crawl a few feet to sit uncomfortably on a rock that was really too small, but it was better than the rough bark of the diseased trees and thorn bushes that covered the area. "What *was* that?"

"Koren," Cecil looked up with eyes that could barely focus. "It had to be Koren. Only that boy and the demon can summon such power-"

"And it wasn't the demon, I could tell that," Paedris agreed. While the court wizard of Tarador was a powerful master of wizardry, he was not nearly as sensitive to magical forces as Mwazo. "What happened?"

Cecil put his head on his knees and breathed deeply, fighting another bout of nausea. Sitting up again, he accepted a flask of water from Paedris and drank deeply. "Koren must have conjured a fireball, no, a *stream*, a raging stream of magical fire. He killed an enemy wizard, did you feel that?"

"No," Paedris shook his head. "It felt like someone hit me on the head with a blacksmith's hammer, I instantly lost my senses. He killed an enemy wizard?"

"An orc wizard, the echo was very distinctive," Cecil explained. "Many other orcs died also. Paedris, the power that boy unleashed-"

"I know. This is not good. Koren may as well have lit a signal fire for our demon enemy. The boy cannot remain hidden now, it will only be a race against time whether Raddick can bring Koren back to relative safety, before the enemy can capture him."

"We do not know if Raddick is with Koren, or even alive. When Shomas died, Raddick must have been with him," Cecil reminded his friend.

"I do not like the idea of Koren still wandering the wilderness by himself."

"I do not like the idea that, wherever he is, Koren was so threatened by the enemy that he somehow acted, in spite of his complete lack of knowledge and our blocking spell."

"Ha!" Paedris snorted. "It is safe to say that blocking spell has been thoroughly shattered now. Oh, this could be a disaster, the end of everything," he wiped away a tear as it traced a line down the dust on his face. "The question is, what should we do now?"

Mwazo thought, taking sips from his water flask until it was empty. "This is unquestionably a disaster, and I am now fearing you and I should have gone to find Koren, instead of sending Shomas on an errand he was ill-prepared for. However, I do not see this changes our plans, particularly as we are now far from Tarador. We must continue as we planned. We cannot do anything else from here, and-" his voice faded and his eyes stared off into a great distance.

"What? Cecil, what is it?"

"Paedris, we might have an opportunity to salvage something from this disaster, turn the demon's eye away from Koren."

"How?" Paedris could not see how any good could come from Koren's uncontrolled use of immense power.

"The enemy has no idea Koren Bladewell exists. To the best of the demon's knowledge, you are the most powerful wizard to oppose the demon. I could place into the demon's mind a fear that the incident we all felt was caused by you, that *you* have developed an ability to summon power beyond imagination. Hmmm, I will need your help in this. Yes!" Cecil liked the idea more and more as he considered it. "Paedris, we fear the enemy will rush soldiers and wizards toward Koren, hoping to capture the course of that incredible power. But, remember, the enemy does not know anything about Koren. If the enemy believes *you* summoned that enormous power, the demon might instead pull his forces away from the area. He especially would not wish to risk his wizards against you."

"The demon surely felt, as we did, that the release of that power was raw and uncontrolled," Paedris frowned.

"Yes, but that could be explained by you being new to use of such power, that your ability to control it is still new. Again, there is no reason for the enemy to think anyone other than you could wield such power."

"It is," Paedris responded slowly, warming to the idea. If even a single orc had survived Koren's massive use of power, that creature would certainly tell a dark wizard that a young boy was responsible for the releasing an astonishing amount of magical energy. Then, the enemy would do anything to kill or capture that unknown young wizard. But, Cecil's idea was worth trying. Paedris slapped his knee. "Cecil, I like it! Trust you to find a silver lining in this dark cloud."

"Yes," Mwazo said dryly, "because I am known far and wide as a ray of sunshine in everyone's lives."

"Speaking of sunshine, we need to get moving, before the day becomes too hot and we need to find shelter from this burning sun. Our mission here is all the more urgent, and I fear we have little time."

Wing and Olivia were also affected by Koren's use of raw power. Olivia was bending down to take a teakettle off a fire when she slumped forward, fortunately to the side rather than face-first into the fire. The hem of her robe did catch fire and she received a red mark on one leg, before attentive soldiers rushed over and beat the flames out with their vests. They pulled the young wizard away from the fire and laid her on the ground, calling for a wizard healer for help, but it was no use. Every wizard with the Royal Army had been affected, some worse than others.

Madame Chu narrowly escaped serious injury or death because she and Ariana were galloping their horses along a road when Koren called upon the spirits for power he could not control nor understand. When Wing collapsed, she pitched off her horse to the left into a drainage ditch filled with scummy water and reeds. The waist-deep water and soft mud broke her fall if injuring her dignity, and jumping into the ditch to rescue the master wizard did little for Ariana's own dignity. "Help me!" The princess shouted as she sank into knee-deep mud, holding the wizard's head above the algae-slicked water. Soldiers quickly jumped down into the ditch, pulling both wizard and princess out of the muck.

One soldier was embarrassed by the disheveled condition of the princess, and the fact that he had touched her to get her out of the sticky mud. "Your Highness, your dress is-"

"Oh, I don't *care* about my stupid dress! Fetch a healer, Madame Chu needs-"

"Forgive me, Highness, but *all* the wizards appear to have been affected," the soldier reported, pointing forward along the road to the army camp. Around the tent used by the wizards, bodies in the colorful robes of wizards were slumped on the ground.

"*What* is going on?" Ariana asked in fear and wonder. She helped the soldiers get Madame Chu into a wagon and brought over to the wizard's tent, where some of the magic-users were stirring. "Olivia!" Ariana called out, dismayed to see the young woman's robe burned at the hem. "Madame Dupres, are you well?"

"Yes, fine, Ari- Highness. I was clumsy," Olivia blinked slowly, her eyes still not focusing properly.

"Madame Chu is not well, can you help her?"

Olivia shook her head. "I don't know how, I might do more harm than good. Highness, someone used an incredible amount of magic energy, that caused a disturbance in the spirit world." She walked over and placed two fingertips on Wing's forehead, closing her eyes and concentrating. "She will be fine," Olivia announced with a shudder from having come into contact with the power inside the wizard from Ching-Do. Will I ever have such power, Olivia asked herself. And could I control it?

Ariana looked around her, where many wizards were recovering, being helped up by soldiers who were wary of touching a wizard. "Why is Madame Chu not responding?"

"Because she is the most powerful among us, her connection to the spirit world is strongest. She felt the effect more deeply that I did." Olivia held up her hands in a shrug, giving the princess a weak smile. "This is a time when I am fortunate that my abilities are still developing."

"Oh," Ariana did not know what to say, so she changed the subject. "The energy you felt, was it Lord Salva?"

Olivia jerked her head silently and motioned for the princess to follow her beyond earshot of the soldiers around them. Ariana held up a hand to signal the soldiers should stay back. "Highness, this was not Lord Salva, he could never be so crude. I recognize magic of this type from my very first days of training, when I had no idea how to control my own power. Except for the amount of power used, this was the act of an untrained wizard."

"Koren?" Ariana gasped.

Olivia nodded, eyes flicking to the soldiers to see if they had heard what the princess said, but they had no reaction. "Possibly. I can't think of anyone else who would have, could have, done this. It was not a dark wizard."

"Koren is learning to use his power," Ariana mused. "Is this a good thing?"

"If he is trying to learn by himself, it is *not* a good thing, Highness," Olivia warned. "He could hurt himself, or others around him. Magic is *dangerous*," the young wizard emphasized. "Even for a master wizard like Lord Salva, pulling power from the spirit world must be done carefully."

"But," Ariana could not help clapping her hands in delight, "Koren used his power! Paedris hoped Koren could save us from-"

Olivia gestured for the princess to lower her excited voice. "Lord Salva hoped Koren could use his power against the enemy, *after* many years of training and practice. Highness, Koren is in great danger. Our demon enemy is now aware someone beyond its control has used a massive amount of power. The demon will surely now be focused on finding that wizard and killing him."

Anger flashed across Ariana's face, irritation that Madame Dupres had ruined her happiness for Koren. After a moment, the princess understood she was being unfair, for Olivia merely spoke the truth. And in that moment, Ariana straightened her shoulders and transformed yet again from a fearful girl to the determined Regent of Tarador. "Then it is all the more important that we prevent the enemy from crossing the river until next summer, to give Koren time to learn about his power. Lieutenant!" She called out in a loud voice, gesturing to a Royal Army officer. "Inform General Magrane we will strike camp within the hour and resume the march!"

Koren gradually became aware he was alive, became aware of anything. At first, he caught glimpses of sunlight during the brief moments when his eyes were open, before he slumped again into a deep sleep. After the light went away, he felt himself being jostled gently side to side, with an occasional jolt or something digging into his back, and that is when he realized he was being carried. Someone was carrying him on a makeshift stretcher, the pain in his back must be from a rock or tree root when the stretcher was set on the ground. He opened one eye painfully, the lids feeling crusted shut. And the skin on his face felt sunburned. Or worse. What had happened to him? It was dark, he could see the moon as a sliver in the sky through swaying fir trees. "Hello?" He tried to speak but only a rough croak came from his cracked lips.

"Koren," came a voice he recognized as Raddick's. "You are with us again. That is good, we feared for your life. Here, drink this."

Koren felt a cup touch his mouth but he could not drink. A wet cloth replaced the cup, moistening his lips and dripping into his mouth. When he was able to swallow, the cup was there again and he sipped slowly, savoring the cool, clean water. "Where?"

"Where is not important right now," Raddick said gently. "How do you feel?"

"Mmph," Koren groaned. "Tired. What happened?"

"You don't remember?"

"Orcs. And fire."

"*Your* fire."

"Mine?"

"Yes," Raddick gave a mirthless chuckle. "You destroyed an entire *army*. Hundreds of them. How did you do that?"

"Don't know. Don't remember." Sleep took him again.

When he woke again, he could see, and the sun was already up. He felt a hand on one shoulder. That time, it was Bjorn's voice. "How are you feeling?"

"How long did I sleep?" Koren struggled to sit up with Bjorn's help.

"All afternoon and all night. It's mid-morning, the Captain was about to order us to carry you again, we need to get moving. Can you stand?"

"I can walk," Koren bit his lip in determination. He did not want to be carried, did not wish to be so weak, to burden others so heavily. "Can you help me up?"

Regin Falco pulled shut the flap of his tent, tying it from the inside. He needed privacy, and he needed to act quickly, while the wizards accompanying the raiding force north along the east bank of the river were busily engaged in strengthening their concealment spells. From the bottom of the pouch attached to the inside of his belt, he pulled a smooth stone and set it on a folding table. His hands trembled and he paused to take a deep breath, listening to the guards talking outside the tent walls. When his fingers no longer shook badly, he unrolled a blank sheet of parchment on the table and set to writing, slowly and carefully in clear block letters. The writing was not pretty and the message neither subtle nor lengthy, for the agent of Acedor had instructed Regin that sending stones could only carry short, simple messages.

When he was done and satisfied his clumsy fingers had not caused the pen to drip too many ink blotches on the parchment, he muttered the words he had been taught and passed the stone steadily over the lettering, working from top left to bottom right. The stone became warm, then briefly flared hot in his hand before instantly becoming cool again. Regin had to hold onto the tent pole to stop his knees from collapsing. He slipped the stone into a pocket, rolled up the incriminating parchment and added a blank piece of parchment before untying the tent flap and stepping outside. The guards stepped back respectfully as Regin tossed the parchment into a campfire, gazing out at the river toward the sun setting over Acedor as the parchment curled, crisped and burned. "I am going for a walk down to the river," the duke announced. It would be dark soon, and he could toss the now-useless sending stone out into the river. He glanced to the north, where Madame Chu had her wizards gathered around her, casting a spell to conceal the raiding party's movements from the prying eyes of enemy wizards. Regin could not prevent a ghost of a smile fleeting across his lips. The haughty woman from Ching-Do may be a powerful wizard, but her efforts were all for nothing. The enemy now knew where the raiding force was going, and they would be waiting to strike.

"Last one," Bjorn grunted a week later as he slapped the arrow into Koren's waiting hand, but this time Bjorn didn't let go. He wanted the boy to look at him, and as Koren felt the arrow wasn't yet his to take, he looked at his companion questioningly. "Make it count," Bjorn stared Koren in the eye and let go of the arrow.

"Have you ever seen me miss?" Koren didn't look back at the older man, and though his words were boastful, his tone reflected uncertainty.

"That's not what I meant." Bjorn loosened the strap of his now-empty quiver, so it would be easier to pull the strap over his head and discard it if needed. His sword belt he tugged on, bringing the scabbard toward the back where it would be out of the way after he drew he sword. "Killing another ordinary orc will do us no good, there are too many of them."

"I know," Koren frowned, dashing out from behind cover to run around a corner of the trail along the steep wall of the ravine. His feet skidded on loose sand and he got a heart-stopping look at the rain-swollen stream at the bottom of the ravine, where rapids crashed over and around jagged rocks fallen from the ravine's sides. "What else can I do?" He ducked back behind cover as he saw an orc aiming an arrow at him, pressing his back flat against the near-vertical wall of the ravine.

"How about some magic?" Bjorn's joking smile belied the seriousness of his question.

"No," Koren shook his head angrily, poking his head out from cover to see where the orc was then. "I told you, I can't do it!" Koren recovered physically within two days, but inside he still didn't feel right at all. He flexed his right hand open and closed, overcome with frustration that since he had poured forth a river of fire, he had not been able to make even the faintest glow of wizard fire appear. "I don't know how, I don't know what I did that one time. It almost killed me!"

"All right, all right," Bjorn waved a hand to calm the boy down. Seeing an orc peek his head around a corner of the twisting ravine, he let fly a rock he had in one hand, watching with satisfaction as the orc was forced to dash backward and the rock clattered where the orc's head had been, shards breaking off and falling down into the stream far below. "Hold onto that arrow until these orcs get closer, uh!" Bjorn was forced to flatten himself to the trail as a pair of arrows came from up the ravine.

"They're not close enough now?" Koren asked anxiously, holding the last arrow to the bowstring nervously.

Bjorn didn't answer, he didn't have to, his actions spoke for him as he sprung to his feet and dashed past Koren, talking cover behind the tangled root of a long-dead tree clinging to the ravine wall. He inched downward to pick up a nice sharp rock, then dropped it. If the orcs saw Bjorn was reduced to throwing rocks, they would soon risk a charge along the trail, and Koren held their only remaining arrow.

"Bjorn! Koren!" Thomas called from down the trail, gesturing them onward. "Captain found the bridge, it looks like they didn't cut it yet!"

"We-" Bjorn had to duck as an arrow hit the rock he was huddled behind, sending stone chips spiraling down into the stream at the bottom of the ravine. Silently, he held up one finger, but Thomas didn't understand. "Koren."

Koren held up his one arrow for Thomas to see, turning to show the quiver on his back was empty. Thomas did understand that, holding up three fingers to indicate the arrows he had remaining. "You can have mine," he assured Koren. "Come now, quickly!"

Another arrow aimed at Bjorn missed, this one wobbling above his head to stick into a pile of sand at the bottom of a side gully. He did not wait for an invitation, rolling over and over until he was no longer behind cover of the rock, when he sprang to his feet and dashed after Koren. They reached Thomas just in time for that soldier to grab Bjorn's vest and yank him to the ground before an arrow could strike him. "Koren," Thomas began but the boy needed no instruction. He spun, his last arrow already fitted to the bowstring, and let it fly to zip up the trail and bury itself in the shin of an orc who was fourth of a half dozen creatures racing along the trail. The stricken orc tripped forward, knocking down three others in front as he fell, and all four crashed onto the trail, arms and legs windmilling frantically, then they all tumbled over the edge.

Bjorn risked poking his head out to watch the four doomed orcs plunging downward, mercifully bashing themselves insensible before they reached the bottom and disappeared into the roiling rapids. "One arrow. Four orcs," he muttered.

"You told me to make it count," Koren retorted without a grin.

"No one likes a showoff, young one," Bjorn grumbled admiringly. "In this case, I grant you permission to show off any time you like."

"Arrow," was Koren's only reply, for two of the original half dozen orcs were still on their feet, with another six coming around the bend of the trail. Thomas slapped an arrow into Koren's hand and the untrained wizard fitted it to the bowstring, drawing back.

That was enough for the orcs, who had seen four of their band die from one magically well-placed arrow. They turned and ran, two of them throwing aside their own bows in their haste. "Hmmm," Koren grunted as he eased strain off the bowstring. He inspected the arrow, surprised and disappointed. "Thomas, this arrow is bent," he complained, "and the fletching is missing a feather."

"I didn't say I had three *good* arrows," Thomas defended himself. "Why do you think I used all the others before this garbage?" He held up the other two weapons, one of which was nearly snapped in half. "Good thing you've got the orcs afraid of you now. Come on, Captain has more arrows. I think," he added hopefully. "This way."

Thomas lead the way down the easy slope of the trail at a dead run, not looking back. The ravine bent to the right, so the orcs behind them could not see the three as they ran, until the ravine bent back to the left and a long, exposed section of the steep-sided canyon gave the orcs a view of the fleeing trio. With a shriek of anger and blood-lust, the orcs resumed the hunt.

Koren pulled his head up, pumped his arms and forced his weary legs to keep running, careful to hug the ravine wall rather than the steep drop-off to the stream below. Did orcs ever get tired, he asked himself?

Their prospects for returning to Tarador, for survival, had seemed much more hopeful the previous day. Koren had recovered from his dizziness and extreme weakness, refusing the offer for him to rest while being carried on a stretcher, but accepting when Raddick insisted others carry his pack and weapons. When his brain shook off the fuzziness that had been the result of him using uncontrollable power, he learned Raddick and Renhelm had agreed to separate, with the dwarf leader assigning one of his soldiers to guide the Royal Army troop at least down to the valley that lead to Tarador. The secret passage was, Renhelm had explained with apology, no longer an option as they had come too far west. Instead, as Renhelm escorted the civilians up to the dour fortress of Magross, Raddick accepted the offer to be guided along a path that was not secret but little-used. Their guide, a dwarf woman named Anrid, hoped the bands of orcs roving through the lower mountains had not discovered the track she intended to take. At first, her prayers had been answered, as the party reached the upper end of the trail without being noticed, and without seeing any orcs, although their howls could be heard echoing off the mountainsides all around.

At its upper end, the trail was a mere shallow gully cut by a rivulet that might ambitiously be called a stream. The party picked their way between groves of trees and clusters of shrubs clinging to the increasingly steep sides of the gully, until it became a ravine and several streams joined to make a roaring torrent of white water at the bottom. At that point, the walls of the ravine were nearly vertical on both sides, with the trail a path hacked out of rock and crumbling soil by the dwarves. All the first day and half of the following night, the party walked down, down, down, with Raddick both encouraged by the speed of their passage and worried about being hemmed in by the narrow ravine walls. In places, the trail became precarious, no wider than a man's shoulders, with a steep drop-off to the rock-strewn stream far below. Gullies and other ravines coming in from the sides were spanned by rickety rope bridges, some of which had been cut and others appeared to have sagged and even collapsed due to lack of care. Anrid had apologized, explaining the paths so close to the border with Acedor were not well traveled, and since Acedor had crossed the River Fasse in Tarador, the dwarf army and engineers had concentrated on building up defenses rather than maintaining bridges that might be useful to the enemy. The dwarf woman had shown how to cross a side ravine, wrapping her legs around a surviving rope cable and pulling herself along hand over hand. Even knowing he was a wizard and should be able to stride across on top of the swaying rope as if it were a broad road, Koren's heart had been in his throat until he felt solid ground under his feet on the other side.

Then, that morning, disaster struck. With the ravine walls so close and the water of the fast-running stream rushing along at the bottom, sounds from above were muffled. Koren heard orc hunting cries throughout the night, he judged none of them close enough to worry about. Before mid-morning, however, three events shattered the party's unspokenly growing confidence. First, they came upon a side ravine, just as deep and steep, where a rope bridge had been cut deliberately, and cut recently as Anrid judged. Going back was not an option, so the dwarf woman had pulled a clever device from her pack and attached a thin cord to an arrow. Koren shot the arrow to fly between the crevice of a stout boulder on the other side, where yanking on the cord demonstrated the cord and the anchor were firmly set. Anrid removed her helmet, chainmail, weapons and even her boots before she slid along the alarmingly thin cord to the other side. After she used the cord to pull across a strong rope, the party followed, but Anrid had warned the danger was not over. "There is another bridge below us, longer, which crosses from one side of the ravine to another. If that bridge is cut, I cannot get us across there."

"What would we do then?" Raddick had asked fearfully.

"Turn back," Anrid answered with resignation. "If this bridge has been cut by my people, they would likely have cut the main bridge also. We should see if by midafternoon, so we could turn around without walking all the way there."

Raddick did not reply that turning around did them no good, though as he had no idea what else to do, he had held his tongue.

They came upon second and third problems almost at the same time. Koren heard voices and went ahead with Raddick to identify the source. With the sound of water crashing over rocks echoing off the ravine walls, it was hard for even Koren to hear, and his eyes could not see around curves or through rock. He inched forward when he felt the sound was growing louder, and then he became confident the source was voices; dwarf voices. Around a corner was a ravine coming in from the east, the trail there little better than a narrow shelf hacked out of rock. A dozen, no, two dozen dwarf women and children were fearfully making their way along the trail toward the gorge of the main ravine.

Raddick had groaned. Civilians. More refugees, people he did not have time to help or care for. Yet, he could not do nothing, particularly not when Anrid recognized one of the women and softly called out to her. Hearing a familiar voice set up a relieved chatter among the civilians, and several of the children squealed with joy.

The civilians had been with a much larger party that became separated two nights before when an orc band attacked. The men had led the orcs away, intending to rejoin the women later, but the men had not returned and the frightened dwarves had walked along barely-remembered paths through the mountains, now they were lost and feared the hunting cries of orcs all around them. Raddick had been about to suggest that Anrid go with the civilians back up the trail, as the path downward was clear to the Royal Army soldiers, but his thoughts were interrupted before he could speak.

Behind the civilians in the side canyon, a shriek arose as a small band of orcs spotted the prey they had been tracking. At almost the same time, another group of orcs from the same band looked down from the lip of the ravine above Raddick, and they, too, set up a cry to call more of their foul kind.

There was nothing for it, then, but to run quickly as they could, down the ravine, hustling the civilians along, and with the soldiers helping carry weary or injured dwarf children. Their only hope was that the main rope bridge was intact; if they could cross it and cut the rope behind them, the orcs could not follow. If. Anrid warned she had no idea whether the bridge still existed, but she also saw no choice but to race down the ravine trail.

Koren, Bjorn and Thomas were assigned to be rearguard, with Koren's arrows slowing the advance of the orcs. Whenever the trail straightened enough for a clear shot, an orc died, though Koren's supply of arrows had dwindled rapidly.

"The bridge is intact!" Thomas exulted as the three ran around a boulder lodged into the side of the ravine, and they could see down the ravine to the rope bridge stretched across the fast-running stream.

"That's not good," Bjorn observed in a flash. "The bridge is fine. The problem is the approaches on both sides. Those orcs behind us can pour arrows down on anyone crossing that bridge, then there is no cover on the other side for a quarter mile or more," he frowned. The near side of the ravine had rocks that had tumbled down, trees clinging stubbornly to the steep wall, and other opportunities for archers to shelter behind. "Once we cross, we will be exposed while the orcs here can take cover."

"You see a choice?" Thomas demanded, irritated. He saw Bjorn was right, and he saw no option but speed.

"No. Let's move," Bjorn announced with a glance behind where orcs were warily poking their heads around the curve behind them.

The race became a rout. Orcs behind Koren lost their wariness after he shot his last arrow, and then they saw the arrow he menaced them with snapped in two when he pulled back the bowstring. Worse, the howling calls of the orcs behind them had attracted others, some of them trying to run through the forest on top of the ravine's near wall. Orcs up there shot arrows down with poor aim and results given the distance and awkward angle, but enough of the distinctive, short arrows rained down that some found targets among the civilians, slowing Raddick's anguished efforts to hurry them along. Seeing their arrows were having less effect than they wished, the orcs above the ravine began dislodging rocks, rocking them back and forth until they crashed down. Some of the rocks collided with other rocks on their way down, starting an avalanche that partly broke away and blocked the narrow shelf of the trail. One particularly large rock bounced its way down and just over Koren as he flattened himself on the trail, pebbles and fist-sized stones pelting him enough to draw blood from his scalp.

"We're cut off!" Thomas groaned in alarm, halted by a pile of rocks blocking the trail ahead.

"No! We go over!" Bjorn slapped the soldier on the back and squeezed past him, scrambling over the loose rock. Stones skittered away under his feet and he nearly fell over the edge, having to launch himself in the air when the slipping debris became a cascade. Bjorn fell heavily on his belly, knocking the breath out of him and he crawled forward on hands and knees, ignoring his inability to breathe and the cuts inflicted to his palms and knees. After reaching a section of trail where the ledge was not covered by the rock slide, Bjorn paused to push his back against the ravine wall and gulp in air. "The two of you come," he wheezed, "on!"

Thomas looked at Koren, the man's eyes bulging with fear. He had watched Bjorn almost slide and fall to his death on the unstable pile of rocks that still partly blocked the trail. Then he looked behind them where orcs were warily shuffling around the curve and beginning to shoot arrows. The nearest orcs were still too far away for the short bows they carried to reach Thomas, but that happy situation would not last, and the orcs on top of the ravine above were rolling more stones down. They could not wait. Koren slung his now-useless longbow over his shoulder and pulled a length of rope from his belt, winding one end around a stone. "Bjorn! Catch it!" He tossed the stone, which arced through the air toward Bjorn but unfortunately it bounced off that man's outstretched hands, bending back one of his fingers painfully and falling toward the raging stream far below.

"Trying again," Koren announced while Thomas helped him haul the rope up. An orc arrow embedded itself in sand near Koren's feet and he turned his head to see that arrow had come not from above but behind. They were running out of time, a fact Koren pushed out his mind as he again tossed the stone. Bjorn was ready and he caught it, not without a scare as he wobbled over the edge until his boot heels dug in and he fell back against the ravine wall.

"Got it!" Bjorn shouted, looking for something to tie the rope end around. There wasn't anything, so he belayed it around his waist. "Come on, quickly!"

"You first, Thomas," Koren urged.

"No, you are the wizard," Thomas insisted.

"Yes, and that is why those orcs will stay back," Koren replied as he belayed the rope around his waist with one hand while he raised the other hand menacingly above his head

"But you said you can't-"

"The orcs don't know that. Go."

Thomas saw the sense in Koren's argument. If Thomas stayed behind to belay the rope, the orcs would rush in, shoot him and then both he and Koren would fall. Without wasting time on talk, the soldier hung onto the rope with both hands, clambering over the dangerously loose rock. He immediately fell, his feet flying out from under him and not slowing his progress at all, for he continued on his knees despite the sharp stones cutting his pant legs and bloodying his knees. When he was close enough he reached out one hand for Bjorn, who grasped him solidly and pulled Thomas to crash into him, both men falling onto their backsides. It was painful and undignified and effective. "Koren!" Thomas called out to the boy unseen just beyond the pile of rocks. "Tie the rope around your waist, hurry!"

"I have a bit of a problem here," Koren warned. It was more than a bit of a problem. While he had stood as still as possible to steady the rope for Thomas, orcs above and behind him launched arrows and Koren had been forced to dodge the projectiles as best he could. Two orcs in particular caused him concern. The first was a hunter, quite ordinary except for the distinctive row of crow's beaks strung around his neck and the black paint covering the left side of his face. He remembered that orc as one who had been chasing Renhelm's civilian refugees, the creature had been behind Koren when he destroyed the army across the meadow with fire. With an icy feeling in the pit of his stomach, Koren realized that orc knew he was the wizard who killed so many of the clan.

The second orc was a chieftain, wearing a helmet adorned with feathers and bones. The first orc pointed to Koren, gesturing to the chieftain as the two spoke in words Koren could not understand but the meaning was clear; the chieftain was being told that Koren was a wizard and would be a valuable prize if captured.

The problem became worse as the chieftain held the first orc back and ordered three others to drop their bows and advance toward Koren. Clearly, those three unlucky orcs had also heard Koren being described as an immensely powerful wizard. Perhaps the orc band did not entirely believe the unlikely tale of one young boy destroying an entire army, but they had no wish to test Koren's power. Testing Koren's power is exactly why the chieftain ordered them forward, and why that clan leader screamed at the reluctant three, waving his axe and screaming threats.

Without a single arrow in his quiver, and without the ability to conjure even the faintest glow of magical fire in his hand, all Koren could do was face the advancing orcs with one hand held high and try to appear haughtily confident and unafraid. For a second, it worked, then either the three orcs saw how badly his hand trembled or the threats from their chieftain overcame their fears, for they raced forward, arms raised to tackle him. "Hang on, I'm coming!" Koren cinched the knot tight and ran to belly-flop on the pile of rock, sliding down and over the edge to drop into empty space.

Bjorn and Thomas held onto the rope, to each other and to anything else they could grasp as they saw Koren fall. The rope jerked tight, pulling both men forward toward the edge and they experienced a moment of panic as one of Bjorn's feet hung out in the air until they stopped sliding. "Pull me up?" Koren pleaded.

With the two men pulling hand over hand, and Koren helping by holding onto whatever came into reach, the three got the boy wizard over the edge to roll onto one side. "The rope's too tight," Koren gasped in pain as it dug into his ribs just under his armpits. Thomas pulled out a knife and sliced through the rope.

"You all right?" Bjorn looked at where the rope had dug into his palms.

"Yes but we have a problem," Koren picked up a stone and threw it to hit an orc who was attempting to crawl over the rock slide. With a cry, the orc rolled down and into the ravine, bouncing off the wall as it tumbled brokenly down toward the stream.

"That'll teach them," Thomas stuffed the knife back into his belt. "Good throw."

"That orc was going to fall anyway," Bjorn observed. He held out a hand and helped Koren to his feet. "What's the problem?"

"Those orcs know I'm a wizard, and now they know I can't use magic. I think their chieftain ordered them to capture me."

Bjorn said a curse word and gestured Koren to squeeze past him on the narrow trail ledge. "Go on, then, move!"

As they ran, orcs above rained down more rocks, slowing their flight along the precarious ledge that was the trail. The last time Koren looked back to the pile of rock that had nearly caused him to fall, orcs were digging it out of the way, and a dozen orcs had already gotten past the obstacle. "They're following us!" Koren warned and his companions barely bothered to glance behind them. Of course they assumed the orcs would pursue.

"Why aren't they shooting at us?" Thomas asked, out of breath. The three could not move fast enough to actually be running, for the trail was littered with stones that had fallen down from above, and more rocks were tumbling down the steep canyon walls. But Koren noted that Thomas was right, the orcs above were shouting and howling and jeering but no longer firing arrows nor throwing rocks. It hardly mattered, for the creatures had dislodged enough loose stones from the ravine wall that they were falling on their own, the material flaking away and breaking loose.

"They're not shooting, because they want to capture Koren," Bjorn explained as he tripped on a stone that rolled right under his feet, throwing him to his knees to sprawl halfway over the edge. Without comment for there was no need, he picked himself up and continued onward, kicking more loose stones out of the way. A shower of pebbles from above pelted him and one fist-sized stone bounced off his shoulder. "Look out!"

Koren shielded his face with a hand as dust and pebbles rained down on him and he pressed himself against the ravine wall for cover. Behind Koren, Bjorn had crouched down on the trail, grunting as stones thumped off his back. Just ahead, Thomas stumbled as a section of the ledge gave way beneath his right foot and he looked upward for something to hold onto. Just as he lifted his eyes to search, a rock larger than his head hit him squarely in the chest and from one moment to the next he was gone, over the edge. Thomas fell silently, perhaps not even aware he had fallen.

Koren reached out instinctively. "No!"

"Koren you idiot, get back!" Bjorn ordered. "He's *gone*, there's nothing you can do." The former Kng's Guard risked a glance upward to see the landslide had spent itself and now only a cloud of dust was falling, then ahead to see whether more landslides would block their way forward. He could now see the near end of the rope bridge, with dwarves walking across one at a time rather than evenly spaced along its length, and four dwarves lined up waiting their turn to cross. The bridge was swaying more than it should, it must have been damaged and Bjorn hoped the flimsy structure would still span the ravine when he got there. In front of him along the trail, dust clouds from prior rock slides partly obscured the view. What- Bjorn noticed the dwarves on the near side of the bridge were panicking, pushing forward heedless of whether the bridge could hold them. Why were the dwarves-

What Bjorn saw made hope die in his heart. "Come with me!"

Raddick's heart was in his throat as he helplessly watched three, then two figures running haltingly along the trail on the opposite side of the ravine, dodging rockslides and stumbling along the narrow ledge. One of the figures fell, tumbling and bouncing sickeningly all the way down to be swallowed up by the fast-moving stream and at first Raddick feared all was lost, until the remaining two figures came around an outcropping of rock and he could see one of them was Koren Bladewell, for the other two had worn leather vests. The person who fell was either Thomas or Bjorn, and Raddick was conflicted about who he hoped had survived. Thomas had served with Raddick for nearly eight years, while Bjorn had a steadying influence on the rash and untrained young wizard. "Lem!" Raddick called out to the man urging dwarves one at a time across the swaying rope bridge. "Make them hurry!" He ordered while scrambling down from the viewpoint above the trail on his side of the ravine. After being first across the damaged rope bridge, Raddick had climbed to better see along the ravine, and what he saw thoroughly discouraged him. He had nearly fallen twice just in climbing thirty feet up the steep ravine wall, there was no way to climb out to the lip of the ravine even though no orcs were at the top on his side. The trail on his side was a ledge cut into the wall, though this ledge was wider and more flat it also was totally exposed and a rockslide a quarter mile up the trail was a serious obstacle. Raddick had immediately put Anrid to work clearing the slide and the woman with three other dwarves were pulling fallen stones out of the way as quickly as they could, but it was not fast enough.

The bridge had naturally been built across the most narrow part of the ravine, where no more than thirty yards separated the east and west walls of the gorge. Arrows could reach from one side to the other and that was a problem for Raddick; he and his people had no more than two arrows each left and some had none. The long, nightmarish pursuit down the ravine trail had exhausted their supply of arrows and they had no materials nor time to make more. Lack of arrows had been the cause of Raddick's current, most urgent dilemma. He had allowed Bjorn to persuade them that, with arrows running low and Koren their most accurate shot, those two should act as rear guard. Raddick had reluctantly agreed and at first remained behind to assure the safety of the young wizard, until he saw the deadly shots from Koren were forcing the orcs to stay far behind. The army captain had then raced on ahead to scout across the bridge, not liking what he saw. From his viewpoint above the trail, he had been first to see orcs were coming toward the bridge from both north and south! A second group of orcs was scampering along up the trail on the same side of the ravine as Koren and Bjorn, and with the trail ahead of them littered with fallen rock, they were moving far too slowly. Shouting and waving his arms, he tried to catch their attention, warning them of the orcs ahead of them!

"Koren," Bjorn said as he waved one arm to acknowledge the army captain on the other side of the ravine.

"I see them," the young wizard gasped, his legs feeling like lead while the two ran along the trail as fast as they dared. "We can make it."

Bjorn did not know if that were true but there was nothing to do except run toward the bridge. The orcs coming up the trail now saw the two people running down the trail toward them and howled excitedly, redoubling their efforts. Without orcs above the canyon shooting arrows or rolling rocks down at them, it was a straight-up race, and Bjorn was again dismayed by how fast the awkward-looking legs of orcs could run. "Koren! Go ahead, don't wait for me!"

"No! I won't leave-"

"You fool! They want *you*, not me!"

"Oh." Koren understood Bjorn was in danger mostly because he was near the wizard the orcs sought to capture, so without wasting breath on a reply he lifted his knees higher and raced ahead.

It was all for nothing. Koren reached the near end of the rope bridge before the orcs in front or behind him, but he couldn't cross! Three dwarves had crowded onto the dangerously swaying span and the thick rope that formed the bottom strand had twisted, nearly flipping two of the dwarves over into the water far below. Raddick and everyone on the far side were screaming for the three dwarves to move however they could, and the one closest to the far side was pulling herself along by hanging onto the bottom rope. When she got within ten feet, other dwarves tossed a rope to her and she swung onto it, bloodying her nose and not caring.

Bjorn arrived, red in the face and cursing in between breaths. "Go!" he shouted at Koren, actually kicking the boy in the seat of his pants to get him onto the bridge.

Koren gingerly walked four, six, then eight feet out onto the bridge, the rope sagging alarmingly, then he could go no farther. The bridge in front of him had twisted so badly there was no way to walk forward, he would have to hang on by his hands, dangling above the rushing water and sharp rocks that waited to smash him to bits. "Bjorn, come with me!"

"Too dangerous."

"You think one more person will make a difference?" Koren asked incredulously. "The bridge will hold or it won't! I'm not going across without you."

Cursing the foolishness of youth, Bjorn shrugged off his pack to save weight and inched out onto the bridge on hands and knees, then wrapping his legs around the bottom strand. It was useless, they could not go forward while the two dwarves ahead of them were entangled in the ropes. From the far side, an over-strained rope snapped, whipping around and making the entire bridge bounce.

"I am never crossing a bridge again," Koren vowed as he closed his eyes and hung on tightly as he could.

"We can't go back now," Bjorn stated the obvious. Orcs from both directions had stopped running at the orders of their chieftain, pointing their arrows at the dwarves huddled together on the far side of the ravine. Raddick and other soldiers had arrows fitted to their bowstrings, Bjorn noted not every soldier who carried a bow had an arrow. If it came to a fight, the far more numerous orcs would quickly slaughter the trapped people on the other side.

"The boy!" The chieftain shouted in the common tongue, his voice making that language harsh and chilling. The orc leader held up his hands, showing he had no weapons ready, though an axe and a sword hung from his belt. "We want only the boy," he pointed a bony finger toward Koren. "Leave him to us, and you may go!"

"Koren, no!" Raddick ordered, knowing how foolish young people could be. "Do not think to save us by sacrificing yourself, you know the truth!" The captain's voice echoed off the ravine walls, the man's lungs straining to make himself heard over the crashing water, the wails of the refugees and the gleeful jeers of the orcs.

Koren forced himself to open his eyes. There were too many orcs, too many arrows aimed at Raddick and the captain's brave soldiers and the defenseless dwarves, there would be no escape. Hemmed in by the ravine's steep walls, the soldiers and dwarves had too far to go along the exposed far side before the ravine broadened beyond the useful range of arrows. Koren had no arrows left, his bow useless and discarded.

This was the end. There was only one thing Koren could do; he would let go of the bridge and fall into the stream. Then the orcs would-

No. That felt wrong. If he fell, the orcs would be enraged at being denied their prize and they would kill Raddick and everyone else on the other side of the ravine.

Falling into the gorge not only would not do any good, it *felt* wrong. It felt wrong the way it felt right when Koren aimed an arrow and knew, simply *knew*, he would hit his target.

He knew what he had to do. It was wrong, but it felt right. He had to trust the spirits, though he knew little of them. "Captain! I must surrender. You will die if I don't!"

"Koren, I warn you!" Raddick shifted his aim to the boy, and his soldiers followed their captain's lead. "You know my orders, I cannot allow you to be taken."

"I know your orders, and why," Koren replied. "Bjorn," he said just loudly enough to be heard over the jeering orcs. "I know what I need to do." As he spoke, one eye on Bjorn and one on Raddick, he slipped his sword under the rope railing to his right, pulling upward slightly and feeling strands of the tough fibers part under the razor-sharp blade.

"Don't," Bjorn knew instantly what the boy intended to do, or he thought he knew. "If you fall, they will kill us all anyway."

"I'm not going to fall." Looking far down to the stream raging white foam over the rocks below, he added "Not far. Bjorn, I have to do this. I *know* it. It's the only way."

"Koren," Bjorn pleaded, stricken. "You don't-"

"This is the only way to win the war." Koren's voice was barely audible over the harsh cries of the orcs and the shouted orders from Raddick and his soldiers. "Bjorn, I know it. I have to do this, or we are *all* doomed."

"Is this like how you know just when to release an arrow?" Bjorn's words carried resignation in them.

"Yes. I am just as certain."

Bjorn did not reply with words, he merely nodded and wrapped a rope around one leg, holding onto a railing with one hand and poised his sword under the other railing.

"Ready?" Koren asked.

Too late, Raddick realized the young wizard's plan. "You fool! NO!" Heedless of the orcs, the captain tossed aside his bow and gathered himself to jump out onto the bridge, when the already-damaged structure sagged wildly. Wizard and former King's Guard struggled to hang on while sawing at the ropes, and with a ripping sound, the bridge snapped in two.

Raddick nearly fell, being snatched back onto firm ground at the last second by Lem's hand and he fell heavily to the ground, reaching for his bow even as he gasped with pain.

Koren and Bjorn swung downward to smash into the ravine's steep side, their lives saved only because they had been close to one side of the bridge and so did not have far to fall. Of the two dwarves entangled in the bridge ropes, one was bashed hard against the ravine wall and hung there unmoving while the other was blessed to thump into a pile of sand accumulated just above a ledge. That dwarf waved an arm weakly and struggled to cut herself free from the ropes biting into her legs.

Raddick accepted help from Lem to regain his feet, picking up his bow and refitting the arrow. He pointed it at Koren, knowing the orc chieftain would hold his own arrows as long as Raddick threatened to take away the prize. "Koren, you leave me with no choice," he called out in a voice less steady than that befitting a captain of the Royal Army.

"Captain!" Koren shouted, his voice steady despite the sharp pain from his ribs. "Trust me. Please! I ask you to trust me. I must do this."

Raddick shook his head, holding his bow firmly, the arrow aimed directly at Koren's heart. He blinked to clear his vision. "I have my orders. You know that."

"Yes, Captain. I am asking you now to trust me. I can end this war."

"I have my orders!" Raddick repeated, but with less conviction, and the arrowhead drooped slightly. Regaining his composure, he steadied the arrow on target. "I am sorry, but I must obey my orders."

"I know your orders, and I know why they were given to you," Koren reasoned with pleading eyes. "Lord Salva did not know what I now know. Captain, please, trust me. I will throw myself down if you wish," he glanced at the white foam of the stream below, and the jagged rocks waiting there. "But I am asking you to *trust me*."

Raddick's tension on the bowstring eased ever so slightly, and he blinked again to clear not only his vision, but his mind. "What would I tell Paedris, if I allowed you to be captured, in spite of his most urgent orders to me?"

"Tell Paedris," Koren considered. "Tell Paedris that I understand now, and he was right to conceal the truth from me, that he could not trust me not to use my power. But also tell him he should trust me now, that trusting me now is our only hope. I *know* it, Captain. Please."

Of all the hard decisions Raddick had in his life, in his Royal Army career, none compared to the choice before him. He had been entrusted with the fate of Tarador, of the entire world, and now he was about to throw it all away because an untrained young wizard, a mere boy, asked to be trusted. Raddick dropped the arrow, lowered the bow and jabbed toward Koren with a finger. Tears streaming freely down his cheeks, Raddick spoke to his soldiers. "Lower your weapons. Lower them! Koren Bladewell. *You!*" He jabbed the finger toward the boy with wild emotion. "You had better be right about this!"

"I am, Captain," Koren's own tears blurred his vision. "Farewell."

Raddick impulsively snapped a salute to Koren and Bjorn, then addressed the former King's Guard. "Bjorn, you take care of him, you hear?"

Bjorn painfully returned the salute, his shoulder grinding as he moved. "I will, Captain. If we don't meet again, it has been an honor. Now, you get out of here before these orcs change their minds, or this young fool surprises us again." He swung around on the rope, turning to Koren. "What now?"

"We let these orcs pull us up, I guess," Koren really had not thought past persuading Raddick not to kill him.

"Ah," Bjorn grunted as the orcs above began roughly yanking the rope bridge upward, bouncing him against rocks and making his sore shoulder protest with hot stabbing pain. "You do have a plan, right?" he looked up at the hate-filled, jeering faces of orcs. "Please tell me you have a plan."

"I do," Koren's insides shivered as he spoke. His plan seemed a lot better before he was faced with being held captive by orcs.

CHAPTER SEVENTEEN

Regin turned in the saddle to watch the last group of boats depart the eastern shore of the River Fasse, taking particular note which boats flew the silver falcon of Burwyck on their flag poles. With pride, he sat tall in the saddle, pleased that the seven boats belonging to his ducal army were evenly spaced and making their way straight across the river in one neat, well-disciplined line. "See that, Kyre, Talen," he spoke to his sons, "our boats proceed as one unit, while the Royal Army boats look like a gaggle of ducklings who have lost their mother."

"Indeed, Sire," Talen agreed, "but then many officers of the Royal Army come from more common stock than do lieutenants and captains of Burwyck." Talen had learned simply to say whatever he thought his father wanted to hear. "What say you, brother?" Talen took the opportunity to put his hated brother on the spot, knowing that despite his conspicuous bravery at the Gates of the Mountains, Kyre was not in their father's good graces. Talen was not sure what Kyre had done to displease their father, but he wanted to give his free-thinking brother an opportunity to further anger the duke.

Kyre could have pointed out that the boats of Burwyck had delayed launching until all seven were ready, an action that put on a pretty show for observers but wasted precious time. If the river crossing had been opposed by the enemy, a massed flotilla of boats would be a sound strategy to overwhelm enemy defenses. As only a few very surprised enemy troops had been on the opposite shore, the raiding force had the luxury of making an orderly crossing. Also, the Royal Army had many more boats that the seven owned by the Falcos, so they could not cross all at once or they would jam up the sandy beach that was the landing zone on the western shore.

But Kyre knew pointing out facts to his father would be the wrong thing to do that day, it would gain him nothing and further split their already tense relationship. "If our army fights with as much coordination and discipline as they display in a mere river crossing, we will acquit ourselves well when it comes to battle. Father, our people fought well in Demarche province and at the Gates of the Mountains, I credit that to your training," he added. That was easy to say, for it was the truth, including the part about his father's long insistence that the army of Burwyck be prepared both in training and equipment. It was also easy to say, for the remark both flattered his father and reminded his father and Talen that Kyre had been in actual combat, while Talen had only sparred in the practice ring. Before he went into battle for the first time, Kyre had thought his extensive training had prepared him well for combat. Now that he had seen the bloody chaos of real fighting, he knew no amount of training could determine how a person would react when a they were faced with death for the first time.

"Yes, you fought at the Gates," Talen spat. "Thank you, brother, for reminding us, we had almost forgotten, as the last time you mentioned it was this morning."

"I said our *army* fought well," Kyre did not bother to raise his voice, Talen had long known how to bait him into an argument, but Kyre felt he was above and beyond that now. He saw Talen as a frustrated and sad boy, a bully who would always be in Kyre's shadow. "They fought alongside the troops of Demarche, halfway back through that province as the enemy poured across the river. Not once did our troops flinch or shy away from battle, not once did they complain about being tired or hungry, not once did I hear any of them despair as we were pushed until our backs were up against the mountains."

"Oh yes, you are so-" Talen began a retort.

"Talen!" Their father barked. "Be silent. Kyre is correct, the army of Burwyck performed bravely, they were a credit to our family. I received letters of thanks from General Magrane and Duchess Rochambeau, even Lord Salva expressed admiration for how our army delayed the enemy's advance. You would do well to study that campaign rather than seeking to snipe at your brother. Really, you boys should be past that now," he added, annoyed. "Now, the two of you, listen to me. Are you listening?"

"Yes, father," the boys chanted in unison, though Kyre saw his brother' attention was focused on glaring at him rather that listening to the duke.

"You may think this is all a grand adventure," Regin looked more at Talen than Kyre, "but this raid is deadly serious. We must advance many leageus into Acedor to reach the road the enemy uses as their main supply line from the west," he repeated the orders issued by General Magrane in the name of the Regent, and Regin still did not believe he knew the true purpose of the raid. Cutting a road, even if the Royal Army engineers could destroy bridges along that road, would only create a temporary impediment to the enemy's ability to provision the host of troops on the west bank of the River Fasse. "You may think a force this size has nothing to fear," he swept a hand to encompass a view of the Royal Army of Tarador and various ducal armies preparing to advance west of the river. "But we have taken only a fraction of our strength with us, we must keep the bulk of our forces east of the river to forestall an invasion. We must move quickly and we will be especially vulnerable during out retreat back to the river. If I fall in battle-"

"No!" Talen cried out. "You will not fall, Sire, you are skilled and strong and-"

"Yes, my son. Soon enough you will see that survival in battle is as much due to fortune as to skill," he nodded to Kyre as he spoke, and his eldest son and heir nodded with a grim expression. "If I fall, you will need to lead our forces safely back across the river. Unlike the Royal Army, we do have the better part of our forces with us here. If the army of Burwyck is lost, or trapped west of the river, we may lose everything we hold dear."

"Yes, father," Kyre agreed. "It does no good to win one battle, if it costs you the war."

"You have learned well, my son," Regin tried to smile but could not manage the gesture. If the duke's plan came to fruition, his heir may not survive, and almost certainly would rebel against his father. Regin considered that this might be the last time he and Kyre spoke in a somewhat friendly manner, and that brought tears to his eyes.

Ignoring the tears welling up in his father's eyes for he knew the proud man would be embarrassed, Kyre held out a hand to his brother. "We will not fail you, Sire."

Talen shook his brother's hand, just long enough to show he agreed but not long enough to demonstrate any affection.

"There is something else," Regin wiped his face with a cloth, pretending to mop sweat off his brow but drying his tears. "This raid is, in my experienced opinion, a foolish endeavor. I know General Magrane has reservations about taking such a serious risk for so little gain, but he is bound to obey our Regent. He is bound to obey a young girl who has never been in battle," he knew that was not quite correct, but Ariana definitely had no experience in large-scale army maneuvers. "If we are overrun, there may come a moment when you must abandon a lost cause and save what you can."

"Sire?" Kyre asked sharply.

"Kyre, while you were in the hospital, you told me about how you rescued General Armistead and civilian stragglers in Demarche. I was proud of your actions, and I was even more proud that you later recognized your actions had been foolish. You risked your force for a few people who could make no difference in the war, while the troops you commanded were desperately needed. A commander must not only lead with courage, he must use good judgment, or lives could be lost for nothing. You must choose when to fight, and when to cut your losses so you can fight another day."

"I fear what you are saying, Sire," Kyre said with jaw set in anger.

"I am *saying*," Regin let his frustration creep into his tone of voice, "that if the Royal Army is overrun, you must save what you can of our forces. I will not throw away our army for nothing, and neither should you."

Kyre sat stiffly in the saddle. He knew his father's words were sound. He also feared he knew what Regin Falco was really saying behind the all-too-reasonable words. That if the battle were joined and the Royal Army hard pressed by the enemy, Regin intended to break away and leave the princess to her own guards. "We are pledged to follow-"

"Damn you!" Regin snapped. "I know we are pledged to follow Her Highness! I will not waste the strength of our family because a foolish young girl will not listen to those who have actually shed blood in battle. No, Kyre," the duke held up a hand before his heir could respond. "Think before you speak. I know you will agree, if only you think with your head and not your heart. This raid is dangerous, far more dangerous than you can know. If all is lost, you must save something to continue the fight on the other side of the river, that is all I am saying."

"Yes, Sire," Kyre's cheeks burned hot from anger and embarrassment. The duke nodded curtly, wheeled his horse and galloped off to greet the last boats coming across the river.

"My brother," Talen's voice dripped with hatred. "If you betray our father, I swear I will kill you myself."

Kyre was not fazed in the least by the threat, his younger brother had posed a threat to Kyre's life for several years. "Dear brother, you may find killing me not so easy as you suppose. And you will not be killing anyone when you have an orc arrow sticking through your throat. Look to your own safety in battle, and try to stay out of everyone's way, little boy." Not waiting for an unimaginative reply, Kyre spurred his horse and rode away up the hill, looking toward the south where the Ariana's guards were assembled around her. His father's words troubled him.

Paedris felt the pouch on his belt vibrate, and he held up a hand to warn Cecil. Inside the pouch was a stone, identical in every aspect to a stone he had given to Shomas Feany, before that wizard embarked on his doomed errand to find Koren Bladewell. With Shomas dead, Paedris had not expected to make use of the sending stone, but as he reached into the pouch for the stone, he considered Shomas must have told Captain Raddick about the stone and instructed the army man in its use, for of course Shomas would have thought ahead like that.

"What is it?" Cecil whispered. A patrol of soldiers had passed by less than an hour before, and the two wizards dared not extend their senses to see where those enemy soldiers were at the moment.

"Sending stone! It must be Raddick," Paedris explained hopefully. He had a flash of hope that Koren might have used the stone, but dismissed just as quickly, for the boy had no idea how to use the magical device. The court wizard knelt on the dusty ground and smoothed out an area of sand with one hand, then held the stone over the flat sand and muttered an incantation. As he waved the stone back and forth, closer and closer to himself, an invisible finger traced words in the sand, to match the words Captain Raddick had written before using his identical stone to record the simple message.

Koren captured by orcs. I could have killed him but he asked me to trust him. Said you should trust him also- Raddick

"Paedris, we need to speak about it," Mwazo gently prodded his friend half an hour later.

"Why?" Paedris did not even bother to sigh, so deep was his despair. The message from the sending stone had been a terrible, awful shock, and Paedris had no way to reply or to ask questions of Raddick. The paired sending stones were linked, they could be used only one way and one time. Shomas must have instructed Raddick in their use, the soldier had scratched out a brief message on the ground and passed his stone over the words. Now the stones were locked, spent. No new message could be sent, nor did Raddick have any way to know Paedris had received the fateful note. "We are lost, utterly lost," Paedris hung his head, scuffing his boots in the dry soil, barely caring where he was going. Seeing that message had destroyed any hope Paedris had for Tarador's survival, broken his spirit. He cared about nothing, for there was no longer anything worth caring about. The world waited for death, and there was nothing Paedris don Salva could do about it.

"We don't know that for certain," Cecil prodded annoyingly.

"What else could result?" Paedris snapped angrily, knowing he was not being fair and not caring. What did it matter if he were fair or cruel now? Nothing mattered, nothing at all. The enemy had Koren, and soon the demon would peel that boy apart to steal his power, sundering the barrier to the shadow world and allowing a horde of demons to overwhelm and consume the real world. Nothing mattered. Throwing up his hands in anguish, he shouted to the heavens "*What* was Raddick thinking?"

"That is the wrong question, my friend," Mwazo replied with a faraway look in his eyes. He took a piece of candy from a pocket and offered it to the other wizard, knowing Paedris became cranky when he was hungry. Since departing the *Lady Hildegard*, the two had often been hungry, often enough that Cecil did not remember exactly what it was to not be hungry all the time. "Here, eat this."

So angry at the world, at everyone and everything but especially at himself, Paedris almost slapped Cecil's hand away in disgust, but a little voice in the back of his mind told him he was being a stubborn, childish fool and Paedris had learned to listen to that voice. "Thank you, Cecil," he muttered as an apology while popping the candy into his mouth. "That is good, it reminds me there are still good things in this world. What did you mean, I asked the wrong question?"

Pleased that Paedris was now in a proper frame of mind for a reasoned discussion, Cecil broke off a small piece of candy and bit into it. "You asked what Raddick was thinking-"

"Clearly, the man was *not* thinking!" Paedris interrupted. "He is a soldier, he is honored to be a captain in the Royal Army, yet he ignored the strictest, the most important order-"

"Why?" Cecil cut off his friend's building tirade. "As you say, Raddick is a fine soldier, entrusted by Grand General Magrane with a vital mission. Then *why* did he ignore his orders, when he knew the stakes, and when disobeying a direct order must go against all of his training as a soldier?"

Paedris looked at Mwazo with raised eyebrows, not speaking.

Mwazo continued. "The question we must ask is not what Raddick was thinking, but rather what *Koren* was thinking. Koren certainly knew the risk if he was captured by the enemy, and the boy's often-demonstrated courage tells me he was not merely afraid for his own life. Yet he asked Raddick to disobey orders and trust him. So, what is Koren's plan?"

"*Koren*'s plan," Paedris whispered. "Cecil, I am ashamed. I lashed out, pouting like a child, while you calmly considered the facts."

"You don't think well when you are hungry," Cecil smiled and gave Paedris another piece of candy.

"That is no excuse for my behavior. However," he smiled, "I will seize on any excuse. What could be Koren's plan?" He pondered, lost for any insight. "Surely the boy does not think he can destroy the demon with magical fire?"

"Perhaps it is just that simple," Cecil mused. "He unleashed unprecedented power, and he must have realized such power is beyond the scope of other wizards. He may believe that he can summon such power again, and consume the demon."

"But he can't! He will fail, and the demon will laugh before Koren is torn apart from the inside."

"The boy doesn't know that. For our purposes, what is important is that Koren believes in his heart he has the power to destroy the demon."

"He does have the power, he doesn't know how to use it, and he lacks the ability to control it," Paedris grew frustrated again, feeling despair well up inside him. "Wait, what do you mean 'for our purposes'?"

"For what we must now do, Koren's actual ability matters not. What matters is the boy *believes* he can destroy the demon, and that is why he allowed himself to be captured."

Paedris did not speak immediately. Then, "Cecil, perhaps my mind is especially slow today. Why does it matter what Koren believes? The demon cares not what he-"

"It matters, because the demon will attempt to read Koren's mind. The boy is strong enough that, in that at least, the demon will not succeed, but Koren will not be able to conceal his emotions completely. Because Koren believes he can and will destroy the demon, the demon will feel that."

Understanding dawned on Paedris. "And the demon will fear Koren."

"Exactly," Cecil nodded without satisfaction. "Paedris, we have no hope to rescue Koren from the clutches of the enemy, and we cannot allow the enemy to gain access to the boy's power. We also cannot kill Koren from here. But," he spoke woodenly, devoid of emotion, "we could make the demon fear Koren so much that the demon kills the boy himself. We came here for me to sow fear into the demon's heart, so it would delay an invasion of Tarador and give us time to find Koren and perhaps begin his training. Now our purpose will be for me to make the demon fear *Koren*, and so destroy the boy for us."

"The demon must indeed be filled with fear, to destroy such a weapon. I do not know whether the demon's fear will overcome its lust and greed."

"The demon has been patient," Cecil reminded his fellow wizard. "It has waited for over a thousand years, and most importantly, it *knows* it can conquer Tarador eventually, without Koren. The question the demon must balance is whether hastening its certain victory is worth the risk of allowing Koren into its presence."

"You think you could tip that balance?" Paedris asked fearfully. His fear was not for the outcome, but for the terrible cost Mwazo would pay for communing with the demon's mind.

"I can feed its sense of fear, I do not know if that will be enough," Cecil made a smile that quickly faded to a frown. "Paedris, I am afraid, I am terrified to my very core. I will not survive touching the demon's mind, but you and I have always known this journey has but one end for both of us."

"Yes," Paedris agreed reluctantly. They had no hope of escaping from Acedor, especially after Mwazo attempted to contact the demon through the spirit world. "However, we did hope our sacrifice would buy time for Koren to gain strength enough to challenge the enemy. Now, our best hope is for Koren to die, and Tarador to suffer slow and certain defeat?"

"We do not know what either, Paedris. The future is uncertain. Not long ago, we did not know of Koren Bladewell. We must act from hope, and not from fear."

"I will try, Cecil, I will try." Lord Salva straightened his back and squared his shoulders. "I do wish my hope was not only that a good boy will die. There is one thing we have not considered," he tapped his cheek while he thought.

"What?"

"Koren asked not only Raddick to trust him, he asked us, *me*, to trust him."

"Paedris," Cecil did not wish to debate an issue that had been decided. "He is a young boy who knows nothing of magic, except that he once managed to unleash uncontrollable power. We are master wizards, we must use our best judgement."

"We have betrayed him before, now we betray him again."

"Because we must. I do not like it either," Mwazo's tone was grim. "We either trust an untrained boy, or we trust everything you and I have learned over centuries of studying wizardry."

"You are right, Cecil," Paedris agreed reluctantly. "Though I do not like it."

"I am ready, Paedris," Mwazo announced in a calm but unsteady voice. Over several days, he had been communing through the spirit world, sending subtle feelings of unease and fear to the demon, gradually increasing the intensity of feeling so the demon would not notice those feelings were coming from outside its consciousness. Here was where Cecil Mwazo showed himself to be not only a master wizard, but a masterful practitioner of the most arcane and difficult forms of wizardry. He dared touch the mind of a demon, though the experience left him drained and shuddering with fear that was genuine. Now, after days of preparing the way, he was rested and ready for the most difficult and dangerous task; that of making the demon believe Koren Bladewell was a trap, a dangerous weapon the demon dared not allow into its presence.

Paedris looked up at the clear blue sky through the brown leaves of the trees they rested under. Clouds were building in the east and the afternoon would become cloudy with rain showers. Now, in the brilliant sunshine that illuminated even the darkest shadows, was the time, yet Paedris hesitated. "Are you sure-"

"I am sure that delay aids only our enemy," Mwazo answered without opening his eyes. He was already partly in a trance and could not spare the break in concentration to look at his fellow wizard. "Paedris, the time to act is now. The longer Koren is under duress, the closer he is to the demon, the more difficult it will be for us, for *me*, to act." He emphasized that the action would be his responsibility, for he knew how much Paedris cared for the boy. Cecil admired Koren Bladewell, and was grateful he had not gotten to know the boy better, or it would be much more difficult for him to do what must be done.

"You are right, Cecil," Paedris looked away, chastened. He knew how very difficult and dangerous it would be for Mwazo to attempt clouding the demon's mind, yet he could not help thinking they were making a mistake, a mistake they could not undo. "Still, I fear we are doing this because we cannot think of a better course of action."

"That is because we have *not* thought of a better option, and time marches on against us. Do you know of another way to keep the demon from seizing Koren's unimaginable power?"

"No. Cecil, I agree we are doing the only thing we know to do, and that Koren will die anyway if the demon takes his power. Yet, a little voice in the back of my mind reminds me Koren told Raddick we should trust him. It haunts me that we do not know why Koren said that."

Mwazo nearly broke concentration, so frustrated had he become with the useless and distracting conversation. "Koren Bladewell is a wizard of immensely powerful potential. He is also a young boy, and young people often have foolish romantic notions. Unless we believe our untrained friend Koren truly has the skill and knowledge and control to destroy a *demon*, we must act as best we can."

"You are right, Cecil," Paedris wiped away a tear. "Please excuse the sentimental weakness of an old man. I am ready." He laid down under a tree, on ground he had swept clear of sticks, stones and bugs, for he could not allow himself to be distracted by physical discomforts. "And, if we are not able to speak later," he added, knowing the extreme danger Mwazo was facing, "it has been an honor to be your friend."

Cecil nodded silently, already falling deeper into a trance as Paedris lent him power.

Koren's legs had become tired from the effort of keeping himself upright on the horse, with his hands bound behind his back he could not use them for balance. That morning he had nearly fallen off twice to the jeering delight of the orcs. Bjorn had fallen while they were crossing a stream and his horse stumbled, throwing the man into the water. For a moment, Koren had feared his friend would drown, for Bjorn had fallen into a deep pool and could not get to his feet. Shouting and pleading by Koren did nothing to spur the orcs to pull the man from the water, only when the enemy wizards ordered the orcs to act did they roughly grab Bjorn and set him back on the horse. "Thank," Bjorn coughed up water, "thank you," he said with a very short and stiff bow to the wizard who had ordered his rescue. Only two days after they had been captured, they had met a larger band of orcs who were accompanied by two wizards.

"Thank me not," the orc wizard snapped with a cruel smile. "When you are brought before my master, you will wish for death, but it will be granted only at a time of his choosing. You are alive only because you can be used to control your young wizard friend."

"I will do nothing to help you," Bjorn retorted proudly.

The orc's smile grew broader. "You need *do* nothing. I sense your young friend will cooperate with us, rather than see you suffer as you should for defying my master."

Bjorn spat toward the orc wizard but he was too far away. "Koren, don't do anything they ask, no matter what happens to me."

"Silence!" The wizard roared and with a gesture, Bjorn's tongue twisted painfully in his mouth and he found himself unable to talk.

"What have you done to him?" Koren tried frantically to use his own power but found he could not reach it, not do anything. When the two wizards, one human and one orc, had joined the orc band, their first action had been to cast some sort of spell on Koren and now he felt sluggish and numb all the time. It was as if the power of the spirit world was just beyond reach of his fingertips and it was slippery, his outstretched hands unable to grasp anything useful. It was intensely frustrating and Koren worried how much of his inability was due to the enemy wizards, and how much was his lack of training and knowledge of wizardry. And, worse, he worried his uncontrolled use of unspeakable power to destroy the orc army had somehow damaged him and his connection with the spirit world.

"His foul tongue, which has often spoken ill of my master, has paid the price. I would do the same to you, if my master had not forbidden me to harm you. But," the orc held up a dirty, bony finger as warning, "a simple gag in your mouth would work just as well if you do not cease your ranting."

Not wanting to risk a disgusting rag being tied across his mouth, Koren held back the words he wished to shout at the enemy, words he knew would have no effect but to amuse the orcs. Using his knees, he nudged his horse closer to Bjorn's. "Are you injured?"

Bjorn shook his head and his eyes glared daggers at the orc wizard. When the two enemy wizards had joined them and Koren had still not acted to kill the orcs and escape, Bjorn began to question the boy's plan, but he remained silent. They had come this far together, Bjorn knew doubts would not do him any good at that point. The two rode in silence, Koren so worried he felt sickness in the pit of his stomach, until nearly an hour later, Bjorn coughed softly. "The spell has worn off," he whispered so quietly even Koren's keen ears had to concentrate on the words.

"Hmmm," Koren thought that was interesting, and might be a useful bit of information later. Magic spells could wear off after a while, maybe whatever spell was making his sluggish and fuzzy would eventually weaken also?

"Don't worry, I have no wish for that to happen to me again, so I will hold my own tongue," he said with a wink.

Koren took that as a sign that Bjorn's spirits were good, and that gave him hope. "Anything we could say would only provide sport for these orcs."

They rode on for what Koren judged was another hour, stopping only once for the horses to drink from a stream and for the orcs to hold slimy water flasks to the mouths of their captives. The flasks smelled bad and the water tasted foul but they were parched, so Koren and Bjorn both drank greedily. They had been drinking from orc water flasks for days already without falling ill, and they had seen the wizards performing some magic ritual over the flasks, likely to purify the water for themselves and their captives. No such ritual was given to the water of the orc band, who had filthy habits and drank from communal bowls. Just seeing their blackened teeth slurping up water, and the bowl passed from one mouth to another, made Koren queasy. The wizards purified water for Koren and Bjorn, and while the food they were given twice a day smelled and tasted awful it also had not yet sickened them. Seeing the slimy, half-rotted food the orcs ate, Koren realized he and Bjorn were privileged to eat the same choice rations as the two wizards.

Having crossed the border into Acedor, they were passing through rolling hills not all that different from the land in Winterthur province on their Taradoran side, though the trees were not as healthy and there were no clusters of neat, well-tended farms. The land also had a constant, faint scent of something unpleasant and burnt, which even after days, Koren found he could not ignore. The road wound around a hill, and despite his fear, Koren was mildly curious to see what lay ahead to the west, deeper inside the fabled, feared land of Acedor, when the two wizards sat bolt upright in their saddles, frozen.

The orcs around them halted, muttering fearfully among themselves and drawing weapons. Whatever was happening, the orcs were familiar enough with the event to be alarmed, many of them making what Koren assumed were hex signs, or clutching various talismans. He also noted the orcs were backing away from the pair of wizards, not letting their eyes off the magic-wielders.

The orc wizard moved first, jerkily swinging one leg around and then falling out of the saddle onto the ground, falling awkwardly and heavily enough to cut his face. Blood flowed freely from the orc wizard's nose and the cut on its cheek but it did not appear to notice. Dazed, the orc shook his head while pawing at its belt for a knife.

The human wizard, a hideous man so twisted and stunted that at first Koren thought he was an orc, got off his own horse less awkwardly, although also moving as if he were a puppet on a string. His arms and legs acted in jerky movements, uncoordinated, making the wizard lurch rather than walk. He, too, reached for a knife, his hand patting along the man's belt until he found the knife by feel, then held it up in front of his eyes as if making sure his sense of touch had not deceived him.

"What is going on?" Bjorn whispered, keeping his eyes straight forward but assessing the orcs around them with his peripheral vision. Only Koren, Bjorn, the two wizards and the orc chieftain rode horses, the other orcs all marched with the shuffling gait characteristic of those creatures. With the wizards off their horses and appearing to have lost their senses, Bjorn judged whether this was their best chance to escape. It would be difficult in foreign territory, on strange mounts and with arms bound behind their backs, but they might never get a better chance to-

The human wizard, after staring stupidly at his knife, slowly lowered the blade and looked around, as if just then becoming aware of his surroundings. After a few seconds, the orc wizard did the same, their eyes rigidly forward, seeing only when they moved their heads. Bjorn felt a chill as they both stopped and focused on the same person; Koren Bladewell.

"Koren," Bjorn whispered loud enough to be sure he was heard, not caring if the enemy wizards saw their tongue-tying spell had worn off. "I will go left, you-"

"Seize him!" The orc wizard bellowed in an otherwordly voice, pointed at Koren with the knife.

"Seize him!" The human wizard repeated his fellow's action, and strode toward Koren faster than Bjorn thought could be possible for such an awkward gait.

"Koren!" Bjorn dug his heels into the side of his horse and the animal twitched, but three orcs quickly stepped in front of Bjorn, trying to grab onto the horse's reigns.

"Bjorn!" Koren replied, his heart in his mouth. "No, don't, they will kill you," he saw a dozen arrows pointed at the former King's Guard.

"What are they doing?" Bjorn repeated the question.

"I don't know! I've never seen this," Koren admitted. It must be a form of wizardry, but one he had never seen. If he had to guess, he would say the two enemy wizards were being controlled by an unseen force, and- Paedris?! Koren was overwhelmed by a mixture of hope and fear. Had the master court wizard of Tarador located Koren and taken control of the enemy wizards through magical means, to set free-

A dozen orcs pulled Koren off his horse, forcing him to kneel but taking care not to injure him, fearing the wrath of their dark master. The two wizards walked hesitantly toward him, their feet dragging on the ground and still moving like they had invisible strings attached to them. Their eyes were glassy, unfocused, looking through Koren rather than at him. They were acting very odd, the orc wizard tried to shift his knife from one hand to the other and stabbed himself in the palm, causing him to drop the blade. He bent down to look at it, nearly tripped on the discarded weapon, then straightened up and resumed walking toward Koren. That orc grabbed Koren's hair in both hands, its claws scraping his scalp painfully, drawing his head back. "Evil one!" The orc wizard hissed. "You seek to harm my master, who is the rightful ruler of this world!"

The human wizard stepped right in front of Koren, so close that one of his knees bumped Koren's chest. The wizard looked down, startled to see he had overstepped. He swayed back and forth until he shuffled his feet backwards, his eyes locked on the knife in his hand and not on where his feet were going. "Fail, you have failed," the wizard hissed. "You hoped to kill my master, you will die instead." The knife swung slowly forward until the blade was pressed against Koren's throat. "Die."

"No!" Koren panicked. "No, please, don't. I have power!"

"Koren," Bjorn warned. "Don't move, you'll make the blade cut you," he saw the wizard was standing rigidly still, the arm holding the knife twitching. No, the blade pulled back slightly, so it was no longer touching the skin of Koren's exposed throat. Then the wizard jerked and the blade pushed forward, only to pull back again. It was as if the evil wizard was trying to make up his mind, or to resist whatever power was controlling him.

The wizard's hand opened and the blade tumbled to the ground, the hilt bouncing off the wizard's own boot. Slowly, the human wizard blinked, while the orc wizard remained rigidly still, unseeing.

"Bjorn, what's happening?" Koren asked anxiously.

"I don't know, other than there's no longer a blade at your throat," Bjorn admitted. "Don't move, don't provoke them."

The human wizard's hands darted out to press palms against Koren's forehead, and there was a red glow of light from under those hands. Koren slumped, his eyes rolling back but the iron grip of the orc held up upright. As the glow grew brighter, the human wizard's head was flung back, his mouth open and pointed to the sky for a second, an inhuman cry issuing from his mouth.

Then that wizard collapsed, nearly knocking Koren over. That action broke whatever spell was controlling the enemy wizards, for the orc shook his head, released Koren and scrambled backwards, surprised to see where he was.

"Koren? Koren!" Bjorn called, restrained by the arrows pointed at him. He could do nothing while the boy lay on the ground, unmoving. No, Bjorn could see the boy's chest was moving, he was alive, which was better than the wizard laying sprawled in front of Koren. That man's already gray and yellowish skin was dissolving, Bjorn saw with horror. As he watched, transfixed, the evil wizard's form began to crumple under his dirty robes.

"Paedris," Mwazo gasped weakly, snapping back to alertness. "I'm sorry. I failed."

"You didn't fail," Paedris barely could muster strength to roll upward, supported by one elbow. "Drink this," he offered his water flask and Cecil drank as much as he could, much of the water running down his face onto the ground. "I saw part of it, I think," as he had given power to his friend, he had been able to glimpse fuzzy impressions through the connection. "At the end there, a wizard died but it was not Koren?"

"No, that was not Koren. I came close, so close!" Mwazo balled up his fists and pressed them to his forehead, tapping himself to relieve his frustration. "I was able to make the enemy fear Koren was a danger, a trick we were playing, a trap. That was easier than I expected because the demon already distrusted a gift falling into its lap. Under control of the demon, two wizards were going to kill Koren, to eliminate the threat. They," he shook his fists, "were so close!"

"I sensed hesitation, confusion?" Paedris guessed.

"Yes. The demon hesitated, it could not decide. It fears doing something it could not undo, and if it killed Koren, it would forever lose that source of power. If I had pressed any harder I would have revealed myself-"

"I know. You did the best you could, the best any of us could. It is my understanding that you cannot make the demon do anything against its will?"

"Correct. All I can do is reinforce a feeling already residing in the person, or demon, who I contact. We knew the demon would be suspicious of capturing an immensely powerful wizard it knew nothing about, so I was able to enhance that fear."

"It wasn't enough," Paedris said simply.

"No. No, in the end, the demon decided to test Koren's power, it sacrificed a wizard to do that. Once the demon saw the overwhelming power the boy can command, its greed and lust for power overcame its fear. Nothing I could do will deter the demon now, Paedris. We are lost."

"Perhaps," Paedris pushed himself onto his knees. "No, Cecil, do not get up, you need rest." Paedris himself almost fell down from a wave of dizziness. "I am drained, it must be worse for you. I will get water, and we will rest here today."

Cecil nodded and tried to relax, shuddering when he thought of how he had brushed against the mind of a demon. "Paedris, I sense something else."

"What is that?"

"You are not disappointed that Koren lives," Cecil's lips curled in a knowing smile.

"No, I am not," Paedris agreed. "Nor are you."

Cecil nodded. "What next? *Is* there a next? I fear we are lost, Paedris."

"I do not know if there is a next for any of us, but we cannot stop now just because we fear the future."

"Then, what next?"

Lord Paedris don Salva de la Murta, leader of the Wizards Council and official wizard to the royal court of Tarador, stood and brushed off the knees of his pants. Pants. Good, sensible pants that were rugged and comfortable for traveling in rough country, not fancy robes what were too hot and got caught on every bramble bush. "I do not know about you, Cecil, but if this truly is to be the end of all things, I would like to try my hand at challenging a demon directly."

"Are you mad, Paedris?"

"Perhaps, but at this point," he winked, "does it matter?"

"I suppose not," Cecil mused. "Better to go down fighting?"

"Exactly. People have long spoken of my legendary power, it is time to put it to the test. At worst, I could at least harm and weaken our enemy, eh?"

Cecil thought the worst thing that could happen would be for the demon to crush Paedris like a bug, but he did not say that. "What are we waiting for, then? I believe the demon's castle is in those yonder mountains."

CHAPTER EIGHTEEN

The incident with the two wizards puzzled and troubled Koren. At first, he had thought the strange, jerky motions of the two enemy wizards might had been caused by a spell cast by Paedris, an attempt to rescue Koren. But when one wizard held his head back and the other had a knife poised at his throat, he feared they would kill him. Instead, the human wizard acted oddly, touching Koren's forehead, and then dying. The orcs had poured oil on the dead wizard's shriveled body and burned it, while the orc wizard had acted dazed the rest of that day. Koren had no idea what to make of the strange incident. Had the wizards meant to kill him, then changed their minds? He did not think wizards of Acedor could make important decisions on their own, which meant the choice to threaten Koren, then keep him alive, came from the demon.

And that terrified him.

Madame Chu gestured for quiet so she could concentrate. As she was almost surrounded by an army, with people making noise though they were ordered to be still and tried their best to comply, she had to mentally block out stray sounds. Wind on the hilltop caused tent fabric to flap, horses whinnied, people coughed, loads shifted in wagons and sentries called out challenges to scouts returning from ranging wide around the army's flanks. There was seldom truly complete silence in the real world, and Wing had long ago developed an ability to ignore distractions.

When she was ready, she withdrew her senses from the world of the real and drifted gently into the realm of the spirits, where it was all too easy to get lost and forget the passage of time. Her fellow wizards lent their power to her, or acted as magical sentries to protect her while she was vulnerable. Two of the most skilled wizards, one from Lord Mwazo's homeland and one from Indus, accompanied her into the depths of the spirit realm, there to help her focus the frighteningly awesome power that could be wielded by more than two dozen wizards from many lands, who had gathered to help Tarador's struggle against the darkness.

Wing knew exactly where she wished to go and exactly where she needed to focus the power, yet though she had been there twice before, it took a frustratingly long time to find the spot again. Going anywhere through the spirit world always took too long, for there were many distractions, and a wizard's mind tended to drift. That drifting adopting the fuzzy sensibilities of the spirits, could be dangerous, a wizard's consciousness could become trapped and slowly absorbed into the spirit world, until the physical body outside was abandoned and the wizard became one with the spirits, never again to remember the world of the real.

After three tries, one less than expected, Wing found the correct spot under the dam and began to release power. Not even the combined power of the assembled wizards could breach the dam made of rock and soil, but when Wing had first examined the area at the request of General Magrane, she realized the dam was already rotten within. Water seeping into and under the dam had eaten it away at the bottom, making the foundation a soggy, slippery mess of slick mud. Below the dam, the old riverbed had steady trickles of water forming creeks though the creeks did not reach far, being absorbed in the dusty ground after less than a mile. In time, perhaps a hundred or less years, the dam would give way on its own, failing as the lake behind it swelled with snowmelt and spring rains.

Neither Wing nor Tarador could wait one hundred years for nature to run its course. With the enemy by now surely alerted to the danger, they would be frantically attempting to move supplies out of the old river valley, an effort that would take days, even a full week considering the mountains of supplies piled up. Enemy wizards were trying to strike Wing, blocked for the moment by wizards supporting her, but that protection diverted their strength away from breaching the dam and they could not maintain that protection for long.

If Wing was successful, the enemy wizards would soon understand they had failed to stop her.

A dam that was undermined by water and rotten within would still be too heavy and solid for wizards to move, but it had occurred to Wing that she did not have to move the entire dam. No, she could get the water to do that for her! All she needed to do was create fine cracks all the way from back to front of the dam, and as water under high pressure shot through the cracks, the water itself would widen the cracks into channels, then gaps and then a full breach until the dam suddenly gave way. With the dam over one hundred feet high and the lake behind it more than a mile wide, there was a massive amount of water pressure on the dam, especially at the bottom.

The bottom of the dam, in the sticky silt accumulated there over the centuries, is where Wing focused the magical power provided to her by ten of their strongest wizards. Under the force of magical energy, the saturated soil gave way in a crack that at first was no more wide than a finger. When water began shooting through that crack out the face of the dam, Wing moved her attention to another spot, and created a thin crack there. Though the amount of material moved to create each crack was small, the energy required was tremendous, and after three cracks were flowing with powerful jets of water, Wing was shaking to hold herself together. One more, one more crack next to another, to make a wide gap between them, and she would be done, exhausted.

Focusing magical power through the spirit world to bore one last, thin channel through the dam was nearly Wing's undoing. As she burned through the last few yards toward the face of the dam, she felt herself slipping away, losing her sense of self and reality in the spirit realm. Alarmed, she tried to pull herself back but it was too late, it was impossible to tell where she was and she could no longer feel a connection to the real. At the last moment as she flailed about, losing hope, she felt a tingle at the back of her mind, gently guiding her up, up, up and outward, pulling and coaxing her, suffusing her with a sense of warmth and comfort and direction.

"Ah!" Wing gasped as she was rudely snapped back into the real. She gasped, choking because she had forgotten how to breathe while in the spirit world, her body responded on its own or she would have passed out.

Beside her, a young wizard also choked but for a different reason, she was nauseous from the shock of suddenly pulling herself back into the world of the real. Trying to breathe while fighting her protesting stomach, she spoke out of concern for the other wizard but also to take her mind off her own troubles. "Are you with us, Madame Chu?"

"No, or it doesn't feel like I am."

Olivia laughed, which was a bad idea as it almost made her lose her breakfast.

"You should not have done that, Olivia," Wing scolded, sitting up and wagging a finger at the young wizard. "You have not been fully trained, you could have been lost yourself."

"You *were* lost, master wizard. You wouldn't allow me to lend you power, or to fend off enemy wizards," Olivia pouted. "I couldn't do *nothing* and watch you fade away."

"Don't ever do that again, until you are ready. And," Wing's expression softened, "thank you. I owe my life to you."

Olivia paused as the ground shook under them. "If you were successful, all of Tarador may owe you today. Can we watch, please?" She asked eagerly.

"I wouldn't miss this," Wing admitted. Other wizards helped the two stand up, and they walked around the side of the hill, where the front face of the dam could be seen.

Regin Falco stood with the crown princess and her commander of the Royal Army, watching water spouting from multiple cracks in the dam. At first, he was disappointed, even anxious, as the jets of water reached impressively far into the old riverbed, but were thin as had no apparent effect on the dam. Could the wizards have failed? Or did their plan work, but there simply had not been enough power to push aside millions of tons of rock and soil? Regin knew that wizards, despite their typical arrogant confidence, were too often guessing about what they could and couldn't do. According to Magrane, Lord Salva himself had not been entirely sure he could actually pull down the Gates of the Mountains until the rocks at the base of those structures began to fracture and shift.

If Madame Chu failed to breach the dam, Regin's plans could be in great disarray, and his own life in danger. He had dutifully reported to the enemy the plan to cross the river and raid into Acedor. But Regin's message had included what he knew must be a bogus story, of the raid being for the purpose of cutting supply lines between the interior of Acedor and the host of troops massed just west of the River Fasse. At the time, Regin strongly suspected he wasn't being told the full truth, and after studying a map he began to believe he knew Magrane's real plan.

When the army column had continued southwest along the relatively new channel of the Lillefasse toward the lake, rather than climbing out of the river valley and striking out due west to intersect the roads used by the supply wagons, Regin had smiled inwardly, knowing he now understood what Magrane intended to do. The smile had been because Regin was pleased at his own cleverness for figuring out what Magrane had tried to conceal for him. The smile was also admiration for the bold and imaginative plan of the Royal Army commander, a plan Regin wished he had thought of. And finally, the smile had been because Regin heartily approved of breaching the dam, because it would suit his own, secret plan.

Regin had agreed to betray his country, to assist in removing Ariana Trehayme from the throne. After the crown princess was dead and he assumed rule of Tarador through control of the Regency Council, he would be in a better position to negotiate with the demon if the invading force of Acedor could not move far because their supplies had been washed away.

Thus it was that Regin anxiously watched the thin jets of water spraying out from the face of the dam. If the attempt to breach the dam failed, the demon would be angry that Regin had not warned it about Magrane's true plan, and the huge mountain of supplies down the old river valley would still be ready to provision a massive invasion all the way to the gates of the royal castle in Linden.

He turned to Magrane and was about to speak when a soldier on horseback called out. "Look!" The man pointed to where a section of the dam's front face was slumping between two of the cracks made by wizards. As Regin watched, transfixed, the slumping soil became a slide, then suddenly the ground beneath Duke Falco's feet trembled and a gap a dozen or more feet wide was opened in the dam, water cascading outward, forcing the gap ever wider. The shaking ground made the dam between the other two cracks also slump, this time the shifting soil on the dam's face only had time to fall a couple feet before water exploded through.

The royal party, Regin included, looked at each other with alarm as the ground they were standing on shook. Was that land, too, about to slide, Regin wondered with fear, remembering too late that a slide in that area had created the dam long ago. Ariana made an exclamation of alarm and Regin instinctively reached out to steady the girl. "Highness, we should step back," he advised, pulling her shoulder gently.

Magrane stood his ground, standing proud and tall, exulting in the sight of his plan coming to fruition. Half the dam was washed away already, with the gap widening every second. A wall of water, foaming brown as it scoured the dry ground of the old riverbed, surged downward toward the enemy's main store of supplies. Magrane knew the enemy's wizards surely knew of the impending disaster rushing down the river's former channel, he also knew there was no way the enemy could move a significant amount of supplies out of the way before the water hit. "Madame Chu assured me the ground beneath this position is secure, Duke Falco," he looked at the man with a hint of disdain. "I would not risk the life of Her Highness."

Regin stiffened and a flash of anger and hatred washed across his face before he got control of himself. "Of course," he said with a bow to the general. "My congratulations to you, General Magrane. This plan was bold, a masterstroke. The enemy will now be unable to cross the River Fasse in force before next spring," he lied, knowing the enemy intended to invade regardless of the supply situation, for the demon cared nothing about the lives of its own soldiers.

"The idea to attack the enemy's supply dump was Her Highness' idea," Magrane bowed tactfully to his future queen. "A general's duty is to find a way to do as my liege lord requires."

Ariana blushed. "Oh, general, you give me too much credit."

"Then credit must go to Madame Chu and her fellow wizards," Magrane pointed above on the hill, where the wizards had gathered to watch the results of their unnatural handiwork.

"Yes!" Ariana clapped her hands. "I must go express my gratitude to Madame Chu. General, Your Grace, please excuse me."

With the princess walking away, Duke Falco was alone with the general, except for a ring of soldiers and guards at a discrete distance, just out of earshot if voices were kept low. "What would we do without wizards?" Regin regretted the inane comment as he said it. "It has not escaped my attention, general, that you deceived me about the true purpose of us crossing the river."

"It was necessary to keep the truth to a small number of people, Your Grace."

"I am a senior member of the Regency Council," Regin retorted hotly. "I am not trusted?"

No, you are not trusted, you snake, Magrane thought to himself. "It was not only a matter of trust, Your Grace," Magrane lied, not caring whether the duke caught the lie or not. "Wizards tell me the enemy might have the ability to read our minds, to some extent. Madame Chu and her wizards are able to shield the minds of a small number of people, but the effort saps the energy of the wizards involved. That is why the information was restricted to myself and the princess. And the wizards knew, of course; they are able to shield their own minds from attempts to pry out their secrets."

"Hmm," Regin was not happy. He did not like the idea the demon might be reading his mind and would know of the duke being less than fully honest. "No matter, you were successful. Again, I commend you for being both clever and bold," he said with full honesty. "What now?"

"Now?" Magrane frowned, irritated at already having to consider the future, his moment of savoring a victory all too brief. "Now we retreat quickly back across the Fasse, and await the enemy's next move."

"Of course," Regin concurred. To himself he thought, the enemy's next move will fall on Magrane before the raiding could cross the river back into Tarador.

"Bjorn, get ready," Koren whispered.

Bjorn tensed, trying to appear exhausted while sitting slack on the ground. "For what?"

"To run," Koren answered, keeping his eyes staring down at his boots and barely moving his lips. "I picked up a flake of rock when those wizards were going to kill me, or whatever they were doing."

Bjorn risked a sideways glance to his companion, who held a sharp chip of rock between thumb and forefinger. Seeing that Bjorn was watching, Koren flexed his arms apart, showing that he was no longer bound. Cutting the rope around his wrists had taken days, working a little at a time. He had to be patient, to avoid the orcs seeing what he was doing, and to avoid nicking himself with the sharp rock. Blood would have caused the orcs to check the rope and he could not have that, nor could he allow them to notice the rope was loose. The worst part of the past four hours had been holding the severed rope together with his fingers, so to the orcs the bonds appeared intact.

Bjorn's eyebrows twitched upward in surprise before he resumed a neutral, exhausted expression. He had looked for a way to cut the bonds on his wrists, but there had been no opportunity for him. The orcs treated Bjorn more roughly, kicking him and jabbing him the with handle of their axes. Koren was not to be harmed, and Bjorn was not to be severely mistreated, but that left a lot of room for orcs to take out their hatred and anger when their wizard was not looking. The wizard could not have missed the bruises and minor cuts on Bjorn's face but he did nothing to stop it, Bjorn had even caught the wizard giving him an evil smirk of pleasure when Bjorn had blood dripping from a cut on his forehead.

What was Koren planning? Bjorn's eyes flicked side to side as he kept his head down, assessing what he would do when Koren gave the signal. The boy could have picked a much better spot to try escaping, for the terrain around them was largely flat and open, with few trees or streambeds in which to hide. Though it was dark and the cloud cover allowed only a thin glow of moonlight, Bjorn was not optimistic about their chances to get away. On foot, they would have to run relentlessly, quickly get far enough away and change direction before the orcs could mount their few horses and pursue. He wondered whether Koren appreciated how orcs could track by scent, for despite their gnarled legs and awkward, shuffling gait, they could move quickly. Bjorn and Koren should be able to stay ahead of the orcs at a dead run, but they would be running through the dark while the orcs would have the advantage of torches. One bad stumble in the dark, a twisted ankle, would ruin any plans for escape.

The orc band would make escape difficult enough, then there was their wizard to contend with. A wizard could surely track them in the dark, might even cast some spell to freeze them in place or render them unable to move. Had Koren thought of that? Bjorn feared their escape plan was from the imagination of a young teenaged boy, a type of person not known for sound judgment and-

No. Koren was a wizard. Of course he had considered the orc wizard, and Koren must have a plan to deal with that threat, although Bjorn knew he could not count on Koren himself using magic to aid their escape. Even before they had been captured, Koren had not been able to conjure any magic, whispering to Bjorn how very frustrated he was that he could not do, or feel, anything related to the spirit world. Koren said he feared his uncontrolled use of magic to destroy the orc army in the mountain meadow had damaged him somehow, that he might be unable to use magic at all.

No matter, Bjorn decided with grim determination. This was the only possibility they had for escape, so he was going to follow Koren's lead.

The single orc guarding them sniffed hungrily at whatever was cooking on the campfire, and even Bjorn thought it smelled good. The orc shifted from one side to the other while seated, then turned to face the campfire, eager not to miss his food ration. As soon as the orc turned his back, Koren's hands came around and he began sawing at the ropes binding his legs. He did not have to cut through where the ropes were wrapped many times around each ankle, only through the single strand connecting them. The orcs had left a rope two feet long between Koren's feet, allowing him to shuffle slowly but hobbling him from running. Whenever the orc sniffed and shifted, Koren swiftly tucked his hands behind his back. Once, the guard glanced back, glaring at the two prisoners who were keeping him from feasting on whatever was roasting over the fire. Koren avoided the orc's eye while Bjorn pretended to be asleep, head slumped over his knees. The orc looked away and got up, walking closer to the fire. When the guard sat down again, he did not bother to look back at the captives.

Not needing to be as quiet with the orc farther away, Koren hacked through the tough, slippery rope, then risked reaching over with one hand to cut Bjorn's hands free. "Careful," Bjorn whispered, "they're handing out whatever they cooked." One orc at the fire was cutting off chunks of the animal they roasted. Soon, their guard would be replaced by someone who had already eaten and would be less distracted.

"I know," Koren grunted from the strain then gave up trying to cut with one hand, crawling behind Bjorn to hold the rock chip with both hands.

"They'll see you!" The former King's Guard hissed. "Go! Run, I'll distract them if I can."

"I'm not going without you."

"You fool, don't-"

"I won't survive out here alone," Koren explained as the rope around the man's wrists parted. He handed the rock chip to Bjorn and sat back down, pretending his bonds were intact while Bjorn furiously and silently cut his own legs free. There was no dramatic announcement to launch the escape, no shouting or words at all, not even a gesture. Bjorn simply looked around to see if any orcs were looking directly at them, then he crouched and slipped away quietly as he could.

"You lead," he said and Koren went ahead, keeping low.

Luck was not with them that night, they were still casting faint shadows from the firelight behind them when a cry of alarm rose in the camp. "Run!" Bjorn urged. Despite not having gotten more than fifty yards before the orcs noticed their captives were missing, Bjorn thought they could at least lead the orcs on a merry chase, so he was startled when an orc who had been sleeping rose up right in front of him. He bowled the orc over, falling onto another of the creatures, and suddenly orcs were everywhere. They had the bad luck to stumble directly into where a dozen or more orcs had laid their filthy bedrolls on the ground to sleep and the orcs were awake in a flash, grabbing for weapons and scratching at the intruders with their claws.

Koren went down under two orcs, kicking them away before three others tackled him.

Bjorn swung a fist at an orc, catching it in the throat and snatching away a knife he then used to slash at orcs circling around him, both sides uncertain what to do next. The orcs by then knew they were fighting the captives and that those two were not to be harmed, Bjorn hesitated because with Koren held firmly by three orcs he did not see the point in continuing to fight.

"Kill me!" Koren screamed, struggling against the orcs, bashing one of the creatures in the nose with his forehead. "*Please*! Kill me!" He pleaded woozily, blood running down into his eyes.

Bjorn had the knife in his right hand, his throwing hand. He had only a second to act before he too was overwhelmed by orcs. For a split second he hesitated, stunned into inaction by the boy's shocking plea. Koren had surrendered to the orcs in the ravine, cutting the rope bridge to remove his only escape route. At the time, he had told Bjorn he knew what he needed to do, and mere moments later he had asked Captain Raddick to trust him rather than kill him as Raddick had been ordered.

Now Koren wanted to die, was pleading for Bjorn to kill him. The sudden turnaround was so unexpected that Bjorn's mind froze for a critical moment. His mind was frozen into inaction but his muscles, reacting on their own from years of training and combat, flipped the knife in his hand so he was holding it in a throwing position before he recovered from shock and saw the blade held ready. An orc launched itself through the air, forcing the taller Bjorn to duck and roll awkwardly the side. With no time left and Koren nearly buried under a swarm of orcs, Bjorn pushed aside all doubts, drew back his arm and threw-

Something hard crashed into his head and right shoulder, sending the knife spinning off course into the night.

Bjorn awoke to find himself draped over a horse, his aching head bobbing painfully as the horse slowly walked along the rough road, his nose bumping against the horse's mud-caked hide with every step. "Uhhh," he groaned.

"Are you awake, Bjorn?" He heard Koren's voice.

"No," Bjorn grunted as tried to get enough moisture in his mouth to speak.

"You've been groaning for the last hour, that's why I asked," the voice continued in a chastened tone. "I'm sorry."

"No talking!" The harsh voice of an orc interrupted and Bjorn heard a thud and a grunt from Koren.

The orcs noticed Bjorn was awake, and halted the horse to unstrap him, forcing him to sit upright. He was sore all over and his head ached tremendously from being upside down so long. Mercifully, an orc held a water flask to his lips and Bjorn drank greedily, surprised when the orc refilled the flask and allowed Bjorn to drink more before pulling the flask away abruptly. Spitting in Bjorn's face, the orc snarled something at him in orc speech, then slapped the horse's flank and the beast resumed walking slowly down the road.

It was well on into morning, Bjorn saw, his vision clearing and his headache slowly fading as the water seeped into his tissues and he was no longer hanging facedown over the horse's back. The horse must have been resentful to have Bjorn's weight draped awkwardly over it for so long, for the beast seemed to seek out every rut and pothole in the road, jarring Bjorn's aching back and shoulder with every step.

Koren's horse was ahead, as the orcs had not stopped that horse while they had gotten Bjorn upright. He saw the boy's arms were now bound with metal, and there were metal chains around both ankles. The orcs were taking no chances with Koren escaping again. Bjorn felt behind himself with his fingers, feeling iron around his own wrists but a glance down showed his legs were free. Did the orcs care less about Bjorn escaping? Yes, he concluded, for if he tried running again they would simply drop him with arrows. His position was clear; Bjorn mattered only as assurance of Koren's good behavior.

Bjorn and Koren had no opportunity to speak until mid-afternoon, when the orcs halted for rest and to eat. The two captives were kept apart, this time Bjorn's legs were tied but only with a rope, so he sat quietly waiting while the orcs built fires and prepared whatever disgusting things they ate for a midday meal. Bjorn was surprised when he was roughly pulled to his feet and made to shuffle over toward Koren, being dumped on the ground next to the boy. Their hands were unbound, then cuffed in front of them with a chain connecting hands to feet. The chain was too short for either of them to stand, there would be no foolish attempt to run that day. An orc brought over bowls of stew that did not smell bad, indeed Bjorn's stomach rumbled with hunger at the scent. He had no idea what kind of meat was in it but he could see potatoes that appeared to be regular potatoes, plus carrots, onions and some sort of peppers. Were the orcs eating so well because they had stolen supplies from the dwarves? Bjorn found he did not care as he slurped the broth and bit into chunks of potato.

Next to him, Koren only slowly and haltingly sipped broth.

"Eat," Bjorn whispered. An orc sitting nearby looked at him but did not order silence, so Bjorn tested the boundaries by adding "You will need the strength."

"For what?" Koren replied, his face completely lost in despair. "We will never escape now," he tugged at the chain to illustrate his point. "Their wizard put a spell on my chains, that's what he told me. If I get too far away from their wizard, these bonds," he shook the thick iron rings around his wrists, "will burn me."

Bjorn let out a long breath. "That makes it harder, for sure. We're not giving up, eh? You're a wizard, Master Bladewell," he winked to cheer up his companion. "You'll think of something, and these orcs will be sorry they ever met you."

"Bjorn, I'm sorry," Koren looked at his bowl, tears streaming down his face, thoroughly miserable.

"You tried, that's all anyone can do."

"No, you don't understand."

"I have to ask," Bjorn looked up but Koren avoid his eyes. "When that wizard held a knife at your throat, you begged him not to kill you. Last night, you *wanted* me to kill you. I do not understand that."

"I'm sorry," Koren sobbed, and Bjorn let him be until he was ready to talk. Sniffling, the boy sat with the bowl cradled in his hands, silently sobbing. Finally, he used a grubby sleeve to wipe his face. "I was wrong, so wrong. I've killed everyone. I ruined everything."

Normally, Bjorn would have responded with some useless platitude that people said in such situations, but something in Koren's tone gave him a chill. Koren was an incredibly powerful wizard. Bjorn had followed Koren's lead at the rope bridge and Captain Raddick had disobeyed his orders because Koren implied he had a plan, a plan he had not revealed to Bjorn. "What do you mean, you ruined everything?" Bjorn said in a hollow voice, fearing the answer he would receive.

"I, I thought I could destroy the demon," Koren looked up at Bjorn, and his eyes welled with tears again. "After I used that power, that destroyed an entire *army*, I thought I knew how to kill the demon. I was sure of it! Before, I didn't know how to make magic work, then after I did it- I still don't know how it works. But I know *what* to do now. I could feel it, the connection to the spirit world, that's where I got so much power. I thought I could do it again."

"When the orcs came at us in that ravine, you told me you couldn't use your power."

"I couldn't! It was there, I, it was like I couldn't reach it, and all I needed to do was, stretch a bit more to reach it. I thought using so much power damaged me or something, and I needed time to recover."

"When you recovered, you could destroy a demon, that's what you thought?" Bjorn asked harshly.

"Paedris said I could! He told Captain Raddick-"

Bjorn interrupted, disgusted. "Lord Salva told Captain Raddick you would be able to destroy the demon someday, *after* you have been properly trained and can control your power."

"I'm sorry."

"*That* was your plan when you asked me to cut the rope bridge with you?" Bjorn was completely exasperated with the young wizard he had pledged to help. "You told me you knew what you had to do! I thought your plan was to allow Raddick and those dwarves to get away, then you would use magic to kill the orcs who took us captive."

"No, that wasn't what I was thinking."

"You weren't thinking at all. Why the *hell* did you think you could kill a demon, all by yourself?"

"Because Paedris thought I could do it. He told Raddick-"

"I know what Lord Salva told Raddick, I was there when Raddick told you. Paedris thought you might act against the demon, *if* your power grows strong enough, and *after* you have been properly trained! You were not supposed to go confront a demon on your own."

"I thought, I thought I could. I used *so* much power-"

"Once. You used that power *once*, you didn't know what you were doing, and it nearly killed you. You could have killed all of us. You were almost more of a danger to-" He stopped, mouth open, then his eyes narrowed with horror. "Paedris told Raddick he is worried the demon could take control of you and use your power to tear a hole in the barrier between this world and the shadow world. If that happens, demons could pour through the hole and consume this world, everything, forever. If I had known your plan was for you to try destroying a demon, I would have told Raddick to shoot. I would have killed you myself!"

"Bjorn, I said I was sorry."

"Sorry? You *have* ruined everything, you *stupid* little child. You arrogant-" Bjorn could not find the words. Then, "You were right to ask me to kill you. You should have killed yourself when you had that knife in your hands. You *coward*. You have doomed us all! At this moment, there are soldiers fighting for Tarador, giving their lives for others, and their sacrifices are all for *nothing* because of you."

"I'm sorry!"

"Sorry? *I* am the one who is sorry. I'm an adult, and I followed, I trusted, a stupid boy who thought he could destroy a demon all by himself, because he thinks he is *special*."

"Bjorn, I-"

"No," the former King's Guard painfully scooted himself away. "Do not talk to me, traitor. If Paedris is right, the demon will take your power and destroy the world. If Paedris is wrong, then all I have done is allow myself to be captured for nothing. I will have time to regret my gullible foolishness when these orcs are cutting out my heart to eat it."

Koren knew there was nothing to say, nothing he could say. He sat in silence, tears falling freely from his cheeks into the cold bowl of stew, more miserable that he had ever been in his life.

After Koren's revelation that Bjorn may have helped the boy send the entire world to its doom, Bjorn fell into a deep depression, barely speaking to any of the orcs and not at all to Koren. When their horses were side by side and Koren wanted to uselessly apologize again, Bjorn squeezed his horse with his knees to make the animal walk faster. After a full day, Koren took the hint. For the first time since that fateful night be met Koren Bladewell in a riverside warehouse, Bjorn Jihnsson wanted a drink. No, he did not want a drink, he wanted a whole bottle. He wanted to drink enough to forget what a stupid, idiotic, gullible fool he had been to trust and follow a boy who had no idea what he was doing. Koren may be a powerful wizard but Lord Salva was right; Koren was too young and foolish to be trusted with any important responsibility.

The next morning, after a sleepless night, Bjorn was no longer depressed.

He was angry.

And determined.

Koren Bladewell was an immensely powerful weapon, and partly because of Bjorn, that weapon was being delivered to Tarador's ancient enemy. Bjorn needed to do something about that, even as every step of his horse's hooves brought them closer to the demon. All that day and the next, he observed the orcs, wracking his brain for a way to get a sword, a knife, even an arrow he could use to stab Koren, kill the boy and end the threat. If he could get close enough, he considered simply biting the boy's throat, so desperate was Bjorn to stop the impending destruction of the world.

All Bjorn's skill, his experience, his inventiveness could not find any way to stop Koren from being delivered to the demon. The orcs would not let him near the boy wizard, with two orcs holding the reins of each horse. They could not even speak with each other, for Bjorn's horse was kept near the rear of the marching column, while Koren rode ahead near the orc wizard. It was as if the orc wizard could read Bjorn's mind and knew the former King's Guard sought to kill Koren Bladewell. When they crossed a long, narrow bridge, Bjorn tried sending a mental image of the boy throwing himself over the side into the rushing river, with Bjorn hoping somehow a young wizard could read his thoughts. Koren did not attempt to leap off his horse over the side of the bridge, and anyway the orc wizard must have feared the boy would do something rash, as three orcs held firmly onto Koren until they were on the other end of the bridge. Thinking furiously that Koren should use his magical powers to kill himself also came to nothing, the boy could near hear any of Bjorn's fervent unspoken thoughts.

One time, when Bjorn was thinking as hard as he could about Koren somehow making himself disappear in a ball of fire, he opened his eyes to see the orc wizard riding beside him. At first, that wizard said nothing and did not need to, the smirk on his face ruined any last hope Bjorn had. "Enjoying the ride?" The orc asked mockingly, its hideous face twisting in a grotesque grin. "Do not worry, soon I will bring your little friend to my master, and I will be rewarded."

"He is not my friend," Bjorn replied through clenched teeth.

The orc cackled with laughter and spurred his horse onward, riding alongside the road until he was again riding near Koren. The wizard was personally taking charge of watching the boy, even checking the food Koren ate to assure there was nothing the boy could choke on. Bjorn knew the wizard was taking no chances of spoiling his prize as they neared the demon's stronghold.

As they had marched along the road, they picked up small bands of orcs, until Bjorn estimated five hundred of the creatures surrounded him. In mid-morning the day after the wizard had taunted him, Bjorn began to lose hope. A cloud of dust in the west came nearer, and the orcs began to murmur among themselves in nervous excitement. Bjorn saw orcs fingering their weapons and talking quietly in small groups, he did not understand their native language and could understand only a few words. One orcish word he did understand was used frequently and with vehement hatred: *men*.

As the dust clouds came closer, Bjorn could see tall mounted figures on horseback and behind them carriages. The column halted and the orcs dispersed off the road, being yelled at by their leaders but many of the orcs still had hands on the hilts of their axes, or unslung their short bows and shifted quivers to make arrows ready. The orc wizard shouted orders for Bjorn to be brought forward, and the wizard rode on ahead with Koren, holding the reins of the boy's horse. Koren had his head hung low, resigned to his fate.

The very last glimmer of hope inside Bjorn died when Koren was picked up off the horse and carefully placed in a carriage. Bjorn was dismayed to see a hideously shriveled human wizard sticking his head out of that carriage, gesturing for the men to bring Koren quickly. Then Bjorn was roughly pulled off his horse and ungently slung into the back of a wagon, where iron bars ringed him in and an iron gate was closed and locked. The clanging sound of his prison door slamming shut might as well be the death knell of the world to Bjorn. His only solace was seeing the orc wizard, after a loud argument with the wizard in the carriage, forced to ride his horse near the rear of the column near Bjorn's wagon. Bjorn got a small measure of satisfaction from seeing the fuming rage on the orc wizard's face. That tiny bit of satisfaction was fleeting and Bjorn tried to get comfortable on the rough floor of the wagon. Dark stains he recognized as layers of blood soaked into the wood made him shudder, when he thought of the fate that surely had befallen previous occupants of the wagon, then the wagon lurched into motion.

CHAPTER NINETEEN

"How did this happen?" Grand General Magrane demanded of the most skilled wizard with the Royal Army.

Madame Chu bit back a sarcastic reply. She could have explained that she was tired, all the wizards with the Royal Army were exhausted from the monumental task of breaching a dam, not to mention the ongoing effort to conceal the movements of the raiding force. She wanted to protest that she and her fellow wizards had done their best in very difficult circumstances, that the entire raid had been for the purpose of fooling the enemy about the expedition's true purpose of collapsing a dam, that the Royal Army's presence west of the River Fasse had mostly been to provide security for the wizards who had been vulnerable during the time-consuming operation of burning cracks through the dam. Madame Chu had not required or suggested the crown princess accompany the raid, indeed Wing had argued the girl who was both current Regent and future queen of Tarador should remain in relative security on the east side of the river.

Wing did not say any of those things she very much wished to say, especially she did not protest that the wizards were all desperately tired. Being tired to the point of exhaustion was no excuse for any person failing to perform their duty in the Royal Army, nor were such excuses accepted by the Wizards Council. Weariness, even great deep weariness what seeped down into your bones, was a given in wizardry, and to complain was a sign of moral rather than physical weakness.

"They fooled us, General," is what she did say in response.

"Master wizard," Magrane added with a slight bow from his saddle, "I meant no accusation, nor do I seek to place blame. What I wish is to understand *how* this happened, so I can plan a proper response and avoid such a surprise in the future."

Wing nodded, grateful for the old soldier's professionalism. "The short answer is the enemy can use wizardry just as we can. We have concealed the true strength, movements and purpose of the raiding force."

"Yes, I understand that, and I commend your efforts, we would not otherwise even have reached the dam site. My question is, how did we not detect the enemy cavalry?" Immediately after seeing the almost complete collapse of the dam, while the lake was surging through the newly-created gap to send a crushing all of water down onto the heaped supplies of the enemy, Magrane had ordered the raiding force back to the River Fasse. The march back was planned to be faster than the journey westward had been; any equipment not immediately useful was discarded as needless weight, and with the river now draining to the south, the course of the river they had used to march west was now wider and easier for travel. The wizards had sent messages through the spirit world to their counterparts east of the Fasse, reporting success in breaching the dam and requesting boats to bring the raiding force back to Tarador. Boats had been readied for people, barges readied to bring horses back, and another part of the Royal Army landed on the west bank to cover the retreat. All appeared to be going well for Magrane, the enemy had reacted and was marching north at a furious pace to intercept him, yet the enemy would not arrive in time. Wizards supporting the Royal Army reported the retreat route was clear and the weather favorable.

Then, scouts riding on the southeast flank of the raiding force ran into an ambush by a large group of cavalry, an enemy formation that did not even exist before it slaughtered many of the scouts, according to Madame Chu and her fellow wizards. "You are now certain your view through the spirit world reveals the true situation?" His tone reflected an anxiety that his triumph was about to be turned into disaster, and that he could do little to prevent doom from falling upon them all.

"We are certain. General, I do not wish to bore you with details about the inner workings of magic-"

"Please do bore me," Magrane insisted. "What I do *not* know about magic apparently can be dangerous."

"On our march north along the east bank of the Fasse, during our crossing and all the way up to the dam, we shrouded the raiding force with spells to conceal the area from prying eyes. We not only created a sort of magical fog through the spirit world, we projected false images showing the vanguard of our force was farther north and west of us, closer to cutting the roads of the enemy's main supply line. Our efforts were successful, for the enemy rushed troops north along the road, and diverted a clan of orcs southward to intercept us, or where they *thought* we were going."

"Yes, you told me," Magrane almost snapped, irritated the master wizard was not getting to the point. The daily briefings he had received from the wizards had been boastful of their successes, and Magrane could not abide boastfulness. "That does not explain why you did not see this sizeable and dangerous cavalry force coming north along the west bank of the river."

"Because we cast a spell to envelop ourselves, we could not extend our senses outside the area covered by the spell. It is like being under a blanket, if you lift a corner of the blanket, flies can get in. We had to rely on our wizards still in Tarador to search the area for us, and because of the distance from which they searched, we had to tell them where to concentrate their efforts. It made sense to concentrate the search to the west of us. They also searched in other directions, but not intensively, such a search drains a wizard's power, and we have too few wizards capable of performing that type of advanced magic. The simple truth, General, is that the enemy did to us what we did to them. They concealed the cavalry force under a spell, and allowed us to see the decoy forces advancing along the supply roads west of us. We were looking in the wrong place. Now that we are aware of the danger and the enemy knows where we are, we have dropped out spells of concealment and extended our senses. We are in grave danger; the enemy cavalry will soon be in position to block our path back to the river. The cavalry does not have the numbers to stop us-"

"No, and they don't have to," Magrane said while grinding his teeth in frustration. "They need only slow our advance until their reinforcements can each us, and those are only a day behind."

"What are your intentions?" Madame Chu would need to prepare her wizards to support whatever action Magrane planned.

"I will do the only thing I can at this point; send ahead my own cavalry force with the princess, to get her safely across the river and link up with our own people on the west bank. They will need to hold the river crossing until our main force can get there by marching."

"That will be," Wing recalled the enemy host she had seen marching rapidly north behind the cavalry, "difficult." The enemy in the area would soon outnumber the raiders, and could bring in more troops while the raiding force was slowly whittled away.

"That is not my greatest concern," Magrane hinted darkly.

"It is not?" Wing expressed surprise.

"No. For a cavalry force that size to be upon us already, they must have set out before we crossed the river. They must have received advanced notice."

"I assure you, General, our concealment spells were flawless."

"I believe you, master wizard. That leaves me with only one conclusion: we have a traitor in our midst."

"Your orders, General?" The cavalry lieutenant asked the commander of the Royal Army only two days later.

"Sound the retreat," Magrane sat tall in the saddle as he spoke words he feared could mean the doom of Tarador. The attempt to rush to the river ahead of the enemy, taking only the princess and wizards with mounted troops who could travel fast through open country, had failed. Scouts reported the enemy cavalry was already ahead in force, blocking the Royal Army's line of advance. Magrane felt his best choice to avoid complete disaster was to fall back, rejoin the main raiding force, then try to push their way through the enemy by sheer weight of numbers. That, too, would be a calculated gamble, a race for foot soldiers on each side to reach the spot on the west bank of the river where boats would be waiting to ferry the raiders to comparative safety. Magrane feared to acknowledge the truth even to himself; even if his backup plans succeeded, most of the raiding force would be lost, trapped in Acedor on the west bank of the River Fasse. His only hope was to get the princess and the wizards safely across, to fight a desperate delaying action while they fought through to the river, boarded the boats and reached Tarador. Those Royal Army troops holding a tiny foothold on the river's west bank were too few for any attempt to sortie out from behind the trenches they had dug as defense.

Destroying most of the enemy's supplies had given Magrane hope he had pushed a full-scale invasion across the River Fasse until next spring, possibly into early summer. Doing that would give the Royal Army time to rebuild fortifications, and for the promised troops from the Empire of Indus to arrive in strength. In the long run, even thousands of fierce warriors from Indus would not stem the tide of Acedor's inevitable victory, but delaying the invasion would give Lord Salva time to do whatever that master wizard had planned. Or whatever he hoped to plan, for Magrane had little faith that even the strongest of wizards could defeat a demon of the underworld.

Now even Magrane's hope for a temporary respite from defeat might be dashed. If he could force his way to the river by sacrificing most of the raiding force, he would give Tarador a chance to stave off immediate disaster; as long as princess Ariana and the wizards escaped across the river Tarador would not quickly fall. But the troops of the raiding force represented a substantial part of his mobile combat power, and the troops he had taken into Acedor were the most skilled and experienced of the Royal Army. Without that strength to bolster defenses east of the river, the enemy might be able to cross before winter and establish a firm presence within Tarador, and once behind entrenched defenses they would be impossible to dislodge with the remaining force available to Magrane. Come springtime, the host of Acedor could merely push forward along river valleys inside Tarador, and the Royal Army could not block every path.

"Sound retreat!" The lieutenant relayed the general's orders, and a horn sounded, picked up by other horns. Soon signal flags were waving. The cavalry column, strung out along the now-drying river valley where the Lillefasse used to flow, began to wheel and trot back the way they had come.

"General?" Ariana pulled her horse to a walk beside the old soldier. "Why are we retreating?"

Magrane explained quickly, adding "Our only goal now is to get Your Highness and the wizards across the river."

"What of my soldiers?" Ariana gasped.

Magrane noted she had called the Royal Army *her* soldiers, and he appreciated her concern for the people pledged to serve her. "Highness, if you fall, Tarador falls with you. The Regency Council will squabble and war with each other, until the realm shatters into seven provinces fighting on their own and only for themselves. Tarador will not last the winter if that happens. Without our wizards, the enemy could use magical means to crush the army no matter how strong we are or how staunchly we fight. I *must* get you and the wizards across the river to safety."

"I should not have come with the raiding force," Ariana regretted her foolishness.

"It was always a risk, Highness. In the end, you are at as much risk on either side of the river. And we had to take the wizards with us, so your royal person is only one complication. Do not worry about the army, Highness. My hope is that once you and the wizards are across, the enemy will lose heart seeing their prize has been denied to them," he added softly with a thin smile, contenting himself that his statement was only a forgivable little lie.

When he got the column turned around and the princess ahead with his best troops, Magrane hoped for a respite while he considered what to do, depending on the next actions of the enemy. The cavalry of Acedor had moved more swiftly than expected, though they traveled north along mostly flat roads along the river, while the raiding force had to gallop across country, mostly following the winding riverbed. Magrane's scouts had already made contact with the enemy vanguard, estimated to be no more than a hundred mounted troops, and Magrane was confident that at least his scouts could harass and delay that vanguard so those hundred soldiers of Acedor would not be a problem. What he feared was-

"General!" Duke Falco called out as he pulled his galloping horse to a walk. "General Magrane, fairy tales are all well and good when talking with a little girl," he looked toward the figure of the princess riding at the front of the column, "but we are men who have seen many battles. I have heard the reports from the scouts, and what our wizards have seen. The enemy is advancing swiftly, battle will be joined tomorrow morning and there is little was can do about it. We must prepare to fight a pitched battle before we can link up with your main force."

"I still hope to-"

"No, you do not," Regin interrupted. "Forgive me, General, but I know you are not a fool, nor do you indulge in wishful thinking. I do not see any way for us to meet with the main body of your troops before the enemy catches us, they know where we are and by now they know we have turned. The enemy can cut the corner and strike our flank, more quickly than we can race ahead for the safety behind the lines of your main force."

"You may be right about that," Magrane admitted. "I had planned to measure our progress at nightfall, and reassess."

"Our progress is slow, and will become slower as night wears on into morning," Regin warned. "We must rest our horses, they cannot travel all night. In the morning, when battle is upon us, we must have fresh horses."

"The enemy cavalry travels with extra horses, they will not rest during the night."

"They can change horses, we cannot. That does not change the fact that our mounts will not be useful in battle if they can no longer stand from exhaustion. General, I agree we must travel as swiftly as we can until nightfall, but if as I suspect we see battle is inevitable by morning, better for us to meet that battle with fresh horses and minds."

Magrane silently, having already considered calling a halt after darkness to be his best option. "Duke Falco, whatever happens, we must get that little girl, as you called her, safely across the river."

"My soldiers of Burwyck know they must protect my future daughter-in-law with their lives," Regin said with determination, though Magrane noted the duke looked away as he spoke. "We are in this together, for better or worse."

"Madame Chu," Ariana said with a jaw-stretching yawn as the wizard passed by the thin bedroll the princess had laid on bare ground, "what are you doing up?"

"I am seeing to changing of the guard amongst the wizards," Wing explained. "We cannot let our guard down for even a moment. Why are you not asleep?" She scolded the girl gently.

"I was," Ariana was mildly embarrassed about being scolded by a master wizard. "I feel so useless. The enemy is rushing at us and we sit here, doing nothing."

"We are not doing nothing, we are resting to prepare for battle," Madame Chu the master wizard reminded Ariana Trehayme the Regent of Tarador. "Our horses could not walk another league without falling down from stumbling." Wing spoke the truth, many of the horses with them had become so tired their soldiers had to drop down and run alongside their flagging mounts, that was when Magrane called a halt for the night. Battle was inevitable, and whether the enemy cavalry closed with them the next morning or afternoon made little difference to the outcome. What could change the outcome was having horses and soldiers rested and ready. Before allowing themselves to sleep, soldiers had unsaddled and brushed their horses, then fed the beasts from the sacks of corn each horse carried. Those horses with mild injuries had been attended to by wizards skilled in the healing arts, but no time nor energy was spared for healing the aches and pains of soldiers, for the wizards would need all the strength in the morning.

"All these people are at risk because of *me*," the princess's tone reflected her misery.

"No, they are at risk because of our enemy. The raiding force would be here without you, having you here gives us something to fight for beyond our own lives."

The words of the wizard were of no comfort to the princess. She looked to the sky, seeking the north star. Not long ago, she had watched the sun setting and wondered if Koren Bladewell was doing the same. Now she wondered if Koren also sought out the north star for guidance that night. "Do you know anything about where Koren is?"

"No. I'm sorry."

"What about Lord Salva? Can he-"

"None of us have been able to contact Koren through the spirit world," Wing let the princess down gently. "Paedris and Cecil are now too close to the demon for me to contact them, it would be far too risky for them to reach out. The best thing you can do for Koren is to sleep now, so you are prepared to lead us in the coming battle."

"I understand that, but-"

"No 'buts', young lady," Wing knelt down and pulled the bedroll blanket over the girl's shoulders. "Rest now. You can do nothing more tonight. Think on this; soldiers who see you awake will be ashamed to get the sleep they must have, if we are to survive the morrow."

"Yes ma'am," Ariana replied with a sleepy wink and turned over to try catching a few winks of elusive sleep. Unknown to her, the wizard from Ching-Do cast a spell to assure the princess would sleep soundly for five hours, long enough to wake refreshed and well before the enemy arrived within bowshot.

Koren Bladewell was seeking the north star that night, straining against his bonds in the jolting carriage as it bounced and lurched in headlong flight toward oblivion. The only time the carriage stopped was to change horses several times a day, Koren guessed that happened every three hours but he had no way of knowing. A trained wizard must have a way to tell time, he mused, but he had neither training nor the ability to use magic. Whatever happened to him when he poured forth raw power to destroy the orc army, it had damaged him somehow, and the enemy wizards had cast a spell to block him from feeling any connection to the spirit world. He could not conjure even the faintest glimmer of a fireball, nor do anything about the magic-reinforced bonds that encircled his wrists and ankles. He was helpless, being rushed along in a dark night to his doom, and the doom of the entire world.

It was only possible for him to see the night sky with one eye, he could not get his head far enough toward the window of the carriage for the other eye to see anything but the grimy ceiling of the carriage. Turning his neck painfully, he sought out the constellation farmers called the Plough and followed it until he sighted the north star, blinking faintly behind high, thin clouds. That afternoon, the carriage had clattered over a decaying wood bridge that spanned a river, just above where another river joined from the west. Koren recognized that river junction from studying maps of Acedor and knew he was drawing close to the lair of the demon. Before the wizard named Mertis was completely consumed by the demon he had summoned and thought he could control, that wizard had gone home to the castle where he had been born, and that is where the demon had lived ever since, having no use for worldly trappings of power.

Soon. Unless the carriage broke down or a miracle rescued him, in the morning Koren would be brought before the demon, and stripped to his bones so the being of the underworld could use his power to unleash a demon horde upon the world.

In a wagon behind Koren's carriage, Bjorn Jihnsson also sought the north star, though for more sentimental reasons. Bjorn found that star to know not which way lay north, but east. East, toward his family, the family he had abandoned to self-pity, weakness and drink. Bjorn sat upright, for it was no use trying to sleep in the harshly bouncing wagon, and prayed. He prayed for his family, of course, that they would be somehow spared the coming cataclysm, or at least die quickly and painlessly. He prayed for his family, but only as a way to pray for the miracle he sought. Bjorn prayed for the strength, the opportunity to kill Koren Bladewell, for only that way could the world be saved.

When Bjorn was done praying for his family, done begging God for a miracle so Koren would die, he added one more prayer, a request for something he thought even less likely to occur than him being able to kill Koren in time to save the world.

Bjorn prayed for the inner strength to forgive an untrained young wizard who had been unforgivably foolish and stupid, for he was only a boy.

CHAPTER TWENTY

The battle was brutal and see-sawed back and forth for over an hour, with the cavalry of Acedor repeatedly disengaging from the fight, reforming their lines and charging into the defenses of the Royal Army. The enemy's strength and ferocity dismayed General Magrane, and made him question his strategy of holding defensive lines, playing for time while the main part of the raiding force marched eastward to join the battle. If he could frustrate the enemy cavalry until the next morning, perhaps a bit longer, he could link up with his divided force and march east toward the river. That had been his plan, but the enemy charges had broken through the defenses three times already and Magrane feared his troops could not withstand another charge.

"We must regain the initiative!" Duke Falco urged. "I will take my cavalry out to hit their flanks before they can reform a column and hit us again. We will throw them off balance and force *them* to react to *us*."

Magrane considered quickly. The Duke of Burwyck was right that to continue a static defense would be certain suicide. "No! I will order *my* cavalry to sortie forth. Can your army hold our right flank, to protect the princess?"

Regin Falco gritted his teeth, unhappy about being denied the opportunity for a glorious charge in what might be Tarador's last battle. "I can guard our right, General, but if later there is need for a second sortie-"

"Aye," Magrane nodded, eager to leave the duke and make plans for his own cavalry to strike. "You will have the honor of it."

The cavalry charge by the Royal Army was successful in that it disrupted the enemy's efforts to reform their lines for another hard push to break through Tarador's defenses, but in the end the cavalry accomplished nothing, for the enemy had been prepared for a counterattack. As the Royal Army charged into the disorganized ranks of the enemy, an enemy cavalry force that had been held in reserve swung around to hit the right flank of Magrane's defense, pushing back the first line of defense and jumping their horses over the hastily-dug trenches there.

"Steady, men, steady," Kyre said though his own hands were shaking and his knuckles were white as he held the reins. His horse was nervous also at hearing the sounds of battle across the field, where the enemy had broken through the Royal Army's thin outer defensive line, and was now charging toward the princess. "It's up to us now," he looked around to meet the eyes of the soldiers he commanded. "Tarador calls us in her hour of need," he announced though his voice cracked with strain. With the Royal Army fully engaged, the ducal army of Burwyck was the major element guarding the right flank, and the only substantial force between the enemy and the guards ringed around princess Ariana. Kyre made sure his sword was ready, and tried to calm himself as he awaited his father's order to send the army of Burwyck into glorious battle.

"Soldiers of Burwyck!" Duke Regin Falco called out in a calm and clear voice, understandable even over the din of battle. Kyre readied his heels to urge his horse forward, his chest bursting with pride that his father, *his* father, would be leading the charge.

Except Duke Falco did not order his army into battle. "Pull back!" The duke ordered. "The enemy is through, we are lost! We must retreat if we are to save ourselves."

"What?" Kyre exploded, and most soldiers under the command of the Falcos joined the duke's heir in expressing confusion, their horses milling around uncertainly.

"Soldiers of Burwyck!" Regin called out again. "The princess is lost, we cannot save her! We must retreat if we are to save anything of Tarador!"

"No!" Kyre exclaimed instinctively in astonishment and fear at his father's totally unexpected action, his voice not carrying as far but heads turned to look at him in confusion. "We must-"

"People of Burwyck," Duke Falco called out as he reared his horse to gain attention. "Think of your families! Think of your homes! If Tarador falls, we must save ourselves or all is lost!"

"No!" Kyre repeated, pulling on the reins and digging his heels into his horse's sides, but the animal only turned to the right, where Joss Haden held the bridle. He could see many if not most soldiers who wore the colors of Burwyck were slowly and warily pulling back, leaving nothing between the fast-moving enemy and the princess. "No retreat! We must-"

"Sire!" His father's guard shouted back at Kyre. "Our liege lord has given us clear orders."

"We can save the princess!" Kyre slammed his gloved hand onto Haden's hand that was holding the bridle, but the man would not let go. Instead, the man's other hand swept around and caught Kyre in the face, giving him a bloody nose and rocking him back in the saddle. Shocked and angry, Kyre fumbled for the knife strapped to his belt on the left, his sword trapped out of reach between him and Haden. He got the knife sheath loosened from his belt, intending to use the handle to hit Haden's hand but the guard saw the knife and hit him in the face again.

"Try to hit *me*, you royal brat?" Haden growled, reaching for his own knife but he pulled it from the sheath, holding the handle in a position to stab with the point. "You father told me I could-"

Haden's words were cut off and the guard gasped in shock, as Jonas reached over almost casually and plunged his own dagger in the chest of Joss Haden. The untrustworthy guard fell backward silently, tumbling over his horse's rump to hit the ground with a thud, his helmet flying off.

"You killed him?" It was Kyre's turn to be shocked.

"I had no patience for a long boring conversation, Your Grace," Jonas explained with a deadpan expression. Around them, four of the other guards assigned by Duke Falco also lay dead, with the last holding up his hands in surrender. As Kyre and Jonas spoke, Jonas nodded, and one of his men smashed the last traitorous guard under the chin hard with the pommel of a sword, knocking the traitor off his horse to lie insensible on the ground.

"But you *killed* him," Kyre sputtered.

"He was about to kill you," Jonas pointed to the dead body of Haden. In death, the man's hand had closed around his knife. "He meant to stab you."

Kyre saw that Jonas spoke the truth, and nodded, unable to speak.

"Your orders, Your Grace?"

"I, I-" Kyre had no idea what to do. "My father-"

"Joss Haden would not have acted without orders from the Duke," Jonas shook Kyre's shoulder, making the stunned young man look at him. "Your father planned ahead to kill you if you disobeyed him, that is why he placed Haden and his crew around you."

"Then, then my father *planned* to abandon the Royal Army," Kyre realized, speaking in a near-whisper, remembering how Regin had told both of his sons they might need to choose between Burwyck and Tarador. At the time, Kyre assumed his father had been warning of an unlikely scenario, but the duke had not hesitated to leave the princess, at a time when the army of Burwyck could make all the difference between Ariana's survival or death.

Jonas shook the ducal heir's shoulder again, making the boy look at him. "You father is either a coward or a traitor. Either way, you now lead Burwyck. What are your orders?"

His father was a traitor. He had not merely schemed to gain more power for himself and the Falco dynasty, Regin Falco had sold out his people to the enemy. Kyre looked down at the silver falcon that adorned his tunic, the Falco family crest. It was now the crest of traitors, a badge of shame. How could he fight on, as the son of a traitor? Jonas gave him the answer as the loyal guard looked to the Falco heir. Jonas wanted not only orders, he wanted a way to redeem the shame that tainted everyone from the province of Burwyck. Kyre would not fight for himself or his disgraced family, he would fight for all those who held fast to their oaths, starting with his own guards. Drawing his sword and holding it high above his head, Kyre stood tall in the stirrups. "Burwyck! To me! To me! We can yet win the day!"

Koren was jolted awake when the carriage went over a particularly hard bump. He tried to rub the sleep from his eyes but forgot his hands were chained, and they came up short of reaching his face, making his already sore and bleeding wrists ache. Why the enemy had bothered to shackle him so tightly he did not understand, the dark wizards had cast spells that rendered his legs useless and made him feel constantly tired, sleepy and his head felt like thick fog. The carriage had fairly flown along rough roads through a landscape increasingly grim, gray and devoid of life as they approached the demon. What day was it? Koren had no idea, he had no way of knowing how many days had passed while he rode in the carriage, a helpless prisoner.

Pushing down on the thinly padded seat with his hands as his legs would not respond, he stretched his neck to see outside the window. At first, the windows on both sides had been covered with heavy canvas curtains, blocking out the world beyond the dark, cramped and stinking interior of the carriage. Some days ago, Koren's slow brain could not remember, the wizard who sat opposite him had torn the curtains aside, unable to stand the stifling hot air trapped in the small space. Feeling the blessedly cooler air, Koren had tried to speak, to thank the wizard, but found himself unable to make his mouth form words. Was that the effect of another spell, he wondered, or had his food and drink been drugged? He was not even allowed to drink or eat by himself, his hands remained chained at all times, the wizard seated across from him held a water flask to Koren's lips and spooned a flavorless mush at mealtimes, which happened only twice a day. If the wizard slept Koren never saw it happen, every time he was awakened from his foggy dreamland, the wizard was glaring at him with pure hatred.

Through the open window, Koren saw it was morning and the carriage was moving through a wide valley between tall mountains, with hills rolling lower and lower into the floor of the valley. Outside, the ruined landscape supported only low grasses and shrubs clinging desperately to life on the eroded slopes, everything he could see was sickly, stunted, yellowed with disease or from lack of nutrients in the dying and dusty soil.

He drifted in and out, unable to remain awake for long no matter how hard he concentrated. Gradually, he became aware of a disturbing presence probing the back of his mind, he kept pushing it away but it came back, stronger and stronger until it took all of Koren's will to force the presence from his mind. The last time, he felt a stab of pain that made him awaken with a gasp, and the presence jerked away from him with a howl of frustration.

Now he was fully awake, the fogginess in his brain wiped away by the anguished howl that echoed terribly, making Koren wince and shudder. He sat bolt upright, jerked to a stop by the chains that bound him. Outside the carriage window, a fortress loomed in the morning sunlight, built into a cliff and towering above a ruined city. The fortress itself was grimy and in disrepair, stones having come loose and tumbled down the soot-caked walls. Roofs of the buildings within the encircling wall had fallen in over centuries of neglect, for the demon no longer cared about the physical structure. Crows or buzzards or other carrion-eating birds flocked around the castle, their harsh calls louder and louder as the carriage rushed down the rutted roads toward the gate. Koren's otherworldly senses could feel the ache of longing filling the demon within, the malevolent presence becoming a pulsing roar as the ancient creature of the underworld trembled with eagerness to finally grasp the prize it had sought for so long. In the seat across from him, the wizard twitched and jerked in agony, unable to withstand being so near the powerful entity within the castle. Wordlessly, the wizard glared at Koren as blood seeped from its nose and mouth. With one last horrible spasm of pain, the wizard's head lolled forward and it slumped, dead. Shutting his eyes, Koren willed himself to block out the roaring in his head, as the carriage rumbled onto the broken cobblestones of the bridge leading to the castle gate. It was no use, the demon was too powerful. The boy wizard felt his will slipping away, the demon encroaching on his mind from all sides until all he could do was hold onto a tiny spark of himself deep inside. Be strong, he told himself, even though he knew no wizard could stand against the demon. Paedris had been right, without training and before coming into his full powers, Koren stood no chance against the power of the underworld.

Koren's nerve failed him when the carriage rolled into the castle, and the massive iron doors closed behind him with a reverberating sound. With an ear-shattering screech, the demon proclaimed its victory, and blackness closed in.

"Cecil!" Paedris called out in pain, the strain of fending off the enemy wizards becoming too much for him. He had wanted to challenge their demon enemy directly, but before he and Cecil came within sight of the evil being's castle, they were set upon by eight wizards. Six wizards of Acedor now remained, and Paedris felt his power ebbing. Being so close to the demon, he had felt his connection to the spirit world becoming tenuous, thin, unreliable as the demon's presence suppressed his power. "Get away if you can, I can't hold them much longer!" He staggered as three fireballs seared through the air toward them and he was barely able to block the magic fire, enough getting through his warding spell to splash all around his feet.

Cecil stood his ground, placing a hand on the other wizard's shoulder, closing his eyes and letting power flow from him into the court wizard. "There won't be much longer for any of us. I will stay here with you," he declared as they waited for death. It would not be long now.

Princess Ariana and her bodyguard had been hard pressed by the enemy, even after Kyre Falco disobeyed his own father and came to her rescue with a third of the confused Burwyck soldiers following the heir to continue the battle while the rest followed Duke Falco in disgraceful retreat. Kyre turned the tide for a hopeful moment, forcing the enemy back with a hard charge that crashed into the enemy lines, breaking up the disciplined wedge of cavalry and turning the fight into a battle of individual soldiers on horseback where the superior training of Burwyck and Tarador began to tell. The enemy was pressed back and Ariana's guards reformed their lines around her, setting pikes into the ground to deter cavalry charges and drawing their swords.

It was not enough, not nearly enough. The enemy forced their way toward the princess by sheer weight of numbers; horses, men, and orcs dying without seemingly any effect on the enemy advance. Finally, after his horse stumbled and fell with an arrow in one leg, Kyre ordered Jonas to disengage, reform the lines and attempt to break through with one last charge by the cavalry. Kyre himself hopped off his dying horse to the ground to fight with Ariana's guards. He found himself only a few yards from Grand General Magrane, who was still on his horse and directing the battle even as their strength faded with every soldier who fell. Kyre slashed at an enemy soldier then feinted another slash, dropping to one knee and stabbing upward with the sword point to catch the enemy under the chin. Not taking time to congratulate himself, Kyre stood and kicked the enemy free of his sword, ready for the next of the screeching, surging, fanatical horde. For a split second, he caught Magrane's eye, and the general lifted his own sword in salute. If he died that day, Kyre might have salvaged some small measure of honor for the Falcos from the wreckage of disgrace. If anyone of Tarador survived to tell the tale.

With ever-smaller numbers her guards had fought to break through the encircling enemy lines, hoping to reach the comparative safety of the Royal Army that was also fighting their way toward their princess. Her guards and soldiers fought bravely and were standing firm even as more and more of them fell to arrows, spears and swords, but the enemy was truly fanatical, under the spell of their demon overlord. Enemy soldiers threw themselves on the pikes and swords of her guards to clear a path for the demon-compelled foul men or orcs behind, forcing Ariana's dedicated guards to untangle their weapons from the front rank of the enemy before they could engage those in the second rank. Her guards had been slowly losing the fight, Madame Chu and her cohort of wizards fully committed to battling wizards of Acedor and unable to help Ariana's physical defense. The superior numbers of the enemy in men, orcs and wizards were too much for the most valiant efforts of her defenders. The chaotic fight reached the point when Ariana had loosened the strap of the dagger she carried on her left forearm. If she were about to be seized by the enemy, she intended to stab herself and deny the enemy a prize captive. Ariana Trehayme was not going to be paraded about as an object of ridicule.

Koren awakened to find himself in a dark chamber, lit only by blood-red torches, and he almost gagged on the choking stench of sulphur and brimstone. On a stone bench in the center of the chamber sat a thin, emaciated figure, clothed in a robe that hung in tatters around its bony frame, the gray desiccated skin stretched tight over the rotted flesh within. Sores oozed openly, running down and soaking the filthy robe but the figure paid no mind to the physical discomfort of the ancient body it inhabited, for that body was no more than a vessel to contain its presence within the world of the real, an anchor holding its tenuous connection to the underworld. Even after all the centuries of restless striving and longing, the demon had not been able to strengthen and widen that connection, for all its incredible power it had failed to open a door wide enough for its demon brethren to follow it into the real world.

Beside Koren, Bjorn suddenly snapped to awareness, finding he was no longer bound with chains at all but unable to move of his own will. He knelt on a cold stone floor, his knees squishing in something he did not want to think about. The seated figure in front of them leaned forward slightly, the action causing brittle bones in one leg to snap and protrude through the paper-thin skin, grayish fluid leaking out. "Is," Bjorn's tongue moved awkwardly, for he had been unable to speak for many days. "Is that, Mertis?"

"What is left of him," Koren answered, his tongue thick and slow. He remembered Paedris telling him the demon pulled the life essence from slaves to keep the body of Mertis from collapsing into dust, discarding the bodies of slaves after they were used up. Were the bodies of slaves what the crows flocking around the castle fed on, Koren wondered, for nothing else lived within that desolate valley.

"So long," the seated figure croaked. "So looooong," the words came out as a hiss, sending a chill through Koren. Strangely, he no longer felt the roaring in his mind, instead there was something squeezing in on him, pulling at his will, demanding his power. The presence in his mind, dark and cold and unspeakably evil, reached within him and Koren found no amount of asserting his will could force the presence out, nor deny it access to the power within him. "Ahhhh," Koren grunted.

"Fight it!" Bjorn whispered, unable to speak louder.

"I c-can't. It is too strong. You can't imagine its power. Bjorn, I'm sorry."

"It's not your fault," Bjorn found himself surprised by his own words. During the painful, endless ride in the wagon, the former King's Guard had found he could not hate Koren Bladewell, though the boy had doomed the entire world. Koren was just a boy, no more and no less foolish and recklessly overconfident than anyone else at that age. Koren had not failed, the adults around him had failed the boy. Lord Salva, Captain Raddick, even Bjorn himself were supposed to be experienced, responsible adults, and they had failed to stop Koren from harming himself through youthful ignorance and stupidity.

"I'm s-sorry," Koren repeated. "I can't fight it much longer. It is *so* strong, ah-"

"Giiiiive it to meeeeee," the demon hissed, its dead eyes glowing.

"No," Koren's shout of defiance came out as a mere whisper.

"Give it to me!" The demon roared, the sound echoing painfully around the chamber, making the oozing fluid on the floor slosh against Koren's knees.

Koren knew he could no longer fight, the tiny spark of self deep within his mind was being snuffed out under the onslaught of the demon's desire. "Y-you want my p-power?" Koren stammered to speak with a jaw clenched in painful tremors, his teeth grinding uncontrollably, tasting blood in his mouth as he involuntarily bit the inside of his cheek.

"Yessssssss," the demon hissed in ecstasy, feeling its final victory so close at hand.

Koren's eyes opened under hooded lids, barely seeing but staring directly into the demon's glowing yellow eyes. *"Then choke on it."*

Koren *reached* into the spirit world, down, down, down into the bottomless depths, hearing the spirits cry out with alarm and ignoring them, *commanding* them to release power and power flowed, limitless. A sun burst forth from the spirit world, more than a sun, pouring through Koren into the demon and still Koren *pulled* more and more power until the spirits writhed in terror and tried to flee but Koren held them fast with his will, draining an ocean of raw, searing power through himself into the demon, holding back nothing. The spirits lashed back and forth to break from Koren's grip and he paid them no attention for they could not escape his indomitable will. He needed power, more power, more more more it was never enough it would never end and the spirits drowned in the power surging through and upward out of their realm.

"*NOOOOOOOO!*" the demon screamed, a hammerblow of sound that assaulted Koren's eardrums and was ignored. Desperately, the demon tried to break its connection with the boy and found itself trapped in an immovable grip. Power, unimaginable, unfathomable, uncontrollable power flowed from the boy into the demon where it had no place to go. Not even a timelessly ancient being of the underworld could use or withstand such a tidal wave of power, the demon stood on the shore between worlds and shrank in panic from the coming wave that broke over it and smashed it over and over and over. Lightning burst forth from its unworldly form until even the demon could not contain a million suns of power and the demon was overwhelmed, power beginning to flow heedlessly through the demon and scorch the barrier between worlds. On the other side, the hordes of demons waiting there had only the most fleeting moment of glee before the power burning through burst forth in all directions to scorch beings who were themselves made of magical fire. The demons howled in pain and fear, shrinking away to the farthest reaches of their dark realm but the power followed them, seeking them out in every corner until the demons screeched in utterly hopeless terror. The power burned, it hammered through the demons, it tore them asunder and they reacted in the only way they could; with the last of their strength they slammed shut the barrier between worlds, cutting off the lone demon in the real world from them forever.

The demon, alone, abandoned and terrified beyond sanity, forgot itself, forgot who it was forgot it existed forgot everything but the searing white hot fire within and the demon ceased to exist, its essence exploding as a deathless creature of the underworld was ripped apart.

Koren was barely aware of being at the center of a maelstrom of fire whirling around him faster and faster, caught in a bubble while everything around him turned to soot and dust and nothingness. The massive, solid ancient stones of the castle were nothing more than loose sand to the tornado of fire that consumed those walls, sending pieces of the castle for miles in every direction, blasting craters with the mere force of air that hit like a solid wall, punching holes in the ground and washing away hills until the landscape around where the castle had been was scoured by a relentless incoming tide of fire.

Paedris felt the shockwave as it hit the enemy wizards, a truly shocking wall of power rolling over them all, knocking them all to the ground and wiping awareness from his mind. His last memory was of Cecil beside him, the man's eyes turning toward Paedris in fear, hope and amazement before he, too, was overcome.

Just when the two guards directly in front Ariana tripped backward under the onslaught of a half-dozen enemy soldiers heedlessly clawing their way in a mindless killing frenzy toward the princess, the entire enemy force froze then stumbled, swaying and crying out in a horrible, otherworldy screeching. Wizards on both sides went rigid, flinging their arms out in shock before slumping to the ground, insensible. Guards and soldiers of Tarador took a wary step backward, momentarily stunned into disbelieving inaction, until Grand General Magrane roared to break the sudden eerie silence of the battlefield. "Kill them!" He ordered, sweeping his own sword in a cutting motion across the throats of two orcs in front of him.

After the initial sickening slaughter while they stood immobile and defenseless, the surviving forces of Acedor shook off the trance that had taken hold of them. The enemy did not fight back, did not even defend themselves. With few exceptions, men and orcs had flung aside their weapons and ran in terror, not even trying to conduct an organized retreat. In the insanity of their fright, some of them ran into lines of the Royal Army, to be cut down. The screams of those unfortunates only added to the mindless despair of the enemy, spurring some to flail about and crash headlong into trees or to leap into the river to drown, weighted down by their boots and chainmail.

As the enemy fled, Ariana's guard regrouped, forming a tight circle around the princess, not yet taking time to aid their own wounded. Not until there wasn't a living enemy within a quarter mile of Ariana did General Magrane pull himself onto a horse and gallop over to his Regent. Saluting her with a bloody sword, Magrane called out in a loud voice, exultant in victory. "Your Highness, I believe we have won the day!"

Her fingers trembling, Ariana firmly refastened the strap of the dagger she had intended to kill herself with, a chill creeping up her neck when she thought how close she has come to plunging that blade into the fine silk jacket she wore over her chainmail. "The day has been won, General, but I think we here do not own the glory of this victory!"

The broad smile on Magrane's face fell into a frown before he quickly recovered. He had not expected to live that morning, and no amount of inescapable logic could tarnish what his soldiers had accomplished on the battlefield. Enough of those wearing the colors of Tarador lay dead or wounded, and they deserved to celebrate their hard-won triumph, no matter how they might have been aided by mysterious events elsewhere in the world.

Before her general could speak, Ariana understood the people who were sworn to follow her needed to be acknowledged. Holding up her own sword, her eye catching the dried blood crusted on it, she saluted Magrane. "There is glory enough to go around today, General Magrane. I salute your soldiers and those of our allies, please convey my deepest gratitude for their courageous stand against our ancient enemy!"

Magrane nodded and spurred his horse to organize a pursuit of the enemy to assure they did not regroup and attack again. Even with the frightful heaps of enemy bodies littering the battlefield, he knew the numbers were substantially against him, if the enemy recovered their senses and resumed their attack.

Ariana did not bother to wipe the dried blood off her sword, instead guiding it carefully into the scabbard with fingers that were still trembling slightly. Her trembling was from exertion and the after-effect of combat and not fear, she told herself, knowing that was not entirely true and not caring. She had survived, while many had not. Ariana gently pushed aside guards around her to kneel by an injured man, when something shining and bright caught her eye on the grim battlefield; it was the blonde hair of Olivia Dupres, waving gently in the breeze.

The wizards! Ariana stood up with a shock and ran toward the young wizard who had risen to one knee, looking around her with unfocused eyes. "Madame Dupres!" Ariana called out gently, taking hold of the young woman's shoulders and helping her to her feet. "Are you unwell?"

"We all, we all received a shock," Olivia explained, not understanding what had happened to her. "Someone used a tremendous amount of magical power."

"Was it Lord Salva?" Ariana asked hopefully.

"No," Olivia shook her head, blinking to make her eyes work properly again. "Not a tremendous amount of power, an *impossible* amount of power. I," she paused to catch her breath. "I did not know such power existed. Highness, I believe the demon is dead."

Ariana clasped her hands in front of her, not daring to hope. "Banished back to the underworld?"

"No, Your Highness. It is *dead*. Someone *killed* it, burned it from the inside with magical fire, and it is a creature of fire. What we, we wizards felt, was this power being used, and the demon crying out as it died. It was," she leaned against the princess as a wave of dizziness swept over her. "A terrible shock to all of us wizards." That reminded her of something. "Madame Chu! Where is she?" Breaking away from the princess, Olivia ran over to where the wizard from Ching-Do lay sprawled on the ground. The woman was alive but breathing shallowly, and Olivia felt the life force within her had retreated to protect itself from the shock.

"What is wrong with Madame Chu?" Ariana asked Olivia, wringing her hands in anguish.

"She is far more powerful than me," Olivia speculated. "She would have felt the shock more strongly. She lives, I can bring her back to us, but my skills in healing are less than masterful. Let me-"

"Olivia!" Ariana grabbed the other girl's shoulder, pointing to the west where six enemy wizards were on their feet. Four were milling about stumbling, appearing dazed and blinded, but two were supporting each other and looking toward Ariana menacingly. One of the two reached skyward and a fireball began to form in its hand. "Madame Dupres!" The princess implored the young wizard for help.

"Oh, we do not have *time* for this nonsense!" Olivia spat in disgust. Standing up, she quickly conjured a truly large fireball and launched it at the cluster of enemy wizards, hitting three of them and splashing the three others with burning magical essence. The six died quickly as their bodies were consumed, burned through to their dark souls.

"That," Ariana took a step back from the young wizard. "That was a rather large fireball, Madame Dupres."

Olivia shrugged irritably, not wishing to spare the time to explain magic to a princess. "The demon is no longer suppressing our use of power, Highness. Please, I must aid Wing, that is, Madame Chu as best I can." Looking to where her fireball had set the dry grass flame and snuffed the life out of six foul practitioners of dark magic, she added with grim satisfaction, "I do not think wizards of the enemy will be bothering us this morning."

CHAPTER TWENTY ONE

Bjorn came back to awareness slowly, falling back into a dreamless stupor several times before he opened his eyes to see black grit raining down and he coughed on black flakes of soot. The air smelled strongly of sulphur, it stung his eyes and the fine grit was clogging his eyelashes, he tried to sit up and pain exploded all over his body, nearly making him faint. Slowly, carefully, he rolled onto his left side, propping himself up on one elbow and wiping his eyes. Blinking helped only so much, his eyes teared up to flush the grinding grit out, and he could see he was in a wide, shallow crater. Of the castle, there was no sign other than piles of blackened sand fused like glass scattered as far as he could see. There were no men or orcs, their weapons were mostly gone also, with only axeheads, the blades of pikes and a few swords and knives half buried in the still-falling soot. Even the hills that had rolled down into the valley were flattened sand dunes under the surrounding mountains of bare rock.

The demon! The demon was gone also, nothing remained that Bjorn could see with his blurry vision. A hacking cough behind him made him jerk his head and a sharp pain made him stop. Moving gingerly, he inched around to see Koren, his face and hands red with sunburn, laying on his back and coughing weakly. Bjorn had to fill his lungs twice to speak a single word, it hurt even to breathe. "Koren."

"Dee," the hacking cough resumed, then, "demon?"

"Gone. Everything else with it." Bjorn developed a rhythm for speaking; two words and two shallow breaths, followed by two words.

"Good," Koren let his head flop back down which was a mistake, as the impact sent a shower of soot to swirling around him, and he choked on it. He was so weak he could barely lift a hand, his toes could wiggle but no amount of effort would make his painful legs budge from where they rested.

"Wha-" Bjorn mistakenly inhaled sooty dust, and when he coughed, there were specks of blood on the ground in front of him. "What did you do?"

"The demon," Koren paused for breath, his seared lungs unable to fill. Gasping for air between every second word, he continued slowly. "The demon wanted my power, it wanted the power to tear open the barrier between worlds, to unleash an army of demons upon us. It wanted that power. I gave the demon what it wanted. *More* than it wanted."

"Ah," Bjorn nodded, beginning to understand. "You couldn't control your power, but you knew how to get it."

"Yes," Koren shuddered at the memory. "I commanded the spirits to drain their world of power, through me into the demon. The power of the spirits is limitless but they gave me all they could and it kept coming, I was scared that much power would destroy us also, destroy this world."

"You stopped it in time?"

"No," Koren shook his head, tried to laugh and coughed until his lungs ached. "After the demon was destroyed, I lost awareness, and the spirits took the opportunity to break free from my will. It was luck that we're alive. Can you see around us? I'm afraid how much of our world I've consumed with fire."

Bjorn staggered to his knees, took in a brief view to the east where white clouds still towered in the sky above black hills, then his strength gave out and he fell into the choking blackened dust. "The world is still here. Far away, but still here."

"Good."

They lay in silence, breathing as deeply as their soot-choked lungs could manage. Bjorn rolled onto his side, looking at Koren accusingly. He pointed with a quaking finger to the boy who was no longer a boy. "That was your plan all along, you scoundrel! You made me think you were wrong, that you had failed."

"I had to," Koren explained. "The demon, and its wizards, could not read my mind, I felt that orc wizard try to invade my thoughts and I pushed it away. But the demon could read *your* mind, and I needed to get close to the demon so I could destroy it. If the demon knew I could kill it, it would never allow me near, it would kill me. *You* needed to believe I had failed, that I could not feel my power, that I was no threat to the demon. The demon read your mind and believed it was safe to bring me within its guard, that I was powerless. I'm sorry that I lied to you, but the deception was necessary."

"Huh," Bjorn slumped, not sure to be insulted or proud.

Koren laughed, an action that made him hurt all over.

"What's so funny?"

"The deception was necessary," Koren snorted. "Paedris I'm sure said the same thing when he concealed the truth from me. So many deceptions, and all of them necessary."

"Lord Salva was right in the end, apparently. Wait. One thing I don't understand. I know now why you were afraid when that wizard held a knife to your throat; if he killed you then, your plan would be ruined. But later, you begged me to kill you!"

"Yes, because I knew you wouldn't."

"You are wrong," Bjorn shook his head slowly. "I made up my mind to kill you. I tried to throw that knife! You are alive only because an orc hit me and knocked off my aim."

"No. I should have said I knew you *couldn't* kill me. The same way I know an arrow will hit its target, I knew your knife would miss me."

"You knew an orc would spoil my aim at the last second?" Bjorn sputtered, incredulous.

"I didn't know. The *spirits* knew your knife would never touch me."

Bjorn's mind reeled in pure amazement. "Lord Bladewell," he bowed with his head as it hurt too much to move anything else. "It is a strange world you live it."

"I don't know anything about it," Koren admitted. "The only thing I know how to do is pull power from the spirit world. That I knew I could do, pull *so* much power the demon could not control it and would be consumed by fire."

"How did we not die?"

"I willed us to be protected, so the spirits did." Koren coughed and spit up black dust. "I should have been more specific," he laughed, which made him cough again.

Bjorn laughed also, making his lungs ache and sore belly muscles spasm in pain. "Oh, it hurts to laugh. What now?"

"Now?" Koren was too dead tired to think of the future. "We, I don't know. My plan stopped with killing the demon. I didn't expect to destroy the castle and all its servants also. I suppose we, walk out of here?"

Bjorn lifted his head again, a bit higher this time. "Koren, all I can see to the horizon is blackened nothing. I remember hills to the east, close to the castle, now that area is almost flat. The castle, the moats, the walls, all of it, is gone. This will be a long walk."

"Oh," Koren was so weary deep in his bones, he found it difficult to care. "We can start in the morning, then."

Bjorn closed one eye and peered at the sun, obscured by the mist of soot and grit hanging in the air. "It *is* morning. Do you think it's the same morning?"

"I don't know. My senses were in the spirit world, where there is no time. It's hard to explain. A whole night could not have passed, could it? That seems awfully long-"

"Koren!" Bjorn interrupted. While the boy had been speaking, Bjorn had caught something odd with the corner of an eye, now he stared at it, transfixed. It was a faintly glowing spark, like a firefly, dancing in the air, flitting lazily this way and that, gradually coming closer to Koren. Bjorn had first noticed the spark as a bright spot in the layer of grit covering the ground, and he had thought at first it was sunlight glinting off the metal of a discarded sword. He pointed with an unsteady hand, his finger trembling. "What is that?"

"What?" Koren turned his head in halting increments, feeling something grinding in his neck. "What are you talk about? No!" His head snapped around so he was looking directly at the object. A stabbing pain shot down his neck and he barely felt it. "The demon!"

"Wha-" With strength he didn't know he had, Bjorn scrambled backward away from the object, pushing with his hands in the loose grit, dragging his wobbly legs. "You killed it!"

"I thought I did! Something, some part of it, must have survived. Demons are powerful, Paedris warned me about that," Koren's lips trembled in panic.

"Can you kill that thing now?" Bjorn watched the evil spark fly about aimlessly, except it was not quite aimless. Slowly, it was drawing closer to the young wizard.

"No. I don't have any power, I can't *do* anything," Koren half sobbed. He was worked so hard and risked so much, been willing to and expecte to die in order to banish the demon from his world, and now saw he had failed. "The spirits won't answer me!"

"We need to get away," Bjorn clenched his teeth and pushed himself to one knee, every muscle in his body sending signals of agony. "Get out of this crater, away from here."

Koren tried to move his legs. He could feel them, and they trembled when he tried to roll over, but they could not move on their own. His arms were like lead, of his left arm he could only lift the wrist. With his right arm, he grunted with effort to lift that hand, palm outward in a warding gesture, but his hand only flopped uselessly onto his chest. "I can't move. I can't!"

"It's getting closer to you. What happens if it touches you?"

"I think it will take over my body and consume me, like it did to Mertis. I will become a new Draylock, and the demon will grow in power," Koren's arms and legs still lacked the strength to move.

"It can take over a person?"

"Yes, that is what happened to Mertis! He stupidly used dark magic and allowed the demon access to our world," Koren was amazed how calmly he was speaking. "Mertis thought he could contain and use the demon's power, but it consumed him instead." No amount of willpower and effort could get his legs to move, he was trapped, and the dancing spark was drifting ever closer, moving more purposefully as perhaps it sensed Koren's presence.

"No, that is not going to happen," Bjorn got onto both knees, slumping forward from the strain until he was crawling on hands and knees. "Here!" He shouted hoarsely. "Come here! Take me!" He waved a hand toward the spark, trying to catch it.

"Bjorn, no!" Koren coughed weakly, his head lolling to the side. The spirits had abandoned him completely, he could not feel any connection to their timeless world.

"Come here, come *here!*" Bjorn thumped his chest to get the spark's attention as it flitted dangerously close to Koren. The tiny glimmer of light drifted up, over Koren, then began to settle down, lazily moving side to side along with flecks of soot in the air.

"Bjorn, no! It will just take you instead. *No!*"

"You come here, now you damned-" With a last, desperate swipe of his hand, Bjorn reached for the spark, and felt it burn hotly into his palm. The shock flung him backward, skidding across the loose grit on his backside. He came to rest rigidly on his back, seemingly dead, his body unmoving.

Then the body moved.

Koren watched in horror as what used to be Bjorn Jihnsson rose stiffly from the waist, and its head swiveled toward Koren. Already, the man's eyes glowed with hellish internal fire. The ghoul stood jerkily, as if unfamiliar with its new host body. Unspeaking, it began walking toward Koren, shuffling one foot then the other, barely lifting the feet and dragging long furrows in the dark grit that coated the floor of the crater. The undead lips curled in an awful smile-

Then the smile froze. So did the creature. As the light behind its eyes faded in and out, it spasmed, trying to bend from the waist and fighting itself. In awkward, halting, jerky motions the creature bent down, its hands twisted into claws seeking a long, thin dagger which lay on the ground at its feet. The hands wrapped around the dagger's hilt, pulling the weapon upward. With a sudden jerk, the being collapsed onto his knees, crashing down and throwing up a fountain of soot.

"Koren-" the being grunted in a voice the boy recognized as Bjorn's, the light flaring in its eyes. "Tell my family I love them." With that, the being pitched forward like a toppling statue, dagger poised in front of it, and the dagger plunged straight into Bjorn's heart.

"Paedris!" Cecil warned, pointing with a shaking hand to the enemy wizards who were standing up, wavering on their feet. In shock, they stared at the two wizards from Tarador, their fear competing with their life-long hatred. With their demon overlord gone, the wizards of dark magic struggled with the innate cowardice that had brought them to practice their evil craft. They had no demon providing them protection and power, they also had nothing to lose, as their hopes for dark victory had perished in unimaginable fire. With a cry that was more ragged than fierce, the wizards of Acedor screamed a challenge and reached upward to summon magical fire.

"Oh, bother. Not *this* again," Paedris snapped with weary irritation. "Begone with you all." Not even using his whole arm or giving the threatening wizards his full attention, he flicked his wrist and the assembled enemy were violently flung far in the air, soaring upward and back, going, going, going and crashing to the hard ground to tumble over and over, their bodies broken, their foul souls leaving the mortal realm.

"Hmm," Cecil remarked, shading his eyes with a hand as he watched the dark objects cartwheel through the sky before they hit far away and sent up puffs of gray dust. "Anything flying that far should have feathers."

"F-feathers!" Paedris chuckled and that started Cecil doing the same and soon they were both on their knees shaking with laughter. "I guess," Paedris gasped, "I guess I was wrong about something."

"What's that?"

The court wizard used a hand to mimic something arcing through the air. "Wizards *can* fly!"

Cecil exploded with laughter, setting Paedris off again and they both laughed until their sides hurt. "Oh," Cecil held his aching sides which twinged painfully. "Why are we laughing at such a time?"

"Because our evil enemy is dead!" Paedris exulted. "That ancient demon is no more."

"And Koren?"

"Koren. I did not sense his death, did you?"

"No," Cecil frowned. "But I cannot sense anything about him now. Paedris, I fear for the boy."

"Then," Paedris looked to the west, where a gray cloud of soot and dust rose as a pillar in the sky. "We must go to him, quickly."

"I wish *we* could fly," Cecil replied with a wistful groan, thinking of the long distance they must walk. "Paedris, that was rather a neat trick, sending all those wizards tumbling through the air to their doom."

"Thank you," the court wizard made a short bow, his aching back protesting. "It was-"

"It would have been more convenient if you had performed that particular trick before, when those wizards had us trapped by magical fire."

"Oh," Paedris' face fell. "I couldn't do it then, you see. With the demon feeding them power, they were able to resist me."

"And now?" Cecil pondered the dissipating clouds of dust where the wizards had crashed down to their deaths.

"Bah," Paedris dismissed the thought with a wave. "They may as well have been scarecrows made of straw. Are you ready, Cecil? It will be a long walk, and we must make haste. I do not sense Koren has died, but he cannot be in good health, if yonder column of smoke over those mountains is any indication."

The Royal Army sent scouts ranging far and wide through the countryside, and set up defenses around the main encampment for the night, though their own wizards assured General Magrane that the scattered, dazed and thoroughly demoralized soldiers of Acedor posed no threat to the unified might of the Royal Army. The only fighting within fifty miles was men of Acedor and orcs attacking each other, and a few men still stubbornly loyal to Burwyck resisting arrest and disarmament. Magrane told the wizards he appreciated their insight, and that he had not lived long enough to command Tarador's army by being incautious and sloppy. Accordingly, trenches were dug and sharpened spikes installed in the bottom to stop cavalry charges, fences of brambles and tangled trees were placed behind the trenches, and sentries posted in depth ringing the camp. Knowing his people were nearly stumbling from exhaustion and the excitement of battle wearing off, Magrane rotated sentries every hour to ensure everyone had a chance to sleep for six solid hours. Everyone, that is, except Magrane himself, who tirelessly rode in circles to check on and thank the sentries. And the injured and healers who would get no rest that night, except those for whom rest would be permanent, having succommed to their wounds.

Neither was there sleep for Ariana, who tirelessly worked throughout the night in the hospital tents. No, not tirelessly, for even before the first light of dawn appeared in the eastern sky, she found it difficult to keep her eyes open. Magrane found her standing over a fire, taking cloths out of a boiling kettle of soapy water. The girl who was Regent, crown princess and future queen was using metal tongs to remove the cleaned cloths from boiling water, rinsing them in a kettle of cold water, and setting them on a line to dry.

"Highness," Magrane bent down stiffly on one knee, or he tried to but his old bones had stiffened after a long day and night in the saddle, so he bent as much as he could, knowing the princess would appreciate the gesture. "After your Regency is over, are you considering applying for a position in the royal laundry?"

Ariana laughed, taking it as a good sign that the commander of her army still had energy for a joke, after being on duty all night. "Actually, yes. When I am queen, I intend to support the royal laundry by changing outfits two or three times every day," she winked.

"I am sure the laundresses will appreciate being kept busy." Magrane leaned on a pole, a wave of weariness suddenly washing over him. He straightened, shaking off the momentary weakness.

"General, you should rest," Ariana chided the man gently, tactfully not mentioning his age as a reason he needed sleep. "Madame Chu was here an," Ariana realized she had no idea what time it was, nor how long ago the master wizard had spoken with her. "An hour ago?" She guessed. "She assured me the enemy has no appetite for a fight with us, indeed there *is* no enemy. The demon is dead, she told me, and with it gone, the compulsion spells it used to control the people of Acedor have been broken." Ariana had been happily excited to hear that good news, until Madame Chu explained this meant many people in Acedor were now able to think freely for the first time in their lives, and they had to be terrified. For a long time, the newly-freed people of Acedor would be unable to feed or care for themselves, so Ariana would be faced with the unexpected and somewhat distasteful task of expending massive amounts of money and effort, on behalf of people who recently tried to conquer and enslave Tarador. How could she sell that idea to the dukes and duchesses of the Regency Council, who were already nearly bankrupt from supporting the war effort?

Ariana did not want to think about that, not just then. She still had many other problems of Tarador to deal with, but she also knew she could not stand by and do nothing, while her former enemies in Acedor starved to death. Those people, after all, had mostly been little better than slaves of the demon, and as such they deserved her compassion rather than hatred or neglect. Her father had dreamed of someday reuniting the kingdoms of Tarador and Acedor as one realm, and she shared that dream. Providing food to sustain the people of Acedor during the coming winter would go a long way to converting them into loyal citizens of a united nation.

Magrane nodded. "Yes, Highness, Madame Chu spoke with me also. I did recall some of our roving patrols and relax the pickets, but soldiers must be vigilant," he said with a wry smile. Then his expression darkened. "Did she have any news of Lords Salva and Mwazo? Or," he lowered his voice, "young Master Bladewell?"

"No," Ariana felt tears stinging her eyes. "She explained the raw magical energy released when the demon died is still reverberating in the spirit world, like ringing a bell. It prevents her from contacting Paedris. She does not think Paedris, or," she swallowed to calm the catch in her throat, "the others have died, but she also told me she might not have been able to feel it." Madame Chu had said the death of a wizard sent ripples through the spirit world, but the effects of the demon's demise were so overwhelming, ripples from the death of one or even many wizards might not be noticeable.

"I have hope," Magrane lifted his chin, in a gesture intended to lift the girl's spirits. In truth, he had little hope that Lords Salva and Mwazo had survived whatever force could kill a demon, and for Koren there could be no hope. Those were the facts and Ariana knew them as well as Magrane did; she also did not need to face the truth right at that moment. Soldiers of the Royal Army were still dying of their battle wounds, and Ariana had enough to worry about within the confines of the encampment. Magrane also knew her thoughts would inevitably wander elsewhere, far the east, to a castle where a demon had resided for centuries.

"I will have hope, too," Ariana also lifted her chin despite her weariness. "Until I have reason to lose hope. General, you won a great victory yesterday, and your army remains vigilant. You should rest," she added with concern.

"Highness, I intend to rest, after we have returned to Linden and your position there is secure from anyone within Tarador who might be tempted to use the disruption of our sudden victory for," he sought out the proper word, "adventurism. Fear of our common enemy kept the provinces united under your leadership, I fear Regin Falco is not the only duke who chafed about being led by someone as young as yourself."

"Oh," Ariana's shoulders slumped. "Do I have to think about that *now*?"

"Someone has to, Your Highness, and since the title of Highness belongs to *you*, you must consider your position. But," he smiled warmly, "I believe you can push aside such thoughts for tonight. I will bring the Royal Army back to Linden with you, see that the ducal armies return to their own lands, and then we may both rest. When that happens," his shoulder shook slightly with relief, "I intend to retire."

"No!" Ariana protested. "But, you have just earned a great victory!"

"Exactly, Highness. The Royal Army has just won a great, a famous victory, a victory that will be talked and sung about for centuries, a victory that will be celebrated in legends and sagas until the full truth has been lost to history. I cannot accomplish anything greater in my lifetime, and," he winked, "there is something to be said for going out on top."

Ariana laughed. "But what will you *do*?"

"My wife and I have always wanted to travel, to see faraway lands," he replied wistfully. "In my career, I have been to foreign lands, but not for the purpose of leisure. Highness, there is much that must happen before I can set aside my uniform, I hope I may retire with your blessing."

"Of course, you will have my blessing when the time comes," Ariana said unhappily, not liking the thought of facing the chaotic future without Magrane in command of the army. The threat from Acedor had bound Tarador together in relative peace, there had not been serious civil conflict or an attempt to overthrow the monarch since- She realized the last time a monarch or Tarador had been deposed was when her ancestor took the throne from the Falcos and began the Trehayme line. That was something she did not want to think about. Regardless, other than minor border skirmishes or foolishly prideful conflicts over matters of 'honor' between the provinces, the seven provinces of Tarador had not fought each other for over a thousand years. Nor had Tarador fought a serious war against any neighboring countries in nearly four hundred years. The peace had been based on fear of Acedor, and the belief that a unified and strong nation was the best insurance against Acedor conquering the world. What would happen now, when the realm of Tarador was weary and in heavy debt from the long war, and those with power both within and outside the realm no longer saw the royal family's rule as necessary to their own survival?

Ariana did not want to face such a dangerous, uncertain future without General Magrane, without Lord Salva-

And most of all, she did not want to think of life, or anything, without Koren Bladewell.

"Your Grace," a soldier repeated, and Magrane cleared his throat loudly.

"Oh!" Ariana was startled out of her dark thoughts. "Yes?"

"Begging your pardon, Highness, the surgeons want more clean cloths," the soldier reported with a bow.

"Yes, yes, of course. Please excuse me, General Magrane," Ariana nodded to the old warhorse, and set about gathering clean, dry cloths off the line.

Paedris don Salva could not remember a time in his life when he had ached more and been more desperately weary to the very core of his being. Nor could he remember a time when he had been more deliriously happy, yet fearful in the pit of his stomach. He and Lord Mwazo had run steadily all that day, stopping only to fill their water flasks and drink after purifying the tainted water. Power from the spirit world gave them energy to run at a punishing pace over the broken terrain, all roads having been blasted away or covered in a fine, choking grit. The wizards had quickly learned to run side by side as their footfalls threw up puffs of gray dust and black soot, blinding and choking any person who ran behind another. By later afternoon, with the sun an angry red ball showing through the dust suspended in the air, they reached a spot where Paedris remembered the ancient map showing low hills and both wizards slowed to a halt, uncertain where to go. "Where is the castle?" He asked, baffled. "There should be, there *was*, a castle here!"

"Paedris," Cecil nudged with a foot the gray grit that blanketed the ground everywhere, "I think we may be standing on what used to be the castle. What used to be everything else also. We must be near the site of the castle."

"Hmm," Paedris pondered that disturbing thought. "The ancestral castle of Duke Draylock stood on the edge of a low cliff, ringed by hills and moats," he recalled from reading ancient scrolls. "The valley below the looming mountains was now almost flat, with no sign of the river that fed water into the moats. Whatever cataclysm happened there, it had swept away hills and changed the course of a river? "This *is* the source of all that smoke we saw this morning. We will have to search, I suppose. I do not see any-"

Cecil grasped the other wizard's arm. "There!" He pointed to a soot-covered object just over the lip of a large, shallow crater.

The two wizards sprinted across the open, fire-blasted ground at a speed that would have surprised anyone who knew their true ages. Cecil reached the boy first, dropping to his knees and holding up Koren's head. "He lives! Paedris, you must help him!"

"Yes." The court wizard knelt, closing his eyes and pressing a hand to the boy's chest, sending healing energy into Koren from the spirit world. "Give him water. Oh, he is near death, this will take considerable time."

It did take time, it was not until well after midnight that Koren cracked open one eye. "W-what happened?"

"We were hoping you could tell us, my young friend," Paedris nearly collapsed with relief. "The demon is gone, utterly. It is not merely banished back to the shadow realm, it is gone, dead. Koren, you killed an immortal being of immense power. How?"

"It wanted my power," Koren answered in a whisper, his mouth still not moving properly to form words.

"Yes, the demon wanted your power to open a door to the underworld. You killed it before it could use your power for its own purpose?"

"No," Koren leaned to the side to cough. "It wanted my power. So, I gave it what it wanted. *All* of it."

Both master wizards gasped, and Cecil slapped his forehead. "Out of the mouths of babes comes wisdom! Paedris, I would *never* have thought of doing that."

"Nor I," Paedris admitted, not at all ashamed of being shamed by a boy wizard who had no training at all. "You burned out the demon from the inside! Koren, how in the world did you get the idea to do that?"

"I cast a fireball, or a fire*storm*, and kill an orc army-"

"Yes," Cecil shuddered at the memory, "we felt that."

"When I used that power, before I fainted or whatever happened, I saw there was no bottom, no limit to that power. I knew that I could have used much, much more power then-"

"It is good you did not," Paedris wrung his hands at the thought of how close to disaster the boy had come. "You could have pulled down those mountains on top of you."

"Oh. Um, but I didn't. Lucky, I guess?" Koren saw Paedris roll his eyes at that remark. "I couldn't control any magic, especially after the firestorm I couldn't do anything at all, but I knew I could reach for that power if I had someplace for it to go."

"Into the demon," Cecil breathed with admiration. "You didn't need any training or skill, the demon would do that for you. It began pulling power from the spirit world-"

"And all I had to do was keep the power flowing, out of control" Koren finished with a sheepish grin.

"Paedris," Lord Mwazo pretended to be washing his hands, flinging his fingers outward in disgust. "I will never again name myself loremaster, for I have just discovered that I know *nothing* about the true use of magic."

"You lured in the demon by giving it exactly what it wanted," Paedris still was having trouble wrapping his mind around a concept so simple. "You used its own greed and lust for power against it, to kill it."

"I didn't kill it, not completely," Koren explained. "Thought I did, but some tiny bit of it survived. It tried to come to me, take over me, make me into its new Draylock. Bjorn killed it. He took it into himself and then fell on a blade, taking the demon with him. Bjorn saved me. He saved us all."

"Ah," Paedris nodded, understanding. Cecil had found a single blackened, shriveled body in the center of the crater, with a twisted blade buried in the chest of the corpse. "That was Bjorn, then? He was a brave man, Koren. Now, rest, that is an order. You are yet weak and need to build your strength. It will be a very long walk home," he added with a frown, wondering how they would accomplish such a daunting task. They would need to find food and horses in a landscape scoured clean of any life. No matter, he thought as he closed his eyes and allowed sleep to take him. The demon was dead. He could rest, truly rest, for the first time in over a century.

Paedris shivered the next morning, cold inside from having so much of his power drained away in the process of healing Koren. "Lord Salva, please stop trying to carry me!" The boy implored. "I am able to walk."

"Koren," Cecil warned, "you are still weak, there is a sickness inside you."

"Yes, but much of that sickness will go away if I get a good meal in my belly and," Koren swept an arm to encompass the lifeless mountains of rock all around them. "We won't get that here."

Cecil shrugged. "He is right about that, Paedris." The two wizards only had enough food remaining in their packs for three days, and that was for two people. With a third mouth to feed, a very hungry mouth, they would run out of food the next day. They dared not eat anything from the poisoned landscape around them, lest the sickness that infected the land strike them down also.

"I am well enough, aren't I?" Koren asked anxiously. "I feel, fine, but-"

"But what?" Paedris asked, dropping to one knee with concern and pressing a hand to the boy's forehead.

"I can't feel anything, *inside* me," Koren tried to explain something he didn't understand. "Even when I couldn't use power, I could feel the connection there. Now, I can't feel anything."

"Ah," Paedris looked to Cecil, sighed and helped the boy stand up. "Listen, Koren. I fear that while your body will heal itself, you may have use too much power. It has, sort of, burned out your power from within. You can't feel a connection because it isn't there. I thought at first that I could find it, coax it back to life, but it is gone. Completely."

"I'm, I'm not a wizard anymore?"

"Koren, I don't know, I-"

"Paedris, we owe the boy the truth," Cecil chided his friend.

"The truth?" Koren looked to the tall, thin wizard with more fear than hope.

"The truth," Cecil said as Paedris looked away, unable to give such terrible news to someone who had saved them all. "The truth is, your ability to use magic, your connection to the spirit world, is gone. It is not something you did, and it is not a mere matter of skill or training. You see, Koren, the spirits have done this to protect themselves. They will not allow you to use magic, for they know you can harm even them. You killed a *demon*, and the spirits fear you."

"I'm *not* a wizard?" Koren staggered, reaching out for Cecil to steady himself. "My Lords, I had just gotten used to the idea of being a wizard."

"Koren, you need never call any of us 'Lord' again," Paedris declared. "I am truly sorry, there is nothing to be done."

"But, what am I to do? I thought-"

Cecil interrupted. "Right now, what you need to do is walk with us, if we are to leave this poisoned land behind. Paedris, this evening, you must try to contact Wing so she can arrange for soldiers on horseback to meet us. We cannot walk all the way out of Acedor, even if the army here is no longer a threat to us."

CHAPTER TWENTY TWO

Kyre Falco was utterly exhausted when he presented himself at the royal tent for an audience with the Regent in midmorning, having been up all night after already being weary from the previous day's battle. While Magrane's Royal Army troops pursued or warily monitored scattered remnants of the enemy army, Kyre had volunteered to deal with those Burwyck soldiers who had followed the orders of his father. He was a Falco and it was his responsibility, he had argued successfully to Magrane, then had to lead people loyal to him on the distasteful task of rounding up those who wore the colors and emblem of Burwyck. Most groups of Burwyck soldiers he found had surrendered peacefully and without comment, other than to say they were heartily sorry for following the now-disgraced Regin Falco.

Kyre had approached those last holdouts of Burwyck personally, holding out his arms to show he had no weapons other than the sword strapped to his waist. "Talen!" He called out to his younger brother. "Father is dead, he disgraced our family. Do not join his dishonor, come forward and join us in victory."

His brother stepped forward warily, holding a bow in one hand and an arrow in the other, glaring hatred at his older brother. "You killed father! You are a traitor to our family!"

"No, Talen," Kyre's head almost nodded from great weariness, most of which was emotional. "Father died by his own hand, when he saw his schemes had come to nothing. He faced hanging for treason, and took his own life as a coward, rather than pay for his crimes. Our family is disgraced, we have nothing. *I* am nothing, I am heir to nothing, the Falco line is dead. Burwyck is lost to us, we must-"

"No! You lie!" Talen screamed in outrage, fitting arrow to bowstring and swing the bow up to aim at his brother. The bowstring twanged weakly and the arrow flew off harmlessly into the air as one of Talen's own guards thumped the boy's helmet with the pommel of his sword and Talen fell to the ground. "Begging your pardon, Your Grace," the guard gave the apology to Kyre rather than the boy he had struck. "It would be a shame for your brother to do something stupid."

"Thank you," Kyre shuddered slightly with relief, as the men around his brother had been the last holdouts of the Burwyck soldiers who had followed the former duke. "I'm not 'Your Grace' any more, I'm not anything. I have no claim on your loyalty," he looked around him at soldiers who had followed him or his father. "No claim on any of you."

The guard went down on one knee. "I followed your father into treason out of habit and stupidity, Your Grace, and I am ashamed. I follow you now because you have the honor I lacked. Ask, and it shall be done."

"Oh," Kyre's tired brain did not know how to react. "See to Talen, please. And, uh," he waved a hand vaguely, "do whatever the Royal Army orders. I must go surrender my sword to the Regent, where I intend to beg for mercy. Not for myself, but for all those who followed my father."

"Highness," Kyre knelt in the royal tent, then unstrapped his sword belt and let it fall to the carpets. "I surrender my sword as a sign of my family's deep shame at the actions of the former duke. He is dead by his own hand," he pulled the heavy gold ducal signet ring from a pocket and tossed it at the feet of the princess. "His treachery and cowardice extended even to the manner of his death, I am ashamed to say."

Ariana held her tongue on the subject of Regin Falco, not trusting herself to hold back from saying something she might later regret. At the moment, she regretted holding back, for how could anyone dispute her thoughts about the vile treachery of Regin Falco? Yet, she knew Chancellor Kallron always cautioned her to measure her words in public. "And what of your brother Talen?"

Kyre stiffened, his troublesome brother being a sore subject for him. "Talen did not see the wisdom of renouncing his featly to our late father, and resisted being disarmed."

"Resisted?"

Kyre nodded, a ghost of a smile crossing his lips. "He was about to shoot an arrow at me, when one of Talen's own guards knocked him over the head. My brother is now under guard, with the other people of Burwyck who did not see fit to repent their actions during the battle. Most of," he coughed into a hand, "those who resisted will not be a problem, because they are no longer with us, Highness."

"I see." Ariana looked at the signet ring of the Falcos, looking down not because she had any interest in the ring, but because she needed time to think. "You father did commit treason most foul, and as his son and heir, you-" She paused. "This is awkward, as you and I are betrothed,"

"Forgive me, Your Highness, but that is not true."

"Uh, what?" Ariana was completely taken aback by Kyre's comment.

"The arrangement of betrothal specified you are to marry the heir to the Falco line, whether that is myself or my younger brother Talen," Kyre began to explain.

"I am *not* going to marry your brother, that, that, horrible, traitorous little boy!" Ariana rose halfway out of her seat before Chancellor Kallron's gentle hand on her shoulder caused her to sit down.

"I would not suggest you or anyone else marry my brother, Highness, for he is a selfish bully, a coward and a fool to follow my father into treason," Kyre glanced up at the princess for the first time. "You do not need to marry any of my father's sons, for his treason has ended the Falco's claim to legitimate rule of Burwyck province. There is no Falco dynasty, therefore there is no heir to hold you to a betrothal contract."

"He speaks the truth, Highness," Chancellor Kallron announced. "Duke Falco's treason renders the betrothal contract null, for there is no Falco dynasty."

"Oh," Ariana felt deflated, for she had been prepared to argue in righteous anger against having to marry Kyre. "That is, good, I suppose."

"Did you really want to marry me, Highness?" Kyre ventured a bold question.

"No! No." Ariana answered honestly without stopping to think which response would be most proper and politically useful to her. "I must admit that, as I have come to see your true nature, and your worth as a person both to Tarador and to myself personally, I have found you less," she found herself actually smiling, "completely repulsive and odious than I expected a Falco to be."

"I am," Kyre could not help a brief chuckle, "pleased that my presence is somewhat more welcome than a skunk at a picnic."

"Oh, I never said that, Mister Falco," Ariana hid her laughter behind a gloved hand. "We have all been marching for many days, then in battle, and now up for a full night. A skunk may understandably complain of the way you smell this day. Perhaps after a bath, you might be less unwelcome."

"Yes, Your Highness." Kyre smiled.

Ariana leaned to the side and sniffed herself. "My own royal person is not immune to the effects of not bathing, either. Tell me, Kyre, did you want to marry *me*?"

"No," Kyre answered without hesitation, speaking without calculation or guile. "I mean no insult, Highness, and recently I have come to greatly admire you despite my having been raised to hate Trehaymes as my mortal enemy. But," he blushed, embarrassed. That, too, was a new sensation for a Falco, especially in public. "We would not be a good match. I have watched the unhappiness of my parents, and I have come to believe a good marriage must be based on more than," he moved his mouth distastefully, "political or financial advantages. I hope Your Highness will not think less of me for speaking my mind."

"On the contrary, it makes me think *more* of you."

"Highness, if I have served you well, perhaps you could see fit to give me a recommendation, when you have time? I have no prospects," he admitted ruefully, "and I am hoping some mercenary company might wish to hire a person with experience in battle."

"Hmm," Ariana made an exaggerated show of putting a finger to her cheek as if deep in thought. "You need something to do? It just happens that, as Regent of Tarador, I find myself in need of someone to administer the duchy of Burwyck until the future queen can appoint a new royal family to assume the dukedom there. But, however could I find someone who is familiar with the province, and has proven to be loyal and trustworthy?"

"Highness?" Kyre's knees wobbled.

"Perhaps," Chancellor Kallron played along with the princess, a sign that he heartily approved of her idea. "You might consider Kyre Falco, Your Highness. He does, after all, know the land and people of Burwyck."

"Why, that is a capital idea!" Ariana clapped her hands in mock delight. "Kyre, would you be willing to act as my royal factor, to administer Burwyck until a suitable person can be found to assume the dukedom there?"

"Y-yes, Highness," Kyre went down on one knee again, partly out of gratitude and partly because he was so stunned by the turnaround in his fortunes that his legs were about to give out and pitch him forward onto the carpets. "I pledge my best efforts as your royal agent."

"I am sure you will. You pledged yourself to protect me, and you have proven honorable, at great cost to yourself and your family. Honorable, and loyal to Tarador." As she spoke, she reached a decision, and spoke before Kallron could intervene. "After I am crowned queen of Tarador, it will be within my power to grant the duchy of Burwyck to a deserving person of royal birth," as she spoke, her mind raced through the complicated rules of ducal succession and the restrictions on how the crown could intervene in such succession. "A person of royal birth," she nodded toward Kyre, "who has demonstrated bravery and unflinching loyalty to Tarador, even at the cost of breaking fealty to his father and liege lord, might be a good choice to assume the dukedom of Burwyck, don't you think?"

"Highness?" Kyre and the Chancellor both asked at the same time, then Kallron smiled at the wisdom of the young princess. "I cannot think of a better candidate, Highness. Appointing Kyre Falco the duke of Burwyck would certainly make a bold statement to the realm that you reward loyalty to Tarador." Kallron was pleasantly astonished at the cleverness of the princess. Making Kyre duke of Burwyck would ensure the life-long gratitude of the boy, and perhaps end the useless and expensive feud between the Falcos and the Trehaymes.

Ariana, Kallron thought not for the first time, would be a formidable queen.

"And," Ariana added, "doing so will make it clear that people should be judged on their own merits, and *not* only on family connections."

"Highness," Kyre looked up with tears streaming freely down his cheeks, "I do not know how to thank you, other than to say Burwyck will be as loyal as my father was treasonous." The princess may believe in him, but he knew many, even most, people in Tarador and the greater world would need to be convinced that Kyre Falco was not fully his father's son. That would take time and tremendous effort, and Kyre was burning with eagerness to get started.

Kyre's bodyguard Jonas waited outside the royal tent, feeling awkward and conspicuous wearing the disgraced and treasonous colors of the Falcos, and wondering when the royal guard force would demand he surrender his bow and sword. Jonas had gone so far as to partly unbuckle his sword belt, so it would drop to the ground quickly, and avoid any excuses for miscommunication that might result in his death that morning. So, he was astonished when Kyre emerged from the tent, head held high, beaming with joy. "Sire?" Jonas pointed to the boy's sword, then gaped at Kyre's tunic. Jonas had expected Kyre to depart the royal tent most likely under arrest, but certainly without his sword, and with the silver falcon crest of his family cut out of his dirty and blood-stained tunic. Yet, Kyre was not in chains, his sword was proudly swinging from his waist, and the Falco crest was blazing prominently on the front of his tunic.

"Her Highness has given me a great gift, Jonas, a gift I must prove I am worthy of."

"Your freedom, Sire?" Jonas asked hopefully.

"Better, Jonas. A chance to redeem my family name, and perhaps restore this," he tapped the silver falcon crest, "to a place of honor in Burwyck, and the world."

"I, I do not know what to say, Sire," Jonas stammered. "What does this mean?"

"It means, Jonas," Kyre looked to the bright blue morning sky and inhaled deeply, "that we have much work to do, and we had best get started immediately." His stomach growled, as one scent he had inhaled was from the Royal Army's kitchen fires. "After a hearty breakfast, of course."

Koren sat taller in the saddle, squinting to see who was riding toward him so quickly, and so awkwardly. Whoever was the lone person who raced ahead of the royal party, he or she was not a skilled rider, bouncing up and down far too much. Yet the person wore fine clothing, with a shiny tunic flowing behind that Koren guessed must have been made of silk, a fabric considered expensive even by royalty. As the person got closer, he waved then grabbed the horse's mane and nearly had to hug the beast's neck to avoid falling off. It was a man, no, a boy and – "Cully?" Koren gasped. What was the servant boy Cully Runnet doing with the royal party, so far from Linden, riding a horse and dressed in fine clothes?

"Ho, Koren!" The boy called out, reining in his horse gingerly. Koren reached out to steady his old friend as Cully turned the horse to trot alongside. "It is *Sir* Cully Runnet now, if you please."

"Sir?" Koren assumed the boy was joking until he saw the crest Cully wore on the front of his tunic, and the silver badge that fastened around his neck. "You are a *knight* now? When, how, when did this happen? How?"

"I taught the princess and a wizard how to swim, is the short version," Cully smiled with embarrassmenbt and Koren knew the full story had to be much more interesting than swimming lessons. "What about you? You're a *wizard*?"

"No," it was Koren's turn to be embarrassed. Ahead, he could see the crown princess urging her horse to a trot as they closed the distance between them. "Not anymore," he flexed his right hand open, remembering when a river of fire had poured forth to obliterate an orc army. Now he had no more magical power than Cully. "I was never really a wizard, didn't know what I was doing. "

"But, you killed a *demon*?"

"I sort of let it kill itself, is all I did."

"Uh huh." Cully knew there had to be much more to that story. "Did you hear they found your horse?"

"Yes," Koren brightened. Paedris had received word that Thunderbolt, having run away from the dwarves, had been located in Winterthur province and was now on his way to Linden with a Royal Army escort. From the tone of the message, the soldiers escorting Thunderbolt would be heartily glad to turn over care of the troublesome horse to Koren. Thinking about his horse made him laugh. "I wonder what adventures Thunderbolt got up to? I couldn't take him into the mountains," he shuddered thinking about the flimsy-looking rope bridges there.

"So, you're not a wizard. Have you thought about what you'll do now?"

It struck Koren right then that he had not thought of the future beyond riding back to Tarador. "I don't know," he said unhappily. "I don't suppose I can go back to being a servant for Paed- for Lord Salva."

Cully saw the lost and sad expression on his friend's face. "I'm a proper knight now," he announced as he grabbed his horse's mane again to steady himself from falling to the ground. "You can be my squire, if you like," he joked with a wink.

"Aye, I can teach you how to ride a horse," Koren snorted.

"And to hold a sword," Cully admitted. "The royal weapons master says I am hopeless. Well, here's the princess," he pulled his horse to a halt.

Koren slowed his own horse, until he came to a stop in front of the princess. It was awkward meeting her again, more awkward with the two of them on horseback, and especially awkward being surrounded by soldiers, wizards and courtiers. "Your Highness," he began stiffly. "I am sorry, I thought ill of you, and I was wrong."

"I thought ill of *myself*, and I was right," Ariana replied with vehemence. At that moment, she wanted nothing more than to fling her arms around the young man, and the irritated glare she gave to the courtiers made them pull their horses away discretely. "You were never treated fairly, you were treated horribly. I was part of that. Please forgiv-"

"Peadr- that is, Lord Salva explained to me why he couldn't tell me the truth. He was right, Highness. I understand that now."

"Koren, please call me Ariana. I can call you Lord Bladewell if you prefer, but," her eyes pleaded as she spoke.

"No. Please, I can't be Lord anything. Did you hear, I'm not a wizard? I lost it all, all my power."

"Well, then, there is no reason I can't grant you a knighthood, is there?"

"Er-"

Ariana reached for a sword, then remembered she wasn't carrying one. "Do you mind waiting? I nearly chopped off Cully's ear when I knighted him," she laughed and Koren had to laugh also, then Koren's expression darkened.

"I should have congratulated you, I heard you are engaged to be married?"

"Oh, to Kyre Falco? No!, No, not anymore. His father committed treason, so the Falcos are no longer a royal family. That makes our engagement contract void, I am told."

"Oh. Were you also engaged to some prince from Indus?" Koren was not sure that rumor was true. It did seem like a lot of engagements for one young woman.

"That was my mother's doing," Ariana was still angry with her mother about that. "The Regency Council declared that contract invalid."

"That must have made the Raj unhappy."

"He was, especially about the money he loaned to Tarador. But, he sent his soldiers here to fight with us anyway," she looked to the north where a hundred soldiers of Indus had accompanied the royal party into Acedor. Grand General Magrane would not be happy until the last foreign soldier returned to their homelands. "We will pay the money back to the Raj quickly. Besides, we heard the prince is already engaged to someone else now."

"Kyre is not a duke now?" Koren asked, confused.

"No, the Falco dynasty ended when his father joined the enemy," she explained. After examining the duke's body, Madame Chu had detected the man was tainted by subtle yet powerful dark magic. Ariana had almost felt sorry for Regin Falco, until Madame Chu stated not even the dark magic of a demon could make someone act completely against their will. Regin Falco had fallen victim to the enemy's influence because he had wanted to, he wanted something he thought the demon could give him. He had been wrong, and he paid for it with his life and the disgrace of his family.

"What about Kyre?"

"Kyre proved his loyalty, several times. He saved my life. As Burwyck province lacks a ruling duke, I have appointed Kyre as my royal factor there. Once I am queen, I can name a new duke, and that *might* be Kyre, *if* he behaves himself," she announced with a wink.

"You trust him?" Koren asked with skepticism.

"I do," the princess nodded vigorously, "and you should also. He has changed."

"We all have," without thinking, Koren opened his right palm, where no flame appeared, or ever would again.

Ariana saw and understood the gesture. Impulsively, she reached out to put his hand in hers. His hand was warm and rough and the touch sent a thrill up her arm and down inside her. "Koren, I'm sorry. For everything."

Koren knew he should pull his hand away, that it was not proper for a princess to be holding hands with a boy. "Ariana-"

"Koren-" They spoke at the same time. "Please, what were you going to say?"

"No. No, please, you first."

She had rehearsed what she would say at that moment, and at that moment, words failed her. Instead, she spoke from her heart. "Would you, would please you come to live in the palace? Please? There are so many books in the royal library we, I mean you, have not even seen yet."

Koren lowered his eyes and smiled, a smile that made Ariana's heart melt. "Do knights need to read a lot?"

Ariana said a silent prayer of thanks. "Oh, yes, they read a *frightful* lot. All day, really, when they are not doing," she waved a hand, "knight things."

"Then," he risked moving his thumb to trace a line along her fingers. "I would like that very much."

CHAPTER TWENTY THREE

"Your Majesty," Raddick bowed to his queen as he came up on deck. "Sir Bladewell," he also bowed to the former boy wizard, now a knight of the realm and, according to strongly-held rumor, soon to be officially engaged to the recently-crowned queen Ariana Trehayme.

"General Raddick," Ariana acknowledged her new commander of the Royal Army. "A fine day, is it not?" She held her face to the wind, inhaling the clean sea breeze, feeling the warm air caressing her face. Since leaving port, the winds had been steady and fair, speeding the ship along under sunny skies.

"A fine day indeed, Your Majesty. Though I wonder how much of this fine weather might be the work of our wizards," he discretely glanced aft to where Lords Salva and Mwazo were gathered with Madame Chu and a half dozen other wizards.

"I am sure it is," Ariana smiled before remembering the subject of wizardry was an unpleasant reminder of misfortune for Koren. "No matter," she added hurriedly, "are you enjoying this sea voyage?" She asked to change the subject.

"Yes, thank you," Raddick replied while avoiding Koren's eyes, aware he should not have mentioned wizardry or magic around the young knight. "This is not my first time at sea, but it has been many years since I last felt a deck rolling beneath my feet. The first days are the most difficult," he said as small talk, knowing anyone suffering seasickness needed only to ask a wizard for a potion.

"Yes," Ariana could not help looking back to where the wizards were gathered. This would be, Paedris had told her, the last time many of them were gathered, as after the voyage and ceremony, many of the wizards intended to take a rest from their long labors. Lord Mwazo would be going back to his homeland, which he had not seen for nearly a century of hard struggle against the forces of Acedor. Paedris and Wing would also be leaving, taking a Royal Navy ship gratefully provided by Ariana, going first to Paedris' home village in Stade, then on to Ching-Do with a stop in Indus. With them on that ship would be the retired General Magrane, now an official envoy of Tarador. Magrane and his wife had wanted to travel, to see the world, and Ariana was only too happy to oblige. When she asked him to consider being her official envoy, he had protested, but she knew Magrane could not simply be idle, and the old warhorse would enjoy the fruits of his retirement. Paedris and Wing, it was hinted, intended to marry when they reached Ching-Do, with the court wizard of Tarador warning Ariana it might be many years before he returned to Linden.

No matter, Ariana told herself as she pushed out of her mind sad thoughts of parting with friends, and looked down through the open hatch to the cargo hold of the good ship *Sir Bjorn Jihnsson.* Down in the hold, covered with an oilcloth tarp, was the ancient Cornerstone of Acedor. Admiral Reed and his fine crew were bringing the Cornerstone to the former pirate harbor of Tokmanto, now renamed Talannon, where the massive block of stone would be transferred to a barge for the trip upriver. At the chosen destination, atop a hill only a few miles from the tainted land where the original castle had stood, the Cornerstone would be set in place, as the first stone of a new castle to be built as a symbol of the newly reunited land.

Seeing his queen was lost in thought, Grand General Raddick bowed silently and strode off toward the bow. Ariana sighed and leaned toward Koren, he put an arm around her. "I so very much want the Cornerstone restored to its rightful place, and to build a castle there, but there are *so* many questions I must answer, *so* many problems to be solved," she complained to the only person she could tell her most secret thoughts to. The people of Acedor, freed from enthrallment by the demon, were now mostly peaceful, seeking only to provide for themselves and their families, and secure a better future. Those former enemies who could not find it within themselves to fully throw off their enthrallment, or who could never be trusted, had been pursued by the Royal Army and either chased out of Acedor into the hostile wild lands beyond the borders, or had fallen in bitterly contested battles. The people of Acedor were still not capable of feeding themselves, Paedris had warned it might be ten or more years before the poisoned land recovered to point where healthy crops could be grown. Even without the problem of feeding the inhabitants, there was the question of how to administer the lands now added to the realm of Tarador. Ariana needed to appoint dukes and duchesses to the provinces established in what used to be Acedor, and of course *so* many people were competing for those coveted positions! "Have you thought about what I asked? Who I should appoint to the new provinces?"

"Yes," Koren smiled outwardly while groaning inwardly. "I have thought about it, and my thought is I have no business being involved in decisions like that. I am a peasant farm boy, I know nothing of royal succession and things like that."

"You are not a peasant, *Sir* Bladewell," Ariana hated to hear her beloved talking that way about himself. Koren had vehemently refused the title of Lord Bladewell, arguing his total loss of magical ability meant he no longer qualified for such an honorific, and besides, he did not care about titles. "If you would allow me to make you a duke, you could take over one of these bothersome new provinces, and make my life *so* much easier."

"No, hon-" he lowered his voice, having almost called the queen 'honey' in public, "Ariana. I don't want to be a duke, I would not have the first idea of what to do-"

"But I could send Chancellor Kallron to instruct you!"

"No," Koren shook his head gently, and looked deeply into her eyes. "I am not cut out to be a duke, I have enough honors already."

"That is not true! You killed a demon and saved us all!"

"*Bjorn* killed the demon, I only robbed it of most of its power."

"You know what I mean," Ariana slapped Koren playfully. "Darling," she whispered, "*why* will you not allow me the pleasure of making you a duke?"

"Because," Koren said with a wry smile and a wink, "there *might* be slight complication."

He held out his right hand, where danced a tiny glow of magical flame.

THE END

Contact the author at craigalanson@gmail.com
https://www.facebook.com/Craig.Alanson.Author/
Visit CraigAlanson.com for blogs and items such as T-shirts, coffee cups etc.

23097523R00140

Made in the USA
Columbia, SC
03 August 2018